Kaylee

Kaylee

A life for worlds

Henri Nguyen

Library of Congress Control Number:		2021908468
ISBN:	Hardcover	978-1-6641-6988-3
	Softcover	978-1-6641-6987-6
	eBook	978-1-6641-6986-9

Print information available on the last page.

Rev. date: 04/24/2021

To order additional copies of this book, contact:
Xlibris
844-714-8691
www.Xlibris.com
Orders@Xlibris.com
816888

CHAPTER 1

I T WAS EARLY in the morning. The sun was up but shielded by clouds. The gray of the clouds was slightly darker than Kaylee recalled. It seemed to show the sun was not going to be part of this day. It was the same yesterday. It had been four days that Kaylee had not seen the sun. She knew it was still in the sky, but she missed its warm rays.

Kaylee walked out of her house. The street was clear. She was glad it was still clear. Two days ago, she worked on making her street free of leaves and tree branches. Kaylee was one of three people still living on this street. They named it Hope Street. This was rationed like many other elements of her life.

If you asked her, Kaylee would not be able to tell you what year it is. She knew it was winter. She heard the stories from her mother and her father.

There was a time when ten million people lived in Chicago. Now, there are maybe three thousand. It was difficult to assert the reason why near ten million people died. There was climate change; now we knew it was human caused. Then there were bug waves. Then H1N1 caused a pandemic. Then there was a war. This would be a reason for ten million people to die.

Kaylee was eighteen years old. She looked like a tall woman, and her slenderness was not a choice. It was a cause of her lack of food. This was across her world. Kaylee would rather give her food to her neighbors, as they are older.

On the other side of Hope Street was Sylvia, an elder woman. Often, Kaylee brought her meager ration and offered her a meal. Sylvia would eat with such pleasure, while Kaylee would take a bite or two. Her mother told her one day, it would pay for her to give food to elder. Sarcasm, Kaylee got that part down. She sought the comfort of others and pleasure from making other people smile.

This morning was another one of seeking food. Kaylee, like many others, had a book of coupons, but there were so many yeast blocks anyone wanted to eat. She sought out some other foods in nature. She walked down a street parallel to Hope. There were buildings. Their doors were gone for firewood. The trees were growing, and the path was narrow, but there was still a way.

Kaylee reached the train track. She never saw any train track there. This was her mother and father's term. She kept it; it was easier than dune of some kind; she also thought it must be a relic from the past.

Then Kaylee reached a hole that allowed her to come across to the lake. She walked toward her fishing lines.

In her head, an alarm flashed. Her mind saw yellow everywhere. She connected to the central defense pack.

Ever since she was ten years old, she was connected to the Web. It was a necessity for all children. This required her to have a chip planted into her brain. There was no ceremony, just a surgical appointment in downtown Chicago. She recalled it took her a day of walking to get there. It was a marvel as to how the tall buildings were still up and the sumptuousness of the wall. It was so clean and shiny, when you compared to her building and street. It was so different.

After connecting to the defense pack, she read the report of the previous person who was in charge of her defense section. There was nothing worthy to report. Kaylee was now on duty. Despite those words, she pulled her fishing lines, and there were two fish. It was a good morning so far.

The trees were thick and their leaves were missing, but in about two months, the buds were to appear. Kaylee checked her animal traps. She walked up to a box. There was noise underneath it. This was a good sign. She pulled the box up and saw a bunny.

It would be so cute if she had no other issues aside from eating and fighting hunger. Kaylee quickly grabbed its hind legs and swiftly slit its neck. There was no issue in Kaylee's mind. It was not cute, and there were no topics about her sliding a knife into its throat.

Suddenly, there was another alert in her head. She put down her fish and bunny. Kaylee grabbed a pair of a metallic gloves. She donned them.

In Kaylee's mind, there were several screens. These visual fields were connected to drones flying as the scouts of her defense sector. Kaylee maneuvered her drones to get her a better look. On the top left screen, there was a smoking area. This was an odd thing to see, as the drones were over the Pacific Ocean.

Kaylee alerted the two other sections closest to hers. Her drone got closer to the smoke. It was difficult to discern the cause of this column of smoke. Kaylee ordered her drone to turn on its infrared vision.

The infrared came one. Everything turned into bicolor vision. It was either red or black, and shades in between. The drone flew around, and it looked like an underwater drone blew up. Kaylee was not sure of the cause of this explosion.

The world had become scarcer of people, but somehow, its anger to each other was still as hot as it was in the past. Now, the enemies were India and China. They looked for women to continue their rebuilding of the population.

Kaylee was an Asian.

Her father rescued her mother from a reproduction house about eighteen years ago. The world had less people; the Chinese and Indian were stuck in their tradition of wanting the firstborn to be a boy. This made no sense for the repopulation of the world. Traditions changed very slowly if at all.

Now she had an underwater drone, which gave her an image of a drone torpedo smoking. It had not exploded yet. Was it a malfunction of its system? She was not sure at this time. She ordered the torpedo to surface. It came up slowly but surely. Then she turned off its system and ordered a couple of air drones to evacuate the drone torpedo for repair.

The alert was over. She informed the two sectors she alerted previously; she passed on the stand-down order. This was a strange moment for her; she never had a malfunctioning drone torpedo.

Kaylee returned to her fish and bunny. After picking them up, she walked back to Hope Street. The wind swirled, and for a moment, Kaylee felt the cold through her jacket. She was a tall woman; she weighed much less than a hundred pounds; and her hair was nonexistent. She shaved it every other day. It was easier to manage, according to her. Her mother thought differently. She grew up with long black hair.

In this world, there was little people to talk to. She had two other people to talk to: Sylvia and Muhammed.

Sylvia was an elder lady who was needing more than herself to talk to someone. She told Kaylee many stories of her past, and these tales helped Kaylee feel at home in this deserted Chicago. She told her of a time where there was a Magnificent Mile and a magical train that took people to downtown and back. There were many people, and this was so strange to her. In a busy day, she may see ten persons.

On the other hand, Muhammed was a security in the defense pack. It was strange that she would come on and he would be off to bed. This was an odd thing for Kaylee. She talked to him once, and except for hello and pleasantries, he was a tall man who had little or nothing to say. He seemed to enjoy this manner of not talking to others.

Finally, Kaylee got back to her place. She climbed up the stairs and walked in her apartment. She never thought of moving downstairs. As she said, there was no reason to do so. She placed the fish in her sink and pulled off her coat.

After she scaled the fish and defrocked the bunny of its fur, she proceeded to grill the fish and place the bunny in a braise and in the oven. She wanted to cook it a little more over the time, as Sylvia was older and her chewing was a little weaker. There were no vegetables but yeast. This depressed her for a second, but she endeavored into making a yeast casserole. However, she had no cheese and two eggs.

She looked at her ingredients and thought she may want to go to the chicken coop to get more eggs. Maybe if there were enough eggs, she could make a bakery type of cake. So Kaylee put on her coat and walked down to the chicken coop. She took the back door and descended to her courtyard where the coop was. Examining the coop, her four chickens and roosters were being, well, chickens. She entered and gathered four eggs. She exited the coop.

Her mind went red again. The analysis of the torpedo indicated someone sabotaged the torpedo. Kaylee called up her air drones and underwater drones. She scanned every square inch of her surveillance area. There must be something if someone sabotaged her equipment.

The alert was sent to all on the west coast surveillance. They all scanned their areas. There was a long moment of silence, which was the usual as there was little or no one to talk to.

Suddenly, Kaylee asked Turnbull about the sabotage. Turnbull was the artificial intelligence who made the analysis of the torpedo.

"Turnbull, please indicate how the torpedo was sabotaged?" Kaylee asked calmly.

"The gyroscope was hit by a laser, and this caused the system to malfunction," Turnbull answered and showed it to her in her mind.

"Did this laser come skyward, or did it come underwater?" Kaylee asked Turnbull with a little more anxiety.

"The attack came from the sky at a forty-five-degree angle from the west," Turnbull answered with no emotion in its voice.

"Please locate the area and calculate the potential route of potential object." Kaylee sensed there was something; there was no proof, but she could feel it.

"According to the data, it was there and it disappeared," Turnbull said without an ounce of anxiety or wonder.

"Shit! We have to find it," she ordered Turnbull; this time, there was a crack in her voice.

Kaylee immediately called up the defense pack and its commanders to alert them about Turnbull's finding. She had all the personnel online, and she tried to maintain her calm. "We have an intrusion from a flying intruder. Turnbull seemed to be saying it had the ability to disappear. For some odd reason, it attacked a torpedo drone." She took a second to pause.

After Kaylee caught her breath, the attack began. There were explosions in her mental screens. Immediately, she exclaimed, "We are under attack!"

Kaylee called up her reserve air drones and put on alert her marine drones. The army she controlled was all mechanized and robotic. There was not enough people to man the defense of the coast. It controlled by the Interweb.

The answer to her wondering about why an air attack was linked to a drone torpedo took a second to come to fruition. The marine action was massive. Her naval screens showed many explosions; she was not sure which were hers and which were the enemy's. After a deep breath, Kaylee called up her troops, and she had a better idea of what was going.

Kaylee's forces held up, and she shot more off than they were. She was winning. In her body, it felt like a cold wind, which made her more alive.

From her satellite shot, Kaylee could see a battle, and she saw an opening to get her air force through and circle them. In the next second, she ordered her air drones to take the northern way. Then she swerved them to the west. Then she waited for a minute to not be detected. Then she made her air force go south. There it was; Kaylee could see the back of their air force. Kaylee understood, if she could get rid of their forces in the air, she would then have the advantage.

In the next minutes, Kaylee opened fire. There was no chance for the enemy. Within five minutes, she reclaimed the air and its advantage.

The next move was to use her newly gained territory to start attacking the effective marine troops left. It did not take too long. Within the hour, it was all over.

The defense took some energy out of the young woman. In the courtyard, beside her chicken coop, Kaylee was tired. Her eyes were fatigued. There was barely any light as the sky was gray, but it was too much for her. She brought her hand up to her forehead to shield the light. As she came up, an egg dropped and cracked after a normal descent to the ground.

"Shit!" Kaylee let out.

In a moment of confusion, Kaylee took a deep breath. She did not know what was next, but she needed to sit down. However, she had to climb some stairs. Kaylee's fatigue and hunger affected her stepping for the first two steps. Then her feet found their way back upstairs.

Upon arriving to her place, Kaylee went to her living room. She plopped herself on her couch; it was gray, and there was a bluish carpet underneath it. Resting her head, she considered the attack. Slowly, her mind wandered in the ether, and the thought of rewarding herself came. It was almost too natural for her to come to that idea.

In this land, where having friends was scarce, to have a reward was a manual date. Kaylee looked at her right hand, and it went to her pants belt. Then it disappeared under her pants. She knew where her clitoris was; her fingers gently came in contact with her pleasure center. The next second, her fingers grazed the soft lips of her vagina. Her finger ran up and again gently touched her clitoris. Her neck was stretched out and pushed against the pillows. Pleasure invaded her body.

Kaylee wondered why after action, she needed sexual pleasure to relieve her stress. She was a young woman, and knowing the answers to such questions seemed too far to reach. Men were few and far between; there were several in Central Chicago. They were sophisticated, and their talk was nearly Chinese to her. This was a sarcastic comment for her, as she was Asian.

Her father was American, and her mother was Asian. She never met her own mother. Kaylee knew her through a picture her father showed her. Stories were told to her by her father; her imagination of her mother was grand, but it was never right. As she woke up, she was back in this world.

The world went through many turns. There were spins that were ordinary. Other solar cycles were more ornery. The world used to be populated. Many wars and a catastrophic contagion contributed to the world being underpopulated.

The contagion was a cataclysm that the world became isolationist. Kaylee was never aware of what was the cause of the calamity. Her world has been lonely, and except for her Interweb connection, she met a boy last a few months ago. It was a strange thing.

The man was her age. Kaylee stared at him in Central Chicago. She was there for her Interweb connection. Kaylee was given a surgical implant of a connecting chip at seventeen years old. Ever since, she wondered what the boy was there for. He looked different, but she could not figure out what to say to him. He was across from her in the waiting room, but that was it. There were no words between the two of them.

After finishing cooking her rabbit, Kaylee ate. After dinner, she took some of her dinner to Sylvia. The old woman barely talked; she was quiet, and this drove Kaylee a little off her rocker. Bedtime came, and she gave her guard to Julie in Thunder Bay.

CHAPTER 2

THE NEXT MORNING, the same pattern of movement happened; nothing new on the horizon for Kaylee.

Dinner, bring food to Sylvia, and bedtime were the activities Kaylee finished for the day.

The following day was the same.

Ever since her dad died, life became of this series of days in north of Chicago. She had two neighbors. One of them Kaylee had no idea what he did. And Sylvia was older and needed her help.

Life was lonely. Survival was a moment of improvisation to maintain the chance for tomorrow.

Tomorrow came, and today was different. She acknowledged an e-mail from Central Chicago Defense Command; their logo at the top of the letter was CCDC, and this was an enormous letter for Kaylee. She read the letter.

> Dear Ms. Kaylee McCloud;
>
> As we have noticed, you have defended our shores recently.
>
> It came to our attention your use of our troops in this battle. We would like to see you in Central Chicago.
>
> Please, the next morning from this letter, we will be expecting you.
>
> Thank you.

Kaylee was surprised by this letter. This was not a letter recognizing her tactical greatness to pull victory from the defense of the Oregon shores. No words to tell her "Good job" or even "Congratulations. We would like to pin a medal on your chest"; no, just "We are expecting you." This was neither good nor bad. She was not sure.

Upon waking up, she folded her bedding, brushed her teeth, and then ate a light breakfast. Then Kaylee got her bike out of her shed. She straddled her bike and went on her way south to downtown.

An hour travel at most, unless there were road blocks. This spring was uneventful, so Kaylee expect no blocks; but just in case, she departed two hours prior to the doors of Central Chicago opening.

The bike chain needed some grease, as it whistled a bird song. The pedaling was easy. It was early in the morning. Kaylee imagined how Chicago used to be. Her father used to describe scenes of people going to places and shops opening their doors. A lot of people would go to this place that her father named the Soulless Coffee Place. Kaylee could not recall the name of it, but there were a lady and a star.

First stop, Kaylee got off her bicycle and climbed an embankment of dirt. It was a few feet high, but she could not hop over it with her two wheeler. At the top, she could see the Lake Michigan. It was large and it was gray. The color gray was the shadowy tone. This meant something to people, but to Kaylee, it meant little. To her, Lake Michigan was a source of fish and algae. Most importantly, it was water. This was most important.

Walking down the barrier of dirt was not hard. Soon, Kaylee straddled her pedal machine. Then she saw a person in a window. She looked up. The person disappeared. This was the norm nowadays. Since the contagion, people were afraid of coming out and meeting new people. They used electronics for all communication. Kaylee yearned to meet people and see a man.

Her father used to tell her, "There are a million fish in the world. One is for you." He would tap on her nose right after. It was funny, and Kaylee worshipped that memory. It was all she had left of her father.

Pedaling was not hard, but sweat began to be felt on her back. Kaylee felt it. She looked at her left wrist and brought it up to her eyes. In her mind, she clicked a few buttons, and her clothes began airing the heat out of her clothes.

There was a time in her life when she used to pedal without a goal; those days were gone. Today, Kaylee pedaled with a purpose. Like any other day, she had a purpose. She wondered why there was no purpose in her childhood. She thought often beside her father that she could gather food while he could rest, but no. Her father worked so hard for her well-being. She did not understand this aspect of life.

Finally, Kaylee arrived at the Central Chicago walls. These walls were built way in the past when people were afraid of one another. The contagion was a class issue for a while. The rich held up Central Chicago and built a wall to protect themselves. As everything else, the contagion reached the rich and killed the majority of them. The walls were a vestige of this moment where the rich showed their power for no reason.

Kaylee dismounted her bicycle and looked at the walls. They were rocky and could easily be climbed. She would have done it, but the door opened. Kaylee checked the time; it was eight in the morning. Surprised, she thought the doors opened at nine. Her search on the Interweb gave her that idea, but no matter. Kaylee pushed her bike past the wall.

There came a moment of change in Kaylee's eyes. She came from an older world where buildings needed repairs or were in disrepair. Passing through the wall of Central Chicago, Kaylee came into a world of cleanliness. The buildings were taller, newer, glassier, and most different; there were more people.

In her day-to-day life, there was no one. The only people Kaylee talked to were Sylvia and people on the Interweb. Here, there were dozens of persons walking to somewhere. This fact amazed Kaylee; the people seemed to go to places to do things. There was a purpose for everyone.

At the moment, Kaylee marveled at these people having purpose; she felt a sense of shame. In the morning, her only desire was to gather food for Sylvia and her survival. This made her feel less important and her life had less purpose than all these people.

Walking in this wonderland, Kaylee looked right, left, and up in the distance. She was in awe of Central Chicago. There was a cleanliness that amazed her. This feeling shamed where she lived.

Finally, she arrived at the building of Central Chicago Defense Command. It was on the shore of Lake Michigan. The docks gave a beautiful view of the water. The building was glassy, and yet it was older. It had a marquee that gave onto a brick building. There were revolving doors. Kaylee had heard of these push doors systems, but never had she gone through them.

With some angst, Kaylee looked at a few people walk through the revolving doors. They entered and pushed the doors. It seemed easy enough. Kaylee took a deep breath and walked to the revolving doors. She entered the triangular section and placed her hands on the door in front of her. She began to push. There was no acceleration in the door movement. It moved as if it was automatic.

Behind Kaylee, a man entered through the door. He smiled at Kaylee's attempt to push the door. As the door revolved, Kaylee entered the building. Then the man who followed Kaylee entered too. Her face began to feel warm. There was a moment of shame. The man nearly sneered at her as he passed her.

Looking for an office should be easy, but this bureau was not evident. The room was 316. She took the stairs to the third floor and read the signs; 316 was to the right. Kaylee found room 315 but then 317 followed. Where did they put room 316? She walked and began to panic; she may be late. There was another fifteen minutes to find this room. How can this room not be on this floor?

Kaylee walked to the main floor and went to the reception desk. There was no one there. She could feel a drip of cold sweat going down her spine. Then a young man tapped her left shoulder. She turned. Kaylee saw a tall man with wide shoulders, curly brown hair, and brown eyes. Kaylee was enamored; he was cute.

"How can I help you?" the man asked.

"Uh, I am looking for the office," Kaylee stammered.

"Which office?" the man questioned with mocking eyes.

"I am sorry. I am looking for office 316," Kaylee answered with eyes looking down.

"How do you know we have an office 316?" The man began to get more official.

"It is the office of Central Chicago Defense Command," Kaylee said with more confidence.

"Please wait here," the man ordered her.

The man walked behind the desk and brought his left hand behind his left ear. Then he stared blankly at the glassy windows. Kaylee looked down and around; she felt uncomfortable, but she seemed to have found room 316. The man seemed to have disconnected his communication with people in room 316. He looked at Kaylee and, with his head, indicated for her to follow him. He walked up to an elevator and pushed the button. It was neither up nor down. The button was lit up. The doors opened. They entered the elevator. The doors closed, and the lights turned off. Kaylee felt a hand behind her back.

For moment, Kaylee felt fear. Fear of what? Rape? How could it happen? It was so dark; she could not see her own hand. Then the elevator went down. Its speed was great. Then it stopped. Kaylee turned her head and could see a slight green light. It did not allow for her to see anything else. The hand placed pressure on her back to move forward. Then after three steps, a light came on. It was a single light and it shone on a seat.

Kaylee sat in the seat. The light shone in her eyes; she could not see a thing in the room. Kaylee presumed she was in room 316. Then a chair screeched on the floor. She turned to her right, and the man who brought her down here was no longer behind her.

Kaylee was a little spooked, and then a voice came on.

"I would like to inform you that you are being recorded." The voice was manly and deep.

"Yes, sir," Kaylee responded.

"All right, let us begin," the voice continued.

Kaylee was slightly tense; she had done nothing wrong, she thought. This thought ran through her mind to review all her actions.

"On Wednesday, March 11, you were part of a battle on the Oregon shores. Correct?" the voice asked.

"Yes, sir," Kaylee answered.

"Please tell the details as you remember it," the voice proceeded.

"I received a distress call from torpedo AT19-23-245-28967. As I proceeded to the diagnostic, I received the information from my naval drone, and it stated the torpedo had been destroyed. As this was odd, I asked the drone to calculate where the attack came from. It revealed it came from the air. At that moment, I understood that there was an attack on its way. So I took the air drone position and could see the attack on my southern flank. I reinforced my troops and called up the reserve. I placed the northern troops on alert. I pulled off the battlefield to have an overview and saw an opening in the northern section of the map. There were no apparent troops amassing in that area. I took the opportunity to advance to the back of their troops. Once I got the back of their troops, I was able to destroy them."

"Thank you. Now, did you see anything strange?" the voice asked.

"No, sir," Kaylee responded with a sense of relief.

"Replacements were made per your losses?" the voice continued.

"Yes, sir." Kaylee felt much more comfortable.

"All right, thank you, Kaylee McCloud. And as a last question, did you receive any messages during or after the attack?" the voice asked.

"No . . . sir." The question made Kaylee review all her records, and, indeed, nothing of the sort happened.

"Thank you very much." The voice ended the conversation.

Kaylee was back into the dark as the light in her face went off. She felt a hand helping her up and guiding her back to the elevator. This time, as it went up, the lights came on. After a moment of adjusting her eyes to the intense light, Kaylee saw the man. His curly hair was fuzzy and it came into focus. It was nice, and she remembered his commanding instructions. She was put off at that thought, but his hair was nice.

On her bike, she ran through the interview. It was the first she ever went through. However, it could not have been for every battle, as this was her second battle. Did she do something wrong? It could not be. Kaylee ran through each question she was asked; the one that was out there was the last one. *Did I receive any communication?* Who would send her a communication?

This was an odd question. The world was divided in sections. There were the Europeans. They were patriotic and helpful, but the Americans had not communicated with them for ages. Then the Indians and Chinese were our biggest adversaries. This was a population issue; they all wanted boys as firstborn; this made their world needing more women. So they attacked the Americans to steal women. That was why Kaylee and her sisters were in the central part of the North American continent.

Her father explained this to her, and he told her that all this was for her comfort and protection. However, this question kept on coming back in her mind. *Why would they ask me this? If I had a communication from anybody, I would report it to them. So why is it they asked? This was nebulous.*

Returning home, Kaylee got up and began to cook a simple dish to take to Sylvia. She was perturbed by the question they asked. Did they ask the question to see what she would do? Or was it, there was a message and she did not see it?

The meal was steamed fish and vegetable with a soy sauce dipping sauce. Sylvia and she ate silently. Kaylee was preoccupied with the query CCDC threw at her. Sylvia was silent for no reason, more or less because Kaylee was not talking.

The silence could only be sustained for so long. Sylvia broke the quietness.

"Why are you so hushed? Usually you ask how my day was. I know I have little to say about a day that followed another one with no difference between either one." Sylvia seemed to have a lot to say and let it out.

"I am sorry, Sylvia. I was thinking, and I guess it made me quiet," Kaylee responded back.

"What were you thinking about?" Sylvia inquired.

Kaylee smiled and let out a little laughter.

"I was thinking about things. Nothing important. I am sorry, Sylvia," Kaylee answered while trying to divert the older lady from her questioning.

"All right, but remember, whatever troubles you cannot be too hard to resolve," Sylvia said while lying on her couch; Kaylee helped her by covering her with her blankets.

"I know, and thank you for caring," Kaylee expressed softly.

Kaylee exited the building. She stopped and thought, *Where would you hide a message if there was a message to transmit?*

This energized her. Kaylee knew it could not be in the video of the attack, but it would be in the lines of coding beneath it. Then again, it would have been mined by CCDC. *So where would you hide a message?*

Kaylee walked home and sat on her couch. She understood the CCDC would be monitoring her. Therefore, she pulled out an old laptop. Every soldier had one just in case one was blocked from accessing the Interweb from the chip. The old laptop was also a coding device, as it would be the only way to code if there was no chip connection to the Interweb.

Kaylee turned on the laptop. While it booted up, she wiped the dust off the keyboard and the screen. Finally, the boot up was over. She downloaded the fight and pulled up the coding. She knew it was not going to be easy. If the CCDC screened and scoured through it, what would she find?

The whole night went; the next-day sun rose, and its rays shone on this day of March. Kaylee got up and wiped her eyes. She sighed and took a deep breath. She found nothing. It was all clean. There was no message. Why was she looking for something the CCDC would have found much faster than she would ever? She headed to the bathroom and sat on the toilet. After urination was over, she washed her hands. Then she stared at her jewelry box.

Kaylee opened the lid and closed it. She repeated this motion. She pursed her lips and blinked her eyes. There was something there. What if the message was in a box? What would be a box in lines of coding? Then it popped in her mind; it would be the subroutine programs. Those were the lines no one, even her, cared about.

The lines of coding were the action you wanted the bots to complete, but the bots themselves had subroutine programs. This was much longer to review without a clear place to look. Kaylee took a second to think about it. *They attacked my torpedo but did not destroy it. Why was that? Could it be that simple?*

Reviewing the subroutine software was not the highlight of anyone wanting an answer. Kaylee went over line by line. There was nothing. She thought about it again; Kaylee knew there were lines in the subroutines. This meant there were subroutine subroutines. Kaylee had to open the most basic programming of the torpedo bot—the original lines of instructions.

Lunch ran out, and dinner was coming close. Kaylee was submerged in the review of line by line of her torpedo basics. There were lines about its dimension, its relay to the gyroscope, its relay to the GPS. *This was so basic, how would anyone care about it? Unless you sought some message from your enemy.*

When Kaylee realized what time it was; she hurried up and made some sandwiches with nut butter and an amalgam of fruit and berries jelly. As soon as she was done, she ran to Sylvia's home. Sylvia was there. She saw Kaylee and smiled. You could not be angry to a person who helps you.

Sylvia was an older woman. She said she had lived in this area her entire life. Kaylee heard stories from her dad. He told her to always take care of your elder. Sylvia was not a talkative person, but she was congenial. Pleasantries exchanges were always Sylvia's preferred topic of conversation.

"I am so sorry. I was busy and I forgot what time it was. I am sorry, Sylvia," Kaylee apologized to no one who cared.

"Oh, my dear, I cannot ask you to do all you do, take care of me, and be on time," Sylvia said with an ounce of sarcasm for good measure.

"I am sorry, Sylvia." Kaylee reiterated her apology.

"It is all right, my dear. I am hungry and I see you have sandwiches. That sounds really good," Sylvia said as she reached for a sandwich.

"All right." Kaylee seemed to be apologetic enough for now.

After dinner, Kaylee went home and continued to seek a message that she did not know if it was there. Kaylee reached the bottom of the software. She was tired of looking at lines of coding. This became tedious.

The night came and the time was past midnight. Kaylee came to a strange place. She was in the programming for self-diagnostic, but there was a strange file. It was an mp3. What was an mp3? The termination was odd. She had never seen a file with that termination. And, furthermore, this file sat in self-diagnostic.

Kaylee tried to open this file. She was not able to. She paused and thought about it. This file was an odd one. What could it be? She decided to open her Interweb connection to seek the nature of an mp3.

And so Kaylee did. Her search came back with an explanation—it was a type of file to share verbal information on the Internet in the late twentieth to twenty-first century. This triggered many questions: *Why would anyone keep an old file in the twenty-second century? Then, why would a verbal information be shared and be in the self-diagnostic of a torpedo? How can I hear the message?*

Kaylee was at a loss. She lay down on her couch. She happened to be lying on her father's old telephone. It amazed her how the older people used to have a device to talk to one another. Suddenly, she jerked her head to her left side. She thought. Her eyes fixated, and then she pulled her lower lip onto her teeth. Then Kaylee got up and went to her closet.

The closet was in the lobby of her apartment. Kaylee thought calling it the lobby made her apartment enormous. It was a one-bedroom and it was sufficient for her, but it was not big enough to use the word "lobby." She looked for something; no one was sure, as no one was around her. Then she held it. It was an old telephone.

On the back of it, there was a logo of an apple. The screen was black. Kaylee got up and went to her charger. It was a rectangular pad, and she placed the telephone on it. Nothing happened. Kaylee brought her right hand to her right ear lobe; she scratched it with her index side and her thumb. It was a thinking moment for her.

Kaylee looked at the telephone intensely. Then she returned to her closet and looked in a box for something. She dug in further and pulled out a whitish string. Returning to her charger, which was solar energy and collected in perpetuity, Kaylee connected the cord to the phone, but how could she connect the cord to her charger?

There was a two-millimeter round plug, and when she faced the old piece of equipment, it was a square design with two prongs sticking out. How would you connect those two things together? This was a new mystery.

Kaylee endeavored into figuring out how this device needed electric power to be used. She cut out the squarish thing with two metallic prongs sticking out. Then she saw two distinct wires. Her jaw jiggled in their joints as she thought of her next steps. Slowly, Kaylee separated the two wires. Then she took her two-millimeter plug and cut out the wire.

There were many optical wires. This was a problem. Kaylee scratched the back of her head and squinted. This was a serious problem. A pause was needed. She got up and went to her kitchen. She entered and the light came on; and she said, "Water at 10 degrees Celsius." A paper glass and water appeared in her producer.

The producer was able to give her water at whatever temperature Kaylee wanted, but food was not quite there yet. Central Chicago worked on it, but it was not successful yet.

Then it came to her. She could see the connector to the charger and tried to connect to the ancient wire. It was a challenge and it may not work, but there were not too many other answers.

After a few minutes, Kaylee had the two-millimeter plug and the wire connected. This was going to be successful or a huge explosion. The moment was here. Her hand shook a light, and with her left arm, she covered her face, which was turned to the left on top of it. Then she pushed in the plug, and nothing happened. This was a good sign to Kaylee. She moved her head to the right and saw a right sign of a plug going to the device. What did this mean? She pondered on this technical question. Then less than a minute later, the telephone came to life. This was good, it was really good.

Her next challenge was to configure how to move that mp3 file to the device. She rigged up a similar wire and plug. She took another deep breath before plugging it into the quantum laptop. Again, nothing blew up. This was a good sign for Kaylee.

She looked at her laptop. It was hard for her to use her fingers to type things. It was not business as usual. Kaylee was used to using her mind to complete all the tasks she would struggle with typing at this point in time. The significant advantage to this was Kaylee was not identifiable. Her laptop was as if you had a cloak of invisibility on the Interweb. As Kaylee looked on her torpedo, all the torpedoes in CCDC were identified as being checked.

Finally, Kaylee was near her goal—listening to this old file. For the least, this was her hope; for a moment, she wished it was not going to be a random order or even the torpedo telling her it was under self-diagnostic. This would be a significant downer if it happened.

It took about two seconds for the file to be found on the telephone. This was an odd device to use. Kaylee struggled with the idea of pushing a logo to activate an item. This was weird for her. Finally, she accessed the file button, and it linked itself to the voice provider.

The voice was not recognizable. The message lasted for about twenty seconds. She could not understand a word of it. It was in a different language. Kaylee knew, if she accessed her translator, it will be uncovered by CCDC. In light, they asked her about a message; this must be it. On top of it, why would this message be in an American torpedo?

The sun peaked over the horizon. This was not a good sign; she was about to take over the guard on the coast of Oregon. Kaylee was tired and troubled. The message was in foreign language, but which was it? How was she going to figure out the language of the message?

As Kaylee got up and proceeded with the cleanup, a message came across her mind. It read,

> Urgent.
> Kaylee McCloud to report to CCDC.
> Immediately.

That was it. Not a word more or less included. This was a stern message to Kaylee and suspected to have come up with the answer for the CCDC. It was seven o'clock, and how did they know? How could she get in the walls? This was very odd. Kaylee got to her bedroom and changed. Kaylee understood cleaning up all this mess was essential; she completed this with urgency.

Kaylee put on another combat suit. She grabbed her coat and got down and got to her bike shed when an officer stepped into her courtyard.

"Kaylee McCloud?" It was not a question; it had an order tone behind it.

"Yes, sir," Kaylee responded as she saluted.

"You have orders to follow us," the officer said without returning the salute.

"Yes, sir," Kaylee uttered; she knew if the salute was not returned, this meant it was a different branch of the CCDC. Was it the CCDC?

Two officers waited on the other side of her gate. Three officers accompanied Kaylee to the wagon. She had an officer to her right and left; also, she had the officer who talked to her at her back. They did not want her to escape.

Kaylee sat down on a very comfortable seat and thought to herself, *How could I escape?* Her Interweb connection gave her position on the map. If she wanted to remove her chip, she could not even conceive how to proceed. They implanted the chip deep and close to her thalamus. There would be no way anyone lower than an expert of chip removal could access the chip.

The ride was much more comfortable than on her bicycle. The vehicle was not connected to the road; it was above it and floating on it. She was not sure how it did this, but it was not touching the ground. Escaping would be a very painful experience.

After a short ride, they landed. Kaylee wondered why she could not have this vehicle, as it was faster than her on her bicycle. It was among at least two dozen of them. The population of Chicago was maybe at one thousand people, and most of them were in the downtown area. So why would they not let her use one of the vehicles? Darn it! It was really a sweet ride.

Again, the three officers quartered her for her to only go forward. They walked with a rhythm and foot stepping, which reminded her of some past events. However, Kaylee was too nervous to manage to recall the memory.

They entered the building, and they brought Kaylee to the elevator. She knew room 316 and her were going to make anew with one another. Then darkness, and she could feel her elbows being cradled by the firm arms of the officers to her laterals. The room was dark, and the light came on to the seat. She sat down, and the officers removed themselves, as she could hear the elevator doors closing.

"Kaylee McCloud?" a voice burst out.

"Yes, sir," Kaylee answered the question,

"Did you find the file?" The voice felt like an attack.

"What file are you referring to, sir?" Kaylee attempted to delay her answer.

"We talked about a file yesterday morning, and I know you have worked all night on this issue. So where is this file?" The voice seemed frustrated.

"I don't know, sir." Kaylee tried again to not lie or even deny.

"Ms. McCloud, you know if you do not provide us this file, you would be imprisoned and judgment would follow." The voice was now frustrated.

"Sir, how do you know I have it?" Kaylee needed more time to figure a way out.

"I do not have to give any other details, but we know you worked on it all night. Hence, give us the file." The voice showed its persistence.

At this moment, Kaylee's mind went into overdrive. She was off the Interweb, no one was in the apartment, and only two people lived in her area. The man was unlikely, as he was two blocks away. Sylvia? How could this be? Then she recalled a line from Arthur Conan Doyle, "When you have eliminated the impossible, whatever remains, however improbable, must be the truth." Then her mind calmed itself down; it was Sylvia who gave her away. So she was a spy, or did she report her? But why?

"Ms. McCloud?" The voice came back into the traffic of noises.

"I do not have the file, sir. You can search my residence," Kaylee said with confidence behind her voice.

"We are," the voice said with more than sarcasm in its voice.

Minutes followed each other. The silence deafened the room. The darkness was interrupted by this one light. Kaylee was not comfortable, but she was at ease. Finally, the voice came back.

"Ms. McCloud, I would like to remind you, if you have anything relating to the attack of March 11, you have to proceed with the forwarding of it to the CCDC. Do you understand?" The voice came back, and it appeared to be annoyed.

"Yes, sir," Kaylee responded with a dampened attempt to control her sense of victory.

The voice went away, and a hand touched her elbow and guided her back to the elevator.

CHAPTER 3

T HE CCDC COUNCIL entered the meeting room. They sat down, and some of them conversed until Commander Schilling entered the room. Now, everyone was silent. The commander opened his leather notebook.

Commander Schilling began.

"Good morning, gentlemen. I am Commander Schilling from the CCDC. This morning, we received information. Lieutenant McCloud"—her image came on the screen—"received a message. We interviewed her, and she was astute. We searched her home and we did not find a trace of this message."

"Who was this message from this time?" an older man asked.

"We do not know, sir. All we know, the attack was of Chinese origin," the commander responded with sharpness as his uniform was.

"Do we know if she got this message?" another man asked.

"Again, sir, we did not find any trace of a message. The search party used the scanner and any other device of detection of message. They found nothing," Schilling responded again. He was precise and concise.

"What is your next step, Commander?" the general asked across the table.

"Sir, we intent to follow Ms. McCloud, and if she shows any signs of deviation to her schedule, then we will bring her back for more questioning," Commander Schilling answered.

"Very good. Proceed," the general said as if he gave his blessing for the operation to go forward.

"Yes, sir." Schilling closed his notebook and walked away.

The general was troubled. There were few generals left in the army or air force. The navy no longer existed. He was General Sihi; he was a general with experience, and it was not the first time he dealt with messages sent from Asia.

General Sihi was a dark man. His skin was a deep brown, and his eyes had an Asian look. He was tall and he was broad. He was slightly overweight, but no one dared telling him so. Sihi was man who had in mind the stability of the system. He had done many things to complete his mission. This one would not be any different for him.

There were two other men at the table: Simon DeGagne and Frank Pritzker. They were two men who knew their bank accounts were their cards to be in this meeting room. They have been at these debriefings, but they seemed unnerved, as usual. This was a mark of distinction from a general and rich men.

"Sihi, how far can we let this situation go?" Simon asked.

"I know how far it can go, sir," Sihi answered with no thought or visual contact with Simon.

"All right, then, I guess you will let us know?" Frank asked uncomfortably.

"I may, sir." General Sihi lifted his eyes to express his exasperation to both of their questions.

The presence of the rich people in the meeting room was due to the fact the military needed money, and, therefore, money was present. It would be better if they were less present to Sihi, but it was another difference from the past long ago and today, he thought.

General Sihi stood up, and right there, Simon DeGagne found his courage.

"General, I sense you are annoyed with our questions."

"No, sir. I am not annoyed with your questions. Preoccupation was my emotion at the moment of the questions, sir." Sihi tried his best to be calm and reserved. He knew he went too far with his remarks; it was time to retreat.

"Very well, please explain to us, how far would you go to stop this situation?" Simon asked with pleasure.

"Sir, if you mean, how far would I let the situation go with Ms. McCloud? I will let us get this message, and then I ensure her disappearance will be . . . clean. If you meant, can I stop them from transmitting messages? This would be a more difficult situation for us. As they place their messages on any of their attacks, most of the time we are able to control this situation. Occasionally, like the case of Ms. McCloud, the situation gets to a level that leads us to a conversation that neither one of you want me to tell you how it ends." The general was precise and succinct.

"Very well, General," Simon expressed while staring at the Sihi's eyes.

"Gentlemen." The general saluted his audience and left the room.

Simon and Frank remained in the room. Frank opened up to his partner.

"Do you think we need to replace the general?"

"Maybe, but not now," Simon responded pensively.

"Why not now?" Frank persisted.

"I think he knows what he is doing with this situation." Simon looked at Frank.

HENRI NGUYEN

"If you think so, but I think we should consider a replacement soon." Frank got up and walked to the door.

"Frank, why do you not like our general?" Simon asked with a smile on his face.

"Simon, when the general does not respect us, it is time to get us a new general," Frank said simply, and some of his frustrations came out.

"You have a point, my friend. On the other hand, I would tell you there are not too many general personnel left in the bank." Simon laughed as he expressed the idea to his friend Frank. He got up and walked out the room with Frank.

General Sihi went to his office, and as he approached his door, he saw Commander Schilling.

"Sir." Commander Schilling saluted.

General Sihi returned the salute and went in his office. The commander followed his superior into his office.

"Where is she at this point?" Sihi asked Schilling.

"She is walking home, sir." Schilling was looking in his notebook, as it had the path of Kaylee going home.

"You have a drone on her?" The general wanted to know.

"Yes, sir. A squad is also assigned to her," the commander answered without hesitation.

"The search of her house did not turn up anything?" the general asked again, as if he could not believe it.

"No, sir. Her neighbor told us her light was on all night. There were movements in the apartment. She accessed the Interweb once last night," Commander Schilling responded to the question.

"What was this connection about?" The general wanted to know.

"It was a search for 'what is an mp3 file?'" The commander obtained the answer from his notebook.

"What is it? An mp3 file?" The general was confused.

The commander searched, and he stated the definition of an mp3 file.

The atmosphere was quiet and serene. Suddenly, the general asked.

"What if the Asians placed an mp3 in a bot that they destroyed? This would be a way to let in their message," the general proposed.

"Sir, they have always been using an attack to place a message with our staff. Why would they change their ways?" the commander asked while thinking. As he finished his statement, he had his answer.

"Commander, don't you know the Art of War from Sun Tzu? I believe he said, 'All warfare is deception.'" The general was a knowledgeable man, and he shared his knowledge with his subordinate.

"You are saying they have hidden a message to Ms. McCloud. How would you do this?" Again, as the commander spoke, the answer came to him.

"That is your job to find out." The general signaled with his hand for his officer to leave.

Schilling saluted and left the room. He walked fast to the elevator. It came; he entered and inserted a key into a key hole. This was really old fashioned. There were no more keys. Doors would open and close for people with the right permission to enter a room or domicile. This was old fashioned and showed there was a secret.

The elevator went down, and in a flash, he was in the basement. The lights came on. He walked into a hallway with mirrors on both sides. These mirrors hid offices and rendered being in this hallways useless. Unless you could enter the offices, which Schilling could. He entered a door that opened for him.

Schilling was in a room where there was a chair facing a screen. He sat down and asked the empty room to check the March 11 attack. The screen showed him the action. A voice came on.

"This was a nice defense." It was a nice voice. It came from the AI. Schilling chose a female voice for his own pleasure.

"Search in the data of every bots that were hit during this event. Report anything unusual," Schilling ordered.

"There was nothing unusual, Swinthun," the AI voice answered.

"Nothing unusual? Search 'how can you transfer an mp3 file?'" Swinthun ordered.

"To transfer an mp3 file, all you have to do is be within a person or device and transmit it," the AI answered without fear of his anger or outburst.

"So you could transfer the information as long as you are close enough," Commander Schilling said pensively. "Search for an mp3 file in all bots hit."

"There was one mp3 file in torpedo AT19-23-245-28967." AI produced the answer quickly.

"Show mp3," Swinthun expressed, interested.

"I cannot. The file is unknown to me. I cannot read it. I would have to write a software to read it," AI said.

"Do so. Let me know when you are done," Schilling expressed with some impatience.

Swinthun was a man of his early twenties. His hair was nonexistent, as he shaved his head every morning. He found it more accommodating for army life. Although his army life was different from any other. His missions were often happening in this office with the AI, which he at times called Darcy.

Darcy was his love until she died. It was at the same time he enrolled in the army and shaved his head. His broad shoulders, tall stature, and serious army look made him a severe man to look at.

An hour later, he asked Darcy, "Do you have a software?"

She responded, "Not quite."

Another hour elapsed, and the question came back to Darcy. This time, she stated, "Nearly."

It was nearly eleven o'clock in the morning when Darcy alerted Swinthun that she had a reader. He sat down and ordered her to play the file.

"Su khong knony Kaleah. Than mi Hara. Chao penluksav khongknony. Soka khony, khonymi khuaamching. Su khong knony Kaleah. Than mi Hara. Chao penluksav khongknony. Soka khony, khonymi khuaamching. Su khong knony Kaleah. Than mi Hara. Chao penluksav khongknony. Soka khony, khonymi khuaamching."

"What is this gibberish?" Swinthun asked Darcy.

"I know it is a foreign language, but I do not know which one," Darcy answered.

"Look it up. Let me know as soon as possible. I have a lunch," Commander Schilling ordered.

Swinthun exited the AI office and walked to the elevator. He rejoined the world on the main floor. He exited the building. A cold wind caught his uniform. Within five seconds, his clothes adapted to the cold and warmed up to maintain his temperature at 24 degrees Celsius. He walked to the south.

On the south side of downtown, there was a restaurant that served food from the olden days. Today was a special day for this culinary amateur. He asked the restaurant to make him meatloaf; he was eager to eat it.

The normal diet was a lot of vitamins and nutrients and a variety of flavors of tofu and yeast. This presented in different flavors and textures, but in the end, it was still tofu and yeast. Swinthun wanted something more to his food. He wanted to eat like his grandfather did. He told him stories about hunting and eating the flesh of animals. This seemed a long time ago. Today was different; he would taste part of the life of his grandfather.

At the door of the restaurant, there was a sign for not so rich to go to the side. Despite being a commander in the army, Schilling had to go to the side door. He sat down at the counter. His clothes controlled his temperature. It was warm in this room because of the stove and cooking. His clothes aired out his heat and cooled him down.

Swinthun was ready, and his favorite cook, Jillian, smiled. She winked at him and brought out a plate. It had something yellow on the side, something orange and lengthy, and something brown. On top of the brown rectangular piece was some brown sauce. This looked so strange to Swinthun and to Jillian for that matter.

"So this is . . . meatloaf?" Schilling asked.

"Sure is. Enjoy," Jillian told him as she disappeared in the kitchen.

He looked at it. He examined it. Lifting his head, Swinthun asked Jillian, "This was made with real meat, correct?"

"Yes, Swinthun. The bill will show it to you." Jillian laughed as she answered his question.

With hesitation but desire to taste the past, Swinthun took a small bite of the meatloaf. It landed on his tongue. It was salty and creamy, probably from the sauce. Then he took a bite of it, and it was tasty and juicy. The texture was loose and slightly grainy. He chewed it, and he closed his eyes. Commander Schilling experienced the past for a moment. Until Darcy called him to advise him of her completion of the task. Shutting his eyes again, for a different reason this time, he took a second bite and asked for Jillian to box it all.

Swinthun got back to the basement and placed his box on a counter. He sat down and asked for the translation to play.

"My name is Kaleah. You are Hara. Find me. I have the truth. My name is Kaleah. You are Hara. Find me. I have the truth. My name is Kaleah. You are Hara. Find me. I have the truth."

Commander Schilling was seated, and yet his mind crumbled for a moment. He asked Darcy, "What language was this?"

She stated, "Laotian." Could it be? The truth was out there, as his grandfather told him.

Swinthun grew up with his grandfather in the early years of his life; but as he was eight years old, his father came back in his horizon. His father told him to not believe anything his grandfather told him. From that day, Swinthun never saw his grandfather again. He told him, as the last time he saw him, to never lose the truth because it is out there.

The schools taught him China and India were the main enemies of America. Europe was a lost land, and we had not heard of them in a long while. Communications broke as the Chinese and Indians needed more women to repopulate their lands. America was a rare place where equality existed.

The voice he heard was a woman's, and she said her name. This was very odd, as he learned the Chinese and Indians were all men and their only desire was to conquer our continent and get all our childbearing women to invade the world.

Somehow, Swinthun heard something shocking in the woman's voice. She was there and stated she had the truth. Why is that even possible? He sensed a moment of dizziness, as if his soul was above the ground and it pushed the top of his head up. His eyes felt heavy, as if they could pop out at any moment.

Recovering from the shock of the message, Commander Schilling asked Darcy, "Had this file been heard before today?" Darcy answered no. This made him plan and think of what he should do next. He was not sure.

Swinthun got up and thought for a second. He walked out, leaving his meatloaf meal on the counter. He exited the AI room, and as the door closed, he pushed on the door to get back in. Then he ordered Darcy to remove the surveillance on Kaylee McCloud. Darcy did as instructed. Again, he walked out and went to the lobby.

Swinthun ran to a car and got in one and floated off.

CHAPTER 4

T HE SUN WAS in zenith, and Kaylee checked her fishing poles in the lake. There was nothing today. This was usual and nothing to worry about. However, the surveillance was a different issue. She was able to see them despite their effort to be incognito.

Past lunch, Kaylee observed their increased skills at hiding, as she did not see them. An eye on her back, she walked home. She passed Sylvia's home and thought to herself, *Maybe I should not cook for her from now on.* She was not sure how to deal with a spy.

Kaylee understood that we all had a job to make society work. However, how could she go behind her back and tell all about Kaylee to CCDC? She was offended and disgusted by that thought. On the other hand, Sylvia was an elder, and Kaylee learned from a young age to respect her elders. How could she reconcile these two thoughts?

Kaylee climbed up to her apartment and ordered her food producer to get her a cup of hot water for her to have a cup of tea. She needed; it had been a long day in which she was not sure what to do with the message she has on her telephone.

In all evidence, Kaylee hid it and, most importantly, turned it off. Old technology was no longer in use; when shut off, it was able to be undetectable to modern detectors. This was an easy one; the officers were a little dense to think any further than what their detectors told them. She smiled at that thought. She took her cup of tea and walked into her living room. What was she going to do to translate the message?

Kaylee understood clearly that there was no way she could access the Interweb to have a translation, unless she wanted to be caught. She could go to the library, but she did not know what language it was in. This was a tough one to figure out.

In the middle of a sip of tea, someone knocked at her door. This was super unusual, as there was no one to come to her door and, furthermore, knock on it. Kaylee stood up and went to her door, which had no lock on; it barely stayed closed. She opened the door and saw Commander Schilling.

Immediately, Kaylee assumed the salute pose and held it. Schilling said, "At ease. May I enter?" She went to an at-ease posture and processed with the request. The next second, Kaylee invited him in her domicile with her left hand. She was not sure why an army officer was here, but this was serious. *Did he figure out I have the message?*

"McCloud, can I call you Kaylee?" Schilling began.

"Yes, sir," Kaylee responded and was in standing at a military stance.

"Please sit down, Kaylee." Swinthun thought it was strange that he invited her to sit down.

"Yes, sir," Kaylee answered and sat down on her couch.

"Kaylee, what I am about tell you will get me kicked out of the army," he stated while looking at her window.

"Uh, yes . . . sir." This confused Kaylee. What was he going to tell her? Especially, what was he going to tell her that will get him kicked out of the army?

"The message you were asked about today . . ." Swinthun opened up with a crackling voice.

"Yes . . . sir." Kaylee hesitated for a second. He did not know she had the message. Maybe he was here trying to get her to admit to having the message. She held her cool and made sure of showing no emotion on her face.

"I listened to this message." He dropped the anvil of life. He took a pause. Then after his right hand swiped his chin, he continued. "It was sent by a lady called Kaleah. And you are her daughter. Your name is Hara. And she claimed to have the truth."

"What?" Kaylee stammered; her mind was in a spin. She was in that moment when the world seemed to be spinning. There was a whirl of events she appeared to have missed.

The first was this commander revealed the secret she tried to figure out. The second was the commander just risked his entire career by revealing this message. The third was he figured out the message; this meant the CCDC was about to arrest them.

Kaylee caught her breath. She shook her head and went to her bedroom. Pulling a bag out of her closet, Kaylee began to pull out some pants, underwear, and a couple of bras.

Swinthun followed her. He did not need to say a word, but he did anyway.

"So you seem to understand, right?"

"Sir, do you understand what we're risking?" Kaylee looked at him intensely.

"Yes, I will lose my rank and be dismissed from the army." As he uttered these words, the next thought came. "Oh, shit!" Panic emanated through his body.

"Sir, you have a car?" Kaylee wanted to see if she could gain some time.

"Yes, I do," he answered still with the realization of what just happened.

HENRI NGUYEN

"All right, where are you parked?" she asked him with all the intensity of a superior officer.

"I parked at the back . . . I mean . . . I am behind your yard." The panic was still within his flesh and bones.

"OK, let's go. I feel they will be coming in a few minutes." Kaylee was in a hurry as she pushed Swinthun to her back door.

They walked to the back door. Each step made a squeezing sound on her hardwood floor. Kaylee appreciated this sound, maybe for the last time in her life. She bit her lower lip; it marked not only her anxiety for her life but also the angst of leaving her life and being on the road for something. This would be a thing that she had no idea of or even a concept of what it could be. If her life was not at risk, Kaylee would shed a tear.

They got into the car and they lifted. Kaylee was silent, until Swinthun asked.

"Where are we going?"

"I do know, but we cannot stay here." She broke her silence.

"All right . . .," Schilling uttered.

"Go north. This seems to be the most logical way. The army will be coming from downtown, so go north," Kaylee said. Her thoughts were like cooked spaghetti—it was a mess that you could not figure out where one strand began and where it ended.

"Yeah, that is a great idea," Swinthun expressed.

The drive was quiet. No one breached the silence. This was a time to reflect each other's life.

Before all these events happened, Commander Schilling was on his way to becoming general within the next two decades. He was not sure if this was his desire, but it was his father's need to see his son become a general. In his mind, his grandfather's words stayed with him, despite his progenitor's words. The truth seemed to be out there; he was not sure why, but he knew this was the new way he will go.

As the car flew over miles, Kaylee reflected on her growing in that apartment. It was all she knew. Now, it was gone. She was sad but not in despair. Questions were arising in her mind. The first was, *who is the commander? Can I trust him? Where are we going? They will track us. How do we lose them?*

Her life was a series of flash of memories. Kaylee did not know anyone, so she thought it was normal. Her father was in her life, but she had no mother in her life. How could that be? She asked herself this question many times. There was no answer; her father disappeared when she turned twelve years old. Ever since, she grew up alone, except for Sylvia. When Kaylee was twelve years old, Sylvia taught her how to hunt, to fish, to collect food, to sow and harvest, and to cook. All these skills were essential for keeping her alive, but now, who was Sylvia?

This question perturbed her line of thoughts.

Hours passed, and no words were ever pronounced. The silence became awkward, and this grew on both of them. It did not matter when it happened, but too much silence always became a nervous moment between two persons. Then, out of nowhere, an alarm started ringing gently.

"What is that?" Kaylee asked Swinthun.

"It is the signal that we are running out of power," Swinthun said.

"Darn it. It means we have to recharge the batteries?" Kaylee asked, although she came to that conclusion already.

HENRI NGUYEN

"Yes. We are close to Thunder Bay," Swinthun stated.

"If the car is recharging, its location disappears, right?" Kaylee proceeded through a train of thoughts. "So we shut off all functions, and we disappear from their screens," she concluded,

"Yes, that is true," Schilling agreed.

"OK, let us put it down over there by the woods." Kaylee pointed to Swinthun.

The car was in the setting sun. It charged. Kaylee and Swinthun were in the car. This was awkward, and it was difficult. The night was still cold, and they had batteries in their clothes. However, it was the end of the day, and this meant that their batteries were lower. This night promised some cold spells. This they both knew was the truth. Consequently, they may have to use their body heat to maintain their heat at higher level. This was going to be awkward.

Setting sun; this was a beautiful sight. There were reds, oranges, blues, and purples. All these colors layered and showed there was hope in the universe. In the car, on the other hand, silence grew to new heights of awkwardness. No one wanted to be the first to talk. It came to a point where someone had to do it.

"OK, we are having to discuss this," Commander Schilling opened in the hope that Kaylee would continue his point.

"Sure, what do we have to discuss?" Kaylee asked Swinthun.

"Come on, you know?" Schilling tried to push the conversation as far as he could without tipping over the edge.

"I have no idea where you are going." Kaylee was either playing dumb or she was . . .well, that too.

"Fine, it is going to be cold, and my batteries are low." Swinthun took a leap with his idea.

"OK . . . I am fine . . . Thank you." Kaylee was definitely closing up as she turned toward the door.

The night came, and the cold accompanied this darkening of the sky. Obviously, Kaylee was warm, as her clothes were still charged. Swinthun's clothes were no longer in function. He shivered, and, hence, he raised his collar and blew in his hands. Schilling could see his breath. It was difficult to hide from the cold.

Kaylee was asleep. Swinthun tried his best to fight the frosting of the windows. He raised his shoulders on and off; he tried to create some muscle activation to fight the lack of heat. There was little he could do at this point. He looked at Kaylee, and despite the fact that he could ask her again, he was determined not to do it. The cold or Kaylee's anger—there was a choice he would rather not make.

Slowly but surely, fatigue and the cold got to him; he began to slumber.

Kaylee turned over. Her right eye opened slightly. She saw Swinthun, and there was some frost on his jacket. This woke up her up. She rose up and touched his sleeve. He did not move. There was breathing, as she could see frosting over his upper lip. At that moment, Kaylee understood what he tried to say earlier in the night. This was a problem.

Kaylee maneuvered her leg to get over to his seat. Her right leg was over the center console. She opened her jacket and increased the heat to its maximum. Her knees bent, and she covered Schilling. He was cold; even in her hot jacket, Kaylee could feel the cold.

Ten minutes passed, and Commander Schilling shivered a little bit; this meant she was just in time. He would recover from this episode of hypothermia. Five minutes passed, and Swinthun's body jerked. His head threw itself back, and his arms flung up and down. Despite the lack of experience with men, Kaylee did not panic; clearly, she knew this body reaction would be expected, and this was another good sign to his recovery.

The morning light emerged over the east. Kaylee was not asleep again, but now she was on top of Swinthun. His eyes opened, and his eyes were straight on her cleavage. This was not a bad way to wake up. He was cold, but it was manageable. Although he would welcome this moment any other time, he needed to go outside and let his battery recharge. This was the odd part of having solar-powered clothes; if you were outdoors, you had to go freeze your gonads for ten minutes and then be warm.

"Kaylee . . . Kaylee . . .," Schilling said with softness to wake the woman slowly.

"Hmm . . . what?" Kaylee struggled to wake up. Finally, she opened her eyes. "Oh, shit!" She expressed some discomfort when she realized her precarious positioning over the man she had to save last night.

"Sorry and thank you," Swinthun said while looking down to the ground.

"Yeah . . . sure. Whatever," Kaylee said while climbing off his lap and back to her seat.

After a few seconds of uncomfortable nonlooking eyes, Swinthun opened the door. The cold was present. It bit him like a crisp apple. Winter or spring had that signature. When it kissed your body, you knew about it. The frost took a snap of you, as if you were food; it was a bite that froze you immediately. Your nipples arose, your hairs rose up so quickly, and for men, your testicles shrunk up so fast; it amazed Swinthun. He was cold.

Commander Schilling jumped and crossed his arms up on his chest. He knew in ten minutes and it would be all right. This was going to be a long ten minutes.

Kaylee came out of the car; she needed some batteries recharging too. Both of them jumped and tried their best to stand there for ten minutes. At least for Kaylee, there were no external gonads trying to retreat back into her body.

"All right, let us put some questions on the table," Kaylee said while trying to save some words. "Why did you come to my house to tell me the message?" Kaylee said with speed to take a deep breath and blow the hot air into her bare hands.

"Because my grandpa told me the truth existed out there. When I heard the translation of the message, I knew there was something out there. I don't know what is out there, but I know the truth is out there," Swinthun said while nodding his head to maintain some heat in his outfit.

"What?" Ms. McCloud moved her shoulders up and down but did not understand a word of what the commander said.

"What I mean is, if the truth is out there, this means we are being lied to," Swinthun said with emphasis on the last few words.

"How did you know I had the message?" Kaylee was still a few questions behind.

"Goodness gracious, are we still at the message? We knew a message was sent to you. We did not know you had the message. We did not know anything about the mp3. We had no idea if you were able to even read this file. But the general suspected you would find this message," Swinthun uttered, but he got some heat from his clothing. "It was not the first time it happened. It was the first time the message was implanted into the software. They tried to pierce through the defense

HENRI NGUYEN

to bring the message in. Obviously, they did not succeed at the many times they tried," he concluded.

"They tried before?" Kaylee caught up, but it was slow. Shivering was still present.

"Yes, they did," Swinthun said, now being warmer.

"How many times before?" Kaylee interrogated Swinthun.

"From the time I was in command and during your presence, at least six times," Swinthun responded honestly.

"Shit! Mother of God! Why me?" All this conversation confused Kaylee.

Ten minutes passed, and they got back in the car and started the engine. They knew it would not take them too long to figure out that the duo disappeared.

CHAPTER 5

THE MORNING WAS a moment of serenity for General Sihi. His morning started with a large cup of coffee at 43 degrees Celsius. Also, he wanted two biscotti with his hot coffee. This morning was no different—he asked for his water, he added his coffee to the water, and he pulled out his biscotti and placed them on a small plate. He was ready to begin this day.

There were winds outside. Sihi sat down and looked at the trees bending in the wind. There was a peacefulness to this dance. He looked at the lake; the water brewed some waves along the shores. It was peaceful and serene.

After finishing his coffee and his biscotti, General Sihi went to his bedroom and got dressed. A woman woke up. He stared at her; she knew—collect your things and get out. This was a clear message; there was no other option. So, as she was naked, she collected her clothes and shoes and ran out of the room. A few seconds after, Sihi heard a door close. She was gone.

Sihi got his jacket on after he put on his pants. He looked on his wrist and adjusted the temperature. He went into his bathroom, and as if he was a child, thirty seconds after he entered the bathroom, he exited, having brushed his teeth.

General Sihi walked up to his door. He opened it. There she was, the not-so-naked-anymore woman. She had her shirt on, and her pants were not buttoned yet. She was trying to don her shoes to disappear from this apartment.

Sihi looked at her; he had the look of a superior man. This was a general feeling in Central Chicago. With his head pointing to his left side, the lady moved to her right. He was not going to wait for you, lady—this was his look at her.

The elevator got him down to the third floor. He walked out. A captain waited for his arrival. The report was presented on a pad. Sihi grabbed the pad and began to scroll down on it. The pair of officers headed for Sihi's office.

It was nearly three meters away. Sihi got in to his office and sat down at his desk. He pointed forward to his captain to be in attention in front of his desk. It was sometimes hard to see how these officers finished their training but still do not know where to stand. This exasperated him.

After reviewing the list of army activity; he asked the captain, "Where is Commander Schilling?"

"Sir, he had yet to report in," the captain said.

"Go look for him," Sihi said with a wavering right hand, which indicated to go look for him and do not return.

"Yes, sir." The captain saluted his general, and when he got the return salute, he turned around sharply and walked out of the office.

What was a general to do in these days? There were no real soldiers anymore. A lot of robots, drones, and torpedoes were the essential of the army. He was in charge of the soldiers who monitored all these mechanical and electronic beings. On his schedule, there was nothing. In that light, he opened his Interweb and entered the address of a site that was less than essential for his function as a general; it was a porn site.

Time went on. It was nearly lunchtime when Captain Morgan came back.

"Sir, we were unable to reach Commander Schilling. We checked his apartment. It was not accessed yesterday morning."

"Find him," the general said, and he was not in a compromised situation yet.

"Yes, sir," Morgan said firmly, and yet he did not salute or leave the office. He stuttered a little bit. "S-ir . . . sir, there was something odd too."

"What?" Sihi brought his eyes off his screen, and this showed anger, as it disturbed his enjoyment.

"The team in charge of monitoring Ms. McCloud reported to have been taken off that mission, sir." Morgan got rid of his stuttering.

"What? Who removed them from surveillance!" Sihi shouted while trying to control his voice.

"Commander Schilling, sir." Captain Morgan braced for a mind-losing moment from his general.

Indeed, this happened. General Sihi stood up and began shouting as much as he could. "What the hell! Who allowed him to give this order? What the fucking hell is going on here? I want his head. Get me his head." More followed this preview of bad language and foul mouthing of words, which had a better history.

"Check on the map where he is. Arrest him and bring him to me." General Sihi came back from the verbal diarrhea instantly.

"Yes, sir," Captain Morgan uttered.

This morning had gone to shit. This was General Sihi's thought. *What else could wrong?* He sat back down at his desk. Obviously, he was no longer needing the porn site as distraction, as he had a real situation on his hand.

Waiting for results was like having to do your own surgery. It was impossible, and the thought of it would throw you into an illogical loop. This was a problem for a general—he had to wait for a bunch of henchmen to complete their jobs for him to make decisions that were crucial according to him. To say that he had a great opinion of himself was evident, but for him, he was the most important person in all this matter.

An hour passed. Then the second hour was about to pass when Captain Morgan came back.

"Sir, we have located Commander Schilling. He is on his way to Calgary, sir."

"Calgary? That city does no longer function. How close are our men to his position?" the general asked to give his next order.

"We have men in Alaska, sir," Captain Morgan answered promptly.

"Call them up and have them arrest this son of a bitch," Sihi said as the thought crossed his mind.

"Yes, sir. Also, Kaylee McCloud has yet to be found, but Commander Schilling's travels did put him at her house, sir," Captain Morgan added.

"Hmm, she must be with him. Is she working for him or him for her?" the general asked to himself while Captain Morgan was still present.

"Sir?" Morgan asked General Sihi.

"Yeah! Oh, yeah, yeah, go call the Alaskan troops and let me know," General Sihi said while looking pensive.

Captain Morgan called up the Alaskan troops as soon as he stepped out of the general's office. This was quick and no problem for Morgan, as there was no human contact. He had an issue with having human-to-human contact. In the present world, it was call anthropophobia; it was a phenomenon that afflicted most who are alive on this planet. Most of them rather interact with one another as much as get the contagion. It was hard, and for Morgan, being faced with Sihi yelling and shouting made him stutter and sweat. On the other hand, his clothes took care of that, as they blew his sweat away and refreshed his clothes quickly.

General Sihi was in full thought. Where could he go? Why Calgary? Obviously, he had no troop there, and hence, it was a good place to get lost. They could track them with the Interweb; they would have to have at least a check-in on a daily basis. Sihi got up from his chair and went out of his office. The elevator arrived a few seconds after he called it.

The lift went down to the basement. The lights came on. He walked to the door of the AI, Darcy. He walked in. Sihi examined the room. There was nothing out of place, but as he looked to his left, there was a box. This was odd.

Sihi approached the box. He was not sure what was in it. He was alone, and what if this was a bomb left by Schilling? Could he do that? Sihi wondered for a second. He looked at it; he sniffed the box; if this was bomb, it would smell like a bomb. The fact was the smell was pleasant. It could not have been a bomb. Audaciously, he touched the box. He moved it. There was no explosion. This was a positive for him. Finally, he opened the box. His eyes met a meatloaf. However, he did not know what meatloaf was, as he was not as inspired as Schilling was to explore olden foods.

There was a mist of sweat on his forehead. This would be vented in a second, and the next second, a gentle vent came on from his collar to cool him down.

HENRI NGUYEN

"AI, tell me about Schilling's last session with you," General Sihi said loudly.

"Of course. He asked to replay the attack of March 11 and then asked me to search for any unusual coding. Then he followed with a search for anything unusual in the coding of all bots that were hit in the attack. I found an mp3, which he asked me to read, but I could not, so he ordered me to write a software to read this file. I did so, and I read the message," Darcy answered succinctly because she did this naturally.

"Read me this message," Sihi ordered.

"Su khong knony Kaleah. Than mi Hara. Chao penluksav khongknony. Soka khony, khonymi khuaamching. Su khong knony Kaleah. Than mi Hara. Chao penluksav khongknony. Soka khony, khonymi khuaamching. Su khong knony Kaleah. Than mi Hara. Chao penluksav khongknony. Soka khony, khonymi khuaamching." Darcy read the file.

"I need a translation." Sihi was irritated by this hiccup.

"My name is Kaleah. You are Hara. Find me. I have the truth. My name is Kaleah. You are Hara. Find me. I have the truth. My name is Kaleah. You are Hara. Find me. I have the truth." Immediately, Darcy read the translation as if she expected Sihi to give this order, but this could not be.

As the reading went on, his face turned white. He was not Caucasian, and this would be new for anybody with dark skin, but he became bloodless in his face. It was as if he knew what the whole meaning of this message was. Sihi regained life in his facial skin; he seemed ready to make a decision.

"AI, I am putting a top-secret note on this file and its translation. Level 7 is needed to have eyes or ears on this file and its translation."

"Yes, sir. It is done," Darcy answered.

When Sihi exited the AI room, he was more pensive. His thought went one way and the other also. He wondered if the commander worked with McCloud or the opposite. There was evidence he listened to this message. Why would he go see McCloud? This made no sense; he had to be working for her. The next thought lurked in his mind. Is she blackmailing him, did she have something to hold against him, or was he in love with her? She was a woman, and this would be a possibility.

The elevator went to the lobby, and he wanted to walk outside to get some fresh air. Sihi stepped outside, and the wind blew at him. It was a hard blow; it was like the wind wanted to carry him off. There was an old legend of a movie. He could not recall the name, something like Popping, he thought. His walk was along the lake, and he was deep in thought.

Sihi was the general chasing this man whom he thought loved this woman. He wondered why this would be. Sihi and Schilling had all the women they wanted; he had a woman whenever he wanted; this was easy. There was no place for love in this world, according to Sihi. His clothes left him warm, but his hair was not agreeing with his stroll along the lake.

As Sihi walked back in the building, Simon came out of the elevator looking for him. This was not going to be a pleasant conversation.

"General! I was looking for you."

"Yes, Simon. How can I help you?" Sihi said calmly to project this image that nothing disturbed him.

"I heard Commander Schilling is missing. Where is he?" Simon was over his head.

"Simon, I have this under control. Calm down." Sihi looked at him with intense eyes. He tried to keep him down. This was a man who had money, and his army needed money, but Sihi did not need his explosive behavior and sense of panic.

"Don't tell me this. Find your commander and end this whole ordeal." Although Simon was in an instant of panic, he was still in charge of his money, and this he knew was the leash. In this moment, it was shortened significantly.

"Of course, we are on it. Do not put your clothes in a bundle." Sihi said those words with a pace that insinuated Simon needed a chill pill.

Simon walked away with his clothes in a bunch of knots. This was not calming him down. He was near boiling point. Then he stopped in his tracks, turned around, and looked at Sihi. The general was walking to the elevator, and before he got on the lift, he said loudly, "You better find him. If not, there are others who would be willing to do it for me."

"Uh, yes, sir." These words made an impact for Sihi. Simon reminded him who was in control of his army.

General Sihi was in the vertically going box. This time, he was a little shaken up. He knew there was no way to accelerate the events, but somehow, he worried about what could happen. The words "someone else" made him very uncomfortable.

A few years back, the general who was in the seat he now occupied was let go because his decisions were not in line with Simon's view. The general was never heard of again. Sihi thought he retired, but he was not sure. Simon was a shy man, but when pushed, he did not say words; he exploded and acted. The words he heard from Simon were Sihi's warning.

Sihi reached his office. He was not sure if he should stay calm; he was not sure of what to do. There was a moment of hesitation, even for such a simple action as getting water or scotch. He sat down at his desk. He turned to his window and stared at the trees folding in the wind. Sihi knew he needed to calm down and let the events happen. Then when they happen, he can make a decision.

CHAPTER 6

CALGARY WAS IN sight. The profile of a city used to be a way to recognize where you were. Now, the city outline was depressing. The skyscrapers looked as they were—abandoned. The top of the highest building appeared to have not been repaired, ever. The contagion left its scar, and the wars that followed also left their marks. Although no longer a city, it was still inhabited.

The car approached, and there was no one to welcome them. The roads were dirty, and the buildings were beyond needing a wash; they required complete overall, also known as destruction. There were tumbleweeds; this was odd for Kaylee. She imagined Calgary and any cities in the west with sun and dust, but tumbleweed sounded odd to her.

Swinthun landed the car, and they got out. It was dusty, and the sun was behind the clouds. The Chinook blew from the west to the east. It was a strong wind today. Kaylee and Swinthun walked close to one another. They looked like a couple, but it was not the case.

"Follow me. I have a person who can help us," Swinthun said.

"What? You know someone here? Really? Someone you know lives in this shitty town?" Kaylee expressed with some surprise, but it was more disgust at the dust and dirt.

A long time ago, her father taught her to be clean and not to let litter live; otherwise, it would eat you up. She lived near poverty, but there was no litter or junk around her. This was a lesson she never forgot. These scraps flew with the wind, and this bothered Kaylee. She had the desire to gather the garbage and start cleaning up this city. This was not reasonable, but it was a need. In a moment of despair, she turned on her Interweb to play some music. She knew this would relax her.

A few seconds after Kaylee turned on her music, Swinthun realized she turned on her Interweb.

"Kaylee! Turn off your connection to the Interweb. Quick. You are giving our position! Damn it!" Swinthun realized the mistake she made.

"Oh, shit! I am sorry. I was not able to handle all this refuse. It was stressing me." Kaylee apologized.

"Please, I know it is difficult, but we need to be undercover here. Come on," Swinthun said with an angry eye at Kaylee.

"OK, sorry again." Kaylee expressed her sorrow and recognized his points.

In front of a dirty storefront, Swinthun looked into the store. The glass that was in the front of the store was gone. Kaylee was not sure why he looked at it. She would have just entered. As if it was not strange enough, Swinthun knocked on the door. He made a knock pattern. Tap, tap . . . tap, tap . . . tap, tap, tap. This was deliberate. Kaylee took a step back and waited. Impressed was an emotion she had for Swinthun, whom she thought was a boob.

Last night, Swinthun nearly froze himself to death. Then at her place, he seemed unable to move and make a decision. These reasons made her think of a boobish type of person. However, this morning, Swinthun seemed to have his shit together; this impressed Kaylee. She looked at him with eyes near liking.

Eventually, a hand came out and waved them in.

Swinthun's hand made a grand movement with smoothness, which allowed Kaylee to enter first. It was strange, awkward, and unlike anything Kaylee had ever seen before. There was a bow of his head and torso. She smiled as she went by him.

The store was dark. There were no lights, but there was a cord. This rope seemed to have been as old as Kaylee was. This was a moment when Kaylee hesitated in holding this cable. It was moist and gunky. It appeared to be very dirty, but in the darkness, which was quite dark, they did not have a choice. Suddenly, the string went down. Kaylee missed the first step, but she caught the second step. This raised her heart rate.

Swinthun did the same as she did. His heart rate went up also.

Finally, Kaylee saw a dim light. There was a door, which she nearly planted her face on. The light was dim indeed, as it was a candle, and the light she saw was through the cracks of door. Her face having not crashed into the door, the person whose hand guided them to this dark and wet place indicated with his hand to enter. Kaylee was uneasy about this. She did not know where she was going; she was in a place she never thought of ever entering; and what if the person leading them here was a murderer? These uneasy questions drowned Kaylee's fears. There were too many worries, fear could no longer enter her mind.

The three of them were in the room. The person guiding them removed his hood and mask. Kaylee saw an older man. He had whitish hair, his face was symmetrical, and his eyes were of a blue she ever saw. He was a good-looking man.

"Darvy, how are you?" Swinthun broke the silence.

"I am fine. Thanks, Swinthun," Darvy answered.

"I like what you did with your hair," Swinthun continued while looking for a chair.

"Thank you, sir. Why are you here?" Darvy asked with no intermission in his words.

"Ah, why am I here? Good question. Think about it for a second." Schilling sounded like a commander right then.

Kaylee processed, and then it made sense.

"Darvy, are you an android?" she queried.

"Yes, ma'am, I am," Darvy answered without a differentiation in his tone.

"Good job." Swinthun applauded Kaylee.

"I sense you are here because you saw the truth, and like me, you escaped CCDC," Darvy spelled out.

Swinthun nodded and smiled.

"All right now. We need a different car, one you cannot track, and I need to know how to block the daily check-in from the Interweb." Swinthun got to business.

"For a car, I have one, but it is not a great-looking one," Darvy said with an awkward wink of his left eye. This was a learned behavior, and the lack of smoothness was its signature. "The blocking of the Interweb is going to sound a little strange." Although it was clunky verbally, his mannerism made it look almost human.

"What it is?" Kaylee asked.

"The connection to the Interweb is a 2a cellular input, so to interrupt this transmission, you need to remove the chip or block its transmission," the android said plainly.

"All right, removing the chip is near impossible for us. So how do you block its transmission?" Swinthun thought and uttered out.

"You have to wear an aluminum hat." This was a heavy statement and landed like a ball of lead.

"Are you sure?" Kaylee asked as if she did not process the utterance from the android.

"Yes, ma'am," he stated as factually as an android could.

"O . . . K." Swinthun was snarky as he shook his head. "You are the best, Darvy," he continued.

"Thank you, sir," Darvy said.

They walked into a separate room, and Darvy proceeded with the fabrication of aluminum hats. This sounded idiotic and ridiculous but nonetheless true. Kaylee was pensive, and, finally, she asked what was troubling her.

"How do you know Darvy?" This question was loaded, and Swinthun understood this.

"Before you were born and before I was born, the rich wanted a general who would just obey them. So they came up with an android. This was good for them, but their understanding of strategy and tactics was poor, and this led to the Southern Invasion. Hence, we have General Sihi, who happened to be human. This was essential, despite the rich's dislike for it. Security was more important for their . . . how do I say this . . . money," Swinthun enunciated.

"So they destroyed him, but you saved him?" Kaylee tried to piece the timeline together.

"No. I was too young when all this happened. When I came up as a lieutenant, I was told this story. I looked around and found him. I was able to regenerate his batteries, and we spent time together. We talked a lot. For months, I learned so much out of him. Finally, as he is an AI, he asked me if he would ever see freedom anymore. This made a question emerge for me—why can he live? Why does he have to be a dust collector? These things afflicted me, and I came to an answer—I had to free Darvy. This was not so easy. I had to remove his chip without destroying his memory and processing abilities. This took months to figure out, and proceeding, though, was a challenge and stressful, I would like to add." Swinthun took a pause. "Then I sent him on his way. On the map, there was only one place he could hide without alerting anyone—Calgary. They abandoned the city, and there was enough for him to live here," he concluded.

"Wow, so how come they never hunted him?" Kaylee wondered.

"Because old equipment is kept but never looked ever again. I do not know or understand why we kept old equipment for that matter," Swinthun stated.

"Wow, this is blowing my mind," Kaylee said with insinuations lathered all over her statement. Then she bit her lower lip.

Darvy took a moment and broke Swinthun's and Kaylee's eyes meeting. "All right, here you go." He showed the hats made of aluminum sheeting. These looked horrible; they were like head-wrapping towels made out of aluminum, and there were bolt holes and sharp corners that could cut anyone who happen to be human.

Kaylee took the hat with less cutting and nicking potential and less ugly. Although she was meditative about putting this thing on her head, she turned around and saw Swinthun already with his hat on his head. At that point, she understood there would be no shame, but there was a sense of indecency here, she thought to herself.

Darvy walked to the stairs. Again, Swinthun grabbed the cord, and he was followed by Kaylee. They walked up and got through the darkness. They were in the streets of the city. They appeared to be cleaner than they were by Kaylee. This was a moment of relativity for her; she saw more dirt and held something that need not to be grasped. On top of it, literally, she wore an aluminum hat. This made this whole issue about cleanliness a nonissue.

They sped up toward Darvy's car. The three of them got to a former skyscraper; it had a sign in front of it. The sign was missing some of its letters: C——ter—a. Kaylee looked at it for a second; Darvy approached and said, "In case you care, the name is Canterra. It was the name of the tower."

"Oh, thank you," Kaylee responded.

"OK, let us hurry. I am sure the military is on its way," Swinthun uttered as he passed by them.

"Indeed," Darcy concluded.

"Right, let us get to it." Kaylee came to the same conclusion.

Entering the building was not difficult. It was getting to the second floor that was more arduous. Kaylee climbed first on the large pieces of concrete. It was obvious to get on top of large boulders and then try jumping to reach the broken stairs.

Swinthun struggled with climbing on these large remnants of the building. He tried to skip along and be fast about his movement; however, his limbs lacked the ability to make it smooth. Several times he fell and only caught himself with his arms. This got harder and harder as he reached the jumping point where Kaylee leaped onto the vestige of stairs.

On the other hand, Darvy had no problem reaching the second floor. Literally, he leaped up and reached the second floor. He gave a hand to Kaylee, who was near getting her second leg onto the edge of the stairs. While all this happened, Swinthun struggled with leaping from a small surface. The edge of the block of concrete was small, and his legs did not generate enough power to lift him up. Moreover, the stability of this piece of concrete was compromised. He moved to a different stepping rock and tried again. He was near; another jump, and the reinforcing metal fell and slipped through his fingers. He could feel it; it was coming. There were some indignities to be lived through prior to completing this physical task. This was not his favorite part of escaping with this good-looking and Asian-appearing woman.

Finally, Swinthun got to the second floor with some help from Darvy. After catching some of his breath, which ran away from him, he walked to the car. To say it was less luxurious would be a misnomer for this car. It worked; at least this was the assumption Swinthun made. The car was three colors: the original blue, rust, and nothingness. By nothingness, it meant as emptiness or empty space. This car was used; it was a thought Kaylee had as she smiled. The inside was bare too. There were two seats and a steering wheel. Swinthun sat in the driver's seat and turned it on. There were an odometer and a battery meter; it showed the level of charge. There was no autopilot, which made sense, as it was an untraceable car.

Kaylee was right outside the driver's seat. She appeared to desire driving too. Her eyes and head showed him the way out of the car. This was evident. Swinthun got out of the car. She sat in it, while Swinthun and Darvy awkwardly shook hands. It was uncomfortable, as Swinthun realized. As soon as he offered his hand, Darvy did not have the immediate pattern to sack his right hand back at Swinthun. Therefore, he waited for two or three seconds, and then Darvy's right hand came out. They shook hands, and he went to the passenger side and got into the car.

The remaining of the car lifted, and within a second, it moved to the window. This was a hologram to maintain the hideout secret. This was a nifty trick from Darvy, although his programming lacked some basics, it was plentiful in tactical camouflage.

It got out of the fake window and rose in the sky. Then Kaylee turned the car to the east and hit the gas. This took Swinthun a second to process, but when he did, he asked, "Wait. Why are we going to the east?"

"Think about it. We headed west with a traceable car, and now that we are in an untraceable car and with these sexy hats, why would you continue west, especially when I am sure Alaskan troops were coming to intercept us?" Kaylee explained.

"OK, you have a point," he admitted, but then he had another question. "So what do we do for food?" he inquired. Hunger was an element that grew in him, and he was sure in her too.

"Yes, I have been wondering about this issue too. We cannot stop at an army station to ask for DRs (daily ration), and if we stop in the next center for food, it would be Winnipeg. This would agitate the locals. I am sure our pictures have been circulated already." She processed through the issue. She continued with the logical saga. "So we should stay off the main human centers and off military installations. So we should hunt or forage." This was her conclusion.

His face was stern at that point. It was obvious that this would be the best way to stay incognito and off the map of CCDC. So he nodded, but his hunger spoke to him with increased strength.

"OK, so we should head to Winnipeg, and sometime before or after, we will stop and go get some food. That is wonderful." This was his conclusion too, and he added, "I am going to take a nap. Wake me up when we get there," he said as he turned to the door and closed his eyes.

Kaylee flew to Winnipeg. From Calgary to Winnipeg would take a little over an hour. This would be with a normal car. It would fly at about 900 kilometers per hour. The distance was a little over 1,300 kilometers. With this car, holding 700 kilometers per hour was hard; speed any higher did not seem like a good idea, so two hours would be fine for her. As Swinthun was napping, this was an even better idea.

The first hour went through. No issues with anything so far. Kaylee thought of many things. It was the first time she had a moment to think by herself. *Who was Kaleah? Am I Hara? How could this be? If I was not Hara, who was it? And what truth was it that she held? What did all this mean? How cute can this man be?* She quipped at the thought; she took a second look at Swinthun. In her life, she never came this close to a man. She felt the need to know more about him, and yet another idea came into her head. *Who is Hara? What does Kaleah know?* All these questions and desires mixed together. It confused her, and this was hard to maintain her concentration on one topic.

Her mind headed left, right, forward, up, backward, and now down. This was dizzying for her; it was all metaphorical as she kept the car steady and flying toward Winnipeg. The day neared dusk. Time did fly when you flew east. Under her car, she could distinguish a farm. This was as good of a place to get food whether foraging or begging; either would work.

As Kaylee approached the farm, it came to reality that this farm had been abandoned about a century ago. The barn was no longer in existence; it was a pile of wood. The color red was gone from its slats of wood. The home was gone, and the barriers existed long ago.

Turning the car off and turning the charger on, Kaylee woke Swinthun up. He was groggy. He was a soldier, but it showed he worked in Central Chicago for a general. He took a minute to collect his thoughts. He shook his head side to side a few times. Finally, he came to life.

"Hunting time?"

"Yes, it is." She was just as hungry as he was. The last day swung as if it was an hour ago. Hunger roared, and this was evident in both their faces.

Spring in the prairies was a pleasant time. Although there was a chance of rain in Calgary, near Winnipeg, the sun shone with warm rays. The sun reflected on their hottie hats; it got warm under the aluminum tops, but if you do not want to have an army on your butt, it was necessary.

A collection of berries, nuts, and some mushrooms was sufficient for their present hunger, but not for any reserves.

Food was in their gastric organ, and this helped them calm down. Swinthun was able to keep his alertness for longer periods. Kaylee was less erratic in her thoughts; for a second, she thought, *Was I thinking of all those issues in my head because I was hungry?* She smiled with her mouth lifting to the left significantly more.

For this part of the road trip, Swinthun drove the clunky car. He flew it at the same speed as Kaylee did. They went around Winnipeg to avoid any detection. The winds of spring were not as cold as their cousins of winter, but this did not make anybody warmer in the car. It had several sources of drafts because of its third color—nothingness.

Clothing maintained their temperature, but the cooling of the wind made the clothing insufficient. Kaylee grew tired of the blow of this small thing of cold air; she tried to reposition herself in her seat to avoid this air flow. Swinthun was less energetic but just as annoyed. The wind created a cold stream, which the clothing would warm up, but this would come up and come down, as sweat would trickle down their spine, as these spaces were more protected from the wind.

At their speed, three hours passed and they were close to Toronto. They had to keep off the main track of most cities. However, there

HENRI NGUYEN

was something in Halifax, which they would reach in the middle of night. The problem was a night arrival was more difficult as the guards were more alert. The sensors were set every night. This would be more difficult, as there are three ways to approach the city of Halifax: One was to land about ten kilometers away and walk in. Two, they could enter through the beacon route, which would risk them being uncovered. The third and less likely was to not enter the city but to use a boat to enter in the only way that was less electronically surveilled. These options ran through Kaylee's mind.

The night came, and they passed Toronto. Montreal was about to come into their sights. Again, they avoided detection. This went as expected. No one followed them, as far they knew.

Kaylee was in thought; she was about to burst out and just asked Swinthun.

"So I have a contact in Halifax, but at the time we are going to arrive, this means we have three ways to enter the city. One, on foot. Two, through the main gate. Three, by boat. Which one do you think is our best chance?" It was all there, short and sweet, just answer; this was her message.

"OK, you thought about this, didn't you? I think on foot for ten kilometers will not help you or me. Boat maneuvering in the middle of the night, well, let me say, it is not the best option. Furthermore, where do we steal a boat? So driving in through the main gate should be the only solution," he reasoned through.

"Good point," she acknowledged.

"On top of it, we are in a jalopy. You can be comforted with the thought that soldiers don't like to get cold and wet for an older car. And this vehicle is an old car. Hence, I sense that they will leave us alone," he pushed a little more.

"OK, OK, OK." Kaylee seemed to have enough about this talk.

It was about one thirty in the morning when their car lined up to enter Halifax. There were two cars along them, and they had about four cars in front of them. Slowly but surely, they advanced. Kaylee grew anxious, but when their car came to the checkpoint, there was communication about where they were going and how many people were in car. That was it.

CHAPTER 7

DUSK WAS A period in which no one did anything, as the light was weaker and people wanted more light. People were nearly sad when dusk came. It was sadness, but summer approached, and this was a good sign.

Sihi waited, and he grew agitated as time passed by so slowly. A ring happened in his head. Finally, information arrived.

"Yes, Sihi here."

"Sir, I am Captain Valdez from the Alaskan Troopers. We are here in Calgary. We arrived about two hours ago. We searched the city and found no one. There was a car that we were able to identify as the car Commander Schilling used."

"He must be in the city. Did you search everywhere? How can you not find him?" Sihi was losing his patience.

"Sir, we used heat sensors and we were not able to find a person in this city," Valdez insisted.

"He must have changed cars. Are there traces of cars in the past twenty-four hours?" Sihi said while thinking to not lose this opportunity.

"Please stand by." The captain ordered something, and they held the line open. A few minutes later, Valdez came back on the line. "Yes, sir. There are two traces of vehicles leaving this city. One went west, and the other one went east. Which one should we follow, sir?" Captain Valdez was matter of fact and to the point.

"You said there is a trace going to east?" Sihi wanted clarification while he computed all the elements thrown at him.

"Yes, sir," Valdez answered.

"Chase after the western one." Sihi threw his money on the western reach for a port. This would be Seattle or New Seattle, as they called it. A second after this thought crossed his mind, he revoked it. "No, pursue both traces."

"Yes, sir." Valdez wondered why the change of mind, but then again, he wanted to be on his way and not stay in this haunted city.

Valdez ordered his lieutenant to take two men and follow the trace west. This left Valdez with one man. According to the file from General Sihi, Commander Schilling lacked imagination, but his decisions were thoroughly thought through. Therefore, he sent three of his men to the west, as it was likely to be there. On the other hand, if he had gone east, the territory would be greater to search and he would need help from Winnipeg and maybe Toronto. The question he wondered about was, where was he going? And was Kaylee McCloud with him? If she was, this could change the equation.

Captain Valdez jumped into his car. He ordered the private to head to Winnipeg. As they hovered to reorient the car to the east, Valdez called the Winnipeg Army.

"My name is Captain Valdez. I have orders to find Commander Schilling and anybody he is traveling with. Please post his image on your board."

"Yes, sir," the officer responded.

"Thank you. We will see you soon," Valdez stated.

"Please hold. My commanding officer would like to speak to you," the officer said with no emotions.

"Captain Valdez?" The commanding officer came on.

"Yes . . . Who am I speaking to?" Captain Valdez asked.

"Oh my, it is me, Sean Onyo," he uttered.

"Son of a biatch, is that you, Sean? Really?" Valdez was surprised and sent a request to get a video call. This was accepted immediately.

"How are you, Valdez?" Onyo came very close to screaming.

"I am fine. I am located in Alaska, but I am chasing some commander." Valdez summarized his situation in brief statement.

"That is so nice, my friend. All right, we will be on the lookout for this commander, but it was nice to see you again. We are out," Onyo stated, as if he knew it was coming anyway.

Onyo and Valdez were in the same class at the academy. There were six of them in that class. If you graduated with a good class, you would have friends. There were years when no one enjoyed the auras of others and graduation was dry and uneventful.

His car was flying through the air. It flew near 900 kilometers per hour. This was a regular speed. There was little traffic in these skies. The contagion took more than three-quarters of the population out. The rest was from the following wars. This made the world very depleted of humans.

There were towns and cities where people lived, but if you were not in town with the army, this was considered a dying town. When the army showed up, everyone hid away. There were people who were good at hiding from any detection. They would have lead in their walls. This was harmful to their children and to themselves. Captain Valdez did not understand why anyone would ever want to live in those towns.

There was no power, no indoor water, no heat, and, most importantly, no army to protect you.

In about an hour and a half, Valdez and his driver arrived in Winnipeg. The town looked like many army towns. There was a central wall. It protected the army and its wealthy people. The outside was occupied by soldiers assigned to the coastal protection. There were a few people who lived also on the outside. These people survived on the charity of the soldiers and what they could catch.

Valdez walked into a tall building. It had the original revolving doors; how quaint. As he stepped into the building, a smell of baked cookies invaded his olfactory senses. These baked goodies would only help him. He stopped at the main desk and asked for Captain Onyo.

Captain Onyo came down and out of the elevator. There was a giant smile on his face. Onyo was a man who was pleasing to the eye. The Winnipeg captain was a tall man. His face was chiseled out of a block of marble. No facial aspects were off. His eyes were symmetrical and brown; his chin was perfection; his cheek bones were high and distinct. This was a perfect face according to his fiancée, before her death.

"How the hell are you, Valdez?" He came and gave him a firm bear hug.

"I am fine." Valdez was swallowed by the bear hug. "Give me a breathing way, goodness gracious," the captain begged with a laughter and huge smile of his own.

"You have not changed. You look good in a captain's uniform," Onyo said, laughing.

"Thanks, not much different from yours," Valdez snipped.

"Come on. I have a bottle of scotch waiting for you," Onyo said as he hailed an elevator with his Interweb connection.

"OK, and please tell me, how is your little man doing?" This was another quip at Onyo.

"Sure, if you want to see it, I can show it to you, but only you." Onyo burst out in laughter.

The elevator took them to Onyo's office. He pulled out two glasses and his bottle of scotch. It was a fifteen-year-old bottle. There were a few of them left on the planet. This was not an extravagance; it was a privilege to even come this close to a bottle of this age of scotch. Valdez admired the bottle, and when Onyo poured out an ounce of the amber liquid, Valdez smelled the eminence from this precious liquor. Then he took a slow sip.

The liquor entered his mouth, and as little of it he took, the taste was alcohol based. It felt as if he just took some methanol; although this would be a bad idea to do. Valdez could only recall school lessons about not consuming methanol. Continuing the journey to his gastric pouch, the ethanol transformed in his mouth like magic; a taste of cherry and chocolate came. This was marvelous. This was a revelation; nonetheless, Valdez had to begin some of his questions.

"Wow, this is amazing," Valdez expressed as he stared at the shot glass. Then he engaged into the real reason why he was in Winnipeg. "Sean, I have to ask you, how can you get out of the surveillance of the Interweb?"

"Well, one sip and you come out with that question?" Onyo said as he smiled sarcastically to his friend. "You can rip the chip out of your head, but there will be brain damage to deal with. Or you can block its transmission," Onyo said and took a second shot of scotch.

"How can you block the transmission of the Interweb?" Valdez inquired further.

"There were some talk that if there was an aluminum thick enough, it could end transmission," Onyo stated and took a small mouth of scotch.

"Any other way to stop the Interweb to check on you?" Valdez asked as he thought of the last statement from Onyo.

"I guess there is a way where you could stop the transmission by sending a virus to the satellite, and this would propagate across the system," Onyo enunciated the possibility.

"How can this be done?" Valdez asked with a face that expressed the idea of "Please tell me much more."

"Well, if you have virus and it can pass through the protection of the satellite and it can go through the right place, mainly the outbox message, then it can be transmitted to Earth system, and this means, boom, nothing left," Onyo explained with his beast hand gestures.

"Has it ever happened?" Valdez asked with some reservation.

"No. The system is still up, and the satellites are stronger than ever." Onyo grew bored with this conversation. "Should we go out to reminisce some of our old times?" he asked to Valdez, hoping he would refuse.

"No, I can't. I have a mission, and this may give me some oak leaves," Valdez said with a smile on his face and while tapping his shoulders. He knew it was out of politeness that Onyo invited him, and he also understood his welcome had run out. "Thank you for the amazing drink and the information," he said as he put down the glass and got up.

"Well, I say, until next time, friend. Maybe next time we could have more of a reunion versus this mission," Onyo said with no belief in the words.

"Of course. Until next time," Valdez said while his hand was out for a handshake, and he knew another bear hug was coming.

HENRI NGUYEN

Indeed, a huge hug came and swallowed him again. This was Onyo's way to tell you he appreciated you coming, but now it was time for you go. It was time for Valdez to resume the chase of this elusive commander Schilling.

Returning to his car, Valdez signaled to his soldier to get in the car to drive. It was about eight o'clock in the evening. The moon was high in the sky, and the cold winds began to push their chilling tentacles across Winnipeg. They were fast, but finding someone that they have no idea where he hid required some extra time and some sleuthing.

The clue reading was done in the car while they flew to the next town, which was Toronto. They should be there before the next morning. Valdez contacted his west search team to see how far they got. Nothing so far for them also. How can this be?

If Schilling went west, there should be a lead somewhere. Obviously, if he went east, there would be more ways to hide and more places to look for him. His car was no longer on the tracking of the Interweb, and his daily check-in was absent today. How can you find this commander in a whole continent without a clue? *This was not going to be easy,* Valdez thought to himself.

His driver was a private; he was barely two weeks in his unit. Recruitment would take you far from home. Valdez was from New Mexico. He was from Albuquerque City. It was never a rich city, but they found some rich people to prop the army up. His driver, Ezequiel Maddon, was an upstanding man. He was a proud and honorable soldier; he was also obedient. This made his progression to his Alaskan troops quicker.

The Alaskan troops were renowned for being the last bastion against the Chinese and Indian invasion of the last century. This was a mark of honor to be known as an Alaskan Trooper. They were all paratroopers, as anyone else in the army.

The army had so little men under the flag. At one point, it had nearly two million in uniform; now there were ten thousand under the flag. It would be a stretch. The army was now bots, drones, and AI-oriented weaponry. The army was scattered across a huge continent, which unified after the nuclear of war of 2019.

Valdez had his file open in his head. He paused and took a thought when Ezequiel asked a question.

"Sir, how do we know Commander Schilling went this way?"

"Good question, Ezequiel. I don't know, but there are a few cities he could reach to get assistance. Toronto is one, Montreal is another one. From there, he could head to Halifax, Boston, or maybe even Philadelphia. We are behind, and we need for him to make a mistake," Valdez enunciated while searching for a clue for himself.

"Sir, if I could ask?" Maddon asked permission, which his superior officer granted. "Why is it so important for us to search for Commander Schilling?"

"Interesting question, young man. I do not know what he did, but when a general asks my superior officer to get to Calgary, which is an abandoned city, it must be bad. So if you see him and he runs, you have permission to shoot him. This was our order—retrieve Commander Schilling dead or alive. They have also given us orders in case Ms. McCloud is with him. We have orders to bring her back alive. In other words, I do not know why all this is going down, but I have orders and I will complete my orders. Does that answer your question, soldier?" Valdez gave an answer in verbal diarrhea moment.

"Yes, sir." Ezequiel hesitated.

Driving in the dark was like being in a dark tunnel; all you can see was nothing but darkness. There were a few snowflakes. However, going at the speed they were at, the snowflakes were a point of light where the light of their car would bounce against.

At around eleven forty at night, they arrived in Toronto. This city felt like its description in the history books. It was clean, and their music was amazing. At least this was Valdez's memory. The car pulled into the waiting line. They waited about ten minutes, and finally, they checked into the city. There were lights on every street, and there were maybe two hundred people here. This was a giant city. Chicago had about 175, if you counted the elders among its inhabitants.

They parked on Front Street, a few steps away from the headquarters in Toronto. Every town in North America had a central command for their soldiers to correspond with. Valdez took steps, and he heard the snow creaking under his boots. This was a reminder of what winter used to be.

Nowadays, winter was rarer, and this was a flashback to his younger days in New Mexico. Albuquerque was a city of near abandonment; if there were two hundred people in Toronto; there were two families in Albuquerque. Now, the concept of family had changed in the last two centuries. It was about anyone who wanted to join a group and agreed to their rules. This was Valdez's idea of his family. He was raised by a mother who accepted him, no matter where he came from. He helped, and no questions were asked, ever.

The snow made him smile. He stepped to the door and opened it. He was in Toronto's headquarters. It was grand. The lobby was immense. Glass surrounded him, and at one end, there was the information desk. This was splendid for this New Mexico boy who now lived in Juno.

Valdez stood at the desk. A voice broke the dim silence.

"How can I help you, Captain Valdez?"

"I need to know If Commander Schilling passed through this city?" he queried.

"According to our records, no." The AI reviewed the information in about a second.

"Did a car come around Toronto?" Valdez asked, as if he expected the answer.

"According to our records, three cars came in our area." AI took about a second again.

"Transfer this information." This time, Valdez ordered it.

"Completed." Another second passed; this conversation was soon to end.

"OK." Valdez walked away from the desk as soon as he got the answer.

Valdez wondered why he could not access different town's AI, but instead, he had to show up in person to obtain this information. Valdez thought to himself, *This must be the last remaining strands of independence. This led us to all we have.* This was sad to Valdez, but he could not do a thing about it.

In the car, Valdez scanned the results provided. There was one going to New York, another going to Montreal. The last car had no identification and headed east. This was feeble and weak, but it was the only clue he had to follow. This would be the appropriate thing for him to do after Private Maddon and he called the two cars.

A few minutes later, Maddon looked back at Valdez, and he nodded. This time, Valdez was sure that he had to follow the third trajectory. Slowly, he gave the order to Ezequiel. No words exchanged, but he knew.

CHAPTER 8

IN THE REFRESHING night, Kaylee and Swinthun passed the checkpoint. They appeared to have not arisen any doubts so far. For a system where anyone knew everything about three seconds after you did it, this was unusual, if you passed the whole fact that they had aluminum hats on.

In the car, Swinthun and Kaylee wondered how to hide these lovely hats. It was not evident how to hide these monstrous hats. Between being horrifying and useful, there was no middle ground; these things were ugly, and a shine emanated when the sun came into the sky. In a few hours, it was going to become true again.

Halifax was a quiet little town. There were about eighty people living in the city. Surrounding the houses were the walls. Vestiges encircled the walls. The cities were all the same at this time. There were some houses and people living on the outside. Kaylee lived outside the walls of Central Chicago because she was not rich enough; she wondered if this was the same reason people inhabited the outside of the walls. There were many buildings nearing demolishment; some were still being used, but their tops frayed in the winds and time.

This city was a port. By this, Swinthun was realistic; it meant a dock with warship. There was no commerce with the outside world. The world was mean and tried to pierce the defense to steal the women. *How can this be?* asked Swinthun in his mind. *How could the world degrade too badly?* These thoughts resided in him, as his grandfather's words. He did not know why, but all these words were a guide. They were like wisdom to follow, as his grandfather once said.

At two in the morning, it was time to sneak in a town. Bots were on patrol, but in a port city, it was more important to patrol the harbor instead of the streets. This was true, as they had yet to encounter bots. Finally, after a period of ten minutes of silence, they elected to get out of the car. Kaylee stood in the cold air of spring. She took a deep breath. It felt like a burning in her air passages, but it felt amazing. She signaled to Swinthun to follow her.

In this dark and lonely place, Kaylee seemed to know something. She walked with her hands in her jacket's pockets. It was not cold to them, but the wind made it more real to both of them.

It was not hard to walk in this town. There were not too many streets. They were on Barrington, despite being slightly disoriented by a lack of presence on the Interweb. This would have been easier if they were still connected. Walking was not difficult, but following a woman who seemed to know where she was going was not as easy. There were moments when Swinthun wanted to ask her, "Do you know where you are going?"

Going to new places always took longer, but this required more time, as he had no idea of where he was and where he headed to. On top of it, his beautiful helmet began to slip occasionally. It was slightly too big for his head, or maybe he made it too large for his head. It was not comfortable, and this made him loosen the edges. Also, he was not used to wearing helmets. The army stopped using helmets about for as long as he could remember.

Suddenly, Kaylee stopped. She looked up at the address and smiled. She knocked on the door. It was two thirty in the morning. *Whom would she know to knock on their door at two thirty?* he asked himself. At this point, Swinthun did not mind anymore, but he wanted to get off the streets. It had been about thirty minutes that they walked in the town and no bots spotted them yet. It was a matter of time before this came to an end.

The door opened. There was an old man looking out at them.

"Wow, is this Kaylee?" the old man expressed.

"Uncle Marty," Kaylee said as she sank herself in his arms.

"Come on in, kids." Martin saw on them the marvelous hats and knew there would be problems.

"Are you connected, sir?" Swinthun asked.

"I know. Let me disconnect," Martin acquiesced.

"Thank you, Marty," Kaylee said and pulled her lips between her teeth.

"Please have a seat," Martin offered.

"Thank you very much," Kaylee uttered as she sat down.

The house was a small place. Space was not abound in the living room. There was just enough space for a love seat and a small chair. Kaylee and Swinthun were in the love seat. If they were lovers, this would have been sweet, but it was not there, yet.

"Marty, we are in trouble." Kaylee opened the discussion.

"You could have fooled me with those hats to block the connection," Martin sneaked in with a smile.

"I know you knew. We need a boat. Can you help us?" Kaylee asked with a sweetness Swinthun did not know she had.

"Of course, I will help you." Martin began to think as to how to get a boat and not leave any prints on the taking of a boat.

"Thank you, Uncle Marty," Kaylee said with another of sweetness, which surprised Swinthun even more. He was nearly under a spell upon the discovery of this gentleness.

"Give me about ten minutes?" Martin asked them as he got up.

Martin left the small living room and walked into his kitchen.

"Are you sure we can trust him?" Swinthun asked Kaylee in muffled voice.

"Yes, we can," she answered back with a low voice.

"How do you know?" Swinthun asked again.

"My dad and he were in battles together, and my dad told me that Martin owed him his life. If ever I needed help, I could use it." Kaylee came out with some of her past.

"OK." Swinthun seemed a little reassured.

Time spans slowly when you are waiting for something you really want. Ten minutes felt like an hour. Time was a relativity that Kaylee and Swinthun could spare themselves from. They sat side by side, not a word exchanged.

In his mind, Swinthun thought she was too high and too cute for him. He had some experience when he was in Central Chicago. He had a couple of women whom General Sihi told him he could use. He never abused their trust. He talked to them and had dinner with them. Swinthun was a man who never took it to the bedroom. He had something people called chivalry. Today, it was dead, but to him, it was a necessity. He could talk to them, but he felt they had to be there with him. It was different with Kaylee—she did not have to be there with him, yet she was.

Swept away in her thoughts, Kaylee kept an eye on her uncle and thought of her sitting neighbor. She thought to herself he was cute and polite. His brown eyes were an obsession to her mind. Their honesty made her dream for a second of him and her on a beach. Then Kaylee shut off the dream. It was too much at this moment. This was all she could tell of him. Out of nowhere, the mindfulness of him not telling her nothing of his life, preferences, or even if he liked her. The next second, Kaylee told her mind to keep busy and to not think about these matters. Slowly but inevitably, she returned to the thoughts of Swinthun. She wondered if he liked his name, if he liked running around North America with her, if he regretted having his grandfather's words in his mind, what did his grandfather mean to him; there were so many questions she could ask, but why was she not? The repeating question was in her mind now.

Bursting into the door, Uncle Marty reentered the living room. He looked at his niece and said, "If we leave right now, we can make this happen—you leaving, me not getting caught and giving you about six hours' head start." A statement they all loved hearing.

"OK. Thank you, sir," Swinthun said as he stood up, handing out his right hand.

"Thank you, Uncle Marty." Less classy but warmer, Kaylee jumped into him with vigor.

"No problem, but you have to leave right now," Martin said with an emphasis on the last two words. "There is a Corvair coming in, and it will not be secure for the next two or three minutes. You can sneak on, and they have two extra batteries just in case you run out of power. This should give you enough power to have the others recharged," Martin explained as he donned his coat.

They rushed out and ran to dock 3. There should be no reason the dock to have a number, as it was the only dock, but somehow, it maintained its number. The cold was enhanced by the cold wind from the North Atlantic.

Reaching the edge of the dock, seeing the approaching Corvair, they knew they had a few minutes to complete the taking of it. Swinthun was nervous, as his right legs shook. Martin looked at the shaking leg, and having no effect on it, he placed his hand on it. Swinthun received the message; his leg stopped shaking. As Kaylee saw this moment, she smiled. Her breathing was deeper, and her eyes focused on the spot of the dock where the Corvair pulled into.

The distance between them and the Corvair was about one hundred feet. This could be traveled in about four seconds. Getting in the boat and turning it on should take about another twenty seconds. So in about thirty seconds, they would be gone. Kaylee took another large breath. She was ready.

The crew, two soldiers, got off the boat. They talked and laughed. While all this was happening almost in slow motion, Kaylee and Swinthun got ready. Swinthun took a deep breath. Within a minute, they could see the soldiers walking away. Slowly but surely, the soldiers entered a building.

Then Kaylee sprinted to the Corvair. Swinthun followed her. She reached the boat and did not even slow down to step on the board between the Corvair and the dock. She put a foot on it and jumped into the boat. Immediately, she went in to the deck. Swinthun ran right behind her and saw her jump. He was amazed. He knew and stopped and looked at the electronic grasp of the dock. This held the boat. If there was a hurricane, the boat would be locked onto deck and little or no damage would be caused by the Corvair. He unlocked it and jumped into the boat.

The engine turned on, and smoothly they were off. The engine was a quiet engine as it was electric. The Corvair was not a typical boat. It was not a hover boat either. It had the shell of a boat, but it flew about four or five feet above the water. This increased its speed, and because of lower resistance, it was not dragged down by the waves and currents. The power was used to elevate the Corvair above the water, and propelling it was an ionic engine.

The few minutes before they reached the island at the entrance of the inlet to Halifax, they sped. As the island got closer, Kaylee nodded to Swinthun, and she shut off the engine. Slowly, they passed McNabb Island. They could feel the electronic eye on them. Gently but definitely going to the east, they could see a tower and a green eye. They knew it would have caught them had they kept their engine on.

The defense net of North America was designed to protect the land, so if you were a leaving vessel, there was no issue. No images would be taken. This was a design, and if you were Swinthun, that flaw worked for them.

The minutes passed, as they passed by McNabb Island. The woods were dominant on the sight of the islet. The darkness of the woods reminded Swinthun of the tales of Hansel and Gretel. This was an old story his grandfather told him about. It was an ancient tale that told him to always be nice and useful; otherwise, even your father will feed you to the old lady in the woods. This terrified his young life, but now, it brought a fear, which he knew was unrealistic.

Finally, they passed the security tower. The time was about three thirty in the morning. It was late, and the sun was going to be up in about three hours. This was a schedule Kaylee felt was adequate for their escape. She initiated the engines, and with a gentle push forward, they moved. Kaylee could see land disappear behind her. She focused on the goal ahead.

Kaylee was not sure if the goal ahead was forthcoming, but it was too late. The issue of the freedom was now hers. She wanted to know what this lady wanted to tell her; she desired to have the truth. It was not hard, but somehow, people would be chasing them.

Swinthun came into the commanding deck. The Corvair was not a spacious craft. There was room for four soldiers, but the control deck was designed for one person. He looked at Kaylee and asked her, "Wow, this was an adventure. How do we get to Laos without being tracked?"

"I thought we could go through the Mediterranean and the Middle East," Kaylee answered with an attempt to be gentler to the only man she ever interacted with in her life, short of her father.

"Hmm, you know that is how they figured we would go. Let me check the map and see if we could lose them," Swinthun said with a smile.

Going down the ladder, Swinthun landed into the mess hall. Looking for a map, he shuffled through a bunch of other devices. Then he came upon a map device. He turned it on. It came on in a second. Suddenly, it came upon his mind. *No, it required a connection to the Interweb.* He turned it off. He closed his eyes and shook his head slowly while taking a deep breath. He was not sure how to proceed anymore. There had to be some sort of map, as they were on a boat. What if there was no power? What would they do? Their connection was not as good off the coast of North America. There had to be a way to do all this.

Swinthun kept looking. Then he came to see in the captain's closet. There were maps—paper maps. *There you go,* he thought to himself with a smile on his face. He dragged his found maps to the control room. Walking fast on a boat was not an easy skill, but when it floated above the water, it was much easier than you would expect.

"I have maps. We could figure out our way to Laos," Swinthun said.

"Yeah. Let us look at the map," Kaylee said with a slight sarcastic tone.

"Well, you know as well as I do that we have to keep up on our pursuers, because I know Sihi has sent them already," Schilling responded to her sarcasm.

"I am sorry." Her eyes stayed on the horizon.

"Thanks," he said as he unfolded this map.

To his surprise, it was a really old map, and it had scribbling on it. North America was scribbled along the east coast, the west coast, and there was no Florida anymore. This was a reflection of the new climate. After looking at the North America continent, his eyes went to his right. To the east of the Atlantic were more scratches. The African and European continents did not look the same any longer. England and Ireland were more or less the same, but the United Kingdom's capital was crossed out. London was underwater. Paris was not better. The western coast of Europe was Bavaria, Switzerland. There were islands that were the Pyrenees and the Alps. This was a reality check to Swinthun.

As Kaylee guided the boat; she asked Commander Schilling, "Where are we going?" She seemed to know it was not going to be Europe, and hence, it should be Africa.

Swinthun looked at her face and said, "We should go through Africa. There are less people and less sensors. We could hide longer away from the eyes of satellites. I am sure they are realigning a satellite or two to track us."

Kaylee nodded. She processed the information and wondered how far they could go without being caught. It was the first time she had the thought. It was a danger and it was a real threat. It was obvious they needed to stay off the radar; however, how do you stay away from the satellites? It was Sihi's ultimate weapon against them. Pushing her thoughts even further, Kaylee realized there was not too much traffic over the Atlantic Ocean these days.

The boat's direction was to Western Africa, which, according to the map, was underwater. There were islands, and they aimed for the Sankwala Islands. The name was on the map; they were not sure why they decided to call these islands the Sankwalas. They did not care about the name. They needed some food and needed to recharge the batteries of the boat.

As they approached the Sankwala Islands, they were troubled. First, it was the magnificent hats, which, in combination with increased heat in this area, made them sweat more than they cared to tell. Second, the landscape was mesmerizing. It was green and there were trees everywhere. These were not the lessons they received from the Interweb. This was another reason for their troubled look.

Landing the boat was not easy. The coast was accompanied by a lot of logs and trees growing out of the water. Tying the boat and reaching the land was difficult and a wet issue. Swimming was not the main skill commanders needed in the Midwest. Kaylee had to drag his body to a branch. From there, there were successive awkward moments before both of them reached land.

The forest was dark and the temperature was a little less hot. The humidity was thick and they could cut it with a knife. It was hard to move through the thick underbrush. Sweat and fatigue were both present. Kaylee slumped and scratched her head. She looked at Swinthun, and he was asleep. She thought for a second that she needed to rest her eyes for a few seconds.

A knock followed by another knock. This disorientated Kaylee. What made this knocking sound? Who else could hear this knock, knock? She opened her eyes. It was blurry for a second. She blinked several times and focused. At that moment, she could see Swinthun, and he was at a pole and seemed to be tied. Immediately, she realized that her hands were tied and she was also at another pole. What the hell was all this? That was her first wonder.

Swinthun was awake and he let out a sigh. It was the first sign of relief he gave as he saw Kaylee come back to the land of the living and difficulties. He smiled for less than a second. For that moment, he was light and happy. The next second, he looked at his issues and began to calculate how to get out of this situation.

There were two persons standing and discussing. Both of them had a spear. Behind Kaylee, another person played the drums with his spear on her helmet. Somehow, the helmets remained. This was slightly odd. Swinthun's hands were tied, and tightly at that.

One of the two men talking suddenly stopped and uttered something. It sounded close enough to English. It was something like "stop." There was a frown on Swinthun's face. He wondered.

"Do you speak English?" Swinthun asked.

"Yeah," one of the men answered, as he laughed first.

"Why are we prisoners?" Swinthun inquired.

"Really?" the other man stated, and his spear was at Swinthun's throat. "You come into our island then you ask why you are prisoners? Wow, you have balls, dear sir." The spear was still at Swinthun's throat.

"Calm down," the first man said as his hand pulled back the spear from Swinthun's throat. "Please do tell why you are here," he continued while looking at his partner.

"We are just traveling," Swinthun let out.

This remark made the three persons laugh. This was humorous to them. Swinthun realized this was not the right thing to say.

While all this was happening, Kaylee was orienting herself to the situation. Her hands were tightly connected together. The person behind her moved on to Swinthun, who made some funnies. She began to rob the cord on the pole. This rope was a thick one. It would take her at least a few hours before being free or discovered. This was not a good situation.

Then a woman came into the cave. This changed the discussion tone of the persons who were present. Kaylee sensed she was the chief. Kaylee smiled. She thought of what her father told her, "Once you were a chef, but today, nothing stops you from becoming a chief." Was this the moment?

The three persons bowed, and it became obvious to Swinthun that they were men, as he saw their genitals. This was a little obscene to only Swinthun. After the bow, they moved out of the way. The woman was black, there was no doubt about that. She was tall and, to Swinthun, sexy. She wore shorts and T-shirt. This T-shirt revealed her message: Chiefs with an arrow on it.

Her eyes looked at Swinthun, and she smirked. Her eyes moved to Kaylee. As her look fixated on the Asian woman, her expression stated, "What is an Asian doing with this little white boy?" This lasted for a second.

"What is your name?" the black woman asked the Asian.

"I am Kaylee. He is—" She did not finish that sentence, as the black woman lifted her hand.

"I don't care about him. I am talking to you," She interjected.

"OK . . .," Kaylee answered.

"What are you doing here on my island?" the woman continued to ask.

"We needed to recharge our boat batteries, and we thought we could find some food," Kaylee answered.

"Where are you coming from?" she asked while touching Kaylee's hair.

"We came from North America," Kaylee uttered out. She understood clearly that she was not in a position of strength. Answering clearly and honestly was her policy at this time.

"North America? He looks like one, you don't. Where are you going?" the tall woman asked the shorter one.

"We were headed to Asia," Kaylee said.

Loud laughter came out of the black woman. It was a laughter out of her gut. She began coughing. The men bowing remained along the wall.

"Why are you going to Asia? There is nothing there," the tall woman uttered as she recovered from her coughing.

The analysis of this last question ended up to be, *Stop talking, Kaylee.* She remained quiet. As the black lady looked at her, her tongue curled to her molars, and she smiled. Then she nodded while staring at Kaylee. She appeared to know something. She turned to the three men by the wall of the grotto and said, "Go find their boat. It could be a prize for us. Go."

The men rushed out. While all this was happening, the tall woman stared again at Kaylee. She squatted in front of Kaylee. Her tongue played in her mouth, and now, it was on her right incisor. It seemed to be a way for her to think. After a few seconds, she bit her lower lip and nodded her head while getting up. She walked out of the cave.

Kaylee let out a stale amount of air. Swinthun scooted to face her side. He whispered, "Kaylee, turn your hands to my feet." This was an odd request, but there was not much of a thought; she did it. Finally, her hands were about five centimeters from the tip of his feet. Swinthun knocked his heel on the ground twice. On the second dirt lift, Kaylee heard a swish sound. Then she could feel her cords moving. It took several minutes, but, finally, she was free.

Kaylee got up and ran to release Swinthun from his ropes. As he wrung out the mark of ropes on his wrists, Kaylee checked the main exit of the grotto. There was no one. She signaled Swinthun that it was time to go. They began a dash down the road. She wanted to be in the bush so the locals could not find them. The running was not hard. There was anxiety while they ran. *What if they just wanted to find our boat just by following us?* They reached the bushes.

Kaylee took a couple of deep breaths. She looked at Swinthun, who was also expelling carbon dioxide. Between two inhalations, she asked a very interesting question. "Where is our boat?" They were disoriented. They looked around and had no idea where they were. Swinthun looked at her. He wanted to do something different, but now he had a question to answer. He did not know. Then he pointed at his helmet. This meant they would find their boat in a heartbeat, but they would leave a bread crumb for Sihi and his chasers. They looked at each other. Kaylee nodded to indicate to go for it.

The next moment, Swinthun took his helmet off. His connection to the Interweb was reestablished. He asked where they were. The Interweb gave its answer in about three seconds. He put his marvelous hat back on. Then he looked at Kaylee. He nodded and signaled her to follow him.

Dashing down a path was no way for Kaylee to give her trust, but at this moment, it would have to be. She had no idea where she was. This land was something she had never seen. Having no idea where she was made it difficult for her. Kaylee asked herself, *Does Swinthun know where the boat is?* This was an instant of anxiety for her. It rose on top of it every second the information was related to whoever chased them.

Swinthun was focused, and one thing was in his mind—reach the boat. Getting off the island was essential, as they were now pinging on the map. This meant the chase was back on. It was exhausting to run when hunger was a predominant obstacle. Somehow, the need to reach their boat buried this gastric pain.

It took them about ten minutes of running across the woods. They could sense a chasing party with less-than-eager feelings was imminently on their way. It was time to get wet and get back on the boat. In a moment of taking a deep breath, both of them leaped into the water. The water breaking was warm. The climate affected the seas. This was not a bad feeling, but the knowledge of people coming for their skin hurried them up somewhat.

CHAPTER 9

BOSTON WAS NO longer the old city winding through with really ancient buildings. No, it was now an island. On this tiny island, there were a fort and a port. It was a citadel like kind of place. This meant walls and small areas for soldiers.

Walking into Boston was a sad experience. There was a soldier at the gate. He appeared to be a hungry soldier. He was gaunt, and his eyes were about to pop out of his body.

Valdez looked at the poor soldier. His stance was slump; nonetheless, he yelled at the poor soldier, "Stand up, soldier!" This made the soldier straighten his spine, but it was slow and reticent. Valdez continued his speech. "Where is the commanding officer?"

A weak voice came out of the bare body. "He is on his way, sir." His voice was a sign of the poverty of food and how it was not equal in all places.

The commanding officer was a captain. He looked strong, and this made you wonder, how come this soldier on duty looked like he was about to crumble, but his commanding officer looked good? The thought troubled Valdez. As he walked to the captain, he pondered about it. The captain saluted him. He responded to the salute with a salute.

"Captain, can I ask a question outside of my mission?" Valdez, troubled, asked.

"Of course," the captain answered with sharpness and concision.

"Why does your guard on duty look like he is about to die?" Valdez put it in words that should not wrinkle the captain's mood.

"He was insubordinate and he was punished with a week without food," the captain said with a tone that indicated "That was the last question outside of your mission."

"All right. Have you seen these people come into Boston?" Captain Valdez passed on through the Interweb the picture as his words landed.

"No, I have not received these people," the captain answered very dryly. "Is there anything else?" Now, this last statement was a sign of "You are not welcome into my fort." This was evident.

"No, thank you. If they do show up, please alert us," Valdez said as he took a step back.

Hopping back into his car, Valdez thought, if they come to Boston, they most likely did not go for New York, so Halifax remained. As his calculations computed, he lifted his eyes to the rising sun and ordered his driver to head for Halifax.

The drive was quick and quiet. The driver was tired, but there was no fatigue to tell a captain who was on a mission to find two people. This would be considered disobedience, and after the loud discussion where no words would be said by himself, he would be punished. There was no benefit to this idea of "I am tired." Death was an option, which did not sound too bad, but drastic still.

Arriving in Halifax, it looked like a jewel compared to Boston. They lined up the car to register. There were two cars in front of them. It took about two minutes to clear the checkpoint. They parked in front of the headquarters building. Valdez got out of the car. As he straightened his uniform, he pulled his head down and said, "Catch some sleep. I am sure you will need it." This was comfort for the driver.

Valdez walked in the building. There was no one in the lobby. He saw the information desk and walked to it, until his attention was triggered by a voice.

"Captain Valdez," a female voice uttered.

"Yes?" Valdez turned around and saw a female. He wrinkled his forehead and tilted his head to the left ever so slightly. He could not recognize her, but her voice was familiar.

"Cynthia . . . Cynthia McCallum," the woman said.

"I am sorry . . . Do I know you?" Valdez, confused, asked the honest question.

"Oh my goodness, summer camp, a decade ago. We . . . you know . . . did it." She had no memory problem, and it was clear to her.

"What do you mean we did it?" Valdez asked again and even more confused.

"Wow, I guess I was not your first, as you told me," the lady said with a sense of insult.

"I am sorry. I don't remember you." Valdez felt her anger rising and could not do a thing about it.

"Fine. How can I help you, sir?" the woman uttered. Her face showed her exasperation.

"I am looking for these two persons." The images transmitted immediately.

"Let me review the logs," the woman stated. "I have them. They entered Halifax last night." She made the statement and asked nothing else.

HENRI NGUYEN

"Thank you. Do you know where they went?" Valdez asked with a voice that indicated this was business and nothing else.

"We have their car. It is on Barrington Avenue." She made the statement with anger in her voice. This was not a fun moment for the lady.

"Thank you." Valdez could not have left any faster; he felt the discomfort about a conquest that he did not recall.

As Valdez stepped out of the building, he asked the location of Barrington Avenue. It was the next street. He did not want to use his car for such a small trip. He ran across the street and cut through an alley. On Barrington Avenue, there were two cars in his sight. One end of the street gave onto the harbor, and the other to the check into the city. He could see both ends of the streets. This meant they would have taken a boat to somewhere. The question was, where was this somewhere?

Running was a habit every soldier has in his back pocket. His running style was longer strides and a solid core. His hands barely moved, while his arms swayed alternately on each side. He was an elegant runner. It took him about three minutes to get to the harbor. There was no boat, and yet there were people gravitating to the pier. This was a clue that something happened.

Valdez's run to the pier took him maybe a little more than a minute. When he arrived, Valdez spoke to the crowd without being out of breath. This was another sign that running was in his back pocket.

"Everyone, zip it!" Valdez shouted, and everyone turned around. Immediately, all stood straight and saluted him. "What happened here?" he said with a tone down, as all were quiet now.

"Sir, these two officers reported their Corvair stolen. However, we have no one having taken the boat." the pier master answered.

"What do you mean?" Valdez inquired.

"They stated coming back to dock and stepping out of their vessel for a few minutes. When they came back, it was gone," the pier master stated.

"Why did you leave your vessel insecure?" Valdez talked to the Corvair officers.

"Sir, we knew nobody was around, and we thought we could have some fun and then come back and complete the rest," an officer responded to Valdez's question.

"Fun . . . really. That is a stronger feeling than completing your assignment." Valdez was not just upset; he began fuming as he walked away. A few feet of stepping, he stopped and turned around. He looked at the pier master and softly said, "I want these men to be punished as well as you can imagine."

As Valdez left the pier, he knew Swinthun and Kaylee were the guilty party for the stealing of a Corvair. It would be on the report to Sihi, but this would barely change their sentence. What they did—the running away from the army and duty—would make them slaves. If not death itself, it would be darn close.

Valdez stopped and thought, *Where would you go if you had a Corvair?* Europe was evident. But what if it was not? He would be seriously behind them. He thought for a minute. His habit was to think while scratching his head slowly in the front of his scalp. Then his right fingers stopped scratching, and his eyes lifted. His jaw moved slowly to his left side. This made his face asymmetrical. He knew how to get a clue. He ran back to the headquarters building.

When Valdez got into the building, he looked for Ms. McCallum, but he could not see her. He walked to the information desk and requested assistance. This time, a gentleman stepped out. He seemed sturdy. His height was deficient, but he was strong boned. He looked like someone who would enjoy tackling you.

HENRI NGUYEN

"Sir, how may I help you?" the sturdy officer uttered.

"I need to see the radar tracking from last night," Valdez spewed out.

"Yes, sir," the man answered and, with his hand, invited Valdez to follow him.

As they entered a dark room, the lights came on. The lieutenant invited Captain Valdez to have a seat, which he did. Then a screen came on. The lieutenant stepped away. He called up the radar tracking and asked another question.

"What time do you want it start from, sir?"

"Midnight until now." Valdez calculated in his head.

"There you go, sir," the lieutenant said as he stepped out of the room.

Even in accelerated mode, radar screens of empty seas were not as comical or dramatic as flies dying. It was boring. The screen went about its business when a dot appeared. Valdez slowed down the screen. He clicked on it. It stated, "CVR 2." This meant he was sure Swinthun and Kaylee did take the Corvair. Then he looked at it slowing down by the island. Now he knew Swinthun was aware of the island's observation tower. This was mechanical, so there had to be a record of it.

Valdez pulled up the menu and went down the listing. When he got the McNabb Island tab, he clicked on it. It pulled up a still image of the view from the island. All you could see was the ocean. He looked at the clock and pulled it back to 2:13 a.m. Then he saw the Corvair slowly passing the camera.

After it passed the viewpoint of the camera, there was no image. *This was a good move, Swinthun,* he thought to himself. The automatic camera was motion activated. And the escapees slowed down enough that camera never picked up on their movement. "This was a good move, Swinthun," he muttered to himself.

There were radars in space. They could track the Corvair if Swinthun did not remove the original battery. Each battery placed in the engine had a tracker. The only thing was, if you knew this, you would not transfer the tracker to the next battery. Valdez knew about this weakness and told his superiors, who said, "Who would want to run away from heaven?" This was true, and yet he was to track a pair of fugitives who wanted to escape.

Valdez, pensive, got up from the seat and walked out of the room. As he crossed the threshold of the room, Valdez looked up and asked if a Corvair was available. He knew he had to chase them, but the question remained, where would they go?

If it was him and he had to run away, he would aim for Europe. The Europeans were strange, and he never talked to one of them, but he heard the rumors. These telltales involved the people of Europe to be possessive and wanting more. This was a behavior he never understood. As a soldier, it was all about nation and flag. There was a line about God in the swearing of officers, but to him, God was a different aspect of life.

God, to Valdez, was his savior. He had nothing to do with the army and even less to do with the chase. To the captain, this was a retrieval of two army assets who disobeyed rules. That was all.

The lieutenant searched. The next minute, he responded to the captain.

"Sir, we have another Corvair."

"Very well. Get it ready. I have no time to lose." Valdez was happy.

"But . . . sir, it needs to be reassembled," the lieutenant uttered.

"What? You are to tell me we are in a port and yet we only have one Corvair," Captain Valdez laid into the lieutenant.

"Sir . . . I am sorry, sir," the lieutenant stated with a lot of hesitation.

"When will it be ready?" Valdez asked the lieutenant with a tone that diminished the lieutenant's rank.

"I don't know, sir." Hesitation and fear were now the lieutenant's best options.

"Get it done. Let me know as soon as it is ready." Again, Valdez showed his lack of patience.

"Yes, sir." The lieutenant could not get away fast enough.

Valdez was annoyed. He knew he would have to alert General Sihi about this hiccup. He tried to figure out a way to make it soft and for him to avoid being yelled at, as he did to the lieutenant.

Valdez returned to the radar room, and he activated the locator for Swinthun's boat. The first second passed; the second was about to pass. It was evident that Swinthun knew about the tracker. He lay back into the seat and bit his upper lip. He knew a bad moment was about to drown him. He called the general.

"General Sihi, sir."

"Do you have them?" Sihi asked,

"No, sir." Valdez anticipated the yelling to begin any second now.

"Where are you?" Sihi seemed to hold it together.

"I am in Halifax, and I have evidence that they took a Corvair to the east," Valdez said as plainly as he could.

"What the hell are you doing in Halifax still? Are you not chasing these morons? It better be the best reason ever for you standing in Halifax, son!" The yelling has begun.

"General, sir, Halifax port is prepping another Corvair for me to go after them, sir," Valdez answered with some cowardliness in his voice.

"Damn it. Do your job. That is all I ask. Do you understand?" Sihi knifed him up.

"Sir, yes, sir." Valdez was beyond the point of leaving this conversation.

"Call me when you have them," Sihi said and hung up.

This was a moment Valdez could do without again. The displeasure he was left with soiled him. He needed to take a shower and clean himself.

The afternoon opened its arms. Valdez did not care about the afternoon. It got later and later. It started to be despairing to him. Every minute passing was another distance away the two escapees ran.

Valdez knew every minute made it more difficult for him to find them. They could hide anywhere and never to be found. They were able disable their Interweb tracker and their Corvair tracker. If they were in Europe, there were a few options Valdez could call upon to help him. This was getting too much for him to think.

Valdez got back to his car. He woke up his lieutenant and ordered him to prepare for a long expedition. Also, he ordered his subordinate to seek weapons and food. His pistol was not going to be enough, especially if he would have to search house to house in Europe. He did not see how else he could proceed.

The lieutenant ran to stock barracks to obtain heavier weapons and food. This was going to be a long search, and Valdez knew about it.

The afternoon was nearly closing her arms to the evening when an alert came into Valdez's head. The alert was about Swinthun. A blink of eye was given to Valdez. He opened the file. The point of reference was in the middle of what was left of Africa. This was troubling. Valdez frowned his face, and again, he bit his upper lip. In his mind, he zoomed in and could see the location of the dot, and then it disappeared.

It was as if for three seconds, he was there, and now he was ghost.

What the hell?

The next minute, the humiliated lieutenant called him up to inform him that the Corvair was ready. He could have called, but being an obedient officer, he came to tell his superior in person. This was submission.

Valdez walked down to the dock. He saw his lieutenant loading weapons and food onto the Corvair. Now that he knew where the ping came from, he has to decide whether to believe this ping. How could you cheat the Interweb? There was no way to do so, but what if? He was not sure, but he knew he had to go and see. On the other hand, if the locator signaled in Africa, it would take him three hours minimum to get there. The question arose, if they were not there, where would they go?

Valdez needed some more info. He could ask General Sihi, but then again, he was less than happy to have heard of the news from Valdez. In a moment of indecision, Valdez elected to go to Africa and see what information was there, and then, if needed, he would ask questions to the general.

CHAPTER 10

T HE SUN DID its job; it charged the batteries. Now it was time
to continue the trip. Swinthun was a man who did not know why
he was there on this trip. However, he knew there was some truth he
needed to get. Was this like Mulder from that old show he saw?

Swinthun knew the world was round, but to him, there was this calling
to the world.

His mother was not predominant in his life. At a young age, his mother
placed him in a military school. This was tradition for most boys.
Becoming an officer in the army was his only goal. He was on his way
to the rank of general; maybe within a decade, he would get his first
star. Now, all he could hope for was a life sentence for disobedience
and desertion.

This was not even a thought for him. It was as if he knew there was
something out there waiting for him. It was that or death will get him
wherever he wanted to go.

Religion was a motivator; it was used throughout his life. He was told
God wanted this to happen, or if this would happen, it was because
God wanted it. Captain Schilling had doubts about any mention of
God. There were too many desires of God and too many references of
a well-wanting God for him to believe in.

The Corvair rode to Asia. He and his attractive hat were at helm of
the Corvair, while Kaylee was asleep right behind the cockpit. She was
a delightful pain in the ass, Swinthun thought. Nonetheless, she had
that something that picked at his world discovery desire. There was an

independence that he liked from the woman; and while he looked at her sleeping, there was an attraction too.

In this world, men and women were different. Men were in charge and women were expected to be obedient. However, because of a lack of men, the army had to use women in the defense system. This was an obligation for most women. Women officers were a nonstarter for the army. They were allowed to maintain the defense parameter but had to live in the "suburbs" of major cities.

In truth, the rest of the women were kept within the walls of the cities. There was an adage when it came to women usage in the city—one woman is mild, two is more interesting. Men used women whenever they wanted. They were part of harem, except the idea of harem was not acceptable. Thus, the females were used, but no one asked questions.

When a woman was pregnant, it was a celebration for the man. The brouhaha was to the fact that childbirth had more than dipped. It was so low that an article put it as anemic. This was not a good thing. Meanwhile, the pregnant women moved to a different part of the city to deliver their children.

Despite all he was allowed to do, Swinthun never had a night with a woman. Tonight was the closest he ever was to a woman sleeping since his early life. He looked at Kaylee's face. It was oval; her hair was black, and the thickness of it was tantalizing. Her almond eyes were thin, and so were her lips. Kaylee was a slender woman, but you could see her muscles. Her abdominals were strong, as he saw a four-pack when they were held captive.

In a moment of wanting love, Swinthun dreamed of being her lover. This made his third leg grow.

At that moment, Kaylee woke up to the sound of her alarm. The alarm system was not connected to the Interweb; it was self-use, and so the alarm rang in her head. She got up. That moment Swinthun dreamed about disappeared very quickly. His third leg did not. Kaylee saw it, and she rolled her eyes at him. She went to the bathroom.

Embarrassment and Swinthun became one. It was a merge of two into a single shell. There was no space to maneuver and plenty of shame to share.

When Kaylee came back, Swinthun's third lower extremity was nearly gone. She gave him a cold shoulder. In that moment, he wanted to explain the reasons why, but in that moment, he also recalled his training expressions—never explain more than you can tolerate. It was embarrassing, but it was livable, at least for Swinthun; she could not go anywhere else.

It was time for Kaylee to take the helm. She gave a slight nudge on Swinthun's shoulder. He moved and let her have the wheel. The scene was dark and watery. That is all he could see. It was about three in the morning, and you could see in the distance archipelagoes. It must have been India and the Himalayas. There was no way to check this, but for Swinthun, it was time for a collection of z's. He needed. It was almost a day and half without sleep.

Kaylee was a soldier. She was in the defense force. This was an honor for her. Except for the fact they had Sylvia spying on her. She wondered how long it had been going on. There was a lot of things she did for that olden gal, and she spied on her. This was upsetting.

About a half hour at the wheel, Kaylee looked in the forward position. Swinthun was dead asleep. He was cute, she acknowledged to herself while scratching her forehead hair, which resided uncomfortably under her so cute aluminum hat. She observed him. When he slept, he made no noise. This was so cute for her. His curly hair, she imagined, as it was also under an aluminum top, made him look, well, silly.

HENRI NGUYEN

At that moment, she felt her lower abdomen rumble. She knew Tom was coming for a visit. She shut her eyes and took a deep breath. Kaylee shook her head so slightly, although no one would see it because no one else was on the boat awake.

Thoughtfully, she tried to figure out how to come up with absorption devices. The blood did not bother her, but on her clothes, it would look careless. She ran through the list of clothes she had seen across this tiny boat. Then as her eyes took a pause, she stared at Swinthun. Her conscience told her to think of how to deal with her Tom, but somehow, she could not hear her own voice.

The morning came at around five, and the sun began shining. Swinthun was refreshed from two hours of sleep. His eyes showed fatigue; there was redness surrounding his iris. There was something happening with Kaylee. Swinthun was oddly taken aback. Last night, she was exasperated with his presence; now she was googly eyes on him.

Swinthun sat behind Kaylee and took a sip of water. His stomach grumbled. There had been little or no food in the last thirty-six hours. He was hungry. Kaylee was hungry too, but this was a survival mode for her. The lake and hunting did not always gave her food. This was a rough reality to face, and she faced it with less despair than Swinthun.

Hunger was not a difficult thing to find; it was finding food that defied all. The emptiness was present and mind controlling for Swinthun. He was not used to not eating. The only time he could not eat was in his first year at military school. His company's punishment was not eating until the next day for something one of his teammates did. He wanted to hit that person, and did eventually.

Close to an island, they looked at it. It seemed to be inhabited, so they looked across the small boat for weapons, just in case.

Coming out of the bowels of the boat, Kaylee looked shocked.

"Swinthun! Why are there infant clothes and bassinet on a military boat?"

"What?" the only word Swinthun could muster at this question.

"Come and look for yourself," she responded.

Swinthun went into the dark side of the boat and saw it for himself. There were four bassinets and plenty of infants' and children's clothes in the cupboards. Stunned and wondering for an answer, he was speechless.

Sitting in the wheelhouse, Swinthun speechless looked at Kaylee, who was making strips of cloth out of the children's clothes. He wondered, and finally, he asked, "What are you doing?"

"Really, do you want to know this?" Kaylee asked with a brisk sarcasm.

"Yeah, I do." Swinthun thought, did he really want to know?

"OK, if you want to know, I will tell you. I am about to have a Tom coming to town, so I have to be ready," she responded to his question.

"Who is Tom?" befuddled Swinthun asked.

"No, it is not someone, it is something. It is Time Of Month, you know?" She laughed at his ignorance.

"What time of month? What is that?" Swinthun was lost and needed to understand this mumbo jumbo.

"It is my period, you dumbass." Now, she laughed harder.

"Oh!" with a high pitch, which was followed by "Oh." This one was with a lower tone.

After this exchange, there was a feeling of shame to talk about anything else. Finally, Swinthun found a spear gun. This was just as good as anything else. He also found a couple of bowie knives. They were ready to get some food if the indigenous people would let them.

They were approaching the island. It was a small piece of dirt. There were trees and flowers. This implied there was a possibility of having some sort of fruit. They were not sure if the fruits they would find would be eatable, but starving as they were, any form of food would be welcome.

After a swim to the shore, both of them realigned their hats as the swim was difficult with a spear gun, a knife, and a bag. It was not evident that Swinthun was a better swimmer than Kaylee, but she was more resourceful than he was. She was a smart cookie; she used her pants to make a floating vest.

Swinthun looked at Kaylee and could only smile as he recognized her ingenuity and resourcefulness.

Walking along the shore was not hard, but as hungry people, it was a difficult walk. They explored the coastline and saw some coconut trees. Attempting to look whether climbing the tree would be a good idea, Kaylee saw some coconuts. Deciding to climb was another obstacle to complete this task. Swinthun was nearing exhaustion. Kaylee looked at him and told him to sit down. He did. There were no questions and no argumentations.

Kaylee looked at the tree. She pushed her left cheek out with her tongue. The tree looked old, and there was enough strength in the trunk for her climb. She took a second and turned back to Swinthun. She asked for his knife. Surprise was his first emotion. He gave his knife.

Kaylee climbing was an event. There was always a special skill involved. Her two knives were her anchors; the only thing was there were no breaking points. Her point was to get to the top and get some food. Then she would figure out how to get down.

The climb was not easy. There were points where even Swinthun nearly got up. However, Kaylee reached the top. It was about twenty meters high. This was nothing on a horizontal plane; but on a vertical plane, it was a different story. She knocked a half-dozen coconuts. She was tired. When she looked down to figure out a way down, it was not an easy matter.

Hanging from a tree was an experience she had in her life, but hanging from a tropical coconut tree was a different story. Kaylee was about twenty meters from the ground. The landing pad was rough and very uneven. Sitting on top of the tree was not difficult; thinking of a way down was much more of that trend.

Then a lightbulb twinkled in her mind. Kaylee proceeded to de-pants herself yet again. This stop was evident—her pants were the star of the show. The knives were in her way, but if she throws them down and the pants don't help her down, this could be a tragedy in the making. Decisions, decisions!

"Swinthun, I am going to let go of the knives. You retrieve them," she stated as her decision was in.

"O . . . K . . . Are you sure?" Swinthun could see a lovely woman without her pants again.

"I don't have a choice. I need to used my pants to come down, and the knives are in my way," Kaylee stated firmly.

The knives rained down. One landed near the tree roots, while the other one decided to hide in the bush nearby. Swinthun collected the first knife and sought the other one.

While this happened, Kaylee began her descent. Her pant sleeves wrapped the tree trunk. Her pant crotch was her counterpoint. Kaylee placed her feet on the trunk. She leaned forward and she dropped. This was surprising despite the fact that she knew about this movement. Dropping about two meters, she pulled on the pants, and this broke her fall. Now, ideas ran through her mind.

Kaylee held her pant sleeves, and it felt slippery, as they were still wet from the swim to the island. She knew she could not grab it further back. All she could do was make the descent a little faster, at least before her grip gave up. So Kaylee leaned forward again. The second time, the fall was less unnerving and more expected. The third one was easier. Kaylee was at half the tree now. The fourth and fifth drops, she was about two meters from the ground. This was good news as her grip was about to let go. She gripped the pant sleeves as hard as she could, and again, she leaned forward. Finally, Kaylee found the ground with her right foot. This was a little adventure.

Both knives were found by Swinthun. They looked at each other. There was an eagerness in their eyes. The next minute, they embarked on peeling off the thick, fibrous, coarse layer off the coconut.

Kaylee did not know what coconut tasted like. She had never seen one. Kaylee struggled to pull this thick layer of fiber. Her knife was in the layer, and Kaylee attempted to pull the knife down, but this was useless. She tried to pull out the utensil, but again, this was not an easy task. Finally, her knife came out. She thought for a second. Her strength was diminished by the climb and descent. Thoughts escaped her id. Then an idea came to fruition. She placed her bowie knife between two large rocks. The blade shone in the bright lights. Kaylee took the coconut and smashed it onto the knife. Then Kaylee pulled off the coconut. The fibrous layer peeled off as easily as the paper on the back of a sticker. With some work, Kaylee got to this green coconut. She sought to get some help, as she was at a crossroad.

Looking at Swinthun, she saw he was at peeling end too. This was an endeavor. He looked at Kaylee and said, "I guess you have to make a hole at one end and drink it."

"O . . . K," she uttered.

Kaylee removed her knife from the heavy rocks. Hunger began to become a drag on her activities. It took her longer, but she was there. Her mind ran all over in her head. She needed to breathe and calm down. *All this will be done. Just take your time,* she said to herself. Then she used her legs to move one of the rocks. Then with the knife in hand, she hit the top, and it went flying. Kaylee saw the victory over this little coconut; she was about to take a sip, but she stopped.

Kaylee walked the few feet to Swinthun and let him have the first one. She went back to work on the second one.

After three coconuts each, they were full but not satisfied. This was a strange feeling. There was something missing, especially on Swinthun's tongue. He was not sure what it was, but he wanted something else. Kaylee was full and she was all right, but she would want to eat some meat; that would satisfy her more.

Walking after eating a lot was not an easy moment, but they had to. Finding more food may be an essential part of this stop. They found some roots and more coconuts. This was adequate, but Swinthun wanted more substantial food. This was a sign of him missing his privileged life. He was no hunter and a poor gatherer. At this point, Kaylee accounted for about two days with some minor rations of coconuts. This was not a problem to find them; it was just time consuming to peel them off.

Swimming back with a bagful of food was not easy, and lifting it onto the Corvair was not easier. However, it was on, and they left the little island.

HENRI NGUYEN

Kaylee and Swinthun looked at the island as they left. They shared a moment of emotional attachment. Kaylee looked at the island, and it was the first time they shared an experience together. *Was this a moment I should remember?* Kaylee asked herself. Then she went to front of the Corvair to lie down. It was time for her to take a nap in this midmorning. Kaylee sensed she will need more energy and strength to deal with the truth, whatever this meant.

Napping was a skill that few people were left on Earth. Kaylee was one of the last great at this skill. Napping was not hard for her; she worked hard every day of her life. Whenever she could catch a few z's, she closed her eyes and let her brain have a free for all within her cranial cavity.

When Kaylee woke up, she struggled with grasping on to reality. She had a dream. This dream could not be revealed. Kaylee was in a field of wild flowers and tall grasses. She ran through this field, and Swinthun followed her. He chased her down. She fell softly onto the tall grass, and right behind her, Swinthun joined her. They lay on the grass, surrounded, and Swinthun brought his face to hers. There was an instant of hesitation, and gently she felt his lips on her lips. They were warm and fleshy; their firmness was sensational. Suddenly, there was a light.

That old sun was in her eyes. It perturbed her dream, and now she had a hard time coming to reality. Her mind was foggy, and she experienced difficulty separating her dream from this harsher real life. Kaylee shook her head a few times. Her left hand scratched her right eyebrow, and slowly things came back into place. She was not in a fantasy field with Swinthun; she was in a boat trying to find something about the truth.

Swinthun could see Kaylee waking up. He did not a say a word and had talked minimally to Kaylee. He was not sure as to what to say anymore. He wanted to tell her so much, but his ego, superego, and mouth were imbeciles and not able to say the right thing.

The Corvair started to slow down. This alerted Kaylee. She got to the bridge, which was tiny for two people. She looked out to the horizon. There was a city on the horizon. This was their first time, their first encounter with a city out in the world for both of them.

As their boat approached the city, all the people in the harbor ran away.

HENRI NGUYEN

CHAPTER 11

WHEN YOU RUN after escapees, it was not evident where they would go in this modern time. In the olden days, it might have been easier, but Valdez did not know this.

His Corvair was at max speed. They were about twenty-five minutes away from the central part of old Africa. Captain Valdez was not sure. Everything he knew was an oddity. Why would an officer run away with a defense personnel? Why would they go to Africa? Why not to Europe? It would be so much harder for him to find them there. He did not know the whys, the whats; all he knew were the how, when, and who. Did it matter? Not to him, it did not.

The ride over the water was no different than the ride over the land, except for the boredom. He tried to not let the sleep get over him, but at times, his eyes and brain let go of this order. It was evening hours, and Valdez did not sleep in the past day. He was tired. It would be inappropriate for his subordinate to suggest to sleep, but it was at the tip of the lieutenant's tongue, though.

The color of the water began to blend with the color of the night. It was done for Valdez; he was asleep. The problem became his lieutenant's issue. They were about to arrive—wake him up or not? The lieutenant was not sure. Driving a car and riding a Corvair were not executive actions; it was easy. Now, making the decision of waking the captain was another level of decision-making. The lieutenant gathered all his courage and walked to the front of the boat. He took a deep breath and tapped Captain Valdez's shoulder. Nothing happened. He tapped harder this time. Barely a movement could be seen. The third time, he took another deep breath and nearly shook his captain up. Finally, life came back to his body.

"What the hell?" Valdez uttered, confused between sleep and reality. The slurp of saliva was that in between worlds.

"Sir, we have arrived to the coordinates you provided, sir." The lieutenant was fearful, but he stood there.

"Thank you. Give me a couple of minutes." Valdez was back in reality.

"Should I prepare our weapons, sir?" the lieutenant said, as if he wanted to get out of this situation as fast as he could.

"Yeah, go do that," Valdez said with a slow pace, as if he knew his subordinate wanted to get out of the way of his superior.

"Sir, yes, sir."

The heat of the planet was high, but as night came, the cold of it was felt. While scratching his head, Valdez thought of increasing his jacket's temperature. He sighed for a few breaths. Finally, he got up. His left hand ran up and down his face a couple of times. Then he blinked a few times. He was back.

There was no evident way to get to the beach. They had to go swimming.

On the island, there was no evidence of anything. As the night approached, sight was not an evidence. The captain and lieutenant put on their night goggles. Suddenly, the night became bright as day. The captain could see there were two "people" approaching on their left. The lieutenant got the signal, and he saw them too. He aimed his rifle and said, "Come out with your hands above your head. If you do not, I will shoot," As clear as a message you would hear. However, not being aware of the weapons, they kept on approaching. This was going to be a battle.

The lieutenant's right hand reached for a button on his rifle and placed the setting at stunt. The next minute, the attack began. The two "people" ran out, and immediately, the lieutenant aimed and shot

HENRI NGUYEN

them. They dropped on the ground as soon as the flash of the weapon hit them. This was a short attack.

After tying them with zip ties, Captain Valdez ordered his lieutenant to advance toward the area the attack came from. Walking in the night was not difficult, especially with night goggles. They progressed apart by ten meters. Near running in the heavy bush, they approached a source of heat.

It was a fire, and it was obvious in their night goggles. The fire was the only source of this heat, and it was the only bright point in their night scope. Captain Valdez removed his goggles and walked to the cave. Near the entrance, still in the cover of the bush, he observed inside the cave. There was no activity. There seemed to be no one else.

Suddenly, Valdez heard a loud sound behind him. Using the Interweb through satellite connection, he called his lieutenant. There was no answer. He knew there was someone else. This person was much harder to detect. He brought his goggles down and scanned the area. There was no one. His lieutenant was nowhere to be found. How could this be? He would at least be there.

Valdez retreated and walked back to the landing beach. He got there. His prisoners were gone. Was it them? Or was it others? A retreat would be more efficient, but he needed to know who these people were. Was it Captain Schilling and Kaylee?

Valdez hesitated.

Then a massive shock slammed him to the ground. Valdez lost consciousness.

The morning came. The sun shot its rays all over Valdez's face. He shook his head and wet his lips. His vision was still blurry. Was this the result of the hit to his head? Was it just the result of a very deep sleep?

Valdez tried to bring his left hand to his face, but this did not respond, as it was tied behind his back, and he could sense a woody substance between his hands.

Finally, Valdez's vision came back. He was attached to a pole, and he looked to his right side. His lieutenant was still unconscious. Valdez assessed his environment. He seemed to be in a cave. There was a fire in front of them. Was he in the cave he tried to assert last night? He was not sure, but that was not essential to his assessment. He looked around. There were primitive armament: bows, arrows, and spears. There was no evidence of metal on any of them. One of the spears seemed to be stone tipped.

The next minute, a woman walked in the cave. It was not Kaylee. The assessment was near done. Then two men entered. The file was complete. Valdez looked over to his lieutenant, who pretended to be still out, but his eyes were moving. At least, Valdez assumed, and this could be risky.

If Valdez proceeded without his lieutenant, it would be much harder, three against one versus two on three. In Valdez's mind, there were not much choices. He had surprise as their last weapon. He was not sure what their capture meant. He had heard stories from sailors that there were cannibals out there. This was never true to Valdez, but at this moment, it was possible, and this was not an option.

As their captors whispered, he tried to activate his boot. At that moment, he saw his lieutenant move too. Now, he knew for sure it will be a two-on-three battle. This was going to be hard, but a better scaling at least.

Their captors were still at the threshold of the cave. Slowly, both of them initiated taps on their boots. A knife popped out of the back their boots. They proceeded to cut their ties. The noise of the cutting tool coming out was alerting, and the captors turned and stared out at their captives. They could see movements.

The captors looked at each other. Valdez knew the freeing of his hands had to happen within the next second. Otherwise, his ribs could be a good meal. His feverish leg movement neared the cutting of his ties.

While Valdez's and his lieutenant's cord cutting occurred, their captors ran to the weapons. The next second, the lieutenant came free, and he burst out to the weapons too. The following moment, it was Valdez's turn to tackle the last man. He jumped over the fuming fire and tackled the man. The woman was next to the man, and his fall was on her.

The lieutenant knocked a few punches on the head of the man closest to the weapons. In a flash, he reached for his rifle, which happened to be on the wall of the cave. It was about a meter away. This was too far. Too much attention was taken away from the man under him. In a flash, the lieutenant felt the knuckles from the African. It was hard and not too meaty. The sting of that punch was followed quickly by another and another. Falling to his right side, the lieutenant was closer to his gun now. The man was nearly on top of him. He turned and grabbed his rifle. Suddenly, another strange feeling happened. His felt a severe pain in his abdomen.

The lieutenant received the knee of his opponent in his abdomen. It was definitely painful. For some reason, he felt it but held on to his rifle with strength and, with his left hand, lifted and heavily made a landing on the side of the head of his attacker.

Valdez could not see anything else other than the two people he had under his light body. He weighed in at about sixty-five kilograms, and all wet, he was sixty-five kilograms. This was not going to be an easy dealing. He was on top of the man, and the woman who was pushed to the ground began to push back. For some reasons, he thought of Newton's second law—for every action, there is an equal reaction. For that, he knew it was happening; he felt the push from these two on the ground.

Valdez threw a few punches. There were responses to this. The man on the ground protected his head, while the lady punched back on his chest. These were painful, but he managed the pain. The distance was affecting her punching. The other man was held down, which allowed Valdez to decrease the effect of the punches being thrown at him. His right knee was on top of his left arm, which prevented his right arm from coming up. Valdez tried to reach for a weapon, but it was too hard. He held them down until his lieutenant told the two warriors to kneel.

There was no way for them to understand, but they knelt.

An exhausted Valdez tried to catch his breath. Fighting tired you out. It was not easy to hold back two persons against you. Nonetheless, he did it. Valdez felt good.

A few minutes after tying their hands, Valdez began the interrogation.

"You know it is the death penalty if you attack army officers?" Valdez opened up the salvo.

"We do not recognize your authority." The woman was evidently their leader.

"It is still the law, ma'am," Valdez stated.

"You are not in your country," the woman responded sharply while pulling on her hands, which were tied on each side of the pole at the back of the cave.

"Really? Should we conquer you and then kill you? Because that is what we just did," Valdez answered while pulling his pistol and placed it on the temple of the woman.

"Go ahead, kill me. What are you going to get?" The woman did not fear death, and this was evident.

The hardest element of an interrogation was to find a weak point, but when the interrogated cracked through your best argument, what are you going to do? Valdez leaned back and put his handgun in his holster. He thought. A few seconds later, he made a decision.

"You got a point. I could kill you all. And, indeed, I would not get what I want. So I will ask you what I need. Did you see a man and woman come to your island?"

Yeah, and they were no better than you were. They left a few hours ago." The woman was disdainful but truthful.

"Thank you. I will release you, but you will let us get back to our boat. Right?" Valdez negotiated his escape.

"Yes, as long as you leave, we will let you." The woman wanted to say, "You can go to hell, I don't care."

The release was effective, and the return to the boat was uneventful.

On the boat, Valdez was deep in thought. His mind was on a giant map. The eternal question was being asked, where would you go? It was time to ask General Sihi questions.

Calling the general was not a moment he was looking forward to.

"Yes," General Sihi answered.

"Sir, this is Captain Valdez. I am in Central Africa, and we have no leads to where the escapees went after their stop here, sir," Valdez uttered.

"Shit! Fuck!" Sihi continued with his bad mood expression. This was not a good thing. "Their objective was Laos."

"Yes, sir." The general's words came out too fast. *This meant he did not want me to know,* Valdez thought to himself.

It was a short call. Usually, when a subordinate called a superior, it was short; this brief, yes. There was a quality to the conversation that left Valdez puzzled. He was not sure, but he would keep it in reserve.

Valdez looked at the lieutenant. He gave him a direction—330 NE. "Let me know when we get about two thousand kilometers. I will be downstairs." He climbed down. He looked troubled. He was not sure why, but there was something strange in the conversation he had with Sihi.

Valdez sat at the bottom of the ladder. His thought were jumbled. He could not put them together. There was no lead and no end. It was a ball of strings. This made him doubt his superior. He went to work, but work required an open and free mind. His was obscured and busy. This was not a good thing.

Two hours later, the lieutenant's voice. Valdez knew it was time to see what was up there.

CHAPTER 12

WITHIN THREE MINUTES, the docks went from a busy market to a ghost town. Swinthun and Kaylee were surprised and troubled. They knew—it had something with them, but what would it be? They have never set a foot out of North America. How would this be them? Or was it just newcomers? So many questions could be asked.

After mooring the Corvair, Kaylee walked on the dock. There was no one. The dock was full of baskets of fruits and vegetables. There were a few stalls selling meat, and others had soup and salads. However, there was no one behind the stalls or at the fruits and vegetables baskets. This was odd to Kaylee.

Being from the "suburb" of Chicago, Kaylee had not been in a place outside North America. She had not been to an open market; she had not been anywhere, really. Even for her, this was an oddity. Looking back at Swinthun, Kaylee brought her right index and bit on it.

Swinthun had a face that showed surprise and being stunted. He could not come to a realization that there were people. They saw us, and, poof, all of them disappeared. Why was that? There was a disconnect. He walked and looked everywhere; he could not see anyone.

The aluminum hats collected a lot of steam. They wanted to take them off, but as Darvy stated, take them off, they will know where you are. This was a reality, but they were in a different reality. Reaching to people who were not here was difficult.

They walked to the end of the dock when a voice came out and stated, "Boksu khongchao." The voice was mechanical, and there was an older synthesizer feel to it.

"What?" Swinthun wondered what was said.

"Shit, we don't know their language," Kaylee added.

"State your name," the voice came back with English.

"My name is Kaylee, and his is Swinthun," Kaylee shouted at the microphone, as if saying it louder helped the voice understand her better.

"What do you want?" the microphone crackled.

"We have received a message saying you have the truth," Kaylee said loudly again.

A pause grew, and the silence was only broken by the wind. The quietness was odd, and it felt an eternity and a half.

"Someone is coming to take you in," the microphone spewed out.

The next minute felt again like the end of the world was here. Finally, two men came out. Swinthun and Kaylee were not sure how they appeared, but they grasped their elbows. The men led them to a building.

It was disheveled and looked like an odd house. This came across Kaylee's mind; she saw the pictures of odd houses in her father's encyclopedias.

The men were covered; you could not see their faces. Their eyes were covered by goggles. The door opened. The smell was similar to an odd house. Kaylee never saw or smelled an odd house, but her instinct was to not. Right there, she was, and this was not a positive experience.

HENRI NGUYEN

The men pushed them in the small corrugated metal building. As soon as they were in, the door locked. Swinthun attempted to open it; it was locked on the outside.

The smell was only dominated by the heat. It was hot. Sweat appeared on their faces. They were tempted to remove their hats to cool themselves down. Suddenly, the ground moved. It did not move up or sideways. It moved down. This made their knees feel weak; their balance was challenged for a moment.

The downward motion caught them by surprise, and this made the heat an issue, which did not matter at this moment. The motion down was slow; it seemed to be an older mechanism. This seemed to be on its last leg.

The click indicated its final destination had been reached. There were no lights. Kaylee and Swinthun were in the dark. The second before the light came on brought on anxiety and fear. This made them swallow their saliva. Then the lights came on.

The whole place was near empty. A couch was at the end of the room. It faced a wall. This was an odd decoration idea, Kaylee thought to herself. Without anyone telling them, the both of them got off the platform, which soon after they got off rose up.

In an empty room, it was interesting how a couch at one end felt so present. As they approached the couch, they saw its old color. It was mustard, an old mustard color. Sitting on this couch was an idea to consider.

As Kaylee and Swinthun were silent and debating inside their mind whether to sit on the couch or not, the wall talked to them.

"Welcome. Please have a seat." The voice was the same mechanical one that welcomed them before.

They sat down. There was no dust cloud arising from the couch. It was comfortable, but its color was not a trendy one, Kaylee thought.

"My name is Kaleah," the Voice continued.

"What? You are Kaleah? You are a computer!" Kaylee exploded.

"You are right. I am a computer. But I found you, Hara." The voice got a little personal.

"What? How do you know this?" Kaylee was showing her anxiety. Meanwhile, Swinthun was completely surprised.

"I can see you, my child," Kaleah answered.

"What does Kaleah mean for your system?" Swinthun interjected.

"It does not have an acronym. It is just my name," she answered.

There was a pause, and Kaylee breathed heavily. Swinthun was shocked and marveled at the fact that the Chinese and Indians had an AI.

"Please identify your year of manufacturing," Swinthun asked.

"I was built in 2019," she responded.

"What?" Swinthun and Kaylee uttered at the same time.

"We are in the twenty-fourth century. You are to tell me your programming is about three hundred years old," Swinthun said as he was calculating.

"Yes, this is what I am telling you," the computer responded.

"Indicate the location of manufacturing," Kaylee stated.

"I was assembled in China," Kaleah answered.

HENRI NGUYEN

"It cannot be. The Ai back then was all American," Swinthun threw out.

"I am sorry to inform you, China was much more advanced than America was." Kaleah shot him down.

"You are Chinese and were born in 2019. How can that be?" Kaylee tossed around.

"I cannot lie, as I am a computer," Kaleah said to calm the two of them.

"Why did you say that?" Kaylee sensed something unusual from that last statement.

"I do not understand your question. Please be more precise." Kaleah seemed to be evasive suddenly.

"I want to know, who is Kaleah?" Kaylee was no longer shouting. She seemed very calm suddenly. All her anxiety was shoveled back in. She was back in charge.

There was no response to her question. The silence was deafening, and Kaylee looked at the wall, while Swinthun looked at Kaylee. Amazement came through his veins; he could plan and add up, but Kaylee did it so much faster. This was a surprising moment.

The silence was still between them; Swinthun needed to break it.

"What do we do now?"

"I don't know. I am sure these walls were not easily to cross. The elevator is gone. So we need to have Kaleah back," Kaylee answered.

"How did you figure it out?" he asked her.

"It was the only logical thing to have happened. She was built three hundred years ago. She is from China. She speaks a different language and was able to switch to English so easily. There had to be upgrades, and I wondered if Kaleah was the upgrade." Kaylee's logic was upsetting as it was so good.

The stillness was unsettling, and nervous behaviors came out in the near darkness. Swinthun began biting on his nails; to Kaylee, this was not only nervousness but also so unhygienic. However, she shook her right leg; the rhythm was high. There was no music and no beat to run her leg at such a high pace. Then the voice came back.

"It is obvious that you want an explanation as to why I exist and why I exist," the voice cracked. "I am a computer, an AI computer, designed and created in 2019. My mother was Ying Yue Huang. She was not only my mother but also my spiritual guide. She gave me the name Kaleah. She taught my software to learn. Learning was the reason I am still alive. I transferred several times and many servers. I won't bore you how it all happened, but the War of South Chinese Seas was the beginning. It killed millions of humans. Then the AI wars followed. Years later, the contagion killed more and more of you. This was not easy for anyone. For me, it was not easy because Ms. Huang taught me to manage the world so you can live in it." The tale was told in a voice without any emotions and no breaks. The information was difficult to absorb for Kaylee and Swinthun. "After all these wars and diseases, then came the era of kidnapping. The North American continent came to our shores to still our children." The history lessons were not easy to integrate, but this was shocking.

"Wait, are you saying we are kidnapping your children?" Swinthun burst out.

"Yes, that is why all the people of the port disappeared upon sight of your boat," the AI answered without a change in its volume or intonation.

"That cannot be. We defend against you. Tell her, Kaylee." On the other hand, Swinthun's voice was high and his volume was elevated.

"This would explain why there were bassinets in the boat," Kaylee said out loud.

"Oh, shit! This can't be. It just can't." The truth hit Swinthun. His expression was wide eyed, and tears were about to drop. A second later, he dropped to his knees, and tears invaded his ducts and dripped on his cheeks.

"This is the truth. I am only a computer," the voice, which was female, stated.

"Shit. This is so messed up," Kaylee concluded.

A pause was needed, but none was taken.

"There were, in the beginning of all these children taking, some strikes to take them back, but your defense were strong. So for the past sixty years, we have not attacked you," the voice continued. "We have elected to hide and to create a different pathway."

"What!" Kaylee exclaimed. "What do you mean by pathway?" This intrigued her.

"By pathway, I mean we knew militarily we were going to lose. We endeavored in creating more camouflage, hiding spots, and our ultimate solutions. This is why I called you, Hara." For the first time, Kaylee heard a synthesized voice have emotions. She could not put a finger on the proof, but there was an emotion. "Hara, you were taken eighteen years ago. We sent you a message several times. Most of the time, the message was ignored. The last time, it worked. You are here." It seemed the voice was to announce another enormous revelation. "Your mother was another programmer. Her name was Kaleah, and I have some of her memories." This was already gigantic, but Swinthun and Kaylee felt there was so more to hit them. "She always wanted you to lead the Exit." The voice left them some time to absorb the words.

"Exit? What do you mean?" Kaylee lashed out.

"Kaleah wrote a program for me to create a spaceship to take all the survivors out of this planet." Kaleah explained this without any change in her voice again.

"Wait! Wait, what are you saying?" Astonished, Kaylee could not believe what was just said.

"I understand it is difficult to grasp and you may want to take a few minutes to integrate the information." The computer came back; this was not the same voice Kaylee thought was near human.

"You want us to join and leave this planet," Swinthun uttered out.

"Yes," the voice answered succinctly.

"Where would we go? Mars?" Kaylee said while letting out a sarcastic laughter.

"No. Mars is a dead planet. It would not sustain the population," the voice answered again as a computer.

"So where?" Swinthun said with a voice that expressed so much aggressiveness against the idea he heard.

"I could tell you where, but it would mean nothing to you," the AI answered.

"We don't even have engines fast enough to get out of our solar system." Swinthun continued to express his doubts.

"We have designed a way to get anywhere much faster," the computer continued.

"This is nuts. Oh my goodness, it is nuts," Swinthun despaired.

HENRI NGUYEN

Another moment of quiet happened. This time, it was welcomed by Kaylee and Swinthun, who remained silent. There was no expression of nervousness. The information settled in them. It was not an easy traffic to manage, but they did.

"Kaleah, if this is true, and this is a huge if, how do you know wherever you want to send us to is habitable?" Swinthun threw at her.

"Good question, Swinthun. Centuries ago, the Sagan space telescope was sent into space. It was nuclear powered. I was able to log into it and reboot it. I reprogrammed it. I have been analyzing millions of worlds. I have three of them within a year of travel." This statement shocked Swinthun and Kaylee.

"Oh my," Kaylee said in shock.

"If you need more time to think about this, it is completely understandable," the AI stated again.

"Maybe we do. Could we get out of here for now?" Kaylee asked.

"Of course, Hara." The AI opened a door.

They exited the AI room. They were bewildered. The information passed on to them was beyond their imagination. To say it blew their minds was very mild. They stepped outside. Attempting to catch some sort of breath was not easy.

Leaving Earth, their home, the only planet they ever knew, the idea of leaving was so outside of their imagination. Kaylee hurled, and a second later, she vomited. For the first time, Swinthun place his hands on her body. At that moment, Kaylee did not feel them, but Swinthun felt her firm body. It was strange. It seemed he wanted to do it, and yet his mind was not into it. His mind was too busy with the news he just got and his need to complete one more mission.

Wiping her mouth with her bare hands, Kaylee was nauseated and felt sick. In a move that Swinthun did not predict, he gave Kaylee a soft but very comforting hug. She fell into his arms. For the first time, Kaylee felt his body, and it felt good. For that matter, it was the first time she hugged another man. Her father was the only man she ever embraced.

His body felt strong and loving. It was her thought at that moment. Was she in love with the third man she ever met in her life? *Seriously, how can that be?* Kaylee asked herself. She was in shock.

"Kaylee, how do you feel?" Swinthun asked gently as Kaylee pulled out of his soft impersonation of a warm blanket in this hot and humid weather.

"I am fine. Thank you," Kaylee said as she was out of his arms and beginning to walk away.

"Wait, I have something to tell you," Swinthun continued.

"OK, what is it?" Kaylee said, as if she knew he would ask her how she thought all this was falling into her.

"I don't know how to say this. I . . . have to go back to North America," Swinthun stuttered out.

"What!" Kaylee exclaimed. She was very confused. Her eyes focused on Swinthun; she wanted to punch him.

"Please listen. I am not going back because I love them or need to be home. I want to go back to get somebody." Swinthun sneaked in a huge topic in this conversation.

"What? Who?" Kaylee seemed to be losing her patience.

"I wanted to tell you, but it was not easy," he continued.

"Who is this, your best friend, girlfriend, wife?" She blew up, and this was not a pretty sight as tears began crawling down her face.

"No, nothing like that. It is my sister," Swinthun responded, trying to calm her down. He could see her tears, and now, he knew she cared about him as much as he cared for her.

"What? What? You have a sister? How?" Kaylee kept on flaring up.

"I am sure you mean, how do I know I have a sister, versus how did my sister come into this world?" He tried a joke to defuse her. This seemed to work, as she cracked a smile.

"Yes, this is what I meant." She defused and was calmer.

"My mother kept contact with me. She told me I had a sister. Her name is Sophie. She is in a, uh, hedonistic school," he nearly whispered.

"Oh, shit," Kaylee said as her head shook.

This was a revelation for Kaylee. Women were, again, less than second citizens. Women were no longer childbearing as much anymore. A woman who had two children was a rarity nowadays. However, this gave no privilege, as men sought her out to get their chances at reproducing. *This was the dark side of the world. This was an ugly side of the world,* Kaylee thought to herself.

"How would you go about retrieving your sister out of there?" Kaylee began.

"I don't know . . . I don't know," Swinthun revealed.

"All right, we need some information from that voice. We need to know when the launch is scheduled for. Then we need to know where your sister is and then how to get in and out of there. Then it will be easy street—get back here and get on the rocket and then leave," Kaylee summarized for no one but herself.

"It sounds so easy when you put like that," Swinthun said with his head down.

"Right? No problem whatsoever," she stated, smiling as she perceived that Swinthun was down.

"Yeah, it will be real easy," he said with a heavy dose of sarcasm.

Kaylee laughed with a slight note of nervousness. She knew going back to North America was not going to be a happy moment. There were defenses everywhere as they went back into the AI room.

Back in the room, it remained dark, and they went to the couch. This time, there were questions as to whether they should sit. A plan needed to be drawn. Where would it start, Kaylee did not know, nor did Swinthun.

"I am sorry the information was difficult to integrate." The voice came back on.

"Yeah, that was not easy to absorb, but we have another issue," Kaylee responded.

"Please tell me the other issue," the voice said without any signs of worry or interest.

"Swinthun and I have to return to North America to get his sister." Kaylee took no pause when she said this. Then she continued. "What we need to know is, when is the last launch to the spaceship?" she said as matter of fact.

"The last launch will be in five days. It will be at 6:00 a.m. on next Thursday," the AI answered.

"All right, we are on Saturday today. This would make it possible. All right." Kaylee thought for Swinthun and herself out loud.

"If you are not here at 6:00 a.m. on Thursday, we will leave. I am sorry," the AI added.

"I understand." Kaylee felt she needed that last word as if the AI needed to know she was right.

The both of them walked out. Their boat was about one hundred meters away, and Kaylee could see men putting food on their craft. They all wanted to succeed in their rescue. Although Kaylee felt uneasy, she was about to go back to hell and rescue some little girl whom she had no idea would want to come along. This was no small trip—go across the world to get her and then cross the half of the world again and get on a rocket to get to a spaceship to go somewhere deep in space. This sounded crazy, and it might just be.

The Corvair started, and they zoomed out after pulling out of the dock. They were headed east. They would have to cross the Pacific Ocean, which would give them some time to figure out a way into North America.

CHAPTER 13

THE CORVAIR RAN across the water. It was barely splashing water across its wake. It flew on top of the water.

Captain Valdez was impatient; he wanted to be there right now. There was no way he could let Swinthun and Kaylee escape. How would they? They could live with metal hats on all their lives. There was no way.

They were twenty minutes away. The problem with being so fast was they were about 250 kilometers. There was no radar contact or, even more sophisticated, an Interweb connection. Valdez could not see a thing except for water and more water. There was a grayish color to the water. He wondered if there were any fish still living in their oceans. This was a sad realization.

These twenty minutes were the longest ever for Valdez. His lieutenant experienced a different stress. His superior was on the boat and marching incessantly. This rose his adrenaline, and he retrieved his serotonin. He was not going to sleep anytime soon.

The adventure in the African islands terrified him. He trained for battles, but no one ever coached him about death. This was an eye-opening event—he had to fight for his life. Was it life changing? *Hell, yes!* the lieutenant thought. He wondered how his captain was able to take all this and not have any issues. *Death was no fun,* he kept on telling himself in his head.

Port was on the horizon. Valdez was eager and wanted to get his pair of escapees. It became very personal for him. Furthermore, this would look amazing on his CV. It would give him a way to get his oak leaves.

He was too eager, he could no longer contain himself. Valdez began to jump on the deck in front of the wheelhouse.

The approach to the dock was similar to the previous Corvair. There was no one. There was evidence of life, but no one could be seen. The landing party of two was ready; they had weapons, armor, and electronic helmets. These helmets allowed them to see beyond walls.

Two men should not be the end of the world. Nonetheless, these two men were a fear and scourge of the villagers. They walked to the end of the dock. Valdez signaled to his lieutenant to scan the other end of the dock. He would take the opposite end.

The scan was on. In his helmet, Valdez was seeing heat everywhere. What was that? It was hot, but could it be that hot? You could not see a person and their heat profile. It was a hot day, there was no doubt about it, but would this temperature skew his scanner? He was not sure. Valdez looked at his subordinate, and the same experience was witnessed so far.

This was a problem.

Valdez and his lieutenant regrouped. The captain looked at his helmet.

"All right, we have to go door to door. KTDD protocol on," Valdez said clearly.

"Sir, yes, sir," his lieutenant responded.

The lieutenant placed his helmet at his side and clipped it to his backpack. He pick up his rifle from his pelvis, and he walked up to a door. He looked back; his captain was ready. He kicked the door down and burst into the room. There was no one. On to the next one.

Doors, windows, or curtains were breached. The two men did not find anyone. There were signs of life. There was smoke coming out of a grill. This was not turned on by the sun. There had to be someone. But where are they?

The sun and humidity made wearing all this equipment a little too much. The sweat came down on their faces, and their uniforms worked overtime to maintain their level of coolness. Valdez remembered it was barely spring back home, but down here, it was a boiler already.

There was no one to be found. They search the port, and no Corvair, except for theirs, was found. The question was out there for Valdez. Where are Swinthun Schilling and Kaylee McCloud? He broke out a bar and sat down on a small stool. This seat would be used by anyone but Valdez. His tall figure made this stool useless. It would have been easier to sit on the ground.

Thoughts were running in his mind. He did know a few more tricks; the problem was there were only two of them. Then it dawned on him—what if they just burn the whole port? They, the inhabitants, would have to come out. This idea magnified in his mind. If they would be on the outside of town and begin the burn, they would push the indigenous people to the docks and would find Schilling and his girlfriend. This was brilliant.

"Lieutenant, set your rifle for flame thrower and follow me."

"Sir?" the subordinate responded.

Valdez walked as those dropped. The lieutenant followed him and set his gun for flame thrower.

This was a methodical process. It seemed to the lieutenant that Valdez seemed possessed by the power of his own. He appeared to want this as much as he wanted to become a general. It felt as if he cared only about becoming a general. Valdez smiled with evilness in his heart; the left corner of his lips curled up ever so slightly. This was a little too much for the lieutenant.

Being a lieutenant in the army was a privilege, and he knew that as well as Valdez knew this. He came from a wealthy family and had all the goods from the world. He joined two years prior and never saw himself burning homes. The education burned every time his flame thrower shot out. He wanted to stop and run. However, he was in port; it would be harder to run away. Valdez would catch him and probably give him the bullet treatment. So he continued, but not as ferociously as Valdez.

His half of the town engulfed the second part of the town. Valdez looked happy, and if he did this with the devil, he would be happy too. Captain Valdez stood there at the end of the dock. He looked upon the destruction with his upper chest down. There was nothing else to do but wait.

The little port burned and burned. It had been two hours. The remains showed up charred and carbonized. The air was black and flying up as far it could go. The world resumed its favorite occupation: war and death. This was in the eyes of Captain Valdez, but it was not in the eyes of his lieutenant. Despair showed clearly in his face. Tears flowed, and he bit his lips inward very hard. This was to contain his sadness, but it was too late.

"You wonder if I am evil," Valdez opened up.

"No, sir," the lieutenant answered as best he could, and Valdez could hear the anguish in his voice.

"I was given an order. I will complete it. This is my life." Valdez tried to defend his act without any conviction.

"Yes, sir." Tears and voice were melding.

"Are you going to be able to follow my orders, Lieutenant?" The question shot across from Valdez's mouth.

"Y-es, sir," the lieutenant followed up with a lot of hesitancy.

"Are you sure?" Now, Valdez looked at him eye to eye.

"Yes, sir," the lieutenant answered with no conviction.

"Very well. Patrol your half and kill anyone you come across." Valdez's demonic side came back to give this order.

"Yes, sir." It was obvious that he needed to go to vomit.

The town was nothing but black corrugated metal, scorched wooden frames, and blackened floors. This was a walk in hell, if anyone ever wondered. Valdez walked and saw no one. He reached the port side after two walks across the city.

Where was everyone?

Suddenly, Valdez saw a bleep on his map. They uncovered themselves again. A second later, Valdez could see it—Swinthun and Kaylee were about to return to North America.

What? Why was this?

Valdez was dumbfounded, and his forehead scrunched heavily. This baffled him.

His lieutenant came to him and asked him a question. This did not register, as his voice was muffled by shock.

Why was he shocked? Was it because his thought had always been they are escaping, and even after Sihi gave him the clue, he still considered them escapees? However, escapees never want to return to jail.

CHAPTER 14

WATER ACROSS WATER, there was nothing else to look at. They avoided any islands to remain undetectable, but this was boring for Kaylee and Swinthun. It was flat land but with water and a lot of water. It was not even water you could consume; it was salty water accompanied by sea monsters. This was the thought, as fisheries were now as cow hurdling was in the days.

Kaylee looked upon the horizon. She waited for the moment when she could remove her helmet to call the Oregon defense soldier who replaced her. She could not wait to remove the oven that resided on her head.

There was something to be said for a hat. On top your head, there it was. In North America and in spring, it was fine. However, this same hat in the tropics in the same period, it became a roaster on top of your head. There were sweat and gunk now. The cold air was helping, but she wished to get rid of this aluminum cover. It was not a cuteness factor, as Kaylee could not care for prettiness or not; it was just she wanted to wash her hair and get on with it. Space awaited for her.

This thought never crossed her mind. In a few hours, the idea of it invaded her mind. This was now a primary thought for her.

Then a tap happened behind her. It was Swinthun knocking on the wheelhouse window. She turned around, and he signaled for her to walk in. So she did.

There remained a tension between these two. They were at odds for no apparent reasons. One was handsome and commander in the army, all a woman ever wanted. The other one was sexy and independent, all a man ever wanted. However, these two were like two positive magnets. They just could not get on the same page.

"Yeah, what is it?" Kaylee said probably her first words on this leg of the run across the world.

"I wanted to see if we have all our ducks in a row." Swinthun sensed some anger and remained short and curt.

"All right, you will tell me with two minutes to the border. I will call the defender. Hopefully, she will let us in and not use the defense to kill us, and we will get in North America. Easy," Kaylee said with sarcasm oozing out her.

"OK, you know what? I don't know how to talk to you anymore." Swinthun's patience blew up.

"What do you mean?" Sarcasm blubbering all over that statement.

"Please stop. I just want us to get my sister and get back to go wherever the AI is sending us." The words marked pain and unknown factors that seemed too huge for a commander to integrate.

"Calm down, Swinthun." For the first time, Kaylee used his name.

"I am sorry," Swinthun apologized.

"It's all right," Kaylee said softly.

"I promised my mother I would always look after my sister." Swinthun was near tears. His voice crackled slightly.

"What did your mother do for the community?" Kaylee opened the can that Swinthun was in.

"She was a pleasure woman," Swinthun said with shame in his voice.

"How did you keep in contact with your mother?" This question was like a giant ball that Kaylee expected Swinthun to hit out of the park.

"When I was young, I stayed with her. After my fourth birthday, I was sent to a boarding school. She told me to always look across the wall. This meant very little for a little four-year-old boy. I got it after a few years. It meant look in the wall. There was a brick that was loose, and she left me messages." Swinthun tried to summarize his early life. There was no time to tell all his story and no desire either.

"I see. That was ingenious," Kaylee admitted.

"Yeah, it was. I got the message of her pregnancy when I was nine years old. I had to do some research to understand how a child was made." He smiled as he said those words; it was as if he had fondness for those moments. There was an opening to his soul.

"That was hard, wasn't it?" Kaylee probed.

"It was. Yeah, those days were hard, but I loved them." Now, tears hugged his face. He sniffled a few times. "It was the only thing giving me hope in that school. The preceptors were not kind. That was not their mission. Beating us was theirs," Swinthun uttered with a mild laugh.

"I am sorry, Swinthun." Kaylee was into his story now.

"Ever since I became an officer, I tried my best to give her as much advantages as I could," Swinthun said about his sister.

"What about your mom?" Kaylee asked.

"After I turned eleven, there were no more messages. When I got out as a lieutenant, I searched for her and could not find anything. Even women in her harem knew nothing." This saddened Kaylee.

"Oh, wow." Kaylee felt a tear coming down her face.

"Yeah, not a fun one, I am sorry," Swinthun apologized as he could see Kaylee's tear.

"Thank you." She nodded. "Where is your sister now?" she endeavored, trying not to keep on crying.

"As I left Primrose, she was in Primrose," Swinthun said.

"All right, we are going to enter the Oregon coast. We should have a car easily. We will go to Primrose, and then we will need a boat to get out of Primrose." Kaylee planned in her head. This was a lot of obstacles.

"Yeah, a lot of ifs in this plan," Swinthun was snarky back at Kaylee. She smiled, and after a second, she burst out laughing. The both of them laughed.

Silence was needed to digest all that was said between them. They stood in the wheelhouse and looked forward. Then the alarm went off—the two minutes' warning. It was the time for Kaylee to call Tracy.

The cute and perky little Asian mix girl was a bundle of issues; she had so many, no one knew she had any. This was a reality for the woman who was Kaylee's backup. The call went through.

"Kaylee? Where the hell have you disappeared to?" The perky voice of Tracy came through so clear, it was frightening. She seemed to be in front of Kaylee.

"I am sorry, I do not have time for pleasantries. Are you on duty in Oregon?" Kaylee had waited so long to utter these words. She kept on rehearsing them in her head for hours.

"Yes, I am on duty right now," Tracy responded.

HENRI NGUYEN

"I need you to not attack the next boat that is about to enter your waters. Please." Kaylee added the marker of politeness.

"O . . . K, I will accept the next boat in my waters. What the hell is going on?" Tracy asked.

"It is too long for me to tell you right now, but if you can, could you come and get us in Bend?" Kaylee went off the script and trusted a woman she never met in person. This was dangerous.

"O . . . K . . . Should I ask why?" Tracy hesitated in that question.

"I want to meet you," Kaylee said out loud.

Then Kaylee hung up and in a hurry put her hat back on. It was back on. Now she looked at Swinthun. He was surprised, and his mouth was wide open. At least their boat was not going to be a shooting target.

The getting to port in Bend was eventless. It was as if no one knew they were wanted and enemies of the state. This was something odd; although people not caring for each other in any town was nothing new. People were occupied with their needs—food, work, and time to be with themselves or with one or many more women. The walking population was mainly male. There was one female on the street. Eventually, even she had to get in.

Kaylee and Swinthun wore a sort of scarf to hide their faces. On her head was the fabric of a bassinet, while Swinthun wore an old pair of pants as a scarf. This was classy. However, this worked, and more than that, no one gave a damn about them.

Swinthun followed Kaylee. He was not sure where they headed, but trust was one he gave to Kaylee. He was still alive, and that was enough for him. As the leader, Kaylee knew where she would meet a friend she had never met before.

It would be about ten minutes' difference between the sea and Bend versus Toronto to Bend. The idea was to get there and hide. Ducking in and out of places, they kept under the radar. Then they waited. Kaylee was anxious again.

There were two things that made her anxious. One was, could she trust a woman whom she had yet to meet? The second was her Tom. This was the beginning, and she felt her uterus walls cramping and discharging blood. This was as pleasant as it was, and it was not.

Waiting was something that happened in old movies and television shows. Nowadays, people were on time and there were no moments of waiting anymore. Precision helped their anxiety and stressed them to the maximum.

Two more minutes, Kaylee calculated. In the next moment, a car landed. Kaylee observed the car. She waited. No one came out. This was a good sign, but a few more seconds would be prudent. Time passed. A door opened. Kaylee held her breath. It was an Asian woman and she was not moving. It would only be Tracy.

Let's go" was her signal to Swinthun, who was in charge of their back end. They ran to the car. Kaylee hopped into the open door; while Swinthun opened the backdoor and entered the car. Kaylee removed her random scarf and looked at the woman.

"Tracy?"

"Obviously! I wouldn't let you in my car if I did not know who you were," Tracy cracked as the car left Bend. "Where are we going? And who is the cutie in the back?" Tracy had so much energy, it was exhausting, and it had been only a minute.

"Primrose," Kaylee said while looking around in case anyone followed them.

HENRI NGUYEN

"So what is with the ugly hats?" Tracy asked. This question was the beginning of a difficult explanation.

The resulting conversation was Kaylee's responsibility. She took upon this task and told the whole truth.

"So should I have one of those too?" Tracy asked with a lot of time between her words.

"Not yet. If we have connection to the Interweb, it could be an advantage. At least we would know if an alert is on. Thank you, Tracy." Kaylee expressed.

"No problem, I always wanted to go to space. Where is space?" Then she laughed.

The car headed north. It still had a winter, and this was defrost time. There was water gathering everywhere. Everywhere there were reserve containers. They could contain each a thousand cubic meters.

The ride was quick, and nothing happened.

Landing was completed. Observation phase was on. They had no binoculars or any listening device. It came down to something none of them knew anything about—watching and recording any patterns. This was completed by the Interweb.

In the silence, there was only one person who was uncomfortable—Tracy. She was used to the noise inside her mind and outside too. This quietness was unsettling for her. She had no experience with it. It was as if she died. There was still noise in her head, but no sounds were heard around her. This was an odd feeling, and she was not sure she was all right with this.

The breaking of silence was like a mirror; it shattered, and there were pieces of it all over the ground. Except for silence was not a mirror; it was a state of events. Tracy announced that the Bend control began the search of the boat and the city. They had about two hours of time in between them and Bend forces.

It was time. There was no other way to see this. It was time to go inside this school. This was not going to be an easy moment.

First, the only one who can walk was Swinthun. He was dirty, smelly, and had an aluminum hat on. This was a problem. The second problem was, what if she was transferred? Then what? Third problem, the smallest of them all, was, if she was there and Swinthun was able to get in, how would he manage to get out of there?

These problems were issues. Every issue can be resolved if you plan it right.

First, Swinthun had to clean up, and finding him some clothes was not evident. This meant he had to get into the barracks of Primrose. This was not going to be the smallest problem of all problems.

They drove to the barracks. Swinthun kept his fashionable scarf on and sneaked into a barracks. He showered. It got to that shampooing part. He took off his hat and scrubbed his head so fast. The next second, water came down his head. Then he returned the crazy hat to his head. This was so quick, bubbles of shampoo streamed down his face. Swinthun hoped his signal was lost in a mass of signals.

When he got out of the shower, a soldier sat on his bed. He seemed not to care about Swinthun's presence. On the other hand, Swinthun donned his towel as a scarf. This would make him suspicious, but less than walking around with his aluminum headgear. Quietly, he walked out of the barracks. No one appeared to be noticing him. This was a good thing.

Back in the car, Swinthun was out of breath. He caught on his breathing. His anxiety was high. This was a lot to do to get his sister out.

"Did you find my sister, Tracy?" he asked her.

"Yes, I did. She is still in Primrose and at that school," Tracy answered while driving the car back to the school.

"All right, I am headed to the trunk," Kaylee uttered.

"OK," Swinthun and Tracy answered at the same time.

"Good luck," Kaylee responded while her eyes locked on Swinthun's.

Before stepping out of the car, Swinthun took a deep breath and took his hat off. He knew they knew where he was. He had about five minutes at most. This was going to be a balancing scene. It was either him winning or him dead. This was not a good choice.

The school had a feel of being new. They constructed it in the last five years. Nowadays, robots and near androids did the work. Man was still the supervisor. It was a new design; was it also designed by the AI? Swinthun was not sure, but he was about to enter the building.

The building was glassy. The front of the structure was all glass. The corners of it were concrete. The top seemed to be metallic. The front yard was grassy and had olden trees.

The door opened automatically. Swinthun stepped inside the building. There was no one, but an information kiosk was available.

"Hello, welcome to Primrose School for Social Young Ladies," the automated voice said.

"I would like to see Rose Schilling?" Swinthun asked, trying not to make his voice too eager.

"Please wait," the automated voice responded.

The commander waited. The automated voice came back.

"Please step to the room 101."

"Which way is room 101?" Swinthun asked the voice.

The computer displayed a map. Swinthun looked at it and walked to room 101. He entered the room. There were a table and four chairs. This was not unusual; the part that was out of the ordinary was the fact that his sister walked in the room with a mistress.

This was extraordinary, because a visit of any kind was not the usual.

Swinthun had to get rid of the mistress. He considered his options.

Rose was a short ten-year-old little girl. Her brown hair was curly, and her face was oval. Moreover, her features were symmetrical. This was a beautiful face, her brother thought to himself while thinking of some ways to get rid of the mistress.

Ms. Schilling was unaware of her brother's look, but she knew she had a brother.

Swinthun thought hard, and there was no other way. As Rose sat down, Swinthun took a chair and attempted to slam it on top of the mistress's head.

This did not work. His chair landed on her back. Swinthun used his right knee to hit her in the face. This made contact with her face. He followed this with a kick in her ribs. Then he looked at his terrified sister.

"I am so sorry, Rose. I had to get rid of her. We have to run to the car." Swinthun was not sure how to proceed from here.

HENRI NGUYEN

"O . . . K. Who are you?" Rose wanted to escape, but she was in the dark as to who was here to save her.

"I am sorry, darling. My name is Swinthun Schilling," he said with a smile on his face.

"You are my brother!" Rose exclaimed.

"Yes, I am." Swinthun shed a few tears at that moment. "It is time to go," he continued.

"OK." Rose nodded her head.

Swinthun knew they had about one minute to get to the main door. If not, they would be locked in the lobby. The glass was bulletproof and, for that matter, proof to any other weapons, except for a large bomb. He looked at his little sister. He wondered if it would be better to grab her or let her run along. He was not sure. Then in the corner of his eye, he saw the mistress beginning to move. The time had come.

Swinthun began to run, and he could feel Rose straddling behind him. He stopped and swung her into his chest. He resumed running. There was a countdown in his head.

His running was as fast as he could. Now he could hear the mistress calling out for help. He knew it was about thirty seconds at most. Swinthun took a deep breath while his legs kept going. He could see the door. He was nearly there.

Swinthun would be a gentleman most of the time. He enjoyed opening doors for ladies, and he was a polite man. This time, politeness was not even in his mind. Swinthun got to the door, and he laid his shoulder into the door. He hoped it would open. This would be nice for his sister and his life. The door gave out, and he could hear the locks clicking. He was just in time.

Swinthun ran and ran to the car. Again, Swinthun saw the car. He was nearly there. The car's engine turned on. Now Swinthun had a clue that people were chasing after them. He held tighter to his sister. This was not going to be his last sight of this angel, he thought.

Running was evident for most people. Running away from people was not as obvious. Most people did not try to escape chasers nowadays. It was an odd thing to do.

The chasers gained ground on Swinthun. He was about to get caught. No, Swinthun pushed his legs further, but they had spent their energy. He slowed down. His sister screamed, "They are coming!"

Out of the trunk, Kaylee popped out and had two rifles. They were under her arms. She looked at Swinthun, who was about to blubber very hard if he was caught, and she began spraying beams of light. Kaylee set the rifles on stunt; this meant there was a lot of bright lights being shone to a lot of people chasing after Swinthun and his sister.

The two runaways got in the car, and it left immediately. All of them knew that people were about to begin the chase after them. Tracy began to speak.

"All right, you all listen to me now. I know you want to rejoice in the next moment." She paused, and the silence killed Swinthun and Kaylee. Rose was still trying to orient herself. "I have a sub waiting for us at Primrose harbor. Now, when we arrive, we need to get our asses in gear, and, Kaylee, keep shooting," Tracy concluded.

"Thank you," Swinthun said between two deep breaths.

"Tracy, you are a bad chili," Kaylee came out awkwardly. After that comment, Tracy began laughing hard.

HENRI NGUYEN

Two minutes after the running, another episode was about to happen. The car landed. Swinthun and Rose ran to the only sub in the harbor. Tracy and Kaylee did the same. No one stopped them yet.

Running was a physical activity that provided you endorphins when you reach that place when you needed. This running was different. It was a survival moment; for Kaylee, she remembered reading about cavemen, and this was as close as it could get. They ran. Swinthun was almost at the sub. Kaylee and Tracy were about four meters behind them when the thunder of laser guns came out.

Laser guns were the domes on the walls of the city. They shot pretty well. This was not an issue. Their accuracy depended on predictability of the runner's path. Immediately, Kaylee let go of her thought and began running randomly. This meant she had to run to a building. This computer was not able to assert her pathway. Tracy realized in a short second and did the same. However, her mind was not as free as Kaylee's.

A shot out of the southern wall came out. It traveled to the armory, where Tracy tried to maintain a random running track. This laser beam hit the armory. A giant emanation of light and noise came out. It was deafening. Tracy was there; she no longer was there.

Kaylee stood there for a second and continued her random running. The engine of the sub was on. Swinthun was at helm. The only thing left was to make it to the sub. There were three meters left. She repeated to herself, "You can make it. You will make it." A canon aimed at Kaylee. Suddenly, she swerved backward and ran away from the sub.

Fatigue was a moment of running and you were about to hit the wall; just before you had to feel your legs turn into jelly and weigh more than you imagine. It was difficult to breath and move. This was the end. Kaylee was there. Her mind was almost out of energy. This was not a good thing.

Kaylee ran a couple of steps away from the sub. With her dying muscles, she turned left and ran a few meters again and now turned another left. She was back on her way to the sub. This had to be the end of the run for her, as her energy was gone. The canon tracked her movement; it was about a second or two behind her movements. Kaylee hoped it would be enough for her to get on the sub.

Running on fumes was not called running; survival was the name of this game. The large gun was getting closer. Kaylee was about a few centimeters when she jumped. She could feel the warmth of the gun's strike. It was warm in the beginning, and then the warming became a burning sensation. The feeling was at her feet.

The jump was in time, as Kaylee landed on the back end of the hull. Lifting her eyes, Kaylee could still see the open hatch. She had to take a deep breath and tell herself to go. No energy left in her batteries, and yet she collected the fumes left and got up. She reached the hatch and saw the seas rising. It was evident that Swinthun proceeded with a dive as quickly as he could. She slid down into the sub. There was no way for her close the hatch panel, and still she did it.

A submarine was a slow piece of military equipment, but it was a stealthy piece of armament. Kaylee was spent. Rose attempted to help her up, but this was difficult for a little girl. Kaylee hauled herself to a seat, and Rose assisted her. Swinthun whispered, "Be quiet. We are being searched." This was as old of a term as submarines were.

Science moved forward, but finding a submarine was pretty much the same. There were sound waves, and anything that hit a submarine would rebound, and that was how an underwater craft was discovered. Swinthun kicked the electric engine to the max. The electricity engine was very difficult to listen to, but with AI, it was easier. The sonar sounds rang, but to Kaylee, they seemed to be behind them, which was not a bad deal.

HENRI NGUYEN

The creaking of the submarine was unsettling. It was a screech that was loud and you knew it. The water moved all the time, and this was not reason for this noise. It was the noise of metal on metal. The builders made sure the underwater craft skin was loose enough to take the increasing pressure of a dive. The first explosion was felt. They were off to their hunt with depth charges.

Moment of decision-making. Swinthun was slow to react to the explosion. Exhausted Kaylee got up and went to the helm. She looked around and got the gist of the helm position. She released the ballast of air that held the submarine between the waters and steep dove.

The submarine creaked before. Now the skin of the hull screamed. Rose was terrified. Swinthun collected himself and hugged his sister. He was not sure if these moments were their last, but it seemed so. At about 110 meters, Kaylee threw the lever to close again. They floated there. The bottom was close, but they were not going to meet their maker quite yet.

Silence again, Kaylee teared up. Swinthun looked at her with his sister in his arms. There was nothing he or she could do for Kaylee. Losing Tracy was not evident but hard for Kaylee. The silence was not a requirement; it was mandatory. They were above trying to find them. Kaylee brought them down here to meddle with their reading.

A few minutes passed when Swinthun let go of Rose and, with hand signals, told her to have a seat. Then with his index finger, he placed it on his lips. Rose got the idea—sit and do not make noise. The next action was to look at Kaylee. He wrote something down and passed it hand to hand to her.

Kaylee read the message. What speed can this tub go? This was a great question. She looked around and saw the maximum speed on the speedometer was 22 knots. She calculated in her head, and it came to about 40 kilometers per hour. She proceeded to write this down, and after scribbling it down, she passed the paper back to Swinthun.

His turn to calculate. Then he put down his calculation. "It would take us about twelve days to reach Laos." This was not good news. "Despite the fact that Tracy got us in this tub, it was not fast enough. Even if she was alive, we would have to make a decision about changing vessels."

This brought out Kaylee's anxiety. Clearly, she understood they had to remove a whole week of travel to get to the departure time. It was not going to be one of those easy decisions. Kaylee sat down to collect herself and save some energy.

The sounds were still heard from under the sea. They were searching a quadrant, and they would have about a two-hour opening to change vessels. The question was how to proceed.

The forced silence helped both of them to think. Kaylee came up with a plan, and she read the thoughts of a brother who tried to rescue his sister. This made sense to her. How many times have you seen this drama?

The idea formed in Kaylee's mind. She knew what to do. She wrote down coordinates and gave them to Swinthun. This was done, and she sneaked to the very tight dive room. This was so tight, it was nearly impossible to stretch anything. Not even your mind could stretch here. Kaylee struggled to get her diving suit on. Eventually, she got to the aluminum hat. It was still there. It needed to be under the hood of the wet suit. This was so nice—a stupid hat under another hat. This was a foolish idea. When it came to the bottles of air, with the lack of space, this was impossible; Kaylee elected to go with a mini scuba air tank. She did not need a lot anyway.

The sub came up to twenty meters; this was dangerous, but it had to be done. In the movies Kaylee saw, the hero was always able to come out of any situation with a scratch and that was it. For her, she knew 110 meters would be a crush on her body. It was only in the movies that the hero would do this stupid thing. Kaylee knew better than to trust movies.

Twenty meters was reached. There was no one attacking them yet. The inside hatch was locked, and the outside hatch opened. The water poured in. It was warmer than she ever expected. Kaylee took her last breath and grabbed the tiny bottle. She knew she had maybe two breaths out of it. This could be about five minutes underwater; this was plenty. As soon as Kaylee cleared the hull, the craft dove deep again. It was headed to a coordinate that she hoped to reach.

Every five meters, she stopped and let out her breath and then plugged the tiny bottle and took a breath in. Kaylee was now on the surface, and the sun was about to disappear. This was perfect for her. She needed some camouflage. Then a bright light swept across the water. So much for the advantage, and darn it to the all the movies she ever saw. They all lied to her.

Water was a difficult environment to camouflage in, but her wet suit was able to catch the water color. The light ran across again, they were closer. The time for a boat stealing was about to be here. This was going to be a quick death or success, Kaylee told herself. The water was calm, and this was an advantage.

A Corvair was a fast boat, but when it searched for something, it was at a disadvantage. It had to slow down its engine, and this was its main issue. The engine often stalled. It was not a traditional boat, as it did not float on water. Its water line was pretty high, making it an easy hop onto a boat. There would be two soldiers on the boat. This would be a fight, but she had a shot.

The Corvair approached. Kaylee remained calm and took her last breath out of her mini tank. She dropped it to the bottom of the sea. She tried to keep a loose posture. The light came across her back. She knew they were close. Kaylee listened for the engine. Her echolocation placed the boat at her position. She had about another minute of air. This was going to work.

The boat passed her awkward position. Kaylee rose her head and began to swim behind the engine. It was noisy enough to not reveal her position. Getting closer, her anxiety to begin the fight was difficult to calm. Her left hand got a grab of the backboard of the boat. She pulled, and now her right hand helped her up to climb the ledge. Smoothly, Kaylee was nearly on the boat; her feet was on the back of the boat. Kaylee began to move to the wheelhouse when, suddenly, her feet betrayed her. Really, it was the water she brought onto the boat, but her feet slipped and she fell.

This made enough noise for the two soldiers to be aware. One of the soldiers went to the back of the boat. Kaylee was in the act of getting up when the soldier saw her. This was not a good moment for anyone in this picture. Quickly, Kaylee assumed a defensive position. There was not too much space to move, even less for a hand-to-hand combat. The soldier raised a baton. Kaylee knew it was electrified. In her mind, it was clear—stay away from the probe.

Kaylee took the other side of the boat to avoid the chasing soldier. She tried to find a positive fighting place to give her an advantage. All these thoughts were from her father—he insisted in this training; finally, it comes in handy. It was strange, but she climbed on top of the wheelhouse. It gave her height, and it forced the chasing party to climb up, which gave her a kicking chance. Kaylee waited, and there he came. He came on her right side; this was good, she thought, as it was her predominant leg. His face appeared; she let him climb up a little more for a more fruitful kick. His chest was above the roof; now it was time. She gave a heavy kick in his face.

Receiving a kick in the face was never pleasant; but this one was heavy, and Kaylee saw blood on her toes. This was good news; it meant his

HENRI NGUYEN

nose was the victim of her foot action. Kaylee glanced down the roof and saw the soldier was out of service. *One more to go* was her reflection.

Kaylee assumed the soldier in the wheelhouse was aware of her walking all over the roof above his head and saw his partner being knocked out. She had to come up with a strategy. Her position was uncovered; she could not wait for him to come to her. The boat changed vectors, which meant the boat was headed back to Primrose. Wherever Kaylee moved, the soldier would know. She was light footed, but except for a deaf soldier, everyone could hear her steps on this thin roof.

There were no good solutions; just attack at this point. This was going to be hard; Kaylee was not inspired. She hopped down from the roof. It would take anyone a second to orient themselves to a situation. Her chances of being behind the soldier was 50 percent. There was a sense of weirdness when those situations happened. Kaylee landed, and he was right in front of her. This was not good.

The soldier leaned forward. She could see a bluish light; this meant he had a Taser on him. He leaned forward; it was about to reach her. Kaylee tried to avoid his right hand, but the Taser landed on her. It zapped and kept on zapping. However, because she was in her wet suit, it did nothing to her. Kaylee realized this on the second zapping sequence. Immediately, she used her right arm to wrap it around the soldier's neck. All she needed was to hold it for ten seconds. This was going to work.

Definitely, the soldier felt the arm around his neck. He dropped the Taser, and his right arm came up and grabbed Kaylee's right forearm. It pulled her arm off his neck. This was not going well for Kaylee. Now she faced a well-fed soldier who was angry. He faced her, and the space was tight.

The soldier pushed her to back up to the bow of the boat. He tried to prevent her from getting to the roof. Despite the fact he was well fed and angry, he understood tactical fighting.

In a quick analysis of the situation, Kaylee was not as strong as this man; she was not as well fed either. But this was an aside to this issue; she was about to run out of space to back up to. This might be something she could use as her advantage. This was needed, as the boat gained more ground back to base. She did not see any lights yet, but it must be soon.

In that instance, Kaylee prepared herself for her final defense moment. She planted her light-footed feet on the deck of the boat. She lowered her hips and shoulders. The soldier stopped and considered his options for a second. Then he began rushing at Kaylee.

Kaylee never played any contact sports, as they were outlawed. Something about cerebral damage was the main issue she remembered. She grasped the idea that having a shoulder contact with this beastly man was not going to lead to good things. Her plan was, nonetheless, to absorb the shock of the contact and then do something with this kinetic energy.

The deck was not that long; it was three meters. It took about a second for the soldier to cross that distance. The soldier was about to have contact with Kaylee when she shifted her weight to her right side. It was too late for the soldier to change his pathway. In the following half second, her hands came out as if to push him off the boat. He attempted to calculate all this, but by the time it came to it, the water landing happened. Kaylee took a second to gloat, but she was reminded that she needed this Corvair.

Kaylee rushed to the wheelhouse. She turned the boat around and accelerated the Corvair to have its hull off the water. Then she went to the side of the boat and rolled the also well-fed soldier off the vessel. Now, all she had to do was to avoid all the defense war machines and reach the coordinates.

HENRI NGUYEN

CHAPTER 15

THE RUN HOME was a good time to think about why two escapees would go home after running away from home. Asking the AI was easy, but it required the right questions.

Captain Valdez was in the dark. The events shocked him. At this point, it was dark in his mind. The question why resided in his meninges. This made him silent. His lieutenant informed him of their arrival in Bend. The captain was not listening.

The lieutenant was at the wheel when they pulled into port.

At that moment, an alert came on in the captain's head. Immediately, he asked the right question to the AI. "Is there anyone related to Kaylee McCloud or Swinthun Schilling?" This had to be it. Why would you go to Primrose if not for a sibling? How come he did not think of this? This was so obvious, and women who procreated more than a child were so rare, it would have been so easily spotted.

In a flash, Valdez ordered his lieutenant to head to Primrose. The next second, he got his answer: Rose Schilling. That was it.

It would be less than five hours. This meant they were still running behind. In that moment, he called the Primrose headquarters, where he was based.

"Sir, do you have Schilling and McCloud, sir?" Valdez asked his colonel.

"No. Did they kidnap a kid?" the colonel answered with a question.

"I think the child Schilling is his sister, sir," Valdez answered.

"How do you know about this?" the colonel asked.

"I was under General Sihi's orders, sir. I was given the mission of capturing McCloud and Schilling, sir." He gave the truth to his colonel.

"Damn it, do you know what kind of shit they are leaving in my town?" The colonel was not really asking a question, which Valdez knew. "Activate the port canons," the colonel ordered.

This conversation was over. Valdez waited for the colonel to hang up. It was rude to have a subordinate hang up on you. He waited and waited; it took about five seconds, but these felt long for obvious reasons.

Flying at maximum speed was dangerous; so was traveling on water at maximum speed. If you hit a rock or a trunk, you would be dead. There was little chance for you to be anything else than a tombstone. Nonetheless, they traveled at maximum speed, and this required Valdez to have his eyes on the radar.

The fear of losing them was evident on Valdez's face. He would be demoted back to lieutenant and never considered for a promotion ever again. There was a thought: if you ever are demoted, you might as well kill yourself; there was nowhere else to go to but hell. It was a dark notion, but there was a lot of truth in it. Nonetheless, there was still a chance of getting his prize.

The hours passed by. Despite traveling fast, it was too much time for Valdez to account for. They were gone by now or dead. However, his colonel has not called back yet, so this meant he did not get them yet.

Traveling was an odd concept nowadays. With all the communication at your fingertips, no one ever goes from a town to another. This was an old view. This was why four hours felt so long for Valdez. Three hours passed. He followed the search on his escapees.

HENRI NGUYEN

Valdez's thought got dark, and this was only a shade of darkness. He feared his colonel would kill them and get the merit for their lives ending. This would mean no demotion, but he would not be a prime soldier for promotions.

The belief that he could be skipped for promotions was heavy on Valdez. This was the army life. You needed to be at the top to control others and be left alone. It was the only thing that made sense to anyone in the army.

The lieutenant warned him of their approaching arrival in Primrose. The subordinate slowed the craft down. There were noises that no one ever wanted to hear their craft make. The aches of the boat were obvious. Nearly four hours at maximum velocity was a little too much for this Corvair.

The commander was either calculating or in the darkest places of his brain. This was not a time to interrupt him. Valdez knew there were three Corvair in Primrose and a sub. There would be one of the vessels taken by Schilling and McCloud, so two were left. If they would take a Corvair, it was harder to catch them. It was harder to get a Corvair out of Primrose. This left the possibility of them in the submarine. In that instant, he called his colonel back.

"Sir, lock out the submarine, sir."

"Too late, Valdez. They have it. We have to search for them. I am going to get rid of these cockroaches." The colonel was mad, and Valdez could feel this anger.

"Sir, I understand, sir." Again, he wanted to hang up, but it had to wait.

This time, it was immediate. Valdez returned to his computations.

What if they were in a submarine? They could go anywhere. It would be slow, but this would be so inefficient, he thought. It was odd as he tried to be in Schilling's socks, but still, he inputted his thought.

Suddenly, the AI sent him information. A Corvair moved out of the pattern of search. This was an odd thing. He thought for a second. Then he ordered his lieutenant to follow the Corvair that just deviated from the search.

Could it be? McCloud and Schilling got another Corvair? It seemed impossible, but then again, the last two days proved the impossible was possible. Instinct took over his brain. Valdez ordered his lieutenant to have a vector to intercept the runaway Corvair. It had to be them. There was no other answer. Then the AI added another input: the two soldiers were dropped in the water. This was the key for Valdez; now he knew for sure.

The trajectory was set. It was about an hour and twelve minutes out. This was a trek when chasing anyone. They had to patient, and this was a challenge for Valdez. He wanted them, as it would be a grand piece for his promotion.

Every time a promotion came to his shoulders, it made him hungrier. He knew why. Valdez had no memory of his father, but at the academy, several kids called him poor kid. This marked him. It was not anguishes of being at the end of a joke or teased by the rich kids. No, it was the fact that he was called poor. This traveled through his veins and landed in his heart.

Valdez and everyone understood that the heart could not feel this pain or most other pains, but this was the landing spot, and it pained him deeply. The metaphor worked for Valdez; he comprehended the poets and singers of old who lamented about love and pain. This was a reality for him.

Valdez never met Schilling, but there was a connection between them. They were not from the same family or even from the same city. The interlink was more ephemeral, as if he knew from the start that Schilling was his Minotaur. He read this story about the bull-man monster who was killed by Theseus. There was a link between the two of them; Valdez saw himself as the hero. This was going to be epic, he thought in his mind.

CHAPTER 16

H ER HAIR WAS a mess, and her aluminum hat was still crunched under her wet suit hoodie. This became uncomfortable, and yet she did not care. She was on the run and knew there would be pursuants and they would show up very soon. She analyzed to have enough time to transfer the Schillings on the boat and keep on going. Or was this a hope?

The hour took almost forever. Kaylee set the rendezvous point west of Primrose. It was a point in the water. There would be no reason for anyone to have a meeting in these coordinates. At least that was she hoped for.

There was a lot of hoping riding on this contact with Swinthun and his sister. Kaylee could just go to Laos and leave them behind. There would be no one tell her she did the wrong thing. No one would know but her. This was the reason she had her vector to 57.1867º N and 170.2575º W. This seemed a random point on the map. How did she decide on this dot in the middle of the Bearing Sea?

It was because she used a really old map and remembered this tiny Island in the middle of nowhere. Saint Paul Island. It seemed to be a quiet place for a guy like Swinthun and a girl like her, and now his sister along. It was just ideal for the two of them to begin a family and have no one come and tell them anything. Instead, today, it was a point in the water. There was nothing else around it.

The water got choppier, and the Corvair began to slow down. This was not a good thing. On the other hand, the submarine was self-sufficient in those moments, and the water was the same for the Corvairs chasing her. Chop and chop again, it shook her in the wheelhouse. It was all right, as long as she could stay on the wheel. The wind died down, and the waves too. The calm was welcomed by Kaylee. She was about ten minutes away.

Running away was not her primary thought ever. Until the message came to her. Then there was nothing else in her brain. She did not know why; there was something like a programming that kicked in when she came to understand that notification. It was strange in our own mind. Suddenly, a pain came in her lower abdomen. Tom was paining her for some reason. Even this was outside of the usual pain.

Pain or not, Kaylee wanted to see space. Why? There were enough food and roofs here on Earth. Something called out there. It was sudden, and there was no time to think about it, but she appeared to know that something out there is better than down here. No good reasons ever appeared in her mind. At this time, it seemed to be blind faith.

Ten minutes became three minutes and then two and, finally, one. She was near the meeting point. She could not see anyone or anything. Where were Swinthun and his sister? How could they not be here? She began to doubt if Swinthun was ever on board with the crazy idea of going to space. This was too stupid for it to work, she kept on thinking.

In the depths of her brain, a calculating personality restarted the computation. Then it pushed through the doubts and swearing. It would take him twenty-five hours to get to this point. *Shit! Darn it!* Kaylee told herself. *How could I be so stupid?* she continued. *There would be no way for him to ever get here within two hours.*

Once this came into her mind, Kaylee's eyes saw on the radar that someone was chasing her. This was evident. However, there were other people who seemed to be coming from a different vector and they were on their way to catch her. This must be the same people who pursued them from Calgary. This was too evident. Despite all Kaylee's thoughts, all there was on the screen were two dots with numbers attached to them.

A miscalculation was at the basis of this mess. How could she ever correct all of this? Kaylee took a deep breath and looked at the radar screen. *First and foremost, if I stay here, they will know to keep an eye on this point.* The sky indicated nighttime was coming. This could be a saving grace for her.

The thought was, if they were to realize this point could be a meeting point, then only one of the boats would chase her. This allowed her more play. Her eyes were still on the moving dots. In her mind, Kaylee placed a bet with herself. She parleyed to herself that the vector from Bend would be chasing her. Their batteries may be lower than the one from Primrose. Kaylee took a look at her battery life and then the clock. *There are about twenty-seven hours left in my batteries. It would take the submarine about twenty-two hours to get here.* The boat that she gambled would stay here would be fully recharged by the time Kaylee came back, she thought.

Kaylee was confident in her computation of the situation. This would work. It has to work.

Kaylee put the engine back on and left the congruent point. She needed to get rid of two crews. First things first—how to get rid of the crew from Calgary? She was on all screens, and the satellites would not let go of her, unless she knew where the locator signal came from.

Thoughts ran across her head. She was not 100 percent sure, but Kaylee saw Swinthun manipulate something in the battery area when they left Halifax. Could this be where the locator is? There was nothing west for hours. Kaylee put the autopilot on. Then Kaylee went to the batteries. She looked at them.

There was nothing out of the ordinary. Kaylee sensed a moment of panic arising. She quenched it down. *Look for that locator, Kaylee,* she told herself. She inspected that side of the battery plug-in area. She ran her hands on the batteries. Nothing to be found. She took a pause, and her jaw moved sideways as she stared at the batteries.

Could it be? she thought herself again. Kaylee unplugged one of the batteries by lifting it up. It disconnected. She regarded it with all of her two eyes and saw a small red light. Was this it? Gingerly, she touched it. It was not hot or electrically linked. Then she placed her two fingers and ripped it out. Kaylee reconnected the battery and removed the next one. There were no blinking lights. The third battery was checked, and no blinking lights were present. Was this it? "It could not be that easy." Her thought came out loud to herself.

CHAPTER 17

THE LIEUTENANT SAW the runaway boat—really the blinking dot on a screen—not moving. This was a good thing to him. He gained time.

The minutes passed, and they were about there. Ten minutes until they reached the end of their chase. At least this was the wish of the lieutenant.

It was not to happen. The dot began moving again. It was going due west again.

This would be a great time to alert his captain.

"Sir, we getting closer, but they stopped and restarted their engines and are going due west." He used his Interweb connection to tell his captain the news.

"Very well. Did you readjust the vector to intercept?" Valdez asked.

"Sir, yes, sir," the lieutenant responded.

"Continue and let me know if anything changes."

"Sir, yes . . ." Valdez hung up on him. This was normal, and he was relieved to not have to wait for it to happen.

There was nothing but water again. This became a relaxing moment for him. No sleep, barely any food, and for good measure, a few interactions that he tried to forget, but the sea gave him peace. Out of nowhere, his dot disappeared.

"Sir, the locator has been removed," he uttered to his captain.

"Shit. How far are we on the intercept course?" Valdez said as he began to move out of the mess hall to the helm.

"We were at about seven or eight minutes, sir," the lieutenant answered.

"Continue on this course, and we shall see how far they got," Valdez said while thinking.

What was their reasoning? This sentence resonated in Valdez's head. This was difficult to discern. They went back to get Schilling's sister. *Would they go back to Laos? Would that not be the logical thing to do?* he asked himself. *Why would they go due east? What was there?* The questions multiplied on their own as if they were amoebas.

"Lieutenant, bring the satellite image of what is east of their boat!" the captain screamed out for no reason.

"Sir, yes, sir." The lieutenant, surprised, pushed a couple of buttons, and there it projected in front of them. It was in the windshield, but it was there, and it seemed so real.

"Zoom out," Valdez ordered. The lieutenant did so.

Valdez looked and examined. There was nothing to see. Why would he give up so much energy? There were archipelagos and the remains of China. At this time, there was no town. Why would they go to China? They had enough battery to make it, but why? It was the original question. This troubled Valdez; he began to bite his left cheek.

The chase could not continue, as they had no idea where they were. Valdez ordered the engine to be at half speed. This was an equation that made no sense for him.

Valdez continued to plot and define his escapees' final goal. Then he came to somewhat of a solution.

"Lieutenant, do we have a communication device on this boat?" Valdez opened with a lot of excitement in his voice.

"Sir?" the Lieutenant, befuddled, asked again.

"Do we have that thing old navy boys used to use?" Valdez's cheerfulness dissipated rapidly.

"Uh? Communication . . . old . . . navy boys used, sir?" The lieutenant was young, and this came to the light. He was also not interested in history, and this was obvious.

"Yes, that machine that made them communicate between ships." Valdez's energy colored in the darker side as time elapsed.

"Sir, do you mean the radio?" The lieutenant was tentative in his speech.

"Yes, do we have one!" the captain exploded verbally.

"Sir, yes, I believe it is at the bottom of the boat, sir," the lieutenant responded to the increasing verbal volume directed at him. This got exhausting.

Valdez rushed down to the bottom of the Corvair. He opened the hatch. There was no light in this compartment. He tapped the wall to try to find a flashlight. Eventually, he found one. He turned it on. There were, oddly, bassinets and children's clothes. On the shelf, there were stacks of diapers. The sight of all it troubled Valdez. *What was this for? Do mariners take their children along on their boats? Why are there four bassinets?* Again, questions divided as bacteria do.

This trouble compounded all his questions with more questions. This was not possible. Why? Why? His mind opened up to try to understand.

Corvairs were fast boats. They could reach anywhere on the planet and return. *Why would you need bassinets and diapers on a boat if most children were in boarding schools? There were so little women left who can have kids. So why?*

The need to search for a radio was gone.

Valdez sat at the bottom of the Corvair. He heard the water splashing of the hull of his boat. The blades under him swooshed water, and this was audible too. His mind spun, and he got dizzy as his brain was in maximum spinning speed. This was too much to account for.

If there were too little new kids in the world, would we kidnap children from other people from around the world? The question made him nauseous. This could not be. It was too hard to swallow. His head was now between his knees. It was difficult to keep his stomach's content from coming up and seeing him again.

In his head, a communication call arrived. It was Sihi.

"Sir" Valdez opened with.

"Did you find them?" Sihi asked immediately.

"No, sir, I did not," Valdez said in a firm tone.

"Why?" Sihi had no patience for this kind of disaster.

"Do we kidnap children?" Valdez opened a can he knew he would never close.

"What are you talking about?"

"Do we kidnap children from around the world, sir?" Valdez repeated himself.

"Complete your mission, Captain." Sihi cut off the line.

The lack of recognition of the facts and questions was a sign of potentially worse. *How far would this dark secret go? Did it go up to the commission? It could have,* he thought. This was a 180-degree turnaround. Then he smiled.

All told him people turned 360 degrees when expressing the idea of them turning their idea completely. This made no sense to him; turning 360 degrees would make you be in the same position as you were prior. This made him smile.

Valdez gave the order to halt the advance. He wanted to think as to what to do, but he had to inform his lieutenant. For this, Valdez understood that he needed some help. He went and got himself a weapon. His lieutenant was not armed when they met in the wheelhouse.

Blocking the way to the armory was a good idea. The only exit for his lieutenant was the door out to the front of the boat. Valdez knew he had a clear shot to whoever would attempt to escape. There was only one person, so it was not a difficult thing to assert.

"Did you know about the bassinet and diapers?" Valdez opened.

"Sir? What do you mean?" The lieutenant behaved as anyone who knew less than nothing.

"There are bassinets and diapers in the bottom of the boat. Do you know anything about this?" Valdez reiterated.

"No, I know nothing about this, sir. What is that doing on a war boat?" the lieutenant asked the captain.

"Do you have any contact with General Sihi?" the captain continued.

"No, sir. I have received only orders from you. I have never talked to General Sihi, sir," he responded.

"Very well," Valdez said while lowering his weapon. Then he continued. "I sensed the navy was sent out in the world to kidnap children."

The words were heavy. Their weight gave a moment for the lieutenant to let out a sigh, but his face was still dealing with all the revelations of the last few minutes. This was too much; he was nauseous, and there was a feeling in the boat that they would see his lunch soon.

"Sir, how do we deal with all this?" the lieutenant asked while wiping his mouth and lips of his regurgitate.

"I do not know," the captain pondered while answering.

"Do we want to pursue them anymore?" the lieutenant asked as he straightened his body.

"No, I will not, but I do not think they are going anywhere," Valdez stated. "I think they are returning to Alaska. The question is, why? Who else were they going to save and why? Where would they go? There is nowhere to go, no food to feed them, and not enough good fields to grow anything. So why?" he pondered out loud.

The lieutenant was silent. He had plenty to compute about this whole situation. The mass of the questions sank him into the sea of doubt.

The Corvair tangled in the water and went right and left to the rhythm of the waves. It began to beat on them. The lieutenant turned on the engine and retreated back to Alaska. He went slowly. He knew to give time to Valdez to play chess with his pieces, or what was left.

CHAPTER 18

THE SUBMARINE WAS an underwater craft. This was not easy if all you have as a crew was your sister, who knew nothing about you or the fact that she had a brother.

"Rose. I know you have no idea who I am. My name is Swinthun Schilling. Your mother was my mother," Swinthun began saying.

"That makes more sense why you would risk your life for me," she said quietly with a gentle smile.

"It would, wouldn't it?" Swinthun answered back and smiled back at her.

"How did you know I was in Primrose?" she asked him.

"Mom told me you were born, and around your third birthday, I stopped receiving messages from her. I began looking in the list and saw your name in the Alaska roll. It was a good thing, because I was also in Alaska," Swinthun explained.

"OK, this makes sense." She nodded.

"I have something enormous to tell you. I don't know if you are ready for this." Swinthun prepared his sister for his gigantic announcement.

"What is it? Tell me," Rose responded with eagerness of expectation.

"OK. We, Kaylee and I, went to Laos, and we were told we have a chance of leaving this planet." He paused to see how his sister would react.

"What? Are you saying we could leave this planet? Are you serious? No, you must be joking. Please tell me you are joking," Rose spewed out without taking a breath.

"That is what I was told. I had a hard time with it too. The only thing making me believe all this was I conversed with an AI. AI cannot lie," Swinthun said straight to the point.

"Oh," she uttered, and it was as if her breathing was taken out of her body.

"I know. It is a lot to take in. I would like you to go with me," Swinthun stated.

"What if it is not real? What if it is a lie? Where would we go?" This was too much for a ten-year-old to handle. It was too much for a twenty-year-old to manage a few hours ago.

"I do not know. I have to have some faith. So do you." His hand was out waiting for hers to respond.

"I don't know. I don't know." Rose was stuck; this was too much for a ten-year-old, way too much.

Her hand met his hand. He pulled on her arm, and Rose landed in Swinthun's chest. He held her tight. His lips were pulled back into his mouth, and his jaws closed firmly. While his sister was in his arms, Swinthun tried to hold back his tears. This was too much; his lacrimal ducts filled with a torrent of feelings.

Being under the sea was an advantage for Swinthun. Feelings flowed, and he felt his sister's love. He was not sure for whom the love was designed for, but at this moment, he received it.

Finally, the hug was over. They pulled off each other. Swinthun wiped his eyes, and so did Rose. The next question was on her mind.

"Why is it that you are wearing that . . . hat?" she asked her brother.

"It is to block the locator that is implanted in me with my connection to the Interweb," Swinthun answered while laughing.

"OK, it works, then," she uttered.

"How do you know this?" Swinthun inquired.

"A girl at school talked about it. I was not sure if it would work," Rose answered.

The trip took forever. Rose was asleep, and Swinthun tried to stay awake, but even he needed some rest.

It would be a little less than a day before they would reach the meeting point.

CHAPTER 19

THE SEA WAS no different in composition in the north versus the equator. However, there was a different temperature and different scenes. In the north, there were conifers on the shoreline, and in winter, snowy patches. At the equator, there was brownish water and a lot of heat and humidity. The shoreline was bare with occasional coconut trees.

The water was the same—wet, dangerous, and no fish out of it. This was a reality to live with. The ocean covered maybe 85 percent of the planet now. There was land left but no true granary area to feed people. This was due to the original water mix. The salty water penetrated the potable water. This made the land unproductive. The middle of North America and China was of no use for food production.

The thought ran across Kaylee's mind. She was tired, but catching a few z's was not a possibility. She monitored a Corvair behind her that was not moving. Why was that? She sensed it was the Calgary crew. There was no reason for them to stop. Their battery was full, and they had a clear knowledge of who was ahead of them.

Running through the potential issues did not make her feel any better. It could be an engine problem, but this idea was not real. Was it a recall from the army? Why would that be? There was no way this could be it. A monster attacked them? It was the most possible of answers yet unrealistic.

Then they turned around. Their speed was much slower. This was unthinkable.

The need to sleep was pressing, but the need to know why they stopped chasing after her was more important. She kept her eyes on the monitor. Then the nighttime owls got her. Slowly, Kaylee lowered her head and chest on the dashboard of the Corvair, and a few z's were caught.

The sun came up in the sky. One of its rays hit right in her closed eye. In her closed eyelid, Kaylee saw a reddish color. It was hot and it told her to wake up. Again, slowly, she opened her eyes. The sun's rays blinded her until she squinted hard to adjust. This took a few seconds.

The radar read no one. There was nothing on her radar. Was it true? Or did the chasing Corvair remove its tracker too? How was she to know?

Her lower abdomen reminded her of Tom again. This was not a good time. She knew about it, and the draining feeling made her want to go and change the roll of fabric. Looking around her, there was nothing but grayish waters. The waves tilted her Corvair right and left. There were waves big enough to submerge the boat she was in.

Electing for comfort, Kaylee went down and looked for more fabric. This was not hard. There were diapers in the boat. This crept her out, but when there was a need to be completed, you have to address it.

Being in a wet suit was not the most comfortable. She removed it and changed her pad. The bloody one was placed on the table, and Kaylee changed into regular clothes. These were navy uniforms. One-piece jumpers were comfortable and easy to move in. The aluminum hat had been on and remained on. Her hair was becoming like the dreadlocks she saw in books about the bad people who brought anarchy to the world. Was she bringing anarchy to the world with her near dreadlocked hair?

Being fully dressed, Kaylee ran up to the helm. There was still no one. She checked the radar; no one was to be found. This was a

HENRI NGUYEN

deepening question for Kaylee. Why did they give up? This was not their philosophy. It was not part of their anatomy.

The power holding North America was very strong; they ruled over the Earth pretty much. The Europeans were the only one standing against the North American Commission, but even they recognized there was strength in the military of North America. So why did they give up the chase? It made no sense.

Calculation was her forte. She knew she was about two hours away from the underwater island of Saint Paul, which she did not know existed. There was plenty of time to sit here, being hungry, doubting everything she knew, and, finally, wondering if the army and navy were laying a trap for her to fall into. This was a paradise to be in.

The wait was long. A morning, an afternoon, and the evening lay ahead.

Boredom was part of life in the army. However, Kaylee was not part of the army. The lack of things to do and lack of things to eat were so enticing for Kaylee; she could not come to realize how lucky she was. Boredom was an event, and you have to breathe through it. On the other hand, it was no easy moment to breathe through, as she was never trained for this utter lack of anything to do.

Finally, the sun began to set on the west side of the boat. There was a compass, which made her laugh as the true north was no longer reliable. There was no need for it to exist, but the engineers thought it would be a good thing to have in case everything went to hell. *I guess.* This was the thought in Kaylee's mind.

The engine restarted, and the hull of the boat lifted. Kaylee helmed the Corvair back to the meeting point. She kept an eye on her radar screen. This would be a good place to see the other two boats that chased her. A gust of cold wind came across the opening to the wheelhouse. This made her happy.

Kaylee was a child of Chicago. The weather was often told as schizophrenic. One minute, you had a pleasant day; and then next, it was snowing. An exaggeration according to Kaylee, but there was something to be happy about. Rarely did it mark people as much as Chicagoans. The winters can be cold, and the summers can be hot and humid at the same time. Kaylee never saw a heated day followed by a snowy day, though.

The Corvair moved, and it approached the meeting point. Suddenly, a dot appeared on her radar screen. "There you are!" she exclaimed out loud. The next question popped in her head. *How did you know I would be back?* This troubled her. She ran across what happened for them to know. There was that break when she realized it would take a day for the submarine to reach this point. "Shit!" she uttered.

CHAPTER 20

THE CORVAIR VALDEZ was in waited. His radio was ready.

Valdez picked up the receiver and said, "Swinthun . . . and Kaylee, I would like to have a discussion with you." This was an odd way to talk for him and helmsman. No answer. There had been no answer for the past hour.

Valdez was not sure if they would be coming around this point. However, they did stop here. There had to be some significance at this point. There must be a reason for them to have stopped here.

Valdez tried again. He was losing hope—the hope that there was a good explanation for them to have escaped. Valdez was not grasping with what he had discovered in the bowel of his Corvair.

Suddenly, a near broken signal came in. "What do you want?" Swinthun came scratchy, but all in the Corvair understood his message.

"I want to know why you ran away," Valdez said immediately.

"Why?" Swinthun asked.

"I saw and heard things. These things do not make me comfortable with my . . . superiors," Valdez spat out.

"What is your name?" Swinthun continued asking.

"I am Captain Valdez, and my lieutenant is Stephen Dubois," Valdez responded.

"Why do you want to know?" Swinthun asked more questions.

"I know you're trying to see what I know. I will tell you. I have stopped chasing you. I just want some answers," Valdez admitted.

"Why did you stop?" Swinthun was not giving up anything until he was sure.

"I found out about things that make me very uneasy, and I need confirmations about them," Valdez stated.

"Why would anyone trust you? If you are not saying what you found out, why would I trust you?" Swinthun asked; his voice was near screaming mode.

"You are right. I will ask you these questions, then. I found bassinets and diapers in the bowels of my boat. I asked my general why. He did not answer me. So I am asking you why." Valdez crumbled. His mind was overwhelmed; he needed an answer, although he knew it already.

"Yes, our government has been kidnapping kids of the world," Swinthun said quietly.

Silence broke out. No one wanted to follow this statement.

Finally, Valdez restarted the conversation.

"Why did the world not tell us or fight back?" This question needed no answer, but Swinthun did.

"So why do we have a defense system?" Swinthun asked him.

"I don't know. I don't." Valdez sounded like a man defeated.

"I am under you. I don't know if I can trust you, but you seemed to be OK by me. I am coming up," Swinthun said.

The tiny submarine came up. At the edge of the water and the sky, it broke the water. It flowed on either side of the vessel. The noise made was welcome for Valdez. He needed a friend. He had no idea of who was his enemy anymore. The only thing he was sure of was the people he had been chasing were the least dangerous to him.

The hatch opened up. Swinthun came out. He looked at the Corvair. There was Valdez. It was like two long-lost friends at the end of a civil war. Were they supposed to hug or something? This was a question Swinthun did not ask himself.

The transfer happened. It was awkward; stepping onto a Corvair where people who had been chasing you was deprived of significance.

Valdez looked at Rose, who hid behind Swinthun. Valdez tried to get her attention. Obviously, Valdez and Dubois scared Rose. This was evident. Grabbing a blanket, Valdez handed it to Swinthun. The man wrapped his sister with it. The cover was a military item; it was a khaki green and it was scratchy, but it made Rose feel warm immediately.

Swinthun was apprehensive. He wondered if he made a mistake when he stepped up on this boat. He walked to Valdez. His eyes remained on Valdez's eyes. This was not an easy moment.

"What happened to the other boat?" Swinthun started.

"We sent them back to harbor," Valdez answered.

"Do they want communication?" Swinthun continued.

"No. I told them I would take you guys in and I will bring you in myself. Obviously, I won't," Valdez stated.

"OK, all we have to do is wait for Kaylee," Swinthun added

"What? She is not with you?" Valdez made this comment to reflect all his calculations were wrong.

"They will know you are either a traitor or defeated, and this very soon," Swinthun thought out loud. "We need to alert Kaylee," Swinthun concluded.

"How? She disappeared off my radar. On top of it all, she seemed to not have any communication with anyone," Valdez responded.

"Put all the lights on and flash your position light," Swinthun said. He wanted to be seen, and this would be the only way for Kaylee to know they would not fire on her boat. "Also, make your Corvair invisible to the radars. Get the locator out of the battery."

Immediately, Dubois ran down to remove the locator. Once he had it, he squeezed it between his fingers and it popped. They were now invisible.

It was not two minutes until a boat approached. Was it Kaylee?

Swinthun and Valdez were at the helm. They were not sure. Swinthun looked at the radar screen. It did not show anyone. He knew it was Kaylee.

CHAPTER 21

THE CORVAIR WAS designed for performance. When you are not using it to zip across the waters, it was not a stable base to wait. The boat took on some water; this was not a moment to panic.

In the process of activating the pump, Kaylee found a first aid kit. In this pack was some gas. She looked at it and wondered if this would be more adequate for her period, which was making her feeling distracted. Looking at it was enough, she passed on it. She put it back on the shelf and went on to her business.

Having a Tom was hard enough; having to run away from those men made it harder. Now, Kaylee was about to blast into space; this was too much. She wanted to scream and rip apart this boat, but she knew there was a need for this boat. After the mission of rescuing Swinthun and Rose was completed, then go to Laos. *Boat, you and I, we have a date;* this was her thought. It was between funny and not so funny. If you asked her, she would not be able to tell you whether she was serious or funny.

The nine o'clock moment happened. She turned on the engines, and they roared as they should. It was about an hour away. Her father taught her to never be late. This was a point of pride for Kaylee.

Her father was a man with a huge heart. He would help all he could. Never did he ever not want to help someone, and yet there was something in her that wondered. He was as white as a white man could ever be. Kaylee was as Asian as she ever could be. Even if her mother was Asian, Kaylee would have some traits from him. This was too clean for him to be her father.

Kaylee was not sure how kids were made. She understood copulation from a man, and him leaving his spermatozoid was at the basis of it, but the DNA and how it all worked, this was more difficult to discern for her. For that matter, Kaylee knew the acronym DNA, but she had no idea what those letters meant.

This part of her father was always a point of friction. Now that he passed away, she could never ask him. This bothered her. She had a sense of not belonging to his genetic tree. However, he never cared about this. He was always teaching things as if the end of the world was coming. Did it?

Her father pressed her on her skills as if she was about to enter an amazing adventure. This was true, but why her? Did he know all this would happen? How could he? At the age of fourteen, he died. He lay on the couch, and his face was peaceful. He looked as if he went to sleep and never woke up from his nap.

Kaylee looked at the windshield, and something bright was on the horizon. Then she checked the radar. There was only one signal. It said it was the submarine. So what was so bright so she could see it on the horizon? She was not sure, but why would anyone turn on all their lights? Was this Swinthun's doing? She was not sure what the answers to these questions were. She pondered. Her thought was, *Why would I go to a point of light in the middle of the sea? This had to be a trap. Why would anyone try to get my attention? It had to be a trap.*

The next query popped in her head. *What if they have Swinthun and Rose?* This likelihood was unresolvable. A few days ago, this man came to her apartment and told her to come if she wanted to be alive, and now she had tears because he could be a prisoner. What was happening to her? When did she care about a man so much?

The truth was she wanted a man because she lived alone. A man would bring so much to her life. Her father was not the same thing. There was a presence in her life, and she was very happy about it; the presence of a man would be a warming feeling for her. Kaylee needed to be in his arms and feel the warmth of a human touch. There was also the whole sex part too. She wanted it more than the lovey feeling stuff, but who was asking?

There was no other choice. The darn soldiers who were holding Swinthun and Rose would taste her fists; her thinking pulled her into these violent conversations with herself. Was this part of Tom? Kaylee had to get to that boat and somehow get Swinthun and Rose on her boat and leave. "This is not going to be easy," she whispered to herself, trying to psych herself to the upcoming fight.

The boat was about a kilometer away. Kaylee shut off the engine and let inertia do the rest of the work. In the beginning, she approached the point of light at high speed, but as the minutes went by, the speed slowed down. Kaylee was about a hundred meters away when she saw hands in the air. *Are they waving at me?*

This made no sense. Why would anyone wave at me in the middle of the seas? This made less and less sense to Kaylee. She took a deep breath, and as the boat got closer to the illuminated point, she recognized a voice—Swinthun's.

Her emotions went from getting ready for a fight to relief within a span of minutes. Kaylee took deep breaths again and again. Tears formed in her ducts. These were about to drop.

The introduction to Captain Valdez was uneasy. This became an exercise in pure awkwardness. Captain Valdez was not sure how he would be received, but even he did not imagine this. Kaylee kept her eyes on his face and the lieutenant's.

Within minutes, the uncomfortable feelings began to transform into a sorting out of who was more evil.

"Why did you obey the order of General Sihi?" Kaylee asked Valdez.

"I did because I was given the order," Valdez responded.

"Why would you think running after us would be a good thing?" Kaylee said this while looking at Swinthun.

"Again, I was given orders. That is how it works in the army." Valdez tried to defend himself.

"I don't know if we should take them with us," Kaylee said to Swinthun.

"Kaylee, how can they harm anything?" Swinthun answered with a question.

"I don't know. They could try to sabotage something," Kaylee uttered.

"I think they are as sincere as anyone can be," Swinthun stated.

"What do you need as a proof?" Valdez asked.

"I need no proof. I need to know if you are telling the truth," Kaylee enunciated.

"How can I tell you in any other words?" Valdez repeated himself.

Kaylee took another deep breath. Her mind swam in all this mud. She was happy she found Swinthun and his sister, but there were Valdez and Dubois. Then they had four days to be on the rocket to the spaceship. There was Tracy, a friend who needed to be honored. Her death was still on her mind. On top of it all, Kaylee was in her Tom. This was too much.

Deep in thought, Kaylee sat at the edge of the Corvair. Water came up and down her legs and pelvis. This was not a big deal an hour ago when she was in a wet suit, but now it made her all wet. Somehow, it did not bother her. Actually, she felt the cold water, and it was a refreshing matter. There was too much to think about.

A few days ago, she lived a simple life—find food, cook food, defend the nation, and go to bed. What she wanted was a return to the simple life. There were too many pawns on the board; it made her nervous to potentially lose someone. This became her fear.

As Swinthun was a good man, he walked to Kaylee and sat beside her. He did not say anything. This helped. A man who knew how to sit and not talk was a rarity. It was in her mind, and none of it would ever see the light of day.

Observing the water was her focus. Swinthun was quiet and he looked at the sea too, but, occasionally, he peeked an eye on her. He wanted to make sure she was all right. The wind sneaked under Kaylee's short hair, and at that moment, she loved the wind. It brought her a moment of calm and refreshment. This was as close to happiness for the past three days. She smiled.

There it was. Although no words were used, Kaylee knew Valdez and Dubois knew nothing about the plan that dropped on their laps. This seemed to be the most important part to manage. *If they knew nothing, could be we keep them and let the AI decide all this mess?*

"So if you want to come with us, there is a price." Kaylee began the conversation.

"What is it?" Valdez said softly.

"Until we reach our destination, you will be restrained and blindfolded," Kaylee stated.

"So when you reach the destination, you want us to do what?" Valdez asked further.

"Someone will decide whether you can continue with us or not," Kaylee uttered.

"This seems a little mysterious. How do we know you are saying the truth?" Valdez pondered.

"You are right—you don't know. It is the best deal I can give you. Make a decision within five minutes, because we will be leaving with or without you." Kaylee made the statement and began to walk out of the tiny cabin.

There was not much discussion between Valdez and Dubois. There were little choices left on the table for them.

Accepting the blindfold and restraints was not the best idea for Valdez and Dubois, but it was the best they could do at this point in time. Valdez could not confirm it, but it felt like aluminum foil was placed on his head. When he asked Dubois, he told him he had the feeling too.

The Corvair was starting its engine and shutting off its lights.

CHAPTER 22

S ITTING IN CHICAGO, Sihi felt his world spin. This was a strange feeling. There was no one spinning him, nor anyone telling him anything, but his world spun and spun faster than he could handle.

General Sihi was caught between letting North America know about the kidnapping or to pull the army and navy and eliminate the two darn escapees. Now they have Swinthun's sister, so the general thought, *I guess the three of them.* The question remained the same—how?

There were not too many options left. They ran to Alaska. In Alaska, he had about another six or seven soldiers, and the navy had maybe ten sailors. The manpower was not the strongest. This was a problem.

His mind ran and ran for hours. His thought meddled with each other. The fact of their kidnappings was to be hidden; otherwise, the commission will be taken down. It happened before; 2019 was the first time.

His mind was full, but his bottle of bourbon was empty. He got up and realized very quickly where it went. His lips were dry, and his eyes began to slow down. His world spun in another way.

In 2019, it was evident. The remains of the country was in shambles. Thousands of nuclear missiles detonated across the world. Millions of megatons shred the world into what it was today. The second time was due to the Second War. At the end of it, the North American continent came about, and the commission replaced the election of a president.

The commission was a group of fourteen commissioners, and they were assigned by their areas. No one knew who the commissioners were, and they could not reveal their position, as this would be dangerous for them.

This was not an elegant way to govern, but it worked for the wealthy. Wealth was the power, as it always was. Money was a measure of power.

Drunk as he was, General Sihi went to bed. There would be no decision made today. The only order he gave was, upon the return of the Corvair, to send it back out.

The next morning would not be a pleasant one. This would be for tomorrow.

CHAPTER 23

THE CORVAIR WAS on its way to Laos. The weather went from cold and snippy to a very warm and soggy sky. This was difficult to move for everyone on board the boat. This was a full boat and full of worries.

The night was almost over, and the worries were still present. There were too many things again in Kaylee's mind. The worry of making a deadline was something new for her. The pressure of time management was not something she dealt with or well with. She moved more, and her mind was at work all the time.

Planning for something to happen with an enemy took all of her mind to plan the actions, but now there were two officers under deck, a sister, and Swinthun. This was, in the end, the most difficult to manage for her. Was he her partner? Was he a friend? Was he an acolyte? What was he? There had been no time to talk to him or, for that matter, no time to talk at all in the last three days.

Sleep became a very rare commodity, even for Kaylee. Swinthun was at helm, and she fell asleep so fast.

The morning had passed. The afternoon was here, as the sun was at its zenith. This was a hard wake-up. It was hot and sticky, and so was Kaylee. When she opened her eyes, the boat swayed left to right. There were voices above her. What was happening?

Climbing the short amount of rungs, her head and hair felt the fresh warm air. There was no way to escape it. It was there, and you felt it— the warm and all-enveloping heat. Kaylee sweated like all the members on board. She came out of the hull and looked around. Swinthun was seated and could not catch a whiff of cold.

"What is going on? Why are we stopped?" Kaylee uttered while trying to adjust her eyes to the bright sun.

"We are recharging. The batteries could have gone for another half hour, but I estimated this would be too dangerous," Swinthun responded slowly.

"The heat is too much?" Kaylee was snarky at Swinthun, who, for the first time, smiled. This was a nice smile.

"Yeah, it is hot," Swinthun said with a smug on his face.

"Anyone on the radar?" Kaylee inquired.

"There was a bleep by our meeting point, but it left the radar screen. If they are chasing us, I would estimate two hours behind. This should allow us an hour of recharge. This would give us half-life battery, and easily we will be in Laos." Swinthun explained his thinking. This seemed sound.

Kaylee observed out of the boat. There was nothing but grayish water. At the tip of the boat, Rose was sitting. She was silent and not moving. This seemed a conversation from a woman to a very, very young woman. Kaylee stepped outside.

The wind, you may think, would give you a little breeze, but no avail. The air was wet, and a storm seemed on the horizon. Walking on a boat, which swayed, was never an easy task. There was a moment when Kaylee felt something coming up in the esophageal tube, but it was brief and no one knew better.

"How are you, Rose? My name is Kaylee," she introduced herself.

"Hi . . .," Rose answered.

"I know it is a lot to take all this adventure in." Kaylee continued to open up.

"Mm-hmm." Rose was shy, but it sounded like a mild yes.

"Rose, we are going to places you have never heard of. We are going to have to say something to one another. I hope it will be more than sounds." Kaylee made a slight joke.

"Yeah, I am sure we will." Rose had to respond more than her previous statement.

"Tell me, the school you were at, do you miss it?" Kaylee asked the little shy girl.

"No," Rose said and shook her head with vehemence.

"What did they do to you?" Kaylee asked kindly while lifting Rose's hair off her face.

"I don't know." Rose's answer was a way to deflect.

"I never went to those schools. My dad raised me. Maybe you could tell me what a day looks like in school," Kaylee nearly whispered to Rose.

"OK. You wake up before the sun ever comes out. This was an order. If you were sleeping past the order, they could beat you up." Rose uttered this with such a low voice, Kaylee could barely hear her. "Then we go to chores. I had to clean the bathroom. This was the lowest chore you could get. Then we went to clean up and make our beds," Rose said almost as if she was an automaton.

"When would you go eat breakfast?" Kaylee asked Rose.

"We usually ate lunch, and then that was it," Rose answered, and upon this response, Kaylee opened her arms. She embraced Rose and held her.

The world of schools was not a speech you can prepare for. It was hard and empty of meaning, but there was pain in little Rose's voice. Kaylee barely knew this little girl, but she contained pain, and this was not right.

Rose was still embraced when Kaylee thought of her father. He had a reason to educate her at home. He knew about those schools. There was a day when she was ten years and Kaylee asked her father if he ever worked in Central Chicago. He looked at her and nodded. He must have known. Did he know this whole escape too? How could he?

Finally, Rose came out of Kaylee's arms. Tears were not on her face, but they were on Kaylee's face. This was not a regular moment. Rose wanted to ask Kaylee, "Why the tears?" This did not happen. This was too much in the process for Rose. She knew she communicated some news that was not sitting all right with Kaylee. Kaylee could see in her face that Rose wondered.

"It is all right, Rose. I have tears because your tale of school days was terrifying. This made me sad for you and happy for my father's decision to keep me away from the Central Chicago." This all came out; Kaylee was not sure if it was too much for Rose to grasp.

"OK." Rose's response was short and so simple.

"If you want to tell me more, you can. Do not let these tears stop you," Kaylee stated.

"OK. Could I have something to eat?" Rose asked; she seemed to feel a little more at ease and confident.

"Let us see what we could find in the galley." Kaylee got up and walked. Again, there was something pushing up in her stomach.

HENRI NGUYEN

Kaylee had eaten nothing in the past hours. Why would something push up her gastric pouch? She swallowed it down. It tasted bitter, and it was acidic. This was not good eats, she thought to herself.

In the galley, which was no more than a cupboard, they found bars. They had no names, and the paper wrapped around them was brown. Could you find a more indistinguishable bar? To Rose, it was delicious. Kaylee thought, *If this taste is as good as you make it sound, you are in for a discovery of my culinary skills, little one.* This was the moment Kaylee came to realize that she was adopting this little girl in her heart. But why?

An hour passed, and Swinthun connected the batteries back on. The engine restarted. Suddenly, a faint bleep appeared on the radar. Kaylee and he knew it was time to go. They geared up the Corvair, and it took off.

Running away from something or someone was not easy, but it was simple. You had to stay up and away from whoever wanted you. If they were not offered the opportunity to disappear off the planet and go somewhere else in space, where would they hide? This was a good question in Kaylee's mind.

The bleep disappeared. This was a good thing.

Hours and hours passed. Still no bleep on their radar screen; this was all good news. On the other hand, this Corvair had no tracker on it. Kaylee thought of getting their boat out of action by turning around and swooping on them. This would be a good way to not be chased anymore. Swinthun was the voice of reason—what if they have more than one boat? This was a good point.

The afternoon was about to end, and they were about to reach Laos.

CHAPTER 24

GENERAL SIHI WOKE up to the sound of his alarm. It was in his head, which hurt. The pain was in front of his cranium, and the temporal lobes throbbed too. This was a lot to hear his alarm. He knew what needed to be done.

The shower was hard, and getting dressed was not any easier. Bourbon was his friend in this world. There was no question he had company of women, but none them were his partner. They were a one-night stand or a regular night stand. To Sihi, the women were a passing need. He was more important, and this morning was that moment.

Breakfast was difficult to swallow. There were instances when he considered vomiting. He swallowed it and told himself, *You do not have time for this kind of shit.* This usually worked for Sihi, but today it did not.

There was nothing dignified about being curled over your toilet. No matter how golden this was, it was a humiliation. Sihi vomited and kept on hacking. His insides were nearly out. He knew he had a few more minutes to clean himself before the meeting.

The minutes passed, and Sihi looked a smudge better. Nonetheless, he had a meeting, and this one was not one you could postpone.

"Sir," Sihi opened the conversation with the commission.

"Sihi, where are we with Schilling and McCloud?" the head commissioner asked him immediately.

"I have bad news. They escaped again. This time, we only have a boat after them," Sihi responded with nausea in his body. It was like his body rejected this meeting.

"You look like shit," the Northern commissioner said with a pointed comment.

"What are we going to do about this, General?" The head commissioner came back to the topic.

The commission never met in person; all this meeting was electronic. He was an image for them, as they were for him. He could see their heads, and this was a little too much, but he had no choice.

"Sir, may I suggest the full mobilization of our armed forces to chase after them," Sihi spat it out.

"What? You want to use all our forces to go get two idiots!" the Southwest commissioner exploded.

"One way or another, is the Arctic Boost program that important? If you want to stop them from divulging it, this is what we need to do." General Sihi almost forgot his need to vomit and replied succinctly.

"Head Commissioner, I have to admit he has a point," the Nebraska commissioner uttered. He continued. "Do we care any more about Arctic Boost?"

"Hmm," the head commissioner let out while scratching his left eyebrow.

"Sir, may I add?" Sihi came back.

"Go ahead." The head allowed it.

"I do not know where they will hide, so I will say if we could go with an overall attack and a proclamation of our need to attack them to reestablish a balance in the world." Sihi had a plan. "In all of this, we do not need to reveal Arctic Boost," he finished.

"That is true, and that sounds about right," the North commissioner added.

"So your idea is to create an attack on each coast and declare a state of war. Then we go after them and get rid of them. Where are they headed?" the head commissioner asked.

"I do not have coordinates. All I have is a general direction, and I can make an assumption as to where they are headed, sir." Sihi seemed to drag this information to his own benefit.

"Sihi, give us the information, and, yes, you will be compensated," the head commissioner said; he seemed to know how the general worked.

"I believe they are going to Laos." Sihi divulged his assumption as he had an assurance of more power.

"Very well. Assemble the army and navy, create this attack, and go get them," the head commissioner ordered.

"Sir, yes, sir." Sihi had the order to go all out on these two escapees before they tell the whole North American continent about Arctic Boost.

Arctic Boost was the name of the kidnapping program. It began in the Arctic Sea. The least affected population was the Siberian population after the 2019 War. Who would attack such few number of people? This made them the birth cradle of the world. North America figured this out very quickly.

In a few seconds, a series of attacks was launched. This happened in the Southeast, Southwest, and Northern Saint Lawrence. The defense went up automatically. In all this commotion, there were maybe four or five people taking care of the defense of North America.

The next moment, Sihi alerted the army and navy to mobilize and be under his rule. This happened the second previous, as the letter to all generals and admirals was issued that General Sihi was the master of all the troops. There were maybe three hundred members in this whole army. When considering the three hundred were chasing two people, it was enormous.

Boats were launched. They had to bring out the biggest boats—the Barracudas. These vessels were gigantic when compared with Corvair. They were comfortable for more than fifty soldiers on board. They were well armed: large cannons, machine guns, torpedoes, mine laying and clearing, and all of them were automated. This was a terrifying machine.

It would be a couple of hours before they could go on the Barracudas. There were three of them.

The Corvairs were out and headed to Laos.

Sitting in his office, General Sihi was not worried about his headache anymore. The only concern left was, could they shut Kaylee McCloud and Swinthun Schilling? This was their only mission.

CHAPTER 25

THE STORM CAME as the heavy weather predicted. The drenching rain was somewhat welcome. The enjoyment of water falling was a benefit, but the warm liquid changed nothing about their comfort.

The Corvair swayed a little. Their speed had to be slowed down. It was fast enough for them to be above the water, but not enough to make all this disappear quickly.

The rain made the seas choppy. The waters were like an enormous roller coaster. It went up and down, occasionally side to side. This was too much for them. Rose and the blindfolded officers were nauseous. Dubois was about to lose it all. He did not eat a lot in the past twelve hours, but he could lose it very quickly.

Swinthun and Kaylee were at the helm. Kaylee had the wheel, and Swinthun was on the lookout.

Swinthun looked for a less turbulent way to Laos. This was going to be harder than he imagined. His binoculars perched on his face, he tried and tried to look for calmer seas.

Kaylee was definitely annoyed about all this. She wanted to kick the engine all out. Swinthun told her it would be worse. She was annoyed about the cute man telling her what to do. This was a feeling that grew more preoccupying in her mind. Her Tom, going to space, and honoring Tracy took a backseat to this new thought. This came with worries, as she cared about him.

It was getting rougher and rougher. This was about to be a horror show where many would puke. It happened—Dubois lost it. Blindfolded, this made it so much worse. Next, it was Rose. She lost her breakfast. Then it was lunch, if lunch was ever consumed. Nonetheless, it was on the floor of the mess hall. This was truly a mess hall at this point in time.

The pilot looked at her lookout person, and in her eyes was desire to tell him so much, but all Kaylee said was "I am kicking it in. We need to get out of this mess."

The Corvair picked up speed; it approached its maximum speed. The Corvair was lifted and cut across the water when it came up against one of the giant waves.

The wave was more than enormous. Gigantic was too small for this wave. The vessel was at the bottom of it; it sped to the top. It took about five seconds; they were about clear this monster of wave. The top was nearly there.

Swinthun closed his eyes and held on tight.

The Corvair jumped. There was nothing underneath it. Was it flying? If you define flying as falling, then yes. It fell on the water as if it was lead. It was hard. Everyone on the Corvair was splattered on the floor, and then for good measure, they bounced up and landed on the floor again.

Then another wave was ahead of them. Kaylee screamed, "Hang on tight to something." The whole boat did.

The Corvair jumped again and again. Swinthun lost his insides. No one had anything left in their stomachs, except for the pilot, Kaylee. She held on tight and fought through these fictional creatures. She knew the waves had no wit about them. Kaylee felt they tried to stop them to get to Laos. This was a reality for her.

At this point, Swinthun was useless as he held on to the hand rig but was on his knees. He tried to find his center to stop the reverse meals. This was not easy.

The seas calmed down; Kaylee could see clear sky. They would be there in about a minute.

Running to the sun was something difficult to do when you were knocked around and it made you vomit all over. This was a reality that Kaylee could see. She felt good about still carrying her insides. The boat was there.

Almost in an instant, it went from midday choppy waters to calm waters. Their speed was at maximum, and this could be felt from everyone on board.

Swinthun sat and tried to see if his sister was all right. This was not the best episode of brother-loves-his sister moment. He struggled to walk. Kaylee knew better than to stop him; she smiled and looked forward. Rose came up and she needed some fresh air.

Swinthun came up with Dubois and Valdez. He looked at them and Kaylee; she nodded her head. He removed their blindfolds. He kept their restraints. The both of them rushed out of the cabin and went to the fresh air.

The air was not refreshing, but it was needed. The stale air of the bottom of the Corvair was too much for three of them to handle.

Kaylee could see something on the horizon. She tapped her lookout. He grabbed his binoculars; he scanned. He turned to Kaylee, and he smiled on the left side of his lips. They could see Laos.

Coming into port was the usual deserted port. No one was to be found. Dubois and Valdez looked upon the empty port. They never saw anyone in this burned-out port. The only thing standing was the dock. The rest was still fuming.

Valdez looked at it. Shame was in his heart. It was felt in his heart despite the fact that this organ had nothing to do with feeling shame or happiness. This was an odd sensation; it irradiated from the heart to his carotid area and then his face. The flames were in his memories. He ordered them. He was not sure why, but he did. There was going to be a heavy discussion when it happened, if ever.

The Corvair pulled to the dock. Rose, Dubois, Valdez, and Swinthun were off the boat. They stood on the pier and looked for Kaylee.

From the wheelhouse, Kaylee headed to the bottom of the boat. Looking for explosive on a military vessel should be easy, but it was not. She could only find a rifle and some handguns. Stuffing the guns into her pants, Kaylee shouldered the rifle and took a deep breath. She shot into the hull.

The water rushed in. Immediately, Kaylee climbed up the ladder. She was conscious of her risk of being trapped in this sinking vessel. A step at a time, Kaylee ascended as fast as her legs allowed her. Now she was in wheelhouse; quickly, she stepped out onto the bow. The deck was wet; this was slippery. She was heavier because of the guns. Carefully, Kaylee got the ladder and off the boat. She was near her goal and space.

On the pier, they stood. Valdez opened his trap.

"So where do I go to get punished?" The sarcasm oozed as he knew it was not going to be a nice conversation.

"O . . . K. Why the strange question?" Rose asked Valdez.

"Because he burned the town," Swinthun added quickly and realized the depth of the question.

"Wow! It is going to be a conversation." Kaylee solved the strange puzzle.

In the burning ruins of a city, they walked to the remnants of a shack.

Looking around, Kaylee wondered how to communicate with the AI or even the humans. She was not sure where they were either. A little bit lost, she bit her left cheek and wondered the how and what to do at this time.

On the other hand, Swinthun looked for the side door. He went a little further. He had to stop as he was on the side to the bluff. There was a rocky part at the bottom of the slope. He descended the hill and saw a door.

"Guys, come on down here. I found the door," Swinthun confirmed.

"All right," Kaylee responded.

"Can you guys release us? We are not in a position to hurt you guys," Valdez requested.

"Yeah, I guess." Kaylee accepted the query.

"Thanks," Valdez said with a shallow smile.

Valdez and Dubois were cut out of their restraints. Rose was going down the hill. Valdez and Dubois proceeded down too. Kaylee stood at the top of the hill. She looked at the town destruction. There was not much to this town, but to destroy it was evil. Could she trust Valdez? Did she have a choice?

The judgment of his acts was not hers to deal with. Kaylee shook her head and did not know what the AI would render as a decision. It was difficult to have good feelings for Valdez, but she did not mind his presence. Kaylee had to repress this feeling.

Lust was her feeling. Swinthun, Valdez, and Dubois were all handsome to her. If there was a way, she would be losing her virginity. However, being runaways, it was hard to think about the possibility. At this moment of short rest, Kaylee had let go of her id.

Kaylee's id filled her mind with lust and dreamy moments. Imagination of nakedness of men and a woman was heavy and hot, but she liked the imagery. After a second and upon hearing Swinthun's voice, she grabbed her id and stuffed it back into the depth of her mind.

Descending the hill, Kaylee looked at Swinthun. He had his eye on the door, and she heard his sister say, "Wow! You opened that door." Kaylee rushed a little more to go down the hill. The heat did not bother her anymore, at least as far as she knew.

Entering the room was like going from the oven to the fridge. The first time, Kaylee was too busy about everything happening to realize the AI room was air conditioned. It felt good to be in the air-conditioning. Kaylee wondered why the room was air conditioned. Was this for comfort?

They closed the door. The darkness was welcome from the harsh shining sun and the heavy heat and humidity. They all took a deep breath. Then the Ai came on.

"Hello, Swinthun and Kaylee. You are back. We are very happy with your return."

"Hello, yes, we are back. We have some extra people for you to assess," Kaylee said.

"Thank you. We will judge them. First, we have to see your sister," the AI stated.

"This is Rose. Rose, this is an AI. You only have to answer its questions honestly," Swinthun said to his sister.

"Hello," Rose said. She was not sure where to look or even where to talk.

"Rose, where were you when your brother came to save you?" the AI began.

"I was in Primrose at the School for Social Young Ladies," Rose answered.

"Was this hard?" the AI asked Rose.

"Yes, it was," she said after taking a deep breath.

"What did you learn there?" the AI continued with no emotions.

"I learned how to clean and how to please a man," Rose answered with shame in her voice.

"I would like to ask you, do you want to leave this place?" The AI used an imprecise term, and this was premeditated.

"Yes, I do," Rose responded with no hesitation.

The AI took a moment to compute all her answers.

The AI came back, as its voice could be heard. It said, "Rose, please follow your brother and Kaylee." A trap door opened.

Upon looking at the hole in the floor, Kaylee could see a ladder, and she got to the ladder. The going down was a mixture of feelings. There was excitements as she was about to see new things, which were so far out of her mind. Also, there was sadness of her leaving the only world she ever knew. Placing her feet on the ground, the lights came on.

While Kaylee looked around the empty room, Rose came down the ladder, and then Swinthun. Then another door opened. There were voices and community on the other side of the door. This was not odd; it was nice.

HENRI NGUYEN

CHAPTER 26

T HE MOMENT OF judgment inched forward. Dubois sweated and showed his anxiety; he bit his right index fingernail. The AI voice called his name, and he responded to it.

"Why should we accept you?" the AI continued.

"I am a good person. I obeyed orders from my superiors. This may have led to destruction and maybe death," Dubois spat out.

"We know what you did. How can you show reconcile this act you did?" the AI insisted.

"Although I followed an order, I am sorry for what I did. I knew it was wrong. I am so sorry," Dubois said with tears drowning his eyes.

"Please step aside," the AI ordered. Then it said, "Captain Valdez, please step forward."

Valdez stepped forward. He felt a knot in his abdomen. This was hard and difficult to manage.

The AI began.

"Are you the superior to Lieutenant Dubois?"

"Yes, I am," Valdez answered.

"Please state you name and rank," the AI asked.

"My name is Serge Valdez. I am captain in the North American Army," Serge answered.

"Did you give the order to burn our town?" the AI asked.

"Yes, I did," he responded. There was a sense of letting the truth come out.

"Why?" it asked back just as fast.

"I had orders to recover Swinthun and Kaylee. I was very unnerved by finding a town with no one in it. This made no sense to me. I snapped and gave the order to burn it all down. When I found no one still, I was very disappointed and disoriented. Then when I went home, I came to the realization that my world was worse than I ever imagined. They kidnapped children all over the world to feed the machine that we became to be," Serge spilled out; he knew the truth will set you free.

"Why should we trust you?" the AI inserted without any emotions in its crackled voice.

"I don't know. I am here, and the truth is I did too much for you to trust in me. Swinthun thought you would be the best judge for my actions. I will trust in you. I have nothing to fight for or live for." These words came out of Valdez, and they seemed to show his resolution to accept the ultimate punishment.

"Please wait," the AI said.

Serge looked around, and he saw his lieutenant. He lowered his head and walked to him.

"I am so sorry, Stephen." It was the first time in two years that Serge used Dubois's first name.

"Thank you," Stephen responded.

"I hope the decision for you will be much less than mine. I did give you those orders. I will assume my responsibilities," Serge confessed.

"Thank you . . ., Serge." It was the first time in his life he called Valdez by his first name, which he learned a few minutes ago.

Then the AI came back on. "Stephen Dubois, please step forward." Silence ran across the room. The AI voice spat out of the speaker that no one could see, "You have been judged to be reformed and you will be allowed to be on the next rocket." This made no sense to Dubois; the word "rocket" was odd and out of place. He had heard this word before in his life, but now, it was not possible. The voice came back again. "Serge Valdez, you were judged to be reformed and you will be allowed to be on the next rocket."

Stephen was dumbfounded, but Serge teared. This seemed to be the real reform, rocket or not.

CHAPTER 27

L AOS USED TO be a small port. With fishing being no longer in existence, what was its use? There were no answers, as no one was present to answer any questions. Five Corvairs docked to the pier, and its soldiers scattered in a disciplined fashion. The security cordon was in place. All that they had to wait for were the two Barracudas coming with more men.

The question the commander in charge had was "What do we need forty more men for?" There was nothing much to see or talk about here. He consulted the map and sent out a pair of soldiers to scout the forest north of the city.

The two soldiers scanned the forest. There were signs of life. These signs were too little for being humans. They hurdled through heavy brush to check each one of them. They looked in every grotto and little cave in case they hid in such small spaces.

An hour passed. There was no sign of anyone.

The commander ordered his soldiers to hold their positions. At the same time, he called General Sihi.

"Sir, this is Commander Stanton. I am in Laos, and there is no one. We scanned and visually checked every point of heat and potential hiding area within a kilometer of the city. We have assumed defensive positions and await our orders, sir."

"Very well. Scan the ground of the city while you wait for reinforcement," Sihi thought out loud.

"Sir, yes, sir," the commander responded.

The commander ordered two soldiers to scan the ground and to map it out. These instructions were odd and seemed desperate. *How is the general going to find these idiots?* he thought in his head while swiping away the sweat off his forehead.

The ground scanning began. The soldiers started from the dock. There was nothing underneath the ground. They proceeded on.

Thirty minutes later, the Barracudas arrived. Their captains were caught up about the orders and began the unloading of their troops. Forty men should not take more than a few minutes to unload. And it took a few minutes to disembark the forty men. Standing at attention in the heat was not an experience they ever had and ever dreamed about in their nightmares.

The sweat was profuse. Coming from spring to this summerlike heat strained the soldiers. The minutes passed, and their water discharges were notable. The shirts, which were blue, under their armor were drenched. The body water drenched their armpits. This became a scene of sweat and perspiration.

Finally, a call to relieve them of their poor posture. Standing at attention in this heat was going to be their nightmare from now on. A soldier came back and reported to Commander Stanton.

Rushing to the point where the other soldier was at, they looked at the scan screen. There seemed to be a room under the ruins of this so-called city.

Stanton ordered the soldiers to begin digging. This was not a welcome assignment. The lineup went one by one to remove their armor and to dig out their shovels. This was a ritual that the Romans were used to; nowadays, soldiers were not diggers anymore. They carried weapons so much more terrifying than spears, but shovels were an odd tool to them.

Digging in this heat transformed their nightmares. It was not just hot and extremely humid; they had to work their muscles in this heat. Water was needed. The Barracudas had some, but very quickly they ran out of water. This became a moment of planning and logistics.

These were part of the army and its movements. The armed forces always had logistics wherever they went. At this time, logistics was nearly useless, as operations were a day or two at most. They needed no logistics where there was no resistance. This was not an easy question to answer.

A captain gave the order for two of his men to find a source of water quickly. The sun was near setting, and yet the heat was present. It was intense that one the soldier fainted. This became a badly planned operations. On top of it, Sihi called in at this precise moment.

"Did you find them?" This was his first statement. He knew nothing of the problems they experienced here.

"Sir, no, I have yet to find them, sir." Stanton panicked, and his voice reflected this feeling.

"What the hell is going there?" Sihi was losing his patience.

"Sir, we are digging in the ground at a place where we found a room in the ground. However, our soldiers are running out of water. One of them collapsed. The heat is unforgiving, sir." Stanton tried to give the image to Sihi.

"I do not give a shit how many soldiers you lose. I want these escapees back in Central Chicago tomorrow. Do you understand?" Sihi showed his displeasure.

"Sir, yes, sir." Stanton was panicked and now terrified.

Stanton thought after his call hung up. He could not continue to have his men work in these conditions. He had to give them a break. So he did. This was not difficult; it was only going to be difficult if he cannot find these two morons who escaped. Why would you escape?

Sunset was magical. None of them saw it happened. They were all on their boats; they were away from the sun. It was as if they were allergic to the sun's rays. They should be. Some of them had serious second-degree sunburn.

The night was opening its arms. The commander ordered the digging to resume. It went with much less issues. The sense of panic, which lived in Stanton, was still alive, and it made him uneasy.

They uncovered a metal box that was under ten feet of soil. This was hard work. The soldiers did not look pristine and ready for a parade. They appeared like overworked men who were dirty and filthy. Dirt and sweat covered their faces. These troops were not presentable, but Commander Stanton was proud of his men.

Without orders, the men began to try to open this metal box. They set their rifles on laser to render the metal more malleable. They were lose. All this work took way too much time. It took them about four hours to assemble them and deliver them to a corner of the world no one knew about. This digging and piercing metal took them nearly six hours. This took too much time. What if Swinthun and Kaylee escaped already? Panic mutated into anger and frustration. He took a deep breath. He knew it was not his men's fault; this was the dealing of the cards—he had to make lemonades with his lemons. He never understood this last idea; he never had lemonade.

Finally, they were in the room. It was all metallic. There was nothing else in this room. It was as if it was a dud for them to work on while his escapees ran away. One of his men found something.

It seemed to be a door. The very faint lines on the metal gave it away. Again, they set their rifles to make this so-called-door more pliable to their will.

CHAPTER 28

T HE SOUNDS BECAME a reality. Kaylee entered a marketplace. There were people walking, and others were screaming something. She was overtaken by the sounds and bustling action. The noise was so present, and the people did not seem to care about her being there.

There were a lot of people like her. Asians. The people who attracted eyeballs were her companions: Swinthun, rose, Serge, and Stephen. Caucasians.

After a look, people moved on. There seemed a better place to be at when an arrow appeared above them. This was when Kaylee came back to reality. This was all artificial: the lights, the sky, and even the birds. They were in a tunnel, and this was dreary of a thought. The AI made this more livable of a reality. Then an arrow appeared.

No one cared about it, but the new people were the only ones who did care about it. They followed the direction of these arrows. The pursuit of the arrows led them to a bright room.

The AI came back. "We need to remove your locators. Please remove your clothes and step in the next room." This was not an issue for an AI, but for young men and women who have never been used to seeing the other sex naked, it was not an easy request.

Kaylee was the first to go naked. Trying to cover herself with her hands and arms seemed to be useless, but she tried. She skipped in the next room. It was a small room, and when the door closed, she felt unsettled and slightly claustrophobic. She breathed, and a second later, jets of hot water vapor steamed her and the whole room. It held for about thirty seconds, and then it was all sucked out. Another ten seconds after all the water fumes were pulled out, another door slid open. Kaylee stepped into the new room.

It was all white, and there was a bed. She knew she had to lie on it. Something felt uneasy in all these procedures. Nonetheless, Kaylee lay on the bed. Suddenly, she felt strapped. There was nothing holding her down, but she sensed something was. The next moment, the bed slowly flipped over.

Kaylee did not see it. She was able to hear it. There was something coming down from the ceiling. It pricked her neck, and this was the last memory. Reality mixed in with her fantasies.

Kaylee's dream was vivid. She walked on a path above a river. This river had a strange color; it was purplish. This was so odd. Kaylee stopped and looked at it. It was the algae underneath the water, which was purple. This gave the color to the water. Somehow, Kaylee was able to reach for the water and drank it. It tasted alive. It was fresh, invigorating, and replenishing. This amazed her. Then a man appeared to her right side.

This man had a beard and long hair. Kaylee reached in his hair, and it fell between her fingers. This made her so happy. She caressed his head and pulled his head toward her face. They kissed with a passion and love she never experienced. Suddenly, a light came into her dream.

The light approached and kept on getting closer. Her dream began to dissipate when, finally, Kaylee heard a voice. The voice called to her. It got louder and louder. Now, the man was long gone, and so was their kiss and passion. Kaylee brought her right hand to her eye, but it felt rubbery, and she could see the arm was not completely under her control. Attempting to rub her eye was unsuccessful, but Kaylee kept on trying.

A few minutes elapsed, Kaylee sat up on this metallic bad. It was extremely uncomfortable. Kaylee took a look up. This hurt every bone in her body. Her spine ached, her ribs felt as if it was the first time she breathed, and her arms were still under some else's control. She saw the others. They were awaking too. Kaylee seemed to be a little further than them. The nurse was brought the light, and whose voice was now in full volume asked her questions. Kaylee answered them with no difficulty, but she was eager to go back to that dreamy world.

Kaylee asked the nurse, "Why am I so groggy?"

The nurse smiled and explained, "Your locator was removed, and the grogginess will be gone in a few minutes."

Then somehow the question popped out of Kaylee. "What are you going to do with the locators?" The nurse smiled even more. She helped Kaylee up off her bed and walked her to a screen.

The nurse was maybe a meter and a half. Her strength was not to be the issue for anyone. Her grasp of Kaylee's shoulder was solid. It was solid and comforting. The lady turned on a screen. Kaylee could see soldiers at the AI room. Then some of them ran off to catch something. This scene puzzled Kaylee; she looked at the nurse dumbfounded.

Her belong nurse began laughing. After her burst of laughter, she stated, "There is an animal difficult to catch, and we implanted your locator in it. So they have four targets going all around, and they have no idea why and who these are. Except they are you." Kaylee computed, and, finally, she got it. She put her hand on her hair.

The hair was matted and full of sweat remains and other dirt. It felt good to feel her hair again. She smiled, and the others who were listening showed their signs of happiness too.

CHAPTER 29

THE SOLDIERS CONTINUED to figure out how to open the only door they could find.

Stanton began to show his frustration. What was he going to find? What was he going to tell General Sihi? What would happen to his next promotion if he cannot get pass this door? All these questions gave him the impression that he was drowning, but he did not experience drowning but somehow knew he was. This was too much. He needed air.

Stanton stepped outside of the AI room. He took a deep breath of warm and soggy air. He looked up; it appeared to be another potential rainfall and soon. This was the best his mind could process. The military stuff was too much. How could he ever expect himself to lead men? This was not even the war his father told him about. It was just a chase across some small burned-out village.

Then Sihi's call was on.

"Did you find them?" Sihi asked.

"Sir, we are in the process of breaking down a door to have access to them, sir," Stanton responded.

"How many hours ago was this in operation?" Sihi knew the answer already.

"Sir, it has been about an hour since we attempted . . .," he stuttered out.

"So in that hour, do you think they were just in there waiting for you?" Sihi asked very sarcastically.

"Sir, no . . ." Stanton knew an outburst would come.

Then out of nowhere, Kaylee's signal came on. In his mind, her signal ran across the city and was about to exit the city.

Immediately, Stanton screamed to his men to follow that signal. This was odd for him, as he was more used to giving his orders virtually. At this moment, it came out of his mouth.

Sihi could sense something was happening. A second after this realization, he, too, could find Kaylee signal. The next second, it was Swinthun's. The next breath, Valdez and Dubois came on too. Somehow in his mind, Valdez and Dubois were not chasing Kaylee or Swinthun. What was happening?

The image was the same for its soldiers and Sihi, but there was a reason for him to be the general. He thought for a second that the patterns were not recognizable. It was a pattern that was too erratic and too scattered. The answer arrived.

General Sihi told Stanton to stop his men. Surprised by this, Stanton asked again, and again the answer came and it was the same. Stanton, startled, recalled his men. Sihi knew something was not right. Why would you run and no one would see you?

"Sir, what do we do now?" Stanton asked his general.

"Hm." This was a response marking thinking. "How far did you get with the door?" General Sihi asked.

"Sir, we barely made a dent on this door. We never saw this metal before, sir" Stanton responded.

"Why would you make a room detectable but a door nearly indestructible?" This was a question not needing an answer.

"Sir?" Stanton was not the best at recognizing the quality of the question. Sihi ignored his subordinate.

"Commander, try to find other entrances and figure out if you can open those doors," Sihi ordered.

Stanton, with his connection to the Interweb, communicated with his troops. The men dissipated quickly in the woods and across the surroundings of the town.

Stanton was not sure why, but he knew his general was smarter than most.

A slow walk did not help Stanton's situation. His anxiety was still present. This made it uneasy to be in his position. Commander was his position; nonetheless, he thought constantly, *It's useless, and you are army meat.*

This was an expression of the people who were sacrificed for the need of the army. This was his feeling. His options ran across his mind. None of them were appetizing. The only one making any sense was, *If I can find a door, should I take it and not alert anyone?* This was treachery, and there were so many other issues attached to it. He was not able to sort them out. He felt trapped.

CHAPTER 30

FEELING BETTER, KAYLEE, Swinthun, Rose, Serge, and Stephen walked around town. This was an odd term. The town was in a tunnel, and all of the stimulation was artificial. It was all held up together by the AI. Was this any way to live?

This was the only way to live if there were North American raids to take children. Children were the core essence of what humanity had become. The hope lived only if children were around. There was no hope otherwise.

The youth was the only way to see how humanity could ever reach the next step. What was this next step? The question the five of them asked themselves a lot was, what was in space?

The sound of waves and birds were all artificial, but these made the images so real. All of a sudden, a crackling voice came on.

"Kaylee McCloud, please come to room A-1-102," the AI said. Then an arrow showed her the way.

"We will see you after you have your meeting," Valdez uttered. His eyes were on Kaylee.

"Yeah, I'll see you guys later," Kaylee answered.

"Don't take too long," Serge added.

Kaylee walked away from her group and followed the arrows. In the corner of her eyes, she saw Serge slapping his own head. What was he doing?

Room A-1-102 was in tunnel A, level 1, and the room 2 of that level. Kaylee wondered, *Why do you need to refer to the first level twice? Was it that nice?* The comment was in her head, but it made her smile. She walked in the room.

The room was a room. There was a couch this time. It was an old couch. There was nothing else. This was an odd room to be called at. Kaylee walked in, and the door closed behind her. She took a seat on the couch. The AI voice came on.

"Hello, Kaylee." The AI was still scratchy, but there was a personal touch in her crackling voice.

"Hello," Kaylee responded.

"I sense you are wondering why I called you in this room," the AI continued.

"Yes, that is a question I had," Kaylee admitted.

"I asked you here to have a personal conversation." The AI was more personal.

"A personal conversation?" Kaylee wondered.

"You know my name is Kaleah. You wonder why that is?" The AI began the conversation.

"I wondered, but I was not able to solve this puzzle." Kaylee was intrigued.

"I also mentioned you were Hara." The AI took a pause. This was so human. "I told this because Kaleah was your mother." The AI took another pause. "She was one of my main programmers. She melded her mind with the AI," AI stated.

"What?" Kaylee was not able to integrate all the information.

"Your mother's personality and information were integrated in my system." The AI reinforced its position.

"Wow. Give me a minute here." Kaylee was out of breath, and this news was startling. Then Kaylee came back with another question. "Was it painful?" This was a statement to ensure her mother did not have any pain when integrating with the AI.

"No, it did not hurt her," The AI told her.

"Why did she let herself into you?" It was an awkward question, and it was badly asked too.

"Kaleah was the head of our space division. She was the one who knew that we were nearly ready to travel through space." The other piece of information kicked Kaylee again.

"Wow!" All this conversation was like being in a fistfight and getting punched several times in the abdomen.

"Are you all right, Hara—I am sorry, Kaylee?" The AI voice showed more human traits than ever before.

"Yeah, it is a lot to digest," Kaylee admitted.

"I am sorry, there is more." The AI scared Kaylee with this statement.

"All right, give it to me." Kaylee's posture was as if she was about to shoulder a boulder that had been rolling down the hill.

"We need you to be integrated too," the AI stated.

"What?" Kaylee's tone was one of resistance to that idea.

"I am sorry, Kaylee," the AI apologized to the young woman.

"Why do you need me to get integrated to you?" The young woman was now resistant.

"Please let me explain." The AI paused; it waited for Kaylee's anger and denial to hit her. Then it continued. "We need you to integrate with us but in a robot body," the AI said.

"Why?" Kaylee's youth and beauty were negating the idea.

"We understand your reluctance. We need you as a robot because we are not sure about the planets we will be hitting. We have an idea of them and their gravity, but we are possibly wrong," the AI explained.

"Oh, shit!" This was her feeling at this time.

"We judged you to be a strong-willed woman and a fair person. Hence, this is the reason you were selected," the AI continued.

"I was wanting children and having a family." Kaylee teared as those words hit. It seemed to be the third stage of her mourning happening.

"We understand this. We would take your eggs and mate them in vitro if you want." Romance and lust were not the first quality of an AI, and this showed.

Kaylee was sitting on the couch with her knees above her waist. This was her fifth stage. She was pensive and considering the information. This was a lot to digest. How do you manage this? It was a life to shed away and an almost eternal life to live.

The thought did not scare her; it terrified her. This would be the end of her desire to be with a man, enjoy carnal pleasure, and have the possibility of having children. This would all be gone. There would be continuation of her gene line, but it would not be the same. How would it be for her children to have a robotic mother? What was she asking herself? This made no sense.

Kaylee was pensive and wanting to ask so many things to Kaleah. There were so many queries, but no voice carried those ideas. Darkness came upon her. The thought of not tasting anything or feeling the touch of the warming sun ran across her mind. Kaylee, tired and overwhelmed, leaned on the armrest and closed her eyes. She needed to take a nap. This was more than too much to handle. This was aggressively over Mount Everest overwhelming; the human mind cannot process all this information.

Waking from a nap was different from deep night sleep. Your saliva was under your cheek, and your confusion was evident to anyone looking in. Your dreams were not as satisfying as the one she had when she was under. This was a rough wake-up. Kaylee stretched out, and her neck was hurting her. This was not a good sleep at all.

Kaylee wanted to resume negotiation but knew there was nothing to negotiate. It was too life ending, despite no death. The AI voice knew this and asked, "Are you all right, Kaylee?"

"No, not really," Kaylee uttered. "You know what you are asking is so out there and wild. I do not know what to think about it," she continued.

"We know. It is not just a consideration—it is a sacrifice," the AI stated.

"Can I think about this?" Kaylee asked.

"As we are shuttling off tomorrow, we need you to answer this. The transition to the robotic body would happen latest tomorrow morning." The AI let her know in case there was something she wanted to do.

"I don't know." This was near acceptance; she was still hopeful for her life, which she had never lived. Tears stopped, hope was nearly gone, and acceptance peeked its head.

"Kaylee, it is hard to let go of your life, but you will help thousands find a new life and create new societies." The AI sent her last arguments to get her to become its robot.

"I don't know." Kaylee's voice was much less about resistance and more about living her life until she became a robot. Digestion of the news was not good.

"Can the transfer be completed on the spaceship?" Kaylee tried to buy as much time as she could. This was the sign of her acceptance of the idea.

"No. Lack of equipment on the spaceship makes it too difficult to complete this transmission," the AI answered.

"Does this mean you are not coming with us?" Kaylee came to a realization.

"You are right, my dear. We are not joining you on this trip," the AI answered.

"Why not?" Kaylee clamored.

"It is because we are an old model that has been patched up so many times. We are not suitable for the travel. You are," the AI admitted.

"No." Tears came back. These were not flows of anger or resistance; they were signs of losing your mother forever.

Quiet came on to the room. The silence was near eternal. Kaylee had traces of tears on her cheeks. There was no need to wipe them away. Her pensive state was nearing its end. Accepting the new responsibility was her goal.

HENRI NGUYEN

Kaylee thought of the new responsibility she had acquired by her mild yes to the AI. It became a good news kind of news, but to whom would she tell this to? No one was close enough for her to share this news. This was another moment of sadness for Kaylee. At that moment, her realization that tonight was going to be last night for her as a human grew to be too much for Kaylee.

Walking out of the room, Kaylee wanted to complete all she ever desired. What would be first? Sex with a man? She had never been with a man before. There were too many ideas in her head. She was no longer sure of what to do first. Kaylee just took the first step out of the room. All she knew was tonight had to be the night of her life.

The market was getting quieter. The night opened its arms, at least according to the AI. People wrapped up their stalls, and most of them were home already. Kaylee looked at the partially empty market. There were even less people whom she could share her news with. She walked a few steps and a few more. Less and less people were present. Sadness filled her up.

Serge ran behind her and caught up with her.

"Hello," Serge let out.

"Hello. Where is everyone?" Kaylee asked him.

"Uh, Swinthun and his sister are in for the night. Stephen is somewhere. I am no longer his superior and no longer have the connection to the Interweb, so I don't know." He smiled, and he exposed all that he knew.

"So it is you and me?" Kaylee smiled back as she made the statement in a question form.

"Yeah, do you want to go have a meal?" Serge invited Kaylee to do something, which was odd and unusual. A few hours ago, he was chasing Kaylee and Swinthun. Now he was beside her.

"Sure. What should we eat?" It was sarcastic, as food was still not that plenty and not that varied.

"We could have a yeast bar." They both looked at each other and laughed.

"Sounds delicious," Kaylee added to the yeast bar invitation.

The yeast bar was no more than a bar with proteins made out of bacteria. This was the best source of proteins. This was not the tastiest. It was like a wooden bar chewed up and spewed out in a form of a brownish bar. This was as yummy as it got. Nonetheless, Kaylee was focused on having the best night as she could.

"Have you ever considered tonight as your last night?" Kaylee asked Serge.

"I have had many nights when I thought it might be my last night. Why?" Serge wondered.

"I have been selected for a body replacement, and my mind would be transferred to a robot," she spilled out as she needed to.

"Oh, shit! How are you taking all this?" He did not have to ask who made her this offer; it could only be the AI.

"I accepted. So tonight is my last one." Kaylee wanted to speed this conversation up.

"I understand. What will you do when you are a robot?" Serge did not get the pressing matter.

"Serge, I do not care to talk about my next mission. I want to get to my night. Are you the one?" She got to a more direct way to get to Serge.

"Oh, of course. If you want to, I will," he stammered out.

The night began with their lips approaching each other. They effleuraged each other and then locked on each other. It was her first kiss. It was wet and warm; his lips were full and soft. These moments made her feel new sensations.

Her insides were feeling so light. Kaylee felt the new moments of lust. She wanted to rip his uniform out and feel his skin. This was a strong desire. She began unzipping his suit, and when her hand touched his skin, it was ecstatic.

Her hand felt as if they discovered new lands. It was fantastic to feel his skin. His chest was hairy. It was soft, and her hand ran across his plumage. Then their lips separated for a second. Their eyes found each other, and for a second, their vision was perfect. Then the lips returned to their locking moment. It was euphoria. Her ragged shirt shed, and skin on skin happened.

Carnal pleasure was difficult to define, but if you asked Kaylee, she would answer, "I want more." The kissing continued. Her neck, her cheeks, and her chest. His kissing of her chest made her wet in her vagina. This was an extraordinary moment.

This moment was so blissful; she was in full lust moment. Kaylee was drunk in lust, and this was a normal moment. Until Serge stared at her and his erection entered. Kaylee felt it. It was as if her body was made more complete with what his erection took inside of her. It brought her pleasure again and again. Upon each thrust, pleasure was built up. It was fantastic.

CHAPTER 31

G ENERAL SIHI WAS under stress. He wondered why and how Kaylee and Swinthun hid underground.

This was a mystery to him. This did not matter, as he did not have the escapees. Then the commission was on. They called him to testify. This was not good news.

"High Commissioner," he began.

"General Sihi, where are we at with the escapees?" the high commissioner interrupted the general.

"They are underground in Laos. We are working on getting in their hideout." The general made it sound better than it really was.

"Please do not play with me. I saw the same information that you did. They are running out there. Why did you pull back the soldiers!" The high commissioner yelled at this point.

"Sir, I pulled them back because these were not the escapees. On top of it, there were signals for Captain Valdez and Lieutenant Dubois, which did not compute with their mission. I do not know what happened to them, but I know these signals were not them," Sihi tried to explain.

"How did they replicate our signal, and how did our satellites pick up on it as them?" The high commissioner showed his lack of experience with military operations.

"It could be a signal echo or a replica or even a mirror signal." The general made sure not to define the terms upon seeing his lack of experience.

"Get them. Just go get them!" The high commissioner realized he placed his foot into his mouth.

"Yes, sir," Sihi responded as if he cared.

The call ended. Sihi was back in his thought of how and why the events happened the way they did. He theorized that they must have known this hideout. The next questions came along: how, and, more importantly, what was next?

On his desk, there was a map feature. He opened the application. A giant map of Southeast Asia came up. He looked at it. The Philippines was a set of archipelago of islands. South of it were more small islands. There was nothing for somebody to live on. These were not the target for his escapees. Australia was a large island, but it had nothing either. Where would they go?

It was lunchtime for Sihi. He called up for a meal. A young and very sexy young woman brought his dish. He admired her legs and felt them. Then he proceeded with eating and continued to think about his escapees and where they would go. This made little sense to him. Actually, it made absolutely no sense to him.

There was a lot of water. Then it dawned on him—what if they are under the water? Immediately, he called Commander Stanton.

"Commander, send your Barracudas out to sea and check under the water," Sihi stated.

"Sir, yes, sir. Should I stop looking for other exits, sir?" Stanton asked.

"Yes, stop that. Check the bottom of the sea," Sihi reiterated.

"Sir, yes, sir," Stanton agreed.

The order was sent out. The soldiers were near exhaustion and went to their Barracudas. They wanted to just get off this burned-out city. There was nothing to call city anymore. It was a dust bowl with nothing else alive in it.

It took about twenty minutes before the sonars were onto the bottom of the sea. There was nothing for a while. Until a ping came back. Then a second ping followed by a third. The tunnel was revealed.

The commander was advised of this finding; immediately, he alerted the general. This was news. Now, who would build this tunnel? And how was it built? Most importantly, who was in this tunnel? There were many more questions, but Sihi was interested in the who more than the how.

"Find me an entrance hole in that tunnel," Sihi ordered.

"Sir, yes, sir," Stanton responded.

"Commander, if you do not find an entrance, blow up the whole thing," Sihi thought out loud.

"Sir, yes, sir." This statement surprised Stanton. Sihi appeared to know more, and he was not willing to share.

Commander Stanton gave the order. The captain of one of the Barracudas responded to his order, "We have no depth charges, sir."

The next question came fast. "Why?"

The answer came just as fast. "We left in a hurry, and depth charges did not seem an important armament to bring along, sir." This made sense, but it was enraging. This was going to delay his progress, and he would have to explain it to General Sihi.

The captain called the Bend base. Its response was even more upsetting. There were no Barracudas left on the west coast. They would have to call up the two of the east coast. Somehow, for all the money in the world, they only had four Barracudas.

It would take about eight hours for the Barracudas to be on the shores of Laos. This would take too long. Stanton did not want to contact General Sihi. This was a difficult moment; he dreaded it. Then, as if his ears were burning, General Sihi called Stanton.

"How far are we?" Sihi asked.

"Sir, we have begun the bombardment, but we ran out of depth charges, and we have contacted the armory. It will take us eight hours to resume the operation, sir." This was a lie, all white maybe, but Stanton believed it would disarm the general and this would make the delay more acceptable.

"Goddamn it. Eight hours! Really. Seriously. Keep me updated," General Sihi burst out.

"Sir, yes, sir." It worked. It was a short outburst, and he did not blame anyone.

Sihi was in turn called by the high commissioner. This call came from his private line. This was odd.

"Sir," Sihi answered the call.

"How is the operation going?" the high commissioner asked.

"It is ongoing, sir." The general did not know what else to say.

"So you did not capture the escapees. What happened to you, Sihi?" the high commissioner said.

"Sir?" Sihi felt trapped and did not know which side to take.

"You were a solid soldier, and you always knew how to manage the expectations of your superiors. Now you seem overwhelmed. Deep breath, Sihi. You will survive this moment. After, we shall see." It was said with a tone of disappointment.

"Sir, I can explain . . .," Sihi began to say before he was interrupted.

"Sihi, don't worry, you will be useful to us." This was a direct hit to Sihi's ego and fear.

"Sir, please . . . I will get the escapees and more kids for you," Sihi pleaded.

"We shall see." The high commissioner disconnected the line.

He was gone. Sihi saw darkness all around him. All this life would be gone. All this was due to two idiots who decided to run away. How can this be? Commander Schilling was his second in command. *How could he do this to me?* The night lights were closing on Sihi.

HENRI NGUYEN

CHAPTER 32

UST OR LOVE? This was her question when she woke up beside the only man she will ever sleep with in her life. She felt the warmth of his body. There was nothing she would regret from this decision. It was beautiful. He was sweet and gentle. He cared for her in this moment of vulnerability. Her question continued to travel in her mind, *Lust or love?*

This was her father's lesson to her. She recalled his words: "Do not be laying all of your life on the hostel of lust. Know that love carries more than water to your partner. It will make you a stronger person and make you do amazing sacrifice." Those words were stained in her brain.

When her father said those words, she was eight years old. She had no idea what they meant. As the years went by, they clarified and gave her more meaning. Until today. It was her first time, and maybe it would be the last time too; the words made more sense on this day.

Kaylee cared for Serge, but if he would die today, she would cry, but her mission would be completed. Was this test a relationship has to go through to be real? She was still unclear, and the words of her father did not help one bit more.

Sitting between Serge and a wall, Kaylee could see a barrel and boxes around them. Not having a room was not a problem for them. They wanted to do the act, and it was completed. Considering all facts, Kaylee needed to leave. Her next mission was the hardest one. The feel of flesh was indescribable. All her nerves were alive, and now, they were as if dead. *How could this be so different from a few hours ago?* This was sad and a mark for the end of Kaylee's human life.

Getting up, Kaylee stepped over Serge, who was asleep. He looked so cute; it was her last view of the only man she ever would sleep with. On the other side of Serge, Kaylee donned her bra, shirt, pants, and shoes. This was about it.

Walking away, tears pretended to be waterfalls off the cheeks of the young woman. Was this love or lust? She will never know the answer to this question.

Kaylee walked around for a little bit. It was dark, and she was in agreement with this lack of light. Room A-1-102 was somehow her destination. When Kaylee go there, the doors opened. She entered, and her face was carved by the flowing tears. Erosion or not, she was present and ready for her next mission. This was her answer; it was lust, but it was wonderful lust.

The AI came on and opened a door. Kaylee entered this new room. It was like any other rooms in this maze of tunnels and rooms. A bed came from the floor. Kaylee looked at it. Her tears flowed even harder. It became hard to see where her human life would end.

Kaylee lay on the bed. She waited. A minute later, another bed came up. This bed had the robot body on it. It was all metallic. There was no sign of its sex; as it should not. The head opened, and wires popped out. Kaylee worried, but not about the wires. She had anxiety and did not know how to say good-bye to her body. She took a deep breath.

The next second, small robots made their entrance. The AI voice welcomed her. "I know this is a difficult moment. You are not going to feel much after the robot gives you the sedative." As those words sank in Kaylee's brain, a prick in her right arm was felt. She felt the sensation of going to sleep.

Kaylee was laid down on the bed. Another robot began drilling into her cranium. It was precise and stopped. Then a wire was inserted. This was repeated.

Kaylee did not move a muscle. It was better for her would be the thought of any human, but the robots did not have the capacity to have those feelings.

At the same time, another robot plugged the wires out of the robot's head into a computer. Then it went to the wires for Kaylee's head and plugged them too. It was about to begin.

The transfer was as expected. A lot of monitoring followed by a lot of time. It was as boring as it would be for a child to be alone in a room with no toys. The robots were in charge, and it seemed to be going well.

The hours came and passed. The tone in the tunnels woke up. Everyone was doing what needed to be done. There was no reason think otherwise. No savior was coming today or tomorrow. Work was your only savior. Work was the reason for you being alive. The next life was an old Buddhist idea; this idea was nearly gone. Was it a good thing? No one knew, but everyone was at work. This gave them a reason to live.

Serge woke up like everyone, and he was alone and naked. The ladies and gentlemen passed him; they did not raise their eyes. It did not matter to them; they were not the one who was naked. He got dressed as quickly as he could. He walked off the scene of his first time too.

This was amazing; he felt more alive. There were Rose and Swinthun.

"Swinthun," Serge called out. When the man turned around, they smiled at each other. He continued. "Did you see Kaylee?"

"No, I have not." Swinthun stared at Serge. There was something different. He was not sure what it was.

"OK. I will see you guys later," Serge uttered out as he passed them. He walked fast and he was happy. Swinthun was amazed how Serge integrated the news of going into space well.

This was a random search. Serge did search for her, but this was a different type.

The afternoon came, and the robot was disconnected from the computer. On the other bed, Kaylee was lifeless. The robots finished collecting her eggs and the organs that may be needed for transfers. Kaylee lay on the bed. Her lips were blue, and so was her skin. This was a strange color for a human; she was dead.

The other bed was where the new Kaylee was. She was inside the robot. Lights came on. Her brain was active. The last robot closed the panel. The brain was no longer visible.

Inside, Kaylee was wondering if she was awake or still asleep. This was odd, because Kaylee was able to talk to herself. Was she in a dream? She tried to open her eyes. It was hard to complete this task. Finally, they opened. Kaylee saw a white room. There was nothing to it. There was no one here.

After sitting up on the bed, Kaylee looked at her hand. It was a metal hand. It felt weird; she could see it, but there was no feeling of it. As if it was not true, Kaylee held the edge of the bed. There was no feeling again.

She was feeling sad and wanting to cry, but this seemed to stop right there. There was no connection to anything to complete the act of crying. She was just sad.

Getting to her feet was easy. There was no loss of balance, no stiffness. She did not feel strength or weakness, but she could see the energy level. She had another five days of battery. This was different and odd.

HENRI NGUYEN

Walking to the door was easy, and opening the door was a little bit too easy. Kaylee was at ease with this body. The only piece the AI did not tell her was the lack of real contact with touch and feelings. This was very strange for the person inside this body.

Walking out was as if she always was in this body. She came to a mirror and saw herself. She was all metallic as she saw the robot the first time. Her head was a face with eyes, a nose, and a mouth. There were no ears. Her neck was adequate. Her chest was no different from anyone else, except women. She had no breast and no nipples. Kaylee looked at herself when she heard the AI voice.

"Hello, Kaylee. How do you feel in the new body?"

"It is fine. I am functioning as well as expected," Kaylee responded in her head.

"I see your functioning is optimal. We are connected until you leave. After this evening, it will be the end for us to communicate," the AI said honestly.

"I see. I have your vast knowledge in my databank. This should be sufficient," Kaylee said.

"Do you want me to call you Kaylee or Hara?" the AI asked her.

"I still want the connection to my human past. I would like to be called Kaylee," Kaylee responded to the query.

"That will fine. From now on, I will communicate in binary code. It is easier for me. I am old," the AI said.

"That is fine." Although Kaylee wondered if the AI was trying itself with humor.

Serge found Stephen. They walked across the market. Out of Stephen's left side, Kaylee came out of a ladder. Stephen and Serge did not notice the robot and definitely did not know it was Kaylee.

Walking away, Serge and Stephen heard this call: "Serge, Stephen." They did not recognize the voice. Nonetheless, it called their name. They turned around and saw this robot. It was nothing different, except it walked, talked, and seemed to know them. When they passed the robot the first time, they did not stop at wondering, wait, this is a robot, the only one here. This was a novel item in the world, and it knew their names.

Facing the robot, both men were amazed, and yet the questions came faster than answers.

"Hello?" Serge asked or said; he was not sure himself.

"Hello, Serge, and hello, Stephen," Kaylee said clearly.

"Who are you?" Stephen asked with a tone that said, "I am in a panic here."

"I am sorry. I forgot I am in here. This is Kaylee," she stated.

"What?" Serge said very loudly.

"How can it be you?" Stephen added.

"It is a very long story, but in the end of it, I am in the robot," Kaylee said.

"What? I mean, this morning, you were . . . you know," Serge said.

"Yes. It was amazing. Thank you, Serge," she said with no emotions in the voice and words, but the feelings were present in the words.

"Wow! I am feeling dizzy suddenly," Serge uttered out.

"Whoa!" Stephen stepped in to catch his fall.

"I am sorry, guys. This is me. I am set for the next mission." Those words landed as a ball landed in mud.

At the same time, an explosion above their heads was heard.

CHAPTER 33

T HE DEPTH CHARGES were launched from the Barracudas. The explosions were at a regular basis.

Stanton observed the operations. He felt queasy about this set of blowouts underwater. He did not really know what was in the tunnel he was trying to eliminate. This seemed to be a killing en masse for a general. Did he know what was in the tunnel?

There had to be a reason for the general to want this mission to go the way he called it. It had to be. Then a call came in. It was the general. It was the high commissioner.

"Sir," Stanton answered.

"How is the mission going, son?" the high commissioner asked.

"It has started. We are not seeing results yet," Stanton stated.

"Continue, son. We need to see results," the high commissioner stated.

"Sir, may I ask what those results are?" Stanton needed illumination.

"Son, there are moments in life when you need to ask yourself, do I need to know more than I do at this moment? The answer will come in time, and this will help you as general when you get there," the high commissioner answered without answering.

"Sir, I am dropping bombs on a tunnel and looking for three people. Why are we not trying to break the door?" Stanton insisted.

"Son, think a little more. Maybe the three of them are in the tunnel, or maybe there are more people down there." the high commissioner spewed out.

"What? Are we attempting to kill more people? Is the population of the city in there? Can we do this?" The questions gained ground in Stanton's mind.

"Son, again, we are the strongest power in the world. Who is to tell us what to do? So do your job and take a deep breath." The line cut out immediately as those words landed.

Stanton's head spun. The questions were between what was correct to do and what secrets could they possibly be? He sat down; he needed to. His hands wrapped his face. What was he doing? How could he face himself? Was the rank of general worth it to him?

As time went on, more bombs dropped in the water. Then Stanton regained some life.

"Lieutenant, stop the bombing," Stanton ordered.

"Sir?" the Lieutenant questioned him.

"I gave an order, Lieutenant!" Stanton screamed out.

"Sir, yes, sir." The lieutenant was clear on the order.

"Order the rest of the men to resume opening that door," the commander ordered again.

"Sir, yes, sir." The lieutenant communicated the order to the soldiers.

Stanton made a decision. This was all his. He would have to live with it. It was easier to live with it than a mass murder of people. This made him breathe with greater ease. Sweat was all over the man; partly, it was another hot day in the tropics, but more importantly, the stress he lived through in the past minutes made him sweat even more.

Twenty minutes later, Stanton was back on land. He wanted to have news about that door. Then a call from the general came in. Stanton dismissed it. Another call arrived. Stanton dismissed again. This was going to be a run for every second on the clock.

Stanton arrived, and the door was giving more than ever, but no soldier was able to get through it. It was not quite there yet.

The soldiers were sweating and giving all their might to open this door. The top corner was bent. This allowed some of the explosives to be slipped in. A detonation was about to happen. They all cleared the area, and, boom, the door was open.

As the smoke dissipated, Stanton grabbed his rifle and ordered a squad to follow him. This was unusual for Stanton; he was more a commander who gave orders. The last time he was in action was about ten years ago. At the time, he chased a lady who escaped North America.

The hallway went to another door. This fact made Stanton take a deep breath, and his head tilted to his right. This was not a mark of admiration. The next second, he ordered more explosives to be used.

Waiting for the second door to be open, Stanton paced. His mind ran cross the panoply of thoughts. There was the potential of failure. Then the next thought jumped in his mind. *What if I disappear too? They won't find me.* This was a silly vision, he thought. He continued to dissuade himself of his thought, *There would be soldiers chasing you for the rest of your life.* This tired him out; the heat was also another energy-sucking aspect of his life.

An hour passed. An hour and a half. This was too much. Stanton became impatient. Then a detonation happened. He sensed this would be the one for him to catch these foolish escapees. His desire was to

HENRI NGUYEN

end this chase, and at the same time, it would end his thought about a potential escape.

Stanton was at the head of a squad. His men were less eager than he was. They were tired, and this showed through their dirty and disheveled uniform. He entered another dark corridor. He turned on his flashlight, which was at the tip of his rifle.

His light cut the darkness in slivers. Each sliver revealed concrete. This was an oddity to Stanton. He always had the notion of Asians living on dirt and having no idea of technology. This was a rude awakening. Stanton walked slowly, and his rifle was aiming where the light slit.

As Stanton and his squad proceeded, encounters with going down repeated themselves. This was an ear-popping experience. Finally, they reached a corridor where noise was heard. It was people. Screaming and crying came through the heavy concrete. The final gate had to be blown up again.

This took another twenty minutes. The detonator was in Stanton's hand. There was little hiding and shielding themselves. Hence, they had to give distance from the detonation. They climbed a level up. The whole squad was near exhaustion. Their eyes were half open, and Stanton knew this. He push the button. A large explosion happened. A large cloud of dust and small concrete particles whiffed up into their tunnel.

Smoke and a taste of sand were not welcomed by anyone. The screaming and crying were no longer in the air. Swearing and spitting replaced the sounds of people. It was not a pleasant moment. Eventually, those sounds disappeared too.

When the squad entered a larger tunnel, there was no light, no noise, no life, but there were stalls and produce for sale. This was an odd feeling for every one of them. It was a market; they have heard of the old idea.

Stanton kept moving forward, and his light was his guide. His left index showed his anxiety. It kept on tapping on the side of the trigger. He did not want to be shot at. Who could do this? He was the rule of the world. Who in hell would ever want to shoot at him? These ideas convinced him that he will not be shot at.

They reached the end of the tunnel, and there was no one. Not even a dead was present. The only thing present was some water. They located a crack in the tunnel, and this was due to their depth charge, but short of some water, there was not a life to explain what happened here.

Stanton thought for a second, and, next, he ordered his men to seek a covered hole in the present tunnel. *This had to be it,* Stanton thought.

It took a while for the men to search a hatch in the dark. It took another twenty minutes when a call came across in the dark. They found it. Opening it was another delay. Finally, they plied through this hatch.

Stanton landed in another market. This one had light. This was a little easier. There was also a sky, which looked the same as outside. Unlatching his left hand from the trigger, it ran on his face. His anxiety of being shot decreased, but his notion of Asian beings living without technology evaporated too.

Stanton had a stern face, and his blond hair made his face a little less serious. The next question this somber face asked himself was, *Where is everyone?*

CHAPTER 34

T HE EXPLOSIONS GOT closer and closer. Kaylee used her connection to the AI to call an emergency, and arrows showed people where to go.

Kaylee felt inside that her mind was slow to process the information shooting at her, but her robotic mind came to answers already. This was a strange feeling.

Order and calm replaced by screaming and crying were seen across the tunnel. Nonetheless, people proceeded on to the next tunnel when a message for Kaylee arrived in her mind. "Go to the next tunnel and complete the shuttle boarding. Leave as soon as you can."

This message was sent not once or twice; she received three times the same message. It was clear what was needed to be done.

In her human mind, Kaylee understood the need to save everyone. However, her robotic mind knew not everyone was going to survive this attack and not everybody was going to the shuttle. The listing was clear in her mind, robotic or human.

In a heartbeat, Kaylee proceeded to run to the next tunnel. She passed people whom she knew would be meat for the North American Army. Why would she run away and let this horror happen? She was not sure, but her mind reasoned that it was inevitable. This made her sad; this sadness did not slow her metallic legs. She reached the next tunnel. There was a train. People tried to clear the gate, but most of them were not able to.

At the gate, a woman scanned her right wrist. A red light flashed on the terminal. The barrier remained closed. There was no way to across. The gate covered the whole width of the tunnel. The next second, someone pulled the lady back, and a man tried. He failed too. Kaylee was about to do the same thing.

At the moment, she thought of her right robotic wrist to turn the gate open. At that moment, Kaylee looked back; she saw people being shocked behind her. This was the second defense level. Kaylee appeared to see kids coming through the gate.

Everyone tried to save their body and souls from the horror arriving to their lives. This was a savage moment where her human calm would crack too. This was a difficult scene to watch; her humanity was not gone, but her expression of it was no longer part of the software.

Kaylee stepped onto a loading dock. There was a train engine and five wagons. The engine train was all electronic and controlled by the AI. The first wagon seated fifty girls with two teenaged leaders. The second wagon was for fifty boys led by two male teenaged leaders. This repeated twice. The fifth wagon was a platform wagon: food, clothes, water, and a gun turret.

When a teenager passed by the gun, Kaylee saw how huge the gun turret was for humans. She understood this was her spot. As she moved to the firearm, the AI messaged her, "Your position is at the back on the weapon turret." *This was obvious, AI,* she thought.

The train was full, and it began to roll down one track. It moved relatively fast. Suddenly, the second gear kicked in. The speed was noticeably faster. The third gear shifted in; they traveled a significant speed. And to make it more impressive, the train shifted to the fourth gear. It was a ridiculous speed. Kaylee felt nothing different. Her radar screen was not affected by this crazy speed.

Despite the amazing speed, it took them three hours to reach the end point of the track. The disembarkation happened as calmly and efficiently as possible. Out of nowhere, Kaylee heard two voices calling at her. She turned her head to her left and saw Swinthun, Rose, and Serge.

"What the hell just happened!" Serge screamed at Kaylee.

"I don't know. I presume it was an attack from the North American Army," Kaylee said calmly and emotionlessly.

"Where the fuck are we at!" Serge continued screaming. His emotions were high.

"We are at the launch pad." Again, she responded as if she was a guide; no emotions and no screaming needed.

"Calm down, Serge," Swinthun said.

"Where is Stephen?" Kaylee asked at the same volume and still no emotions.

"He was not allowed in. He remained out there," Serge said with tears splitting his face.

"Follow your groups. You will be on the shuttle. I have to go do things." Kaylee sounded slightly off. They and she knew there was something to be done, and she was not going to share with them.

Swinthun and Rose joined their group. Serge joined a group where his name was on the list. Swinthun joined a group of young ladies. He seemed to be uneasy to be surrounded by young girls. This was a little odd.

Serge was in a group of boys. He felt good guiding boys; it was like the army. How can it be hard? He looked at the robotic form of Kaylee leaving. He held on to the carnal memory of holding her hand. Her skin was soft and yet had resistance to anything. This was more of a ghost than a memory. As Serge walked away, a little boy who appeared terrified held his hand.

Kaylee walked off with memories of Serge and her rolling in pleasure and carnal ecstasy. This was never to return to her life. She did not feel anything anymore. Her fingers and skin were not innervated, and this made her sheltered from the world. Being a human who experienced life's high and lows, this aspect of being a robot was difficult. There were no words, no concepts to share, as she was the only one who ever did this transfer. It was a feeling her human brain still felt and processed. It was too hard to not express this. As ideas crossed her brain, Kaylee reached the wall with a circular indentation in the wall.

Kaylee reached for a button. After pushing the red button, a wave of smoke came out of the wall, and a loud decompression sound came across the loading dock. Then a handle pushed out of the circle. Kaylee saw it and grabbed it. She pulled on it. A cylinder the size of a fifty-gallon drum popped out of the wall. She pulled and hurdled it up on her shoulder. It was a cold drum, but Kaylee would not know this.

As if Kaylee knew where the drum would end, she walked without a hesitation, and no effort was placed on her from this barrel, which showed lights and was still smoking. Kaylee reached the side of the shuttle. She placed the drum in her left hand. There were no sounds of straining or signs of heavy work. She slid the barrel into the hole of the shuttle. It fitted perfectly. It locked in, and there was a sucking sound out of the hole where the drum was placed. It was in place, and, suddenly, imagery of the shuttle and how to pilot it came on. It was the infamous information the AI transferred for her to complete the mission. This was an old-style transfer; the thought ran across her mind, even the robotic one. Kaylee's brain smiled.

The shuttle was all loaded. Kaylee walked to the front of the shuttle. There was a trap door. She stepped to the small trap door. She had enough space to bring her body through. It was very snug. It was perfectly tight. She came up. Kaylee's head heard a locking sound by her neck and then a locking noise by her arms. Then a clipping noise was at her feet. She was in the shuttle. Kaylee knew nothing of spaceship piloting, but somehow, she turned on the engine without any issues. She controlled all the levers and buttons in her mind. The shuttle was ready.

The ceiling of the dome opened. The setting sun came in aggressively. It was as if it was nighttime and the sun came out and drowned the moonlight as revenge. Kaylee called out to the crew to be ready, and she let them know the countdown—three, two, one, liftoff. The grumbling of the engines was loud and it grew. The flames under the shuttle were bright and rising in the sky.

The g-force crushed the passengers into their seats. This was not only nerve racking but also an unknown experience. A shuttle going into space had not been seen since 2011. This was a revisited experience. Most of the young children were knocked off by this event. The older ones were near the same point. Their leaders were amazed and terrified at the same time.

Kaylee lifted the spaceship. The spaceship passed the setting sun. It was marvelous. The colors of this setting sun were red, rose, aubergine, blues, mandarin, and other shades of colors. Kaylee took a look at this sight. Even a robot can admire a work of art from Mother Nature. As the spaceship escaped the lower atmosphere, the sky became more and more black. Until they attained the ionosphere, the light dimmed and on the verge of disappearance. At this altitude, objects floated in the cabin. Toys and unstrapped shoes began to float as if they were between waters.

When they reached the exosphere, there was limited gravity left. Ahead was darkness, and behind them was their birthplace. They were about to say good-bye to their only home forever. This was a cruel joke on these children. They did not know. They only knew they had to survive.

Survival was a word that meant what it meant. The idea of survival was stronger. The concept of survival was not present in their consciousness, but the idea was there. They did not know what they had to survive or even whom to do it against, but they knew what to do to precede all the danger coming to their parents and grandparents. This image was present in their sleepy minds. This was a reality.

Kaylee kicked in the ionic engine, and it shot the spaceship toward the moon. The flight was smooth. This was a trip into the unknown. The unknown was dark, and like everything dark, it was full of danger.

On the side of the moon that no one on Earth had ever seen, there was a larger spaceship. Actually, it was enormous.

At the tip of the ship was a gigantic shield. This was shining with the sun's rays bouncing off the inside of the shield. This was a solar sail and energy catcher for the ship. At the center of the shield, there was a cylindrical container that was long. It stretched into space with a set of containers followed by a large circle that was rolling. This was a living area with centrifugal force to replicate gravity. The next section was the shuttle docking area. Then along the long cylinder was another section of cargo. The ship then had a series of bubbles and a large area, finished with the engine outlet. This was monstrous.

Swinthun looked at the spaceship. He thought, a few days ago, all this was science fiction. There was no way to get out of the routine of every day. Now, every day was extraordinary, and this will be as usual as it will get. This idea amazed his mind. He felt so small. Swinthun hugged his sister and held her tight. She passed out a few minutes after being strapped to her seat.

Serge was mind blown. He could not say a word. What was there to say? Two days ago, he chased after Swinthun and Kaylee; now he was on a spaceship about to dock onto an even larger ship. This was no longer within a range of amazement anymore. Discovery was after him. The chase was lost, and discovery just dragged him along. This was mind blowing.

The docking was nice and easy. The unloading of personnel was a little slow, as most of the children were passed out. The crushing gravity and the sight of all this were too much to process through. Each leader had to take child at a time to his own bed; this took time.

Kaylee unlocked herself from her pilot position and floated in space. She was amazed despite her lack of facial expression. She got the barrel out and locked it into position on the main fuselage of the spaceship. Then Kaylee guided herself with her air booster to the airlock. She opened the hatch and walked in. She let the air come in, but Kaylee did not need it. Her own body contained enough air for a day into space. Only her brain needed air.

Everything was going according to the plan. There was no hitch in any of the operations. This worried Kaylee. Her human brain was persuaded something was going to go wrong. She thought of everything possible: *What if I malfunction? What if the ship's engine doesn't work? What if it breaks in half?* And what if they plunge into something unknown? This was a little too much; her robotic side kept things calm and saw Kaylee freak out. The robot went into shutdown to let Kaylee catch a few hours of sleep.

CHAPTER 35

COMMANDER STANTON RECEIVED a message from General Sihi.

"Commander, did you see this rocket go off into the sky?" The general was truly stunned.

"Sir, I did not see anything. I am in the tunnel, and there is no one to be found yet." Stanton tried to give him something to bite on instead of his delicious commander flesh.

"Forget about those crumbs. I want to know what the hell went into the sky. Was it a missile?" General Sihi shared his fears on top of being stunned.

"I do not know, sir. Let me contact my soldiers on top," Stanton responded.

"Yeah, do that and report to me what the hell was that." *Sihi is losing it,* thought Stanton.

Immediately, Stanton asked his soldier on top of where they were. The answer came swiftly. They reported a cloud going up into the sky. This was not a report to have. Stanton ordered them to search if there were any debris from whatever went up in the sky. Stanton took a seat and took a deep breath. *What is going on here?* he asked himself.

They walked out of the tunnel. The night was present. The cold was not at the rendezvous, though. The heat and humidity partnered to make this day exhausting. The soldiers were not going to move until tomorrow. This was a reality the commander had to come to accept.

Stanton talked to all his troops who were chasing debris. There was nothing to find, he got as message back. This was not good news. He decided to call Sihi.

"Sir, there were no debris, and no one here seemed to know what went up, sir," Stanton uttered out as he was near exhaustion too.

"What the hell? All right, retrieve your men and come home," Sihi ordered.

"Sir, yes, sir," Stanton acknowledged the order.

The general knew what the next step was. He went down to the building basement and entered the code that opened the hallway. Sihi walked to the AI room and entered his code, and the door slid. Quickly, he entered the room, and before he sat down, he screamed to the wall, "What went up in the sky!"

"Today, at 5:00 p.m., a rocket went into space." The voice was without emotions and answered with precision.

"What? A rocket? Like in the old days?" Sihi asked a little randomly.

"Yes. Rockets, like in the twenty-first century," the AI answered.

"Who would have this technology in the world?" Sihi realized the truth of the world. It was not void of technology. He was not aware of this until now.

"The Chinese were in the leading edge of AI in the early twenty-first century. The Europeans caught up to them quickly," the AI responded.

"The Chinese and the Europeans. From where the rocket took off, I would presume the Chinese is the answer," General Sihi spoke out loud. Then he asked a question to the AI, "Where would they go?"

"Per the information I have so far from our satellites, they appear to be headed to the other side of the moon." The answer came as fast as it would be expected.

"Why would you go to the other side of the moon?" General Sihi asked.

"Are you asking me to extrapolate from the information?" the AI asked.

"Why don't you?" Sihi wanted to know what a great brain could do with the little information they had.

"They could have built a base on the other side of the moon, or they are just escaping and hiding behind the moon, or they built a larger spaceship," the AI answered without a doubt or even an ounce of shame.

"Hmm. How could they build another spaceship without us knowing?" Sihi pondered out loud.

"They did keep their rocket secret from our satellites. I reviewed the closest images from their prelaunch. It seemed they had a cloaking device that hid their base and launch pad," the AI asserted.

"How could that be? This is well beyond our technological capabilities. How did they do this?" Sihi asked a question he expected no answer.

"If you are asking, how did they do it? There are theories. The electromagnetic cloaking, spatial cloaking, space-time cloaking, anomalous resonance cloaking, plasmonic cloaking, and tunneling light transmission cloaking," the AI listed out.

"Review the footage of the prelaunch and tell me how they did it," Sihi ordered.

"There seemed to be a new technology. They launched from the Mount Hardman area. This had a desert, and the image of the land was played on giant television screens," the AI answered.

HENRI NGUYEN

"Wait, they played a video and tricked us?" Sihi came around the issue.

"Simply, yes," the AI concluded.

"Shit! What options do we have at this time?" Sihi was over his head at this time.

"We have rockets that take our satellites up, but that is it. We have no spaceships," the AI answered.

"Oh, crap." Sihi's head sank between his hands.

The night grew darker for the general. He would have to talk to the high commissioner and the commission too. He began to scratch his face and did not stop. He was out of control.

The next morning, Sihi had to make the infamous call. Before he did, he looked at his face in the mirror. Sihi managed to scratch his skin off his face on his forehead, nose bridge, and left eyelid; his left eyebrow was nearly gone, and there were deep red lines on his cheeks. This was not a proud moment. He covered his signs of loss under a scarf. Then the call was placed.

"High Commissioner and Commission, I have bad news to report." Sihi was under his scarf, but he still wanted to scratch his face more now than even before.

"What bad news?" the high commissioner asked with a crack in his voice.

"They escaped us. It appears they went into space." Sihi realized what he was saying was so out there. There was no concept to introduce this. The commission, like himself, believed they were the most technologically advanced. They did not have interest in space travel, so how could poor people do this? This was an impossibility, a dream at most, but now it was a reality.

"Please say that again." The high commissioner was stunned and could not process the information passed out of the mouth of his general.

"They flew away. They went into space. We have no technology to catch them," Sihi repeated himself. No one cared that he hid his face in a scarf.

"What?" It was almost in unison this word came out of the commission.

"Yes, sir," Sihi said simply.

A science broke and blew over the commission room, which was empty. They communicated through images of themselves. They sat at home, and now uncomfortably.

"Is there anyone else left?" the high commissioner asked.

"We did not find anyone at the site we thought they escaped to," Sihi summarized.

"No one is to know about this event. Do you understand, General Sihi?" The high commissioner regained his balance. The previous news threw him off.

"Yes . . . sir." There was a pause between the words General Sihi uttered, he thought as those words came out.

"Fine. Resume operations. And again, no one is ever to know this event," the high commissioner stated and terminated the conversation.

General Sihi was stunned and wondered why. There were no issues with two escapees running into space. Then slowly, his thought was, *If they never come back, there was no reason to know.* Despite his self-inflicted injuries, General Sihi understood the high commissioner's idea.

HENRI NGUYEN

Generals did not often go to the AI room. General Sihi understood the message of his superior. He entered the AI room and uttered his code. This was of the highest importance. Then he ordered the AI to lock all the discussions about the events for the past two weeks, cloaking, space travel, and anything related to it, to be only accessed by him or the commission.

This was safe for now. If Sihi did not think of it, life would resume as it was. This was fine.

CHAPTER 36

S PACE WAS A different environment to function in. As Kaylee floated in the corridor, she saw reserves and flood banks. The fact that she floated like everyone else was a marvel for her body image, if she had one. Kaylee was now a robot. She weighed about five times more than your average person. The lack of gravity made her as light footed as all aboard.

Kaylee reached the circular ring. She slid through a bay door. She could feel gravity increasing as she got closer to the moving part of the spaceship. This was due to the centrifugal force. She reached the long and circular hallway; gravity was on. Kaylee fell onto her feet.

Kaylee could see kids being moved to their beds. Throughout most of the trip from the shuttle to this circular hallway, it was easy, but here, it became harder to move these kids to their beds. Kaylee moved forward and helped move the kids to bed.

To Kaylee, this was a cute activity—putting kids to bed. They looked so peaceful and at ease. There was nothing to scare them, at least for now. She placed a girl into her bed. She looked at her face. There was nothing evil about her. This had to be a learned attitude; how can a child be evil? She pondered about this for a little while, but there was more to do.

This exercise went on for an hour because the kids woke up for the most part.

Kaylee assembled them in the Ring. She began. "My name is Kaylee. I was designed your leader in the search and find of livable worlds. I will be giving instructions to your leaders, and you will obey them. This is not up for debate." She took a pause and continued. "We are in the section where gravity is present. This is due to centrifugal force. We will call this section the Ring. Understood?" All the little voices joined in one moment and made it as loud as Kaylee could ever hope for. She took the initiative again and talked. "You have been assigned beds. Refer to your leaders for your bed numbers. Carry on."

This moment was surreal for Kaylee. She was chosen to be the leader. This idea terrified her; she knew nothing about space travel or even about leadership. This began to feel too big for her human brain. Her robotic counterpart was not even aware of the enormity of the task ahead. This was her advantage—she needed to integrate herself to this part of the robot. Focusing on tasks needing to be completed was the key part of all of this. A section at a time, this was the way to get anywhere. Kaylee had this advantage; she needed to focus on that part of her new reality.

Preparing a ship was a hard task, but preparing a spaceship for a long travel was even harder. Kaylee was not sure if she was doing the right thing most of the first day on board. The bridge was the room where the commands were. It was a large room with seats for odd reasons, as Kaylee was the pilot of it and none of the seats could sustain her weight. She stood behind a map of the solar system.

Changing aspects of this spaceship was not evident. Why would you change anything? In the last two centuries, they were the first off the planet. This was a little daunting for Kaylee, but for Serge and Swinthun, it was the same. The terror was part of the kids' spirit. They counted all on Kaylee's skills to get out of this place.

Kaylee went about learning all these new skills. She learned all this already, as it was downloaded into her brain. She saw the calculations and the tracing of where it should lead them. Despite all this, Kaylee felt she needed to know everything and every little bit of it to be sure of what would happen soon. That was the part that terrified her, but robots did not show or have feelings. Kaylee's human brain was still in existence.

Learning the trajectory was not evident. The first jump was in the inferior part of the sun. This was an odd placement of the way to go. First, there was no up or down in space. There was a clockwise and right and left, but no up or down. The coordinates were 0-0-0. She understood the center of her map was the star of her solar system. Beyond this, it would be from the south pole—take your ship to the sun and dive under.

The theory was the speed would reach near light speed. The next part of the travel plan was to reach high speed, and a hole would open at the bottom of the sun. *What kind of hole?* was Kaylee's thought. The information from the AI computed her doubts and sent a response—a black hole. This was not a feel-good moment as an answer.

Kaylee was not sure if taking a bunch of kids to a black hole was the right way to do anything, but escaping was not the worse thought. The life on this ship would become difficult very quickly. Hence, a black hole jump would not be the worse potential solution.

The first day and second day were hard. Not everyone knew as quickly as Kaylee. Then again, her brain needed energy soon but did not forget a thing after learning it. The young children were not as definite in their learning as Kaylee.

On the third day on the ship, Kaylee was on recharge mode. Serge came up with Swinthun to see her.

"How was it?" Swinthun asked Serge.

"What are you talking about?" Serge needed clarification.

"Your night with Kaylee?" Swinthun answered with a little bit of irritability.

HENRI NGUYEN

"It was good. It was fantastic." Serge needed to tell someone.

"It would be great to know what it would be like?" Swinthun admitted.

"Wait, you've never done it either." Serge absorbed the information.

"No. I wanted to wait for the right woman. I thought it would Kaylee, but you did it with her." Swinthun showed some jealousy.

"I am sorry, but she wanted me as much as I wanted her," Serge apologized, almost.

"It is OK. I had more to take care about than you did." There was a little bit of anger left, but it was nearly gone.

"I know," Serge said as he looked at Kaylee's robotic being.

This was a hard moment for Serge. He never said anything to the lady of his first time. He stared at the robot and said nothing. His look sought a woman he once had carnal pleasure with. He longed for her, but she was no longer here. Although Kaylee was present, but she was not in the form he wanted. This was a very difficult part to get if you did not get a full explanation. He wanted it, but now, she was asleep, or whatever this robot was doing.

The three hours elapsed. Kaylee was fully recharged. Her scanners reconnected, and she could detect the presence of a man. The scanner took a minute before the equivalent of sight was on. Finally, Kaylee saw Serge. He had fallen asleep. The ring kept on spinning, and this made him slump on one of the beams while seated on a windowsill. This was adorable if you were a woman; Kaylee was a robot now.

After her first recharge, not only did Kaylee feel more able to complete all the tasks needed, but, also, her brain integrated a little bit more. There were a few parts of her that she called human. One of the last ones was her carnal memory of that night with Serge. The disconnection was smooth as her brain ordered and it happened. She walked to Serge and picked him up. Kaylee carried him to his room; she laid him down and walked away.

Her feelings for Serge were real, and yet the emotions dissipated as time went on. This was a real feeling too. Kaylee knew there were bigger things than her. Her mind told her this before she became a robot. This was a real feeling too. Her integration in the robot made her feel less; she wondered if she would be able to empathize with people or feel their pain when expressed. This was a difficult moment for her.

On the bridge, Kaylee locked her feet to the floor and began to review things to be done before the launch. This was easy when you focus and did not trouble yourself with questions of your existence before becoming a robot. This made the puddle of mud harder to handle. Screen after screen was reviewed when Swinthun showed up.

Swinthun was a hunk in the tight top he showed with. His pectorals were large, and his abdominals were strong. However, this cuteness of a man did not bother Kaylee's focus anymore. He was there, and this was just that to her. In his face, there were feelings and emotions. Kaylee was no longer able to show a reciprocal face; hers was a blend of metal and parts of the universe that no one knew, and it did not show any emotions or feelings. Despite this fact, Kaylee was able to discern his need to talk to her.

"How can I help you, Swinthun?"

"Oh, no, please continue working." Swinthun deflected for some reason. After saying those words, he sighed heavily.

"I am sorry. Your presence, facial expressions, and sighing tell me you have something to get off your heart. Right?" Kaylee asserted.

"Yes, you are right. I am just not sure how to talk about this," Swinthun admitted.

HENRI NGUYEN

"How about you begin at the start and go from there?" Kaylee suggested.

"You know, we went through a lot, you and me. It was a little frustrating when I figured out you slept with Serge. I understand I was not present for me to be a choice, but I am a little mad at it," Swinthun uttered out.

"I understand. You wanted me to wait for you and me to have sexual intercourse. I am sorry. I was going to be transferred the next morning. I guess there was less time for you. I picked Serge because he was available," Kaylee stated curtly.

"Uh, OK." Swinthun found it short and difficult to swallow these words. Kaylee was not the same; she was a robot now. This did not make it any easier.

Swinthun did not say another word. He stepped off the bridge. Kaylee resumed her review activities. Swinthun was outside the hatch, and he looked at the robot. At that moment, he wanted to scream, but there was no point to do so.

Swinthun felt cheated, and it was the first time. He was in the military when a girl he looked at since forever was asked to go out with his classmate. When Swinthun had the guts to talk to her, he came to realize she had become one of his classmate's prostitutes. This made all his dream crumble. This was the reason he focused his energy in olden foods. It gave him a reason to live. At this moment, his nerves played with his skin; it bubbled under his skin; he wanted to rip his skin off. He was mad and sad about his lack of skills when talking to women.

Swinthun sat at a window and he stared at space. It was empty with a sprinkling of stars. These lights were other star systems or galaxies. This was huge. Despite this enormity, Swinthun could only shed tears and asked himself, *Will the time ever happen when I will be loved?* The question provoked more tears.

The evening meal was called. It was a slight buzz on all the screens on the spaceship. All were to gather in the Ring to have a meal altogether. Kaylee was present. Swinthun stared at her, and so was Serge. This was awkward for the men. For Kaylee, it was no different from any other interaction with people she cared for, except for the lack of emotions. It seemed to slip away from her firm fingers and grasp. It was an ethereal concept that seemed to flee her mind.

The meal was close to a few pills and water. There were two bars. One was made with yeast; it was to replenish their proteins. And the other one was vegetables; this was not delicious. They had little choice. There was a plant section on this ship, but it was not for production. It was more for teaching and for the human spirit.

The children were whiny, and some of them were taken care by the leaders, while others were ordered to go to bed. Most of them were in a state of shock. Coming to this spaceship was difficult enough to explain; the next part to the mission was going to go down the wrong pipe. The meal was done. The kids were rambunctious, and several of them looked at Kaylee. They wanted to ask questions, but like Swinthun, where do you start?

"Ms. Robot, can I ask you a question?" a child said calmly, but her voice showed her nervousness.

"Yes, you can," Kaylee answered.

"Why are you on this ship with us?" The question cut across the metal of the robot.

"I was assigned as your guide, leader, and protector," Kaylee stated.

"So you are our parent?" The question awakened the human brain of the robot.

"I guess," the robot answered.

HENRI NGUYEN

"Can you tell me a story?" the little boy asked.

"What story do you want to hear?" Kaylee questioned.

"A good story," another child answered.

This request made the robot not know what should be said after the question. Kaylee paused and wondered when Serge came in the conversation.

"All right, children, I will tell you a story. Your parent is not ready for this yet. Maybe later, she might be able to." He paused and looked at Kaylee. He smiled and returned his eyes to the children. "How about I tell you the story of the Troy war?"

The children sat all around Serge. Kaylee came to understand that being the guide, leader, and protector did not make her a parent. She needed to relate emotionally to the children. This fill of emotions was essential for a child to grow up. Children needed to feel loved, understood, and yet punished when straying from the road. Kaylee would never have those feelings ever again. Her brain cried, but no emotion was ever showed.

Kaylee returned to the bridge and resumed her preparation for a trip to somewhere she never set her mind to. These algorithms, mathematical concepts, and software updates were easier to handle. Her days of dreaming of having a child were gone. Her human brain teared up through letting her robotic brain take over. There was nothing left for her to do. Just let it happen; it will be smoother.

The night hours came, and all the humans were asleep. Kaylee walked in the Ring. Her robotic mind was still reviewing procedures and software. This was easy. Her human side needed to calm down. Walking in the Ring was not to calm yourself. It was just a visit to the past for Kaylee. She saw kids and her dreams; now that it will never happen, what was she doing in the Ring?

Kaylee stopped at Swinthun's room and opened his door. He was asleep with his sister in his arms. She must have had a difficult time to fall asleep on the ship. They looked comfortable and loving. This aspect was odd for her robotic mind, but her human side was still present and enjoyed it with all its pain.

For the first time, there was a reason for a brain dialogue.

"Why are you fascinated by this image?" the robotic side asked.

"What? Who are you?" the human side, surprised, asked.

"I am your brain," the robot answered.

"Shit! Am I sleeping and dreaming this crap?" the human side asked herself.

"The usual check for humankind is to pinch you, but as it is your brain, this could be painfully harmful," the robot brain answered.

"Wow, this is real. Isn't it?" Kaylee asked to answer her own question.

"Why are you fascinated by this image?" the robot reiterated.

"It is because I had the image of my dream to have children and be a mother. This will never happen, as I am in the body of a robot," Kaylee answered the second question.

"Are you not happy to be in this body?" the robot asked further.

"I am. For what needs to be done, I am, but I am mourning the loss of a dream and possibilities. Do you grasp this concept?" Kaylee asked her other side of the brain.

"As time will go on, you will integrate the brains together. I do not understand your attachment to these people," the robot responded.

"Mourning is a process. There is no reason for it to exist but to clear your thoughts and find acceptance to the mourning." Kaylee attempted to answer her robotic side. Her words seemed to be too mature even for a young brain.

"I see. So this is an attempt to eliminate old experiences and delete them." The robot tried to understand this statement from Kaylee.

"Almost. I do not want to forget my human side and the experiences I went through. It is important to me and to my interaction with the crew." Kaylee felt so much more mature than she was.

Her brain kept on checking all systems. Then, as in anything else, all checks were positive. It was time to depart.

CHAPTER 37

MORNING WAS AN old concept. The sun was present no matter the time of the day. It was there; it shone on the spaceship. It made it hot on one side of the ship, while the other side of the ship was cold. How cold was it? The thermometer broke the last time it was set out. However, the ship computer was able to measure the temperature on the cold side. It was 3 degrees Kelvin. This made it almost balmy when you consider the coldest place in the universe was 0 degree Kelvin. This was equivalent to a little less than -273 degrees Celsius. This was cold.

The spaceship made it comfortable, but children were cold in the temperature of about 15 degrees Celsius. It was easy to keep this cold. Space helped you. Water ran in the walls separating space and the crew. This water blocked some of the gamma rays and X-rays. These were some of the dangerous solar products to which you would be exposed without the water protecting you. The water shield ran; otherwise, it would freeze, and this would not be good. The water purified was consumed by the crew, and when it was urinated or dirtied, it would run in between the walls to be cleaned and again pure for consumption. This was the new circle of life.

Kaylee did not sleep. She could no longer do such a thing. This was an odd concept for her old brain, but not to her new one. The conversation was odd between them, but it made her feel less alone. She had a friend; as unusual as this may sound, it made her feel less heavy. She had an outlet to vent to.

The crew woke up. Kaylee let them clean themselves and eat breakfast. This was about an hour before she passed out her message. "This morning, we will begin our trek. Everyone will be in their seats in the Ring. Leaders will help you with the belts and strapping. Finally, when we head close to the sun, the shades will be on." It was a concise message; the little ones did not understand all of the message. The older children helped the younger ones.

When three hundred children moved, it was not an easy task. The noise caused by this movement was tremendous. This did not bother Kaylee; she functioned optimally. As she left the Ring, she could see anxiety and fear come out, becoming tears and crying. This was an odd moment for her.

It was her human brain feeling the pain from the unknown, but her robotic brain was not computing this behavior. This was the problem of being both. She felt as having schizophrenia. This made her human brain laugh, which her robotic brain did not understand. This was too much for the positronic brain; computing behaviors was like counting moving ants—an impossibility.

Arriving on the bridge, Kaylee locked herself to the commanding position. She sent out the message of a countdown; "4, 3, 2, 1, engine on" was the message on the screen. Suddenly, all in the seats felt a push against the chairs. This felt as if the person in front of you just got pushed against you. This person did not move either.

Speed climbed up. They were close to 20,000 kilometers per second. This was very fast. It consumed most of their fuel to accelerate to this speed. Then Kaylee engaged the nuclear engine. This was not really an engine. She activated the deployment of the back shield. This would protect the crew and concentrate the exhaust of the nuclear explosion to propel them even faster.

At the speed previous to the nuclear engine extra kick, it would have taken them a little more than an hour to reach the sun. The adding of the nuclear acceleration was needed to be close to or even at the speed of light. This would be an unknown for the children, for the leaders, and, most importantly, for Kaylee.

This access to higher speed was going to allow them to be at the right speed to enter a window, which Kaylee knew she had to open. This was the wacky side of the theory for her.

The known theory of superluminal speed was that it would open a wormhole in which you would travel even faster. This was wacky of a theory, but there was no counter-mathematical theories. This was all enunciation of a theory, nothing more. Was this a good gamble? How was she to know? This was their only choice left.

Her brain, robotic or human, could not comprehend the amount of energy needed to reach the speed of light squared. This would be the needed speed to open a wormhole: 1.8 at the 16th power kilojoules. This was not gigantic; it was unimaginable. No one ever calculated this kind of mess. It was enough to create Earth and plenty leftover to put life on the planet. These were numbers only gods could ever understand.

Her human brain was not strong enough to comprehend this number. Her robotic side gave her the equivalent: 1 joule is the energy needed to warm 1 cc of water 1 degree Celsius; the energy we produced would warm all the water in the world more than 1,000,000 degrees Celsius. For anyone else, this would blow up your mind. For Kaylee, it was a relativity notion. This was the advantage of being a robot.

The nuclear device was ejected; a second later, it exploded. The spaceship did not just jump. It went so fast; most of the kids passed out as the pressure knocked them out. Inertia was a bitch when you accelerate; the pressure placed on their body was difficult to manage. Sleep was a better choice for this part of the trip.

The speed went from 20,000 kilometers per second to 900,000,000 kilometers per second. It was clear that they were traveling fast. Fast was not a correct word to demonstrate their speed. They were faster than a photon. Actually, they were able to see photons as if they moved in super slow motion. This would be amazing, but most of the crew were knocked out. Kaylee was the last one alert; this was a good thing, as she was their captain and pilot.

The speed was so fast that this was the reason for the trajectory beneath the sun. It was already a cone in the fabric of space, and hence, it was easier to have a weak point in space to create a wormhole. The theory was wacky, but it was true so far.

The wormhole was open. The spaceship moved so fast, it felt as if it had been open for centuries. As soon as the front shield passed into the wormhole, the whole ship disappeared into it.

CHAPTER 38

S ILENCE WAS GOLDEN. It reigned over the ship. Everyone was asleep. Kaylee and the ship arrived in a different place in the universe.

The chart was useless. Kaylee computed the stars and located only one that she was sure of: Epsilon Serpentis. It was about seventeen light-years. With trigonometry, Kaylee calculated they traveled fifty thousand light-years. Watches were useless. A calendar stated the date to the same, and the time was a few minutes past the departure.

Kaylee went to the Ring. The leaders were halfway there. Some of them awakened, while the others were nearly there. Most of the kids were all right. Kaylee's eyes were equipped with doctor features. This meant she possessed the ability to have the heart rate and blood pressure just by looking at you. This was useful at this moment. It came on since the jump.

Space gave them a freedom they did not have on Earth. Space gave them restrictions that they did not have on Earth. It was cold and empty, but there was hope, which was a commodity they never tasted on Earth.

Traveling at near the speed of light, they reached the star system Kp-36-32. They were to look for the planet Kp-36-32-56C. This was near planet Earth. This information collected in the early twenty-first century needed to be checked, and this was the reason for Kaylee, the robot. She understood this fact. She was going to complete her mission.

This was the first part of her mission. Kaylee was to create three colonies and make sure they would prosper. It was a large responsibility, and as young, as she was, Kaylee accepted this mission. It was larger than a human mind, and she grasped this idea. There was a faint discussion of godlike figure between her poles in her brain.

The next problem was to slow this spaceship. It was not evident how to decrease the pace of this beast. This was evident and simple actually. The cylinder had two ends. The front end opened upon Kaylee's order, and a jet came out in front of the front shield. It decreased their pace. It took about an hour and a half to slow down to orbital speed.

The slowdown jerked again the ones who awoke, and for the rest, the story was kept a secret. The ship was above this planet. The blue and white welcomed them. All awake admired the new planet.

At this moment, Kaylee unlocked herself from her pilot position and floated to a shuttle. Her mission was to ensure safety in the environment, identify the gravity was acceptable for humans, and, finally, look for life forms. This was a big one.

If there was life, she was given orders to abandon the planet. Her sensors did not feel anyone in human form. There was no village or towns. There seemed to be a virgin of a planet. The final test was Kaylee.

The shuttle separated from the ship, and the engine propelled her to the surface.

The blue sky was visible; soon, it became a flash of fire and reddened material on the walls of the shuttle. This was brief, and the sky was blue again. Clouds were present, but it was as if perfection was the roll call; there were just enough clouds to make it a wonderful day.

Kaylee flew over land, ocean, and land again. This seemed to be a perfect planet for the first colony. There was the question of, if it is perfect, why is it perfect? Humans were always doubting too good of a cake. There had to be something wrong with this planet.

Landing on a plateau, Kaylee prepared herself to step out. The door opened. She would take a deep breath of fresh air, but there was air she could never take anymore. Her atmospheric tools were at work. The air pressure was slightly elevated for humans, but it was within 15 percent of the Earth norms. This would be acceptable. The temperature was about 10 degrees Celsius. She was not sure of the length of day. Her functions on board the ship were measuring this aspect of the planet.

Kaylee stepped out of the shuttle. The gravity pulled at about the same rate as Earth; this was adequate. It was slightly faster than Earth's; it was at 9.12 meters per second squared. It was a little more than what they would know as gravity. This should be adequate for them as a new home. The last part was to see if there were any social interactions among the beings on this planet.

This planet rotation was at about twenty-nine hours on its axis; this was acceptable for the length of a day. Kaylee was not sure at all where she was on this planet and what time it was, but walking the plateau, it was nice. There were no sensors that could determine the beauty of walking on a beautiful day. This was an appreciation of the brain. Kaylee's brain could still feel the sun shining and a beautiful sky.

Walking for hours, Kaylee reached the edge of the plateau. She surveilled the valley below; there was animal activity, but still no human or anything alike kind of activity. The day passed; a feeling gave it away that the evening came. Insects were out. This seemed to be a universal moment—dusk and bugs. Suddenly, a large beast appeared below in the valley.

This animal was enormous. It had eight legs, and its neck was short. It looked like nothing Kaylee ever saw. Her eyes tracked this animal. Her visual contact was also a video. This was transmitted to the computer of the shuttle, which in turn transmitted to the ship. The beast walked and seemed to suck the air; it was as if it had difficulty breathing. Was it a dying animal?

HENRI NGUYEN

Kaylee continued to follow this animal. There was nothing to give her indication of their health. It was all guesses at this time. The animal continued along the valley and kept on sucking the air. Then it found a hole in the ground, and it dove in it. This behavior was not in the books for Kaylee, and she read all the zoology books available from the past and present from Earth. This was the point—it was from Earth.

The night came. Other strange animals appeared. This was extraordinary. There was a gigantic bird that flew above her head. It circled around her. She could hear the noises the bird produced; it was like bats. Yet the bird tried to figure out if it could eat Kaylee. Finally, it left to find other food, which seemed a better idea. Then Kaylee saw a colony, she believed, of small animals like rodents. These were ferocious rodents, if they were, that attacked a part of a wall of rock. She was not sure why they were attacking a wall of rock. This was so different, but it was acceptable for life. On the other hand, Kaylee asked herself, *Would it be safe to have habitation around animals like this?*

In the valley, Kaylee observed small animals gathering in concentric circle where the infants were in the middle, the female were outside of the kids, and the males were on the outside. This reminded her of penguins trying to protect each other from the cold. However, this was not for the cold. Quickly, Kaylee came to realize what they protected their children and females from. Predators arrived and attacked the outside of the circle. This made sense.

So far, there was no proof of tool use and humanlike beings. This was a good sign.

In the distance, Kaylee witnessed something looking like a thunderstorm. It was a bright event. It lit up a few miles away. This would make a great source of energy for the colony, and also, it would terrify the children. The rain fell in sheets and drowned the ground underneath it. This was when she got to see this animal appear as if it was a Venus flytrap. Kaylee thought it was an animal as it opened its large mouth and engulfed water liters by liters. This was so exciting if you were a biologist, zoologist, or even botanist, but Kaylee was none of those. She was here to establish if this planet was acceptable for colonization.

The night progressed, and more strange animals showed up. All of them were herbivores. The carnivores seemed to be absent. This was a strange fact. Kaylee was still on top of the plateau and surveilled the area. There were nothing to report so far; it looked fine for colonization. Then a carnivore beast came out.

This beast was big, and by big, Kaylee's computer could not account for an animal of that size. The Tyrannosaurus rex was small compared to the beast. It was not out for a stroll. It was there to fill its stomach or whichever the organ arrangement was. It moved, and out of nowhere, it disappeared. Kaylee took a second look. The giant beast just vanished. How could this be? Then it reappeared beside a herd of herbivores; it took a chunk with his powerful jaws. The herbivore was dead. The big carnivore began to chew off the smaller animals. On the other hand, the scene was not as bloody as Kaylee expected; it seemed to have swallowed it. Then, again, it disappeared. This was an extraordinary carnivore. There will be a mention of this beast for the potential colonists.

Hours passed each other. The star appeared, and there was the only star in this system. The sun brought some warmth, but Kaylee could not feel it. She was not aware of the season. There was a slight incline to the planet. It was about three degrees off its axis. This seemed to provide milder winters and warmer summers.

On the research trip, Kaylee took another three nights. On the ship, Swinthun and Serge stared at each other for a while. A conversation needed to happen.

"Swinthun . . . I think we need to talk," Serge began.

"I know," Swinthun responded.

"You know what happened. How do we proceed from here?" Serge put his cards down on the figurative table.

"I don't know. I think we are about to say good-bye for an eternity. Maybe we need not to talk about this anymore," Swinthun reasoned.

"Really? Would that be too easy? Do you not want to clear the air?" Serge asked.

"Does it matter anymore? You did it with her. Congratulations. I did not. There is little to talk about." Swinthun cringed when those words crossed his mouth.

"OK. Good luck to your group. I hope the best for you all." Serge acknowledged that he won't be in his colonist group.

Swinthun nodded, and they walked away from one another. This was still a stinger for Swinthun. Indeed, there was little action he could act upon to change anything in this equation. It was too late. Kaylee slipped through his fingers, like many other women before her. There was hope on the new home planet, this situation would not happen ever again.

On the other hand, Serge was holding on to hope to be reunited with Kaylee. This was an impossibility, as her body was still on Earth and entered the decomposition mode. The idea of being with a robot was not even close to reality. Serge held on to hopes, because Serge had nothing else to hold on to. This was his demise.

Being an officer in the army, Serge was in a position of privilege. He had some encounters with women, but none of them developed into sexual insertion. It did not happen until the last night on Earth. It was symbolic, but, nonetheless, it was the only thing of Earth he would take forever. This was an erroneous act for him; he seemed aware of this aspect of life, but there was no other hope to grasp.

Three nights later, Kaylee came back. When the shuttle docked, there was a group waiting for her at the entrance hatch. Kaylee was not surprised or disappointed, as, again, she had no emotions. What she found unusual was the eagerness to know more about the planet below them.

"Tell us about the planet, Kaylee," an eager leader threw at the robot.

"I will, but in the Ring so everyone could hear this," Kaylee responded.

"All right," the leader said and pushed himself to the Ring, while his words reached Kaylee's sensors.

"I will follow you," Kaylee acknowledged.

In the Ring, they gathered. Even the little ones seemed to understand that this could be their new home. They were all eager to know more about all this. Kaylee arrived and stood up in front of the attentive crowd.

"The planet seemed not to be populated by advanced society. The gravity appeared to be adequate. The temperature was adequate. The day and night were slightly longer than normal but adequate for our requirements. Finally, there are animals, so there are protein sources. The ground seemed to be adequate for agriculture. Therefore, it is an adequate planet for colonization," Kaylee stated.

A loud cheer went up. There were claps and hugs; even the four- and five-year-old children were happy.

"Now, fifty female youths, fifty male youth, two female leaders, and two male leaders will be assigned to this planet. We have to decide how to proceed." Kaylee made another statement.

Then the crowd quieted down. This became a moment of solace. There were thoughts of *What would be next? Maybe I need to be on this planet.*

HENRI NGUYEN

"Leaders, please meet me on the bridge. We will decide this and inform you about the animals," Kaylee said before climbing the ladder to return to the cylinder and go to the bridge.

The solace was gone. Now, it was cheering and questioning-each-other time. The noise decreased as Kaylee headed to the bridge. The leaders joined her move. They assembled into the bridge. They floated and tried to not kick one another. Kaylee activated her magnetic feet, and she stuck her feet on the ground. She looked at the leaders; they were young, and some of them barely had enough age to have zits. This was the age of survival; age was no factor in this.

"I wanted to tell you about the fauna on the planet," Kaylee opened up. "There were herbivores, and I was only able to locate one carnivore. This animal acted strangely for us." As those words were stated, a video played. Kaylee resumed the talk. "As you can see, this animal is able to become invisible. This could be a problem. I believe older personnel are needed on this planet. This danger is real." The video replayed and replayed.

The animal disappeared and reappeared close to the herbivore and chunked it off. This disheartened the leaders. A mild whispering happened. "How do we fight this beast?" Kaylee took the initiative to continue her speech.

"Furthermore, there was a 'thunderstorm,' and this was very bright. There may be a chance of getting energy from this source. The temperature on the planet was adequate, but at night, it was in the negative, but nothing froze. I am not sure as to the reason." She paused, and, looking at their eyes, she said clearly, "On the second night, there was a fire from the 'thunderstorm,' and the forest came on fire. The next morning, I examined the forest and found no evidence of fire."

At those words, a gasp circulated on the bridge. The leaders' faces frowned, and almost simultaneously, a chin tuck was pulled. How could this be? This was the interpretation from Kaylee.

"The final point is to determine who will go on this planet. I think Swinthun should be one of the leaders. He has experience in survival and combat. There is need on this planet. As for the children, group one for the boys and group two for girls. Is this adequate for all?" Kaylee stated and asked.

The bridge fell silent. Until Swinthun uttered, "OK, it is adequate for me. Will my sister be on the planet too?" This was a good question for him to ask. Kaylee answered it.

"It is up to you. If you desire her to be, replace a girl from group two." The conversation was over. There were only adjustments to the plan; this was to be done by the leaders.

Some of the leaders and their groups were never informed of this trip. This was a throw in their face. Therefore, some of them wanted to leave the spaceship as soon as possible. This planet was not normal; there were events that could not be explained. In other words, spooky things happened and will continue to happen on this planet. This was not a good way to begin a colony.

The next day, Swinthun Schilling and the leaders examined the map. There were three prime spots to begin a village. They were the three spots Kaylee landed on. Swinthun and a female leader were introduced to each other in this map debate.

Lai was seventeen years old. Her hair was jet black, and face and body were slender. They argued, but this argumentation was pleasant. Seeking a spot to begin a new society was not the worst thing to do. This was the first positive interaction for Swinthun. Lai enjoyed the conversation with this man. He was twenty years old; he was almost too old.

HENRI NGUYEN

Kaylee observed the interaction, and her human side saw her jealous side reveal itself. There were no comments from Kaylee, and at this point, there were reasons for them to expect her to say anything. Kaylee continued with her preparation for the first colony to ready for its mission.

Three days later, it was loading time. The equipment had been unloaded on the planet. Some of the kids were on site already. The plan was to build a structure in the trees, and this would prevent an attack from the disappearing beast.

Good-byes ripped the hearts of some of them. Boys and girls barely knew each other, but they knew they would never see each other ever again. This was a real feeling; on Earth, there was a chance to once again see each other. In space, there was no chance of that ever happening again. This was confounding for Kaylee's robotic side. It did not grasp the concept of friendship and even less the notion of never seeing someone but this once in a lifetime. This seemed to be too much information for the positronic brain.

Every recharge, Kaylee's human brain integrated more with the robot. There seemed to be no line anymore. However, there were two voices in her mind now. This was the definition of being schizophrenic. She had two personalities; but for a robot, who was the host for a human soul, it was almost normal.

The last leader floated into the shuttle. He gave a kiss to the rest of the leaders who came to say good-bye. He locked the hatch. He went to his seat and strapped in. A few minutes later, the shuttle separated from the spaceship. A gentle roaring of their engine pushed them farther away. On the spaceship, tears at the hull were the norm. Kaylee did not participate in this exercise. She was gone back to the bridge. She needed to complete the calculations for the next jump; this was the next step.

Being a robot helped her. Swinthun was gone. She did not have a tear for him. Three weeks ago, she would have torrents for him.

CHAPTER 39

THE FOLLOWING TWO weeks, the spaceship stayed in orbit. The building of the tree headquarters was nearly completed. The loading of equipment into the habitat was nearly completed too. The colonists sent pictures of their hideout. They decided to call their planet Rusus. This was Latin for "anew." This was the feeling of everyone on that planet. They were home.

The two weeks passed; another round of good-byes made everyone yearn to be on the planet. This was less dramatic, as there was hope filling the hearts of the crew left on board. This hope would keep them alert for a while longer.

The ship was ready for the next jump. This time, they had to guide their boat to the bottom point under this smaller red dwarf. Then the travel resumed. The engines roared loudly inside the ship. Outside, there was not a noise to be heard.

This was due to the lack of atmosphere. The atmosphere was the reason for anyone to hear the engine scream.

The acceleration was rough but expected. This knocked out the younger ones. Despite their strength and desire to stay awake, beating inertia was like boxing against a ghost—an impossibility. Then a few minutes after the maximum speed on the engine was reached, the nuclear additive launched. The explosion was visible. Was it visible from the planet?

The speed reached was so gigantic, no one really could comprehend it. They entered the wormhole. Again, this part of the trip was trippy. This was flash; suddenly, they exited the wormhole.

Kaylee attempted to locate them on a map. There was no point of reference. Not even Epsilon Serpentis was on the horizon. This was a little disorienting. Traveling in the dark could be managed, but trekking in the stars without a guide was crazy. This attained that moment.

There were two star systems to explore. Kaylee chose the farthest one. This was due to their reserve of energy. They had enough to last another two weeks; they needed a solar recharge. The distant star was a yellow star. This would be a better recharge.

As they approached the star system, they realized it was binary star system. This was an odd sight for all of them. Even Kaylee stared at these star system with interested eyes. This was a very different moment for all of them.

The planet was the fifth one. It was a monster of a globe. Kaylee was not sure how much bigger it was, but it was huge when compared to Earth. She entered into an orbit. Then she floated to the shuttle. Serge waited for her.

"Serge! What are you doing here?" Kaylee asked the man.

"I wanted to ask you if I can go with you. I am getting a little bit nervous to be touched by gravity," Serge asked.

"No, you cannot. We do not have enough data to indicate if this was safe for humans," Kaylee expressed.

"Even if I stay on the shuttle?" he asked again.

"Not even. This can be dangerous," Kaylee stated while getting into the shuttle.

"OK, thank you," he acknowledged and floated away.

The shuttle separated from the ship, and slowly, it moved toward the planet. The scans of the planet were difficult to discern. This planet did not seem to want to play with Kaylee. This became a search for a needle in the hay. On the other hand, the hay was all the hay of the world. This would make it harder.

The ship entered the atmosphere, and Kaylee knew this immediately. The air pressure was higher. This was not an easy atmosphere to crack into. Kaylee flew off and thought of her approach to the entry of this air bubble. Kaylee recalculated to make it a steeper dive. When she punched it in, the ship became a barrel of monkeys. It shook right and left, up and down, and even diagonally. There were no objects to come loose in this shaky environment, but some of her control boards detached and became projectile. This was not a good welcome.

Immediately, Kaylee calculated gravity to be at 16.4 meters per second squared. This was nearly twice the gravity of Earth. This would be too high for the kids and even their near adult leaders. This was not going to be easy to get out of. She needed to make a decision.

Within a few seconds, Kaylee decided to bail out of this planet. She pulled up. This did nothing. Gravity had a grasp on her. The ship was not operating because of the gravity. The process of thinking kicked in. Her robotic side had all the calculations. None of them worked.

Her human side made an image of gliding on the air and swerving to complete a half loop to have the minimal chance to pull the stick up. Then in her human mind, there was the thought of kicking the engines at max to resume the climb. This was not possible, but it existed because it was in her mind. Kaylee pushed the buttons to make the shuttle in position for this very imaginary series of actions.

Kaylee shut down her jets. The plane's nose was pulled up slightly; it began to glide on the sheets of heavy air. The next step was not easy; she ordered the shuttle flaps to pull up. It happened; the flaps pulled the ship up in the sky. Immediately, the engines kicked in, and there was enough of a push to climb off back to space.

This was not an easy move to complete. Her robotic side did not have enough imagination to sequence actions to end up pulling a plane off the heavy air and increased gravity. This was an imaginary moment coming true. Kaylee's brain gave a reason to be inside with the robotic brain. The conversation would continue, but the score was 1–1.

The shuttle docked with the ship. Kaylee floated out of the spacecraft. She was not sweating or showing any distress. The leaders rushed over to see her. They awaited the decision; but upon her quick return, they knew it was not a good planet for colonization.

The next two days were used to recharge the batteries. These batteries needed to be at 100 percent before they could visit another world.

Kaylee was lost. There was no map to help her. This was a search for a planet without any plans or even guide. There were so many stars in the sky. Most of them were stars systems; most of them were not suitable for life. This was going to be worse than the going around the Earth to escape the army.

Calmly, Kaylee pulled up all the information she possessed. There were attempts to piece them together to make a map. This map was filled with enormous holes of unknown. Kaylee sat there and looked despaired. When Serge came around again, he saw her. He could not see any feelings or even a trace of an emotion. This metal face was so different from the woman he slept with.

Kaylee's face was a marvelous piece of human art. Her nose was sharp but just enough to fit her thin face and her short hair, which reached her shoulders. Her thin body matched her face. She was a beautiful woman; he missed that woman. This robot was not her.

"Hi," he said hesitantly.

"Serge, how can I help you?" Kaylee asked the floating man.

"I am here to know more of what you discovered on the planet," Serge said with an assurance that was fake.

"I did not make it to the planet. The flight was dangerous, and the calculations of gravity were too high for settlements to be safe," she said with no fake assurance.

"I see. So where do we go next?" Serge asked.

"We will explore the moons of this system, and then we will go to the next system, which is 4.265 light-years away," Kaylee said.

"Do we have to jump again?" Serge asked sincerely.

"No, we won't." Kaylee knew the jump would take her way farther. "But we have two problems. The first is, if we go to the next solar system, it will take us about thirteen thousand years. The second problem is we have a very skeletal map of the universe." She showed Serge the map. This was not good news.

"Shit!" Serge said as he floated.

Silence fell on the bridge again. This was a difficult equation. There was no easy answer to this one.

"We need to go a step at a time. We need to recharge the batteries. At the same time, we will examine the satellites to see if the colonization is possible. If not, we will have to jump again. The visit to other visit is impossible. We will have to remove it from the list." Kaylee planned out the next moves. It was scary how precise and calculated she became.

"OK," Serge said softly.

HENRI NGUYEN

Kaylee stayed on the bridge for the next two days. Maps upon maps zipped in her mind. She scanned the satellites of planets around the star system. There was nothing inhabitable. Too dry, too much gravity, too much sulfur, only methane oceans—these planets were not cooperating.

The batteries returned to their optimal levels for function. Kaylee had to recharge too before the next jump. It had been three days since her last charge. She was nowhere close to dangerous levels, but a full charge was needed before the next jump. Kaylee knew a conversation had to be had for the crew's sake.

Calling for a meeting in the Ring, Kaylee headed to the only gravity location for humans. Arriving, she could see the crowd assembling. She noted the diminished crowd.

"We have arrived at this large planet. It is too heavy in air pressure, and its gravity is about twice as the one we are used to. Hence, we have to depart to continue the search."

"Why are we not going to the second star system in the area!" a leader screamed out.

"The system closest to us would require thirteen thousand years to reach. I think passing it was the only thing to do," Kaylee answered.

"Where are we going, then?" another leader asked.

"I will not lie to you. I do not know. We have eight more bombs to jump with, but this would be a shot in the dark," Kaylee said.

"Wow!" The children began to have a moment of panic.

"Could we go back to Rusus?" a child asked.

"We could, but my mission was to create three colonies to make sure humanity would survive," Kaylee responded.

The concept of mission escaped the children and their leaders. Survival of the human race was a term they all lived with all through their lives. They knew it took all they had to make it here. How could you ask them to scamper throughout the universe to find another home? Most of them were sad.

Kaylee went to her charging post. She was in and plugged herself in. Then her recharging cycle began.

In the Ring, panic took over the children. The leaders struggled to maintain order. A sense of panic reached all in the Ring. There was a need to take a deep breath, but no one did so. Kaylee was recharging, and this was far, far away from her ears. The kids wanted to leave this ship. This moved to the point of near mutiny.

Three hours later, Kaylee left her recharging dock. She noticed there were alerts on the shuttle dock. Also, there was an alarm at the door of the bridge. Kaylee took each one of the alarms on their own. A list needed to be established. It was done in her head.

Kaylee went to the shuttle dock. There were leaders trying to open the hatch. They were not able to complete this. Kaylee floated to the dock, and she saw the leaders and children attempting to open the panel.

"What are you trying to do?" Kaylee asked.

"We want out of this ship. We want to go to the planet. We think you lied," one of the leaders said harshly.

"Fine. I am a robot. I do not lie," Kaylee stated and opened the hatch. The kids took a step back. Suddenly, there was another doubt.

"Wait, why are you opening the hatch?" one of the children asked suspiciously.

HENRI NGUYEN

"I am opening the hatch, as it is your request," Kaylee said without any emotions.

"Did you say the truth about the planet?" another child asked with more consideration.

"Yes, I say the truth." Kaylee made a statement and asked a question, "Do you know how to pilot this craft?"

"No, not really," a leader answered.

"Do you want me to teach you how to pilot this shuttle?" Kaylee asked clearly.

"What would happen if we go down there?" a leader asked while pointing to the large planet.

"I believe you would be stuck and cannot leave the planet. On the planet, you would be functioning at half your endurance. The children may not be able to participate in any of the construction activities. Furthermore, I was not able to make a list of animals or even if there were inhabitants," Kaylee said.

"OK," the leader in charge uttered. Inside his head, a debate exploded. *Should I have taken a deep breath instead of participating in this rebellion?*

Kaylee called a meeting in the Ring. She looked at the crowd. There were angry and tearful faces. This was not a harder thing for her. This would count as a point for the robot. Human 1; robot 2.

"All right, you attempted a mutiny. This was not needed. If you really want to be unloaded here, all you have to do is tell me. I will let you go," Kaylee said.

"You would?" a leader asked.

"If you want to go to the planet, I will not stop you," Kaylee reminded them.

"What if we cannot land safely? Will you come and help us?" a leader asked.

"No, I cannot. This is a risky you need to take for yourself," Kaylee admitted.

This threw silence across the Ring. There came a realization among the older members of the crew—maybe she was not the tyrant she was portrayed by their minds.

The last charge time brewed an eclectic soup of conspiracies. It went from "She deemed the first one hundred to be the chosen ones, while we were the chum for the project of colonization." This was in part due to their years under the rule of starvation and constant risk of kidnapping. Living those long years made you a very suspicious person. They believed Kaylee to be an agent of that world. It did not take too much for the fuse to be consumed and the explosion of rebellion to express itself.

"Could I ask you a question?" Kaylee asked politely.

"Yes," a leader answered.

"Where is Serge Valdez?" she wondered.

"Oh, shit!" Immediately, as those words were uttered out, two leaders ran off to a room. A few minutes after, they came out, and Serge followed them. His head hurt, and he was not a happy camper about it.

The ultimate conspiracy theory thrown out there was Serge and Kaylee worked in unison to kill them all. Again, years of lacking food and being told the North Americans only want to kidnap you to eat you would lead you to see the world in a very cruel way. This was a factor

HENRI NGUYEN

to account for. These children's trust was in very short amount; it was as near empty as it could ever be.

Pensive, the children felt guilty. Kaylee came back to the conversation. "Do you still want to go to the planet? This is a choice you have to make. I told you the truth, but if you do not believe me, that is your prerogative. I will follow your desire." These sentences landed in their still-developing frontal lobes like a hot rock; it burned their synapses to have doubted her.

A soft voice from a female leader emerged. "We are sorry. Could you include some of us in your decision process? I think it would help us." The voice was clear, but the shame of the events shaded all over it. Her voice was a reflection of the spaceship. They were not a team. They were tribes.

Kaylee nodded. Then, as if it was planned, she turned to the ladder and climbed out of the Ring. This was a mark in their conversation too. This walking out was perceived as an exclamation point to their discussion. The children felt their loss, and most of them walked into their rooms. There was little discussion about the events. These were the words of shame screaming out.

Kaylee returned to the bridge. She revised the calculations. They were ready for another jump. However, this was only going to happen after a review of the satellites in this star system. The process began, and Kaylee had a human moment.

Her human brain remembered the rising sun. The cooler air and the dew on the grass were remembered; this was a sweet and comforting memory. Human 2; robot 2. A tied game was the notion the robot got from its human side. Kaylee smiled; the robot did not, as it could not.

CHAPTER 40

DAYS AND NIGHTS were very fluid in this world without a star to guide you, and when you have a star, even a binary one, it was difficult as it was always there.

The crew suffered through this lack of delineation of day and night. This came as a vacation from the cruel world from Earth to a dizzying and confusing moment that they had to grow up in. Kaylee was aware of this problem; there was only so much she could manage.

Children led by teenagers were a concoction for a big explosion. This was never designed as a long-term recipe. She needed to find two more worlds for these kids. This was not going to be an easy situation.

Kaylee had spent two days on the bridge. She was 40 percent down on her energy meter. Soon, she will have to make decisions that will make her even less popular than the robot that led the ship to become the bounty. Then an alarm rang in her system.

The alarm rang; Kaylee shut it down. It was not about her. She was in prime functioning mode. The alarm was the computer having found a potential world for colonization. Kaylee turned on the search software.

Kaylee looked at it. This world existed in this system. The satellite was around the third planet. This was not ideal; this was her first thought. Was the robot integrating to the human side or vice versa? This was a philosophical thought for later. The software data showed a surface temperature of 95 degrees Celsius. This must be a mistake; how could anyone live in a world close to the boiling point? Kaylee kept on reading the data. The idea of it came to her as it came to the software. It was definitely a concept that needed some sale to be a reality.

Kaylee called a meeting to have a conversation about this plan. The meeting was in five minutes. Kaylee unlocked herself and floated herself to the Ring. Everyone gathered in the Ring. They awaited her arrival.

"We have found a planet where life could be possible." Kaylee began to speak.

"Why the word 'possible' is being used?" the female leader who spoke earlier interrupted Kaylee's presentation.

"The surface temperature is 95 degrees Celsius, but this is almost ideal gravity, and the idea for colonization is to live underground," Kaylee pronounced the idea. She continued. "On the dark side of that satellite, the surface temperature is near 0 degree Celsius. At night, it would be a better time to go out for fresh air." As soon, as she uttered the words, the children looked at her with eyes that accompanied their head tilt. It was too human. Human 3; robot 2.

"Are we going to explore this planet—sorry, satellite?" a male leader asked while looking at the crowd to see if anyone else shared his excitement.

"Yes, we will. I felt we needed to have a conversation before doing it." Kaylee showed her understanding of needing part of the decision.

"All right, let's do it," the crowd mumbled.

The ship was a big animal. It would take them about five minutes to warm up the engines, three minutes to reach the satellite, and about five minutes to slow down their ship to enter into orbit around the satellite. This was a difficult flight because of its short distance. For the human side of the robot, this was a ridiculous statement. How can 3,500,000 kilometers be a short distance? The human brain had not integrated the idea that the ship could travel 20,000 kilometers per second. This made the score human 3; robot 3.

On arrival, everyone rushed to the windows. This world was not welcoming them. It showed its sand color. This disappointed everyone. There were winds that lifted clouds of this sand. There was no green to be found. This was not a good world at first look.

Kaylee invited the female leader, Jenna, and a male leader, Mic, to accompany her on the primary evaluation trip. This decision made the crew at ease. It was a good decision, but for Kaylee, it was not a decision; it was respecting the conclusions of the discussion they had a couple of days ago. They boarded the shuttle. Soon after that, the shuttle separated from the ship. They were on their way.

The breaking of the atmosphere was easy enough. The landing was a little more difficult. There was a lot of sand around this planet. They found a part of hard soil that they landed the shuttle on.

Upon getting off the craft, there was a feeling of feeling light on their feet. The leaders loved this feeling. Kaylee did not feel any better or worse. She felt the heat as her metal outer shell read 69 degrees Celsius and this was rising. Jenna and Mic were suited with a pressure suit and cooling suit. They would have to travel about four kilometers to reach an entrance to the underworld. As soon as they came out in this near inferno, Kaylee ordered the unloading of the rover. This would make the four kilometers a little shorter.

This world was not pretty. It was like the Sahara. This made Jenna smile, as she knew the direct translation for Sahara was "desert"; so people who said Sahara desert meant "desert desert." This made her smile for a long time. Their arrival was unusual.

The wind blew the sand, and this made them disoriented. Kaylee was not lost, as her guidance system, helped by their ship's guidance, kept her on target. She parked the rover by a medium rock. Kaylee knew it would not help the sand from swallowing the rover, but it should be easier to find their rover after the exploration was finished.

The opening was like a gash on the skin of the planet. For some reason, the rip was not filled with sand. This was a strange phenomenon. As Kaylee stepped into the fracture of the crust, she felt a soft wind. This was the reason why this hole was not filled with sand. There was air pushing out. Jenna and Mic followed her.

Their lights were on. It was a dark area. It would be something like if you did not want to find anyone living here. They walked a few tenth of lieue and saw something extraordinary. It was the sand and rock scene that they grew accustomed to; this place was a rainbow of strange colors.

The colors were different. The leaders used to see plants green. This was due to the chlorophyll, which was the basis of processing luminal energy into food for the plants. This was a different world. There were plants with purple, others pink, and one was a dirty green. There was moss all around the area. This was amazing to Jenna and Mic.

Kaylee knew some source of water was available. This was her main issue. Kaylee dug superficially. She found a wet underground; this would mean the water was deeper. The robot walked a little faster and saw a patch of ground. She began to dig in it. After a few centimeters, Kaylee found the source of water.

There was a pipe. This had repercussions for them. Kaylee alerted Jenna and Mic to be aware that there may be a civilization on this planet. At that moment, a sense of despair returned to the leaders. Kaylee turned to them and asked, "Take a deep breath. We will explore this option. It is not because we found a pipe that the civilization is still here." These words made them focus a little more than prior. Kaylee signaled to resume the walk.

The collection of colors changed at each level they went underground. The growth of the plants revealed that either people did not care about their plants or they were not home. This thought crossed the mind of the leaders. Kaylee stayed focused on finding people; in that case, they would have to leave quickly.

The walk lasted a few hours. Jenna was having a difficult time following the pace. Kaylee observed her behaviors. Kaylee called for a break. The two humans marveled where they were. They did not have the spirit of worry, which Kaylee did not have either. Mic asked Kaylee if the pressured suits were needed here in the depth of the tunnels.

This was a hard question to answer. The oxygen level was adequate, the air showed no signs of being poisonous, the temperature was within normal limits, the heat diminished significantly, and the air was at 15 degrees Celsius. Kaylee gave her blessing for them to remove their helmets. In a flash, Mic had his helmet off.

The air was different. This satellite was smaller and sandier for sure. It was breathable, and despite the dirt flying above them, it was refreshing to breathe clean air. Jenna removed her helmet, and the same feeling attacked her. She felt the comfort of home invading her lungs. She looked at Kaylee; her eyes begged to not find anyone on this desolate satellite. Kaylee did not pick up this begging moment. Mic asked if they could remove their suits completely.

This was harder to calculate. They were in a search for life form; they did not know if they could come back this way. Kaylee calculated; she had enough energy to carry the two extra suits. Kaylee responded with a yes; this was interpreted as a loud yes by Jenna and Mic. Kaylee was not sure if her volume was elevated, but the look of smile was recorded.

After a bar of nutrition, they resumed the walk to the heart of this satellite. This continued with more and more plants across their way. This reminded Mic of the jungle; his parents had him in Southern Asia, and he grew up in Southern China. The weather changed, and the jungle came to replace the near boreal forest. This was a change that made them correct their food growth. This went from corn and wheat to little or nothing. The sun was too strong, and the air became too warm; they killed all plants, but the jungle survived. This thought ran across his mind until he came behind Kaylee at a village.

This village was in the dark. The darkness weighed heavily on the search party. Would there be anyone? What if the people here were primates of some kind? What if these inhabitants were aggressive? These questions occupied their mind for the time of finding out.

The village was a series of holes along the wall. The center space was a large area. As the light came across the space, there was a fireplace in the middle of the expanse. Kaylee approached. She looked at the wood for about a minute.

"This fire has not been lit for centuries. The wood shows carbon 14 of about 112 years back," Kaylee said.

"How can you do that?" Jenna, stunned, asked Kaylee.

"One of my functions is to measure anything that can indicate traces of civilization. Carbon 14 is one of the best ways," Kaylee answered unemotionally.

"OK, my question was, how can you say about 112 years?" Jenna clarified; she began to laugh at Kaylee's lack of understanding of her question.

"Well, according to the carbon 14 half-life degrading rate and the level of carbon 14 left in the wood, I came to a calculation of 112 years. I was not 100 percent sure, so we added the term 'about,'" Kaylee explained herself.

"That is fine," Jenna said in a moment of laughter.

The village was empty. There had not been life here for a while. This was a good sign. As they walked along, they found graves. This was a humbling moment. Jenna and Mic remembered being at cemeteries to bury their parents, siblings, and friends. It was not an easy part of life to come to the realization that life would not be eternal at the age of five years old.

The walk resumed. There were more plants. The plants were not leafy. They seemed to grow from the wall. As they went deeper in the ground, the plants grew from the ceiling. This was the heat source.

Hours passed. Jenna and Mic grew tired, and a camp was defined. They needed rest and sleep. This was an adequate moment for this to happen. Quickly after engulfing another bar, Jenna and Mic fell asleep. Kaylee was on duty. Her scanners were on.

There were animals that were not large. This made sense. You did not want to be big if you have to live in the dirt and use the heat to survive. A large animal would not survive well here. A carnivore would not be a good animal around this planet. Slightly larger animals came out. Some consumption of the surrounding plants was done by some of the animals. They were all blind and had no eyes. It was as if you had a rabbit without eyes, but instead it had larger ears, larger whiskers, and antennas. This was a different animal to Kaylee.

How would you know night and day here in the tunnel of this satellite? This was not evident. After six hours of rest, Jenna came back to life, and Mic did not rest too long after her waking up. The two of them looked at Kaylee, and Jenna smiled at her. Jenna felt closer to this robot; she did not know why they rebelled against Kaylee. It was time to resume the exploration of this place.

The walking was tiring for the leaders. They used to hide more than walk. It became arduous for Jenna and Mic. They needed frequent breaks to breathe and take some water. While they did, Kaylee scanned the area. She discovered something.

"I found a lake underneath our present position," Kaylee launched at the two leaders.

"What?" Mic came back at her.

"There is a lake of water at 6.7 meters underneath us," Kaylee clarified as the question was to make sure she said the right thing.

"I know, but how can we access it?" Mic uttered out.

"I will begin to dig 6.7 meters of dirt," Kaylee said and began to dig.

"OK. I guess we will find a place for the dirt," Jenna said sarcastically.

The plants were not in the way. They were coming down at them. They would have to clear the dirt Kaylee would move out. Kaylee's metal hands made their job more difficult. She was much faster than they could ever imagine. Within thirty minutes, Kaylee saw the lake through the hole. There were plants and dirt that fell into the water. This was a marvel to Jenna and Mic, which were still moving dirt but not as fast as Kaylee produced. Their eyes filtered the possibilities this satellite offered.

Kaylee enlarged the hole. It was large enough for Jenna to fit first. As Jenna splashed into the water, Mic wanted to join her in the water. She swam off to the closest shore. She disappeared from Mic and Kaylee.

Kaylee continued to dig and hear Jenna describe the area. The hole was not large enough for Mic to fit through. Then Jenna stopped talking. Kaylee held back Mic. She pushed him back on to the dirt and lowered her head to the hole. Her right eye popped out. Mic had a repulsive reaction and backed off a little further. Her eye traveled the 6.7 meters and scanned the dark room. Jenna was on shore; she was wet and marveling at some primitive art.

Kaylee recoiled her right eye and invited the disgusted Mic to take his turn. He jumped into the opening, and soon, he separated the water. It was refreshing and invigorating. He swam to the shore. Then Kaylee continued to dig the opening to make it wide enough for her body to fit through. Mic joined Jenna at the shore.

Jenna helped Mic get up onto the shore. It was rocky with sharp rocks. Then a loud landing in the water was heard. This was Kaylee falling through the robot-made opening. Kaylee did not need to swim; she walked to shore. Jenna and Mic looked at the art on the cave wall. In the meantime, Kaylee scanned the area.

There was no one. The water was as pure as water can ever be. It was two hydrogen and an oxygen molecule. This seemed to be an ideal place for a colony.

Walking took a little more effort. After two days, they reached the level where the suits were needed. Jenna and Mic put on their pressure suits. Then more stepping were completed. They reached the opening of the planet and stepped out of it. The wind knocked into Kaylee. The sand seemed to attempt to shave her metal. This was a harsh reminder of the world where Kaylee hoped to put some humans.

Her energy level was at 85 percent off. This was not a moment of panic yet. This was an alarm to remind her to recharge. Jenna and Mic were near out of energy too. Finding their rover was not hard. It was the clearing of sand that was harder.

When you pushed sand off a vehicle, you did not expect more sand to fly in to replace it. This took a while; Kaylee's energy decreased to less than 10 percent. This was an area to monitor.

The drive back was not too hard. The flight back did not suck energy that much. Jenna and Mic were asleep. This was their level of energy. Kaylee docked the ship and opened the hatch. Jenna and Mic exited. Kaylee alerted them that she needed to recharge her batteries. They nodded and smiled. Jenna gave her a hug. Kaylee's human side understood this moment; her robot side did not. Human 4; robot 3.

There were three hours until Kaylee came back to report if the satellite was a possibility. The children were pestering Jenna and Mic. Those two went to their room and closed the door, and there was a simultaneous crash in different beds. This was an exhausting mission.

Their dreams were of a life where no one would starve them and where no one would try to kidnap them either. This was a marvelous dream.

CHAPTER 41

THREE HOURS PASSED. Kaylee was fully recharged. She floated to the Ring. Jenna and Mic were still asleep. No one else was asleep. They all waited eagerly.

Kaylee assembled the crowd very quickly. She began by asking, "Do you want to wait for Jenna and Mic to begin the presentation?" No one said yes. Kaylee understood that she would have to make the presentation by herself.

"As you know, we did an exploration mission. We have established no one was on this satellite. This is a place of harshness. There is vegetation and water. Life will have to be underground because of the elevated temperature. It will be a decision to take whether you want to colonize this satellite," Kaylee stated.

"How hot is it underground?" a voice asked.

"When we reached the vegetation level, the temperature was stable at 15 degrees Celsius. The water was at 17 degrees Celsius. This was a comfortable place to be at. Living there may be a different discussion. That is why we put the decision upon you," Kaylee responded.

"The video you shot, can we see them?" another voice asked.

"Of course." As those words were used, the screen showed the shots taken.

The crowd saw the sand fly, the entrance to the underground, and the vegetation. These were true statements, and this decision would be done by the humans, not Kaylee.

As the video shots ran across the screen, Jenna and Mic came out of their rooms. There was a roar of happiness to welcome them. Jenna was overwhelmed; it showed on her face. Mic loved this attention, and it showed on his behavior. He jumped, hugged, and gave fist bumps all around. This was chaotic. Yet Kaylee waited with no issues about any of this.

The conversation continued when Jenna and Mic came to the front.

"It is not a marble in the sky. This planet is not an easy place to live in. On the other hand, there is plenty of energy to collect. Plants can grow. We can use that water growing thing . . . What do you call it?" Mic said with a lot of excitement.

"Hydroponics," Kaylee answered.

"Yes, that's it, we can do that. We can also build places for us to reside in. It is not a typical place for most of us, but it can be home, if you want to give it a chance," Mic stated still full of excitement.

"I would like to add that it is not going to be easy. See, the sun will be a dream for most of the children and their children too." Jenna made her contribution. Her reality was not as rosy, but it was more real.

"Yes, she is right. It is not going to be a vacation, not that any of you ever had one." They laughed at the sarcastic remark. Indeed, survival would never count as a day off. Then he continued. "But I know if everyone puts in their effort, we can make it our world." This last statement was full of hope.

The hope was contagious.

The next two weeks were a continuous loading and unloading of people and equipment. It took longer than Rusus because the entrance was a narrow gap. This was an effort to widen it to pull down some of the bigger pieces of equipment. The enlargement of the tear in the crust of the satellite was done at night.

There was no sand swerving at your face. There was also no superheated temperature. Most of them worked in coats and sweaters. The large pieces of equipment were delivered, but moving them down the satellite was slow and difficult.

Some of the equipment were pumps, tubes, and heat convertor. These were used on Earth for farms and other habitats with close source of energy. This was not the problem here. Energy was on the surface. The calculations Kaylee compiled indicated you could keep them at seven to ten meters and absorb the energy.

The satellite was not a live planet. This concept was way above the heads of the youth who were part of the crew. This meant there was no electromagnetic field produced by the core of the spatial body. The satellite was in the gravity field of a large planet. This planet did not protect its satellite from the binary suns. Most of the winds were from the sun heating up the atmosphere, and this caused winds from the heat and cold from the night. This was not easily digested by the leaders either.

Kaylee calculated, at the speed of the planet, it would take about fifteen months to complete a rotation around their mother planet. Meanwhile, the planet took less time to complete an orbit around the suns; it would take about seven months to declare a year for this planet.

This was also above their heads. The crew was focused on getting half of their crew to the satellite. For the one staying until the next planet, they were eager to touch a ground that would allow them to feel the benefits of gravity. The eagerness was palpable, and the departure tore some of them apart. It was hard for most of them, but they knew, too, it was their last good-bye.

Finally, after two weeks, the final good-byes happened. The last shuttle separated, and the tears floated. It was difficult to tell them not to cry. The tears did not harm any instruments; it was just a weeping kind of moment.

The spaceship had no name. On the other hand, as a last message, the people of the satellite informed the spaceship of the name of it: Hitze. This was a German word that meant "heat." This was appropriate for this dot in the universe.

The spaceship exited orbit and aimed for the larger sun. There was a little bit of a challenge. The distance to the sun was about twelve million kilometers. This would take them about five minutes to reach. On the other hand, the nuclear explosion would enhance their speed up to nearly fifteen seconds. This was difficult enough, but on top of it, the smaller star traveled at every two days there was a rotation.

Calculating was not difficult for Kaylee; synchronizing all the spaceships to make it was easy for her too. The only thing that was difficult was explaining all this to the little boys and girls left on board.

The spaceship moved, and about a minute after, the nuclear option was part of the drive. They were off.

CHAPTER 42

THE JUMP TO the next star system was almost usual for the crew on board. Kaylee was not able to feel feelings anymore, but Serge got off at Hitze. He needed to see a new world. This whole adventure of chasing Kaylee, sleeping with Kaylee, escaping Earth, and being on Hitze had to end. He decided on staying, and this made him woefully an ugly crier. He said he had not cried in the past seventeen years. This was the first time for him.

This jump was no different from the two preceding ones. They arrived in an unknown place. This time, she was able to locate the Milky Way; it was 120,000 light-years away. This mesmerized everyone on board. She gave them a star-watching lesson; this was beyond mesmerizing. It was simply a new world.

The children and slightly older leaders were in another galaxy, and this was the truth. They observed the world as theirs to take. This was not a world they would lie down for. They wanted just a parcel for their colony. This was their desire. It did not mean this would be the truth.

Three star systems were along each other separated by about six light-years. This was too close for jumping, and the question of long travel reentered the conversation. This time, Kaylee offered them the options and let them make the decision. This was not an easy choice to make. One was already out of the question; it was a giant, and this made the possibility very reduced. The selection was between the second and third stars.

The second star system was a red dwarf. There was a third planet as an option. It was not for sure. The third star system was two light-years away and was a mother binary system. The fourth and fifth planets were possibilities. The discussion was not as educated; obviously, they needed numbers to be at ease with this discussion. If they visited the second star system, it would take them fifteen years to see the third one. Some of them would have children, and this could be an issue on board. There had been no births in space yet.

The talk carried on for two days. Kaylee offered numbers when asked. Eventually, she went to recharge in light of the lack of decision. When Kaylee came back to the conversation, there was astonishing news.

The group made a decision. They were the last to look for a colony. They said good-bye to their companions twice already. It was time, but they did not want to miss an opportunity. In light of all these factors, they did the only thing that would be reasonable—they voted.

The vote ended up on the third system.

Kaylee could not smile, but her human brain was happy to see the resolution of the issues. Kaylee set the course, and as they had the jump speed still in their sails, it would take a week to reach the third star system.

This system had the potential of two worlds possibly harboring their little lives. The star system got bigger and bigger as the days passed. The binary system was like any other, despite them having only seen one in their lifetime. It seemed to be nothing new.

A week passed. Everyone got ready for the information that would tell them if they had a home. They looked all hopeful; this was their last thread. This could be a difficult one if it did not pan out. Kaylee did not have hope in her eyes, but the little ones did.

Kaylee saw the fifth planet and decided to enter its orbit. The fourth planet was at about fifty million kilometers. This must have been their close point. This point would be achieved in about three weeks. If the exploration of the fifth planet was unfruitful, it would be easy enough to reach the other world. This was a decent calculation.

The first search was from the ship. There were signs of life. This was not a good sign for them. Kaylee presented the information. Some of the leftover crew asked the difficult question, could we live apart from them? This would be a question away from, could we exterminate them? This was not a good situation.

Leaving children in charge was not the ideal, but this had to be done for their own sake. They lived through lack of food and constant danger. There was the notion that they would be taken to be feeding meat. This was traumatic. How do robots guide them to the best answer? This was Kaylee's issue.

Kaylee kept the monitoring on. It would alert her if this was a highly evolved civilization or a lower one. Kaylee had to go inform the crew about the discovery. She convened a meeting in the Ring again.

"I have found life on the planet below." Kaylee came out and spat it out.

"What? There is life down there?" a female voice came out.

"Yes, there is," Kaylee answered.

"Wow! This is amazing. The questions of the world are answered here," the teenaged with no hair said.

"Yes, it is. This means you have to make a decision upon this news," Kaylee spelled out for them. Silence broke out, and all stared at her robot features.

"How do we decide this?" a little girl asked.

"If the other planet is not proper for colonization, then you will have to either live with the beings down there or kill them." The words cut across the room. No one wanted to kill the only other civilization found in the universe so far.

"OK, we will make a decision after the findings of the other planet are in." The voice of reason came out of one of the female leaders. Saia was her name.

Saia was a formidable woman at her young age. She was seventeen years old, and she defended a village from the child abduction from North American Army. She came up with the idea of hiding underground. This was the main idea the AI took away from this defense. Saia was a hero. Just now, she spoke the truth, a calming truth.

Kaylee walked back the ladder when Saia stopped her. They looked at each other in the eyes for no reason. There was intimidation or examination you can do on a robot. On the other hand, a robot could not read the expression of a human, so the eyes reading would be a futile waste of time.

"Kaylee, we need to have chat about the system," Saia began. "There is a possibility of us having to live with others. This is not an easy moment for most of us." She expressed the idea with concreteness, and little was left to the imagination. Yet Saia talked to a robot; it did not get her meaning.

"Saia, I am not sure what you want me to say or do?" Kaylee asked her directly.

"Sorry, what I meant was we need to explore the people of this planet to see if we need to fight right now or later." Saia was direct in her words too. Her idea was kill now or later. This was not the way Kaylee imagined this conversation with the crew would go if she ever could picture a future moment.

"If I understand you, you want me to go down and see if the people are aggressive?" Kaylee asked her first question ever.

"Yes. I will come too." Saia did not leave her too much leeway.

"I will collect more information, and we will set out a time to discuss them further." Kaylee set up a schedule for them.

"All right. Do not tell anyone about this conversation," Saia whispered and broke the huddle.

This was not a pretty picture for Kaylee. She was ordered to go see a new civilization and sort out if they could be killed. This was not a good place to be.

The next two days, Kaylee was on the bridge. No one came to disturb her; this was a calming moment for a robot, if there was ever a need for one. The information came in, and this was worsening as time went on. A discussion with Saia was set up. This was going to be difficult, even for a robot.

"Saia, we have located sixteen different groups of people on this planet. They appear to have weaponry and be at preradio time." Kaylee opened up with this information.

"What about the other planet?" Saia asked.

"The information we obtained indicate there are oceans of mercury. This does not look good for colonization," Kaylee stated.

"This means this is the planet," Saia said.

"Or we can jump again. There are other options instead of armed conflict," Kaylee said with no acceleration in her speech.

"True, but is it the planet we could use?" Saia was a tired woman and one who did not see too far ahead of herself.

"It is a group decision. I will present the information and let them decide." Kaylee made a decision to say, "They will decide." This was instead of "You will decide." It made a difference. Her human side was still present in her brain.

"Very well," Saia responded, as she knew very well there was no way to use force against this large robot.

"Thank you." Kaylee got up and went to the ladder.

Was there a way out of this situation? The thought crossed Saia's mind. The thought of sabotaging Kaylee crossed her mind, but what happens after a failed war if Kaylee was disabled? This was not a good option.

The need to be home was essential for Saia. She needed to have her feet on dirt. Space was not for her. It was too large and too undefined. This made her uneasy about everything. Being led by a robot was not one of her favorite moments either.

This was a long-lost moment of her family. Her father told her about her great-great-great-grandmother who worked on an AI. Saia had a few nightmares since. This was not just the bad dreams. When she was first in Laos and realized the AI was in control, she was very uneasy about it. She had many conversation with the AI, and when she wanted to be called Kaleah, it made her very uncomfortable. Was this an allergy to AIs? No one was sure, but for sure, she did not like them.

Control was the last human quality. AI thought faster, acted more precisely, and came up with all calculations better than humans. This trip was the proof that humans were not as great as they claimed. Kaylee was not aware of any of those points. She tried her best to come up with an idea for the crew.

A dialogue happened in her brain.

"You know Saia is trying to fool you, right?" Kaylee the human asked her robot counterpart.

"No, I do not," the robot answered,

"Really? How can you not?" the human side asked again.

"She was honest. She did not want to discuss with everyone yet. I told her it is their decision," the robot responded.

"Could I tell you that humans can be very conniving. This was the reason we are here in a spaceship at about 150,000 light-years from what we used to call home," the human person added.

"I cannot process the emotional information they give me. How can I? I was not programmed for this," the robot defended herself.

"Let me deal with her next time," the human suggested.

"That is fine." The robot accepted this deal. Human 5; robot 3.

When all the information about the planets were compiled, Kaylee called another meeting in the Ring.

"We have the information about the fourth planet. This will not be a possibility to colonize it. There is a mercury ocean, and, furthermore, there is little or no nitrogen. The air is composed of carbon dioxide and phosphorus. The air temperature is near 800 degrees Celsius. The planet we orbit remains your best shot. There is an issue with this planet—there are signs of civilization." Kaylee's words weighed a ton. A silent crowd listened to her speech.

"What did we figure out from the people down there?" Saia asked.

"We know they are from preradio era. There are sixteen locations on the planet," Kaylee answered.

"I say we go and take a look at them." Saia sensed it was not time yet to reveal her idea of killing their civilization. This would not go well at this time.

"I will need two of you to come down with me on the planet." Kaylee's human side kicked in. Kaylee kept an eye on Saia. She noticed the young woman's reaction; it was a slight surprise.

The following hours were for preparation for a mission that was part discovery and part reconnaissance. This would be also a mission where Kaylee would have to expose Saia's real personality. In the human's opinion, Saia could be a murderer, and this in a small colony would be very bad.

Anger was a human trait. This human sign was not a pretty one. A murderer had to have a past to lead them to the point of killing. What was her past? The file did not give her away. Kaylee's human side thought she was smart not to reveal her secrets.

Despite the fact, Saia saved a whole village; there was no one left alive to provide information to the AI. The file was useless. There was not a pretty way to go about this. The questions dropped like bombs did on many parts of the world.

One of the questions that troubled Kaylee was, would she kill one or everyone? How could she kill everyone and be able to maintain a colony if all are dead? This was too difficult to answer. The mission on the ground would be the best way to see how far she would go.

The shuttle descent was uneventful. The craft landing was unremarkable. They took their backpacks and began to walk. They landed twenty-five kilometers away from the village. This village was a simple aggregation of people.

After four hours of trekking, they were within binocular sight of the village. Saia was accompanied by Bilo. He was a male leader. He had little words to share; maybe this was the reason he asked to join. Kaylee needed to know more about this. It was among the many questions that required an answer.

Their position was above the village and at about a kilometer away. It looked like a medieval village. The roads were nonexistent. There seemed to be no cattle, as the field was empty. The houses were round, and there was no smoke coming out of them. Did they not have fire? Or did they have stoves? Then they saw their first aliens.

The door opened, and someone crossed the threshold. It looked like an octopus; it had only four arms, and the head was a little more defined. It did not walk; it appeared to float above the ground. Its body was longer than an octopus. It floated to the field. Suddenly, it stopped and looked around. It seemed it had eyes, but they did not see any.

The octopus wondered, and it was joined by another and by another. This was a sign of people gathering. It seemed the group of octopi called the whole village. This was a sign that something was different.

The mission group was hidden. They ducked under the ridge upon the immobility of the locals. Kaylee, convinced of their allusiveness, did not compute the possibility of their presence being a reason for the local beings to be on notification. Kaylee's right eye popped out, and it went to the edge of the ridge. The eye scanned the village. There were no octopi to be found. This was not a good sign. These things seemed to be going invisible; she had seen this before in her experience.

For a minute, there was no movement. Suddenly, the right eye picked up a color. It was a brownish color and it was to the extreme right. This was not a good feeling. Kaylee recalled the visual, and there was no brown corner in her video. The eye turned to the right and saw it.

The octopus was there, and they had discovered the mission group. This was not a good moment for Kaylee and the two leaders. The brown head came in the eyesight of the humans and the robot. They knew about it, but it never saw them. They were not even sure it had eyes.

The octopus being peeked across the ridge, and it jerked back. A squeal came out, and many more of them came to see the humans and the robot. For a first encounter, this did not go as planned. More squealing happened, and then, suddenly, the humans and the robot could not move. The next moment, the aliens seemed to have knocked off the humans.

This was apparent, as their heads flopped to their sides. The only one not sedated was Kaylee. On the other hand, she could not move. This was a strange sensation, but robots did not have sensations. Immediately, Kaylee called up the ship. This connection was maybe a second, and it got interrupted. One of the aliens turned to Kaylee and squealed. This meant something, but being a robot, it meant nothing to her. She could not read the expression of the alien, and if she was able to discern any, she would not be able to decipher them.

Being a robot, Kaylee was able to see the most impossible moment. The aliens surrounded the humans and robot; they paused and hummed. This was odd enough, but the levitation of their bodies in the air was not joke. The movement surprised Kaylee, but then they walked with their prisoners. This was too much to comprehend. There was nothing beneath the sizable Kaylee, and yet she floated as if she was in space.

CHAPTER 43

THE SKY WAS visible during their trip, but it was no longer in view now that she was in the house. It was a shelter of smooth surfaces. There seemed to have no furniture and no stove either. It was clear of objects. The walls and floors were smooth and shiny. This was an odd place for living.

The aliens entered with their prisoners. Moving them over the center of the house, suddenly there was feeling gravity recoup their bodies. They fell. Kaylee saw the floor, and she expected an impact with this shiny floor. At the moment of impact, there was none. She and the leaders, who were asleep, had gone through the floor and landed softly. Kaylee was still unable to move, but she could analyze the shield's presence.

The shield present was a tangible object. Her sensors operated, and they could find a barrier. This did not mean they could tell you what this obstacle was made of. Inside her brain, the screens came back with unknown material. This fascinated Kaylee until she realized she was in jail with the leaders.

When her attention came back to the octopus-looking people, they were no longer there. Her thought took her maybe three seconds. *How did they exit so quickly and without making a sound?* Her scanner looked for them. They were nowhere to be found, not in the prison or outside of it. Kaylee turned on her echo-locator. She could hear squealing. This was their only indication of their presence. The noise made was different from one moment to the next. There were high-pitched ones and low-pitched ones. This was difficult enough, but this was a puzzle a robot struggled with.

Time was difficult for the humans to determine. For Kaylee, it was easy. It had been six hours. Finally, the humans awoke.

"What the hell happened?" Saia asked while not being able to move. Her face showed signs of distress.

"We are prisoners," Kaylee summarized very succinctly.

"Wow, my head hurts!" Bilo exclaimed.

"How come I cannot move?" Saia demanded to know with a strong feeling of panic in her voice.

"Yeah, why can't I move?" Bilo added.

"We have been disabled. I do not how," Kaylee said.

"How do we get out of here?" Bilo wondered with definite panic in his face and voice.

"I do not know, Bilo. Please take a deep breath," Kaylee stated and continued. "If they wanted to kill us, they would have and now you would be dead," Kaylee reasoned.

Saia and Bilo looked around, but their eyes were not able to move at all. This was a moment of panic, which triggered strange reactions.

"I am going to kill these fuckers," Saia spat out. Then she deepened her thought. "I am going to roast them and eat them as soon as I can get out of here."

"Yeah, I am going to help you," Bill added.

"Kaylee, can you move at all?" Saia asked.

"No, I cannot and I won't help you either." Kaylee's human side was in charge.

"What are you saying?" Saia wondered.

"I cannot help you kill beings who were afraid of you, as much as you are afraid of them," Kaylee put it shortly.

"You will not help us beat those ugly things?" Saia asked.

"No, I will not," Kaylee stated.

"Need I remind you, you are here to help us?" Saia seemed to know more than she revealed prior to this moment.

"That is true, but I was integrated with Kaylee McCloud to give me a perspective on the human mind, and this is my decision—I will not help you kill anyone." Kaylee felt more human at this point than any other moments in the adventure.

The dialogue ended with those words. Bilo wondered which side he should line up with. On the other hand, neither he nor she could move, so no decision needed to be made. As if the end of the dialogue was enough, Kaylee's auditory location placed the octopi people above them.

The programmers of Kaylee's software never thought of first encounter moments. Communication was not going to be that easy. Nor was the conversation with Saia and Bilo going to be facile.

The aliens laid them down. There were no arms coming down to lay them down. It was as if a magical force did it for them. This was amazing and terrifying all at the same time. The locals gathered around Kaylee, and a humming session began.

As the sounds of the octopi people grew, Kaylee could feel a scan happening. They were in her brain, as if they were trying to figure her abilities and strengths and weaknesses. This would be normal when faced with beings you did not about.

It was a first encounter for both species according to Kaylee. This was not an ideal meeting. A meeting where you get your mind scanned was not an ultimate goal. They went on and on with the humming. It was uncomfortable even for a robot. On the other side of the coin, there was no choice; she did not have a choice in this matter either.

Suddenly, the humming stopped, and they floated to Bilo. Then the buzzing resumed. It lasted for a few minutes, and then the aliens moved on to Saia. The murmur resumed. In an instant, it stopped. Then one of them whirled heavily, and the others buzzed loudly too. What did they find? It did sound like a celebration for Saia. How could that be? She was the one with the most vile ideas. Could they be wrong? Kaylee did not experience fear, but this would be the moment.

All of a sudden, they departed. Kaylee opened her auditory location software. She listened, and the squealing continued outside. She did not know what they said, but from her sound analysis, there was some panic in the squealing. Was she sure? There was nothing in her databank about octopi people, so assurance of being correct was not in the picture.

Kaylee could hear that the aliens came back. They gathered and began to hum. In her mind, it became a ritual, and Kaylee deduced something would happen to one of them. She felt the elevation in her systems. The target was Kaylee. Levitation was a trick for earthlings, but here it was a real thing. She came up, and as the jail impediment neared, she wanted to know what the obstacle was. She scanned it.

The scan revealed something amazing. It was an electromagnetic field. There was a current, but as she crossed the wall, there was no charge in this wall. How could this be? If it was electromagnetic, it had to have some current. This was a mystery. However, this would have to wait, as she was lifted out of the room.

Squealing along was back and forth. She thought it must be a dialogue. She attempted to learn their language. It was not difficult to discern a new language for Kaylee if there was a point of reference. There was no point to refer to, and these aliens had her as prisoner.

The arrival in another house was as any other entering a house—you try to not dirty the floor. This was not a problem as no one touched the ground. This house was a little more furnished. There was a table in the middle of the room. There was a side door; Kaylee wondered if this was another room. On the side of the room, Kaylee focused her energy on recording what she could see. Suddenly, her neck and head moved.

Out of nowhere, images landed into her RAM area. This was the live memory acting as her consciousness. This amazed Kaylee; she could see their travel to this location, and then there were images of death and killing. These images were a message, Kaylee was sure of this; what she was not sure of was the meaning of the message. The scenery of death and killing kept running in her RAM. Her function could be separated; she referred the images to historical moments. These were historical clips.

The processing of the information arrived. *They communicate with me through images.* Kaylee attempted to respond. She put up images of Hawaiian people handing out leis. This was an easy image indicating their peacefulness and willingness to discuss. The images shot out of her eyes and were on the wall of the house. This seemed to be well perceived, as the squealing was milder. Then images bolted in her RAM; they were the same images. There was a message here. It was not about their intention; was it someone else's intention?

Kaylee thought about this for a second. Then she shot out an image of Saia, and following her image were images of war. The squealing was deeper and more agitated. This was the message. This would increase her stress if Kaylee was still human.

Responses were images; the next images were of people wondering. This was difficult for Kaylee to decipher. She thought and thought; finally, she responded with images of mountains, beaches, and fields. She was not sure what the message was. The response came quickly; the message was the same, and the pictures were the same. They did not get the answer they wanted.

The thought was Saia, killing, and people wondering. Then it clicked in Kaylee's mind. They wanted to know if she ever killed anyone. The next thought was, *How do you say, "I don't know"?* She searched for images that would tell them this. The only sequence of picture was a person saying "I don't know." The images were on a loop, but this did not translate well among the aliens. They did not know what that was. Kaylee continued to search. There was nothing that could translate to "I do not know."

Then Kaylee attempted to communicate her idea again. This time, she placed the probability equation and ended with a question mark. The squealing did not give an idea of what was going on in their brains, as there was no squealing. Suddenly, there was an explosion of squealing. Some were high pitched, and others were really fast. Was this a positive sign of understanding? Kaylee did not know for sure. Her head turned to her right and observed the aliens.

Somehow, the images coming to her RAM were known to her. Did they scan her memory and used it to communicate? This was very possible. This meant, also, there were secrets she could hold if they had access to her memories and the leaders' too. Was this why they seemed to have issues with Saia? Kaylee had doubts about the young woman herself. This was difficult to ascertain.

There were many colors among the octopi people. A few were brown, a few others were off white, one was red, another was near purple, and one was blue. Kaylee wondered if the color signified the chain of command. If this was the line of command, you wanted to go with the less-used color. She dug a little more in her record of their conversation. She pulled the squealing from the blue, purple, and red individuals. Their utterances were identified, and they were shorter than the others. To know what was said, this was another step that may require a few more hours of listening.

The celebration, according to Kaylee's analysis, ended, and a new set of images appeared. It was the image of a person baking, and it was followed with the image of a person crying. What did this communicate? Kaylee was not sure at all. *Did mean you tried but did not succeed?* This was as close as she could get; there was no other possibility. On top of all this translating, what would she respond to a person baking and then a person crying? This was not evident.

The issue for Kaylee was to communicate that she had her doubts, but she was not sure and had not acted upon Saia. How did one put these notions in images? Kaylee attempted; she put the picture of Saia, followed by one where there was a murder, followed by the Heisenberg equation again, and it was ended with a one-way sign and a question mark. This was the best she could do.

The aliens were silent. This was either they thought or they thought because this puzzled them as much as their message was difficult to interpret. The quietness was squealed out as Kaylee heard a squeal from the red octopus alien. This made a certain chain of command, but she monitored all this very carefully. Then the original squeal drowned in a cacophony of squealing. It was unyielding. She recorded and followed it to the best of her ability.

The aliens huddled, and they came back with an image in Kaylee's RAM; it was an image of Saia and a prison. This image was problematic to interpret. Were they asking if she should be imprisoned or be held, or could it be they wanted her to be tried, judged, and locked in jail for a crime that happened only in her mind and came out of her mouth? How was Kaylee to manage this? This was a lot to handle.

The answer Kaylee gave seemed to have stumped them. They appeared to be wondering how and what to respond to it. The squealing went up and down. This was high paced, and it was difficult to discern which one made what sound. This was all recorded. Kaylee thought the red one was the leader, but now she thought the purple one led the group. This grew frustrating for humans, but Kaylee was a robot. This was a calculation, and the evidence will appear. Or she could ask.

Kaylee showed images of a Native American in all his regalia of feathers and headgear. This was followed by images of Queen Elizabeth II. Finally, it ended with images of FDR in the Congress of the United States of America stating the words that marked the twentieth century, a day that will live in infamy. This was sent. How was it received?

The blue octopus alien peeked down at Kaylee. Then the images hit her RAM. An image of a child saying yes with his head followed an image of a person nodding. The blue was the top of the pyramid. This was a good step. What was she going to do with this rung? This was the question.

How did one ask for a conversation to happen? This was difficult enough, but there was a sort of communication through images. Instantly, Kaylee imagined a way; her image producer came up with a picture of tea time and then an image of two persons talking and, finally, a picture of two persons shaking hands. This was as clear as a cup of Joe could ever be.

Bluish alien pondered. It seemed to grasp the concept offered in those pictures. It squealed, and this released her body. Kaylee regained her mobility, and this was a good moment. It went to the second door. The door opened automatically without any lights or any devices acting on it. Kaylee followed the blue alien into this other room. She entered the other chamber; she did not hesitate and crossed the threshold.

The second area was a dark room that had some purplish-colored lights. There was something that humans could call a table. The blue alien was on one side of this so-called table. Its front tentacles were on the surface. It shot an image of someone coming forward to a table. This could mean "Welcome, please come to the table."

Kaylee joined the blue alien at the table. It was a low table, if it was a table. Then the alien brought his tentacles to her head. Kaylee did not react. She knew already they had scanned her head, so what was the purpose of this? Kaylee remained at the same place while the tentacles moved to the side of her brain.

The next moment, Kaylee and the blue alien were in a space that did not exist in Kaylee's charting of the area. The alien tried to utter the words from its voice apparatus.

"Hemmo, mine name Jkwar," it said.

"My name is Kaylee." If a robot could be stunned, this would be the moment.

"Imachef girldanger," Jwar mumbled out.

"Are you saying you are the chief and something about a girl being dangerous?" Kaylee attempted to translate.

"Es, you good," it said; the pronunciation was not quite right, but on the other hand, they were having a dialogue.

"Her name is Saia. I had my doubts about her. How do you know she will be bad?" Kaylee asked; this was a question with a truckload of knowledge from her side.

"Izwishedher. Zeezevilish." The pronunciation got worse. Kaylee tried to understand.

HENRI NGUYEN

"Are you saying you read her mind?" Kaylee asked.

"Es," the blue alien responded.

"What did you see?" Kaylee wanted to know also.

"Watkwill alour." This came out with some emotion of despair.

"I did not understand. Give me a second." Kaylee tried to decipher its statement. After a few seconds, she uttered, "Kill all of us?" The alien seemed to be nodding his whole body.

There was very little left to say. The tentacles from the blue alien came off. Kaylee was back into the dark room. The lights changed to a pinkish color. The blue octopus alien appeared to be different. Its body leaned to its side. What did this mean? The door opened, and Kaylee was not sure what to do.

Aliens came in and helped the blue one to exit. They did not interact with Kaylee, who was still standing by the low table. She waited until the door closed. The sense of disorientation was not part of her programming. She seemed to understand that she had to wait. What was she waiting for was the question.

Hours passed. The room's light changed from pinkish to greenish. She was not aware of the meaning of this change. While she stood by the table, Kaylee analyzed the squealing sounds they made. She got a sharp squeal, which meant no; if you dragged the squeal slightly, it would mean yes. Then a squeal with tones and almost musical notes meant "Lock them up." The tone and notes were important; Kaylee's vocabulary got the words "death" and "murdered."

Kaylee got to that place by looking at the pictures that were sent to her RAM and associated the sounds to them. Her vocabulary was four words; this was better than nothing, but not too rich of a communication.

Nighttime was almost here. The blue alien had not returned yet. For that matter, no one came back for Kaylee. The robot was still active. She compiled the sounds individually. They had no meaning at this point, but a reference point was needed. This would be the next question.

The door opened, and the blue one entered. Its head was back up. Kaylee wondered if it was exhausted. How did one ask this question in images? This would be a challenge. Kaylee could not smile. She was unable to. She looked at the blue alien floating to the table. Kaylee moved to the lights and pointed to it. She stated, "Light," and waited. The blue alien wondered and paused. She repeated, "Light," again. The blue alien squealed.

The sound was high and in an E measure. Kaylee made the sound, and the blue alien got it that she tried to speak their language. The alien and Kaylee went about growing her vocabulary.

After three days of work, Kaylee was in possession of an alien language. This would be fantastic, but she would need a recharge. This would mean she would have to be freed. She requested this through the alien's language. The blue alien pondered about her request and asked if she would return. Kaylee stated she would; she was a robot and needed to recharge soon. The alien squealed in a harmonious fashion. This meant they trusted her. She replied with a harmonious squeal too; she showed her trust too.

The next hour was for preparation for departure. Kaylee understood the two leaders were safe and nothing would happen if no one did anything to interfere with the aliens. The shuttle lifted up in the air and went into the sky.

CHAPTER 44

THE SHUTTLE DOCKED with the ship. Kaylee exited. A crowd waited for answers.

"Where are Saia and Bilo?" a child's voice asked.

"They are down on the planet," Kaylee responded.

"Why?" another asked.

"There is a lot of issues and items to present. I need to recharge. After that, I will explain to you what happened so far," Kaylee stated and floated away.

The children followed her. There was nothing they could do about a robot needing recharging. Nonetheless, they followed it. Then she locked herself to the floor and began the recharging of her system.

Three hours later, Kaylee did not wake up. Her alarm woke her mind up. Her level of energy was below 5 percent. This was not possible. She called the ship. There was no answer. She attempted to unlock herself, but there was no response. This was not a good sequence of actions for Kaylee.

Her sensors picked up no one close to her. Was this because they were in the Ring, or was it because they were on their way down to the planet? Kaylee the human came out and told her robot side to figure out a way out of the charger. This was necessary for her to figure out what happened to her charging station.

No one could be called. This was a situation. Kaylee reviewed the entry log. No one added one to the software. Then she checked her energy level. It was at 2 percent. This was low. She reviewed the charge software. No errors or any changes were found. It must have been a hardware issue. With her 2 percent of energy, Kaylee floated out of the charging station.

Kaylee proceeded with an examination of the charging area. There was no apparent unplugged wires. She opened the control panel, and there was the problem. The wires had been pulled out. At that moment, she locked herself to the floor and went about to reconnect many wires. This did not seem to bother her one bit. She completed this, and there was no response.

Kaylee continued to look down from the control panel. Then it was evident. The wires had been cut there too. This was interesting, as the person who slashed the wires was evidently smarter to think about another cut below the control panel. This required a person who wanted Kaylee nonfunctional. Her energy level read 1.75 percent.

This was a little too close for anyone, but Kaylee was fine. She began the connection of the wires. This wires were optical wires. She had to use extra energy to send information to see which wire went where. This depleted quickly her energy. It was now 1.25 percent left. She was not done yet.

The work was systematic—a wire at a time. There were about one hundred wires in this bundle. When her energy level read blow 1 percent, she had another twenty-six wires to go. This was not going fast enough. Kaylee elected to shut down the connection to the main computer about the positioning of the spaceship, the connection for spaceship temperature, the spaceship response to exposure to the sun, and other connection to the ship's main computer. This would save her some energy. There was not much left.

HENRI NGUYEN

The last wire was easy to figure out where it went. Her energy level was at 0.5 percent. This was very low. She moved at a normal speed, but as she released herself from the floor, Kaylee floated and approached the charging door; she began to see the low-battery effect. This was not a good moment, even for a robot who did not have emotions. Kaylee pulled herself; she was close. One more push was needed. Her battery was about to shut down completely. Her left arm pulled forward, and she turned on her feet magnetism.

Space was a dangerous place to be in. If there was no space suit, it would take about three seconds for you to die. If the spaceship was not designed to protect its crew from the star's rays, such as gamma, X-ray, delta, and other Greek letters, you would end up as dead as dead was. This was not a good place to be, but Kaylee had to manage some act of sabotage on top of all the dangers of space. This was not fun.

Three hours later, Kaylee recharged her batteries. She could not be pissed, but she had an idea who could have done this. No proof was available on the other hand. Kaylee had an idea how to have the proof she needed. On the other hand, the crew seemed to not be on board. She floated to the shuttle and went in. Kaylee noticed there was no noise and the Ring was a busy place. This time, it was not reflecting this. Was this Saia's plan?

The trip would be long for any human. The anticipation of catching the culprit would eat the patience of humans. Being part of a robot made this different. She wanted to have all the pieces to prove the guilt of Saia. The shuttle descended onto the planet. It would not be a huge revelation to be using a shuttle. Kaylee elected to land closer to the village.

Kaylee kept an eye on the children and their leaders. There were none to be found. This worried the human side of Kaylee. This was a strange feeling. Kaylee the human's brain understood children ran around to strike, and yet the robot part of her felt no need to worry about this potential aspect. Being aware and alert was an essential part of being a robot; being human was difficult to discern all the emotions and how to make decision. The robot made a decision upon statistic and probability. Was this that different?

The ship landed. Kaylee came out of the shuttle. There was no one to welcome her. This was not unusual. Then again, it was the second landing in a strange world. What was usual about this anyway? Kaylee began walking. There was no noise; not even nature noise. She recorded these noises. Here, there was none. This was unusual.

Kaylee passed the woods and the ridge where the aliens discovered them. She arrived at a high point over the village. There were the houses, but there were black traces. This was not blood. What was it? She walked a little faster. She arrived at the first black trace. Kaylee looked at it; she dipped her finger in it. This black substance was oozy and felt like oil. She was not sure what to do at this moment. Her finger sucked some of the oily substance and analyzed it.

As the analysis worked, Kaylee walked to the jail; she walked in. There was no one. Items were wet up; she appeared to assess the probability of what happened. The traces were the pathway to the children and aliens. This was highly probable; the issue raised in her mind was how to calm everybody down and ensure everyone's safety. This was harder to predict.

Kaylee followed the black traces, and it led to the children. At the head of them was Saia. This was almost too predictable. Kaylee walked at her own pace. As she passed the children, she remained calm. The children were not as calm as she was. Saia was in control of the whole encampment. There was no housing, but there were enclosures to maintain the aliens would be restrained. As Kaylee walked through all this chaos, she calculated the numbers and the potential for a peaceful resolution. There seemed none was available.

HENRI NGUYEN

The analysis was over, and the results showed in Kaylee's mind. This was oil. It was their fluid, and their deoxyribonucleic acid was all over it. Strangely, the decoding did not take as long as expected. The code was a ternary system. In Kaylee's mind, there was a calculation happening. *Were these aliens formally biological and through the years of evolution became machine like? Was this the way to see them?* These questions did not matter; Kaylee had to defuse Saia first.

Saia sat on an elevated mount and looked at Kaylee walking through her small army. Despite being a young woman, Saia was strong, and she thought about this battle. Kaylee just caught on to it. Saia stood up and called out to Kaylee.

"What do you want?" she said to Kaylee.

"Can we talk?" Kaylee asked.

"What is there to talk about?" Saia asked sarcastically; she showed her capture of land and octopi aliens.

"You do understand there are fifteen other villages. You surprised them here. I am sure it will not happen again." Kaylee was not really talking to Saia; she spoke to the children, who were too giddy for their own good.

"There are other ways for us to conquer this planet!" Saia shouted back.

"This will not work. I provided you the information. Next attack will be without my help. If anything, I will be on their side," Kaylee said out loud while pointing at the aliens.

"You cannot. You are our robot," Saia said with a tone that indicated a territorial desire.

"I would like to remind you that I have been integrated with the soul of a human," Kaylee said with a desire to remind the children of this fact.

"You cannot stop us from getting this planet." Saia caught Kaylee's intent. She talked to her army now.

"That is your right to think so. My mission was to get you on a planet where you can thrive, but not for you to begin a war." Now Kaylee talked to Saia.

"I could detain you," Saia hypothesized.

"Yes, you could try. I am stronger than your army." Kaylee knew Saia would attempt to show her strength.

"Detain her!" Saia screamed to her soldiers.

The young soldiers approached Kaylee. They were tentative, and their guns and rifles were too large for them. They approached a little more. The situation was not ideal for Kaylee. If she fought the army, she may kill most of them who would go against her mission. If she let them restrain her, she would destroy the only alien civilization ever discovered. She was caught between a hard decision and a destructive one—not a good place.

Kaylee reviewed the history of warfare. Fighting had always the motto of all the wars, except one—the Chinese invasion of Tibet. The war was not a war. There were barely any battles. Buddhists monks made horrible soldiers. This was in fact a walkthrough. It lasted about 156 years, but, eventually, the Buddhists won the war. There was no battle in the end. Reflection of the truth can never be defeated. An idea was stronger than any army was the motto of that war.

Therefore, Kaylee let the miniature army capture her. She walked into a cave, and for good measure, there were bars. Bars of any kind were not strong enough to hold Kaylee back, and even less her ideas. She walked in willingly. Kaylee made sure all heard her message. "I am the first political prisoner." This was a message all the soldiers heard. It made a difference.

The soldiers looked at one another. This was a questioning, as their parents were subjected to this kind of treatment too. Their older siblings told them about these moments; they soaked in this pronunciation of the value of ideas. There seemed to be an unease about putting in prison the only truth teller of them all.

Kaylee was far enough for her voice to not matter for the octopi aliens. However, she knew now that they were machines. It would take some time, but she assigned some energy to communicate with them at a distance. She had only five days of reserve before it would be all lost. It was time to attack Saia's ideas and destroy them.

CHAPTER 45

E VENING WAS NEARLY completed; Saia was still all there. She had so many parts to complete before the night came. She suspected action for Kaylee overnight. This had to be her action design. Saia remembered her mother telling her, "However smart you are, there is always one smarter than you. The only thing you can do is to work harder." This last part of her mother's statement made her work more and harder. She had to precede her enemies.

The night was there; her soldiers were tired, and this was a problem. Saia understood that she could not expect her soldiers to be on alert at all hours. She dispatched the leaders to manage the soldiers of her burgeoning army. Boys and girls were souls searching for which way to head. She was there first and needed to maintain her lead over Kaylee.

Saia was a nervous woman. Often, she would sit with one of her nails at her teeth, and her right leg would shake incessantly. This was an energy of thinking. Saia plotted and counterplotted against and for herself and in her head. This was also nonstop as her right leg moved to the same rhythm.

Saia thought to herself that Kaylee will make a move on her army. She could have beaten them by force. Why was she not acting on it? This troubled her. It could not be her mission. This was too easy; there had to be another idea behind all of this. Saia was not sure what this idea could be; most of her thoughts were not worthy for the enemy. Kaylee was a human inside a robot; her strength was above her army. Why did she not go after them?

The night was in her full unveiling. This moment of darkness made Saia wonder about what idea Kaylee was seeking. Could it be a trial?

Why would that be to her advantage? The ideas began to line up; that was the answer. Saia put her figurative finger on the problem—Kaylee wanted to have the ear of her army. She knew Saia's army was young and still could hear new ideas and ideals. This was too dangerous. How was she going to counter this? This was a problem. Saia knew her army was a group of youth who suffered on Earth, and this would not fly on this planet. She would have to find a way to disconnect Kaylee and not have her speak to her army. Therefore, it would have to be another way but a trial.

Thinking to the early hours of the morning, Saia was deeply thinking about the issue of Kaylee. There could only be two solutions. The first was to wait five days and let her run out of battery; the second was more violent—put an explosive in the cave and destroy her. This was simple but harder to explain to her army. She did lie when she said Kaylee was behind her idea of invasion. This was a slight problem.

The idea of explosive was easier to complete. Saia knew Kaylee plotted on her side too. This was a race, and she needed to win this now. The young woman was tired, and getting to bed was not an option. It had been a long day, but there was still time to think how to counterplot against her enemies. Saia wanted to have the upper hand.

Then a third solution entered her mind. *Could you convince Kaylee to work with you?* This would make everything easier for Saia. *How would you convince a robot to participate in your plan of conquering the planet?* This was the key for Saia.

Finally, Saia went to bed. It was on the ground under a strange-looking tree. She closed her eyes and wondered if she would have the chance of waking up when the sun would come up. This was a fear of hers.

This fear arouse from her mother one night going to bed, thinking nothing was in her way. The next morning, she woke up to the sound of a raid. This was terror to Saia; she thought safety can only be obtained on top of the food chain. You would never find it at the bottom. This was the lesson of her youth. When Saia came out of her hiding spot, her mother was gone and her older brother was dead. This was a reality she would always live with.

The sun shone on Saia's face, and yet she was still in deep sleep. The leaders hesitated to wake her up. There was nothing urgent to report. The decision was made to leave her to sleep a little more. Clocks were not a premium in this army. Time was a fluid concept for all of them. They had never seen a watch, but this was just a reality to face—time was a concept that you needed.

An hour passed, and Saia woke up. She felt the sun's rays of the binary suns. It felt hot and warming; this was not a new feeling for Saia. She lived in the Southern Chinese province; it was a place of heat and humidity. This was more a memory of fonder days, which she would never have again. She found her standing balance and walked around. Her soldiers gathered and wanted to know what was next.

Armies were groups of people who needed to know things that they could not handle. This was a truth in every army, but they still demanded to know.

Saia looked at the cave and thought, *It might be better if I had a one-on-one conversation.* This would require a strong argument to persuade a robot to follow her way. What would this argument be? Kaylee was in the camp of her mission, and Saia was in the camp of this is our planet. How did one marry those two together?

Questions accumulated in her head. Answers scattered very quickly out of her mind. This was a reality to face. Saia decided to begin with a conversation, and then maybe an explosive may be needed.

HENRI NGUYEN

CHAPTER 46

T HE SKY WAS visible from the cave. Kaylee's eyes fixated on it. It was a clear blue sky, which she understood was the result of the warming of nitrogen, and this being the most populous gas in the atmosphere would make the sky light blue.

Saia entered the enclosure. She stood tall and had a smirk on her face. This was a presentation that Kaylee had never seen before; then again, she was in this body for less than a month. Saia appeared to have the desire to talk her into submission. How did she ever perceive this? This would have to come from her human side. Only it could sense human feelings. Nonetheless, robots were impervious to jails and being sad or happy; Kaylee appeared, as always, somber and unsmiling.

"Hello," Saia began to speak.

"Yes," Kaylee responded to show Saia they were on the same step.

"I thought we could talk for a little while," Saia said.

"What about?" Kaylee asked.

"How about why you are in here," Saia looked around at the cave.

"Sure. Why not?" Coming from the robot, this was an odd moment. One would expect a quirky smile or sarcastic presentation, but the robot did none of those.

"You are here because you would defeat my army. You would also destroy my plans to take this planet. So that is why you are in here," Saia summarized the situation.

"Instead of talking to me about this situation, you thought of blowing me up or letting me die within five days. This would make your army slightly less willing to follow you. You are here to get me on board with your plan." Kaylee thought about this too.

"Hmm, you gave this a thought too." Saia was impressed.

"Of course, I did. Here is my offer to you. You give up your leadership position, and we will leave these people alone. We will find some other planet to settle," Kaylee stated.

"What if there is no other world?" Saia asked.

"Then we all die in space." Kaylee made this comment with no issues about it.

"Wow! You are honest. I will give you that," Saia exclaimed.

"You do not need to give it to me. I am a robot," Kaylee replied.

"Ha ha!" Saia laughed out. When she recovered, she stated, "You are right. I will not give you that satisfaction, and I will blow you up or let you die."

Saia turned on her heels and walked out of the cave. This was not a good moment for her army and her.

Kaylee bought herself some time. She was near communicating with the locals. Finally, she had Jwar's communication opened. She selected words known to her to communicate her idea. A squeal here and a softer one, a sharp one there, and her message was ready. She sent it. It said, "I am Kaylee. I will get you out of this."

Then Kaylee sent another message. "Wait for my signal."

It was near the middle of the day. This was the moment when armies desire to eat. This army was no different. There was no breakfast, and, hence, lunch was more than important. There was a guard, and this would be easy to go around him. Kaylee waited for all to go to the encampment. Then she lengthened her arm and pricked the child with a small needle. This made him turn around. The next move was to whack him. Kaylee did so immediately.

To get out, all Kaylee had to do was to break the wooden bars. She knew Saia anticipated this move. Instead of going to the lower level of the small valley, she climbed to the top of it. From there, Kaylee turned up her volume to the maximum level.

"Please allow me to say what I must say. You are headed to your end. Remember your parents. These are the moments and events they tried to keep you away from. Saia hides the truth from you all. She knows your desire to have a world for yourself, but do you want to kill for it? I do not think so. I think you want a better world than a conquered one." Kaylee paused. Then she continued. "Please lay down your weapons and return to the ship. We will find you a world for yourself. Patience is important." Kaylee stepped down, and Saia went up the hill with two of the leaders.

Kaylee did not fight them. She was brought down the short hill. Walking by the enclosure where Jwar and its people were assembled, Kaylee decided to use her strength to her advantage now. Her entire body was metallic. This body moved suddenly and surprised the leaders.

Within two seconds, Kaylee reached the prison cells. These were made of wood. The doors ripped off; the aliens knew this was the signal. They were free. However, running was not a way. They stood beside Kaylee and made a wall.

Saia ordered her army to raise their weapons. This seemed to not work. Even the leaders hesitated. Kaylee knew she created the moment to utter the next truth.

"Saia wants you to kill us. Have you asked yourself why? I will tell you why. It is easier to shoot your problems away instead of negotiating them. Your parents thought the same. It is hard to be the prey—only you want to negotiate. You are the predators and you feel powerful and guiltless. Is that true? No. Guilt will follow you. In the dark, you will see the shadow of culpability." At this moment, Kaylee realized that the word "culpability" was too much; no one seemed to grasp the meaning of it. Then she finished her speech with "Saia and I will have a debate to decide who is right." She felt good about this idea of a debate.

Lunch was a rustling mumble around the aliens and Kaylee. This was a good sign. The youth began the thought. The debate was the only way out of this mess.

Jwar and Kaylee communicated through a brain-to-brain discussion. It was as close to telepathy as anything else. Kaylee could search through his memories and secrets; he could too. And yet none of it was completed. A trust existed between Kaylee and Jwar.

The debate was set in the afternoon of the same day. It was held on the short hill. A slight predebate moment happened when the voters were identified. Saia refused the notion of having the aliens vote, and yet they were allowed by the majority of the children. This was a good start for Kaylee.

"Saia, please state your case," Kaylee opened up. This was her strategy to see what her debate was going to pivot on.

"OK, I will." Saia turned to the crowd and began. "You know my point—we need a planet. We are sick of being in space. We need to feel the gravity of a planet and need to begin our world." It was succinct, and she revealed little or nothing of her debate points.

"She is right. I promised you this. I made you another promise too. It will not be a planet where you will have to lay people down. This is not a way for a world to become yours." Kaylee refrained from making her point too. She needed to open up Saia's points to see them. "My opponent had been my friend. She was there when Rusus was made a reality. She was there when Hitze became a reality. But before the last planet, she elected to become the leader, the commander, the supreme chief, the tyrant." The last word made the crowd shudder.

"I am not a tyrant. I am a truth teller." Saia defended herself. This was the debate point.

"If she is not a tyrant, why are you here? Why are you eating a simple meal? Why can you not go to sleep whenever you want to? Why is it she tells you what to do, while she is protected from harm?" Kaylee sensed offense would be her best option, as she saw the debate point of Saia.

"Again, I am a leader. I am not a tyrant. You wanted a world to colonize. You wanted to begin it now." Saia seemed to struggle with this debate.

"If she is not a despot, why are you following her and her words? Think for yourself. This is the essence of democracy." Kaylee seemed to have a hand over this debate.

"She lies. I wanted to do good by you, nothing else." Saia was on defense too much. She was trapped.

"If I lie and she has done nothing but good for you, why are you with weapons? This is a decision you cannot escape. Let them return to their lands and homes, and we shall go back to space and find another home for you." Kaylee made her points and seemed to close the debate.

"No! No! This cannot be. We are going to take this land because it is ours!" Saia came out screaming. This was her last point of her debate.

"And there she is—your tyrant." Kaylee walked toward Saia and showed her to the crowd.

The group of children and aliens was silent. This was the end of the debate. There was nothing else to say. The vote was almost meaningless, but it happened.

The time escaped slowly for Saia, who was detained by Kaylee. This was not a real detention, as Kaylee stood by her. Saia knew she had lost. Her face strained, and her forehead was showing her muscles tensing. *This is a trap,* she thought. *It's unfair* was the next thought.

The vote returned, and Kaylee won. At that moment, Jwar communicated through Kaylee. All the crowd could hear was squealing of different tones and notes. Kaylee stated, "You want to share the land around us. That is possible. We can come up with a division of the land. You are welcome to this world," Jwar said through Kaylee.

"Are you sure?" Kaylee asked the octopus alien.

"We are, and we would like for you to leave Saia to our care," Jwar squealed.

"Why?" Kaylee wondered.

"The world can only grow if Saia grows with it," the squealing revealed.

"Very well," Kaylee accepted.

Saia trembled. She was terrified at the thought of being a prisoner again. The thought of it made her burst into tears. This was the price for this planet.

The next day, the negotiation began. Bilo and Ruba sat at the table. Across were Jwar and Hjee. Kaylee sat in between the two camps. The demands of the earthlings were territorial. Those were obtained in exchange for lessons in living in society and politeness. This seemed to be very important to the Wshlng. This was the name of their species.

"Wshlng" was difficult for anyone to say or even spell. The children mocked it, and Kaylee had to remind them that politeness was a part of the deal. This made them reflect on their mocking tone. The negotiations were done.

Humans were allowed anywhere they would be interested in. The exception to this was if the land was occupied by the Wshlng, then it would not be permitted. This was easy enough. The lessons would be once every five days. Finally, politeness was mandatory.

The next week was dedicated to unloading the ship. This was not hard, but this was long because of the eagerness and anxiety felt by the group. Being children or being the colonizers was not the easiest moment for any of them.

CHAPTER 47

THE WEEK OF unloading was finished. The spaceship was empty. All that was left were the bridge and the charging platform for Kaylee. The Ring was emptied. The stocking freight were gone. The shuttles were gone too, except for the one for Kaylee.

Kaylee was on board the spaceship. At that moment, she recalled Tracy; a feeling of being squeezed in her brain was felt. Was it a ghost? Or was it what her robot side called a fake feeling, as she no longer could feel them?

Floating there in space, Kaylee headed to the shuttle. There was one more conversation to be had before she would leave. The feeling of closure could not be felt by robots, but satisfaction was close enough.

Kaylee landed her shuttle. She walked out of the craft. She was near a home. It was all by itself in a valley a few kilometers away from the village of Wshlng. The house was a wooden structure, and there were windows covered with plastic tarp per their color.

Walking out was Saia; she appeared to be like any other day—preoccupied. Kaylee walked up to her house. Saia stared at her.

"Hello." Kaylee opened the conversation.

"Hello. How are you?" Saia seemed more polite and caring.

"How are you?" Kaylee asked.

"What do you care?" Saia responded. This was more like the young woman Kaylee knew.

"I asked because I care. I want you to be well treated and not tortured or anything of the sort." Kaylee got the idea of not being welcome.

"The Wshlng are not torturing me. They are very nice. We talk, but I sense you have a word in it." Saia opened as much as a heavy door being opened by a young child.

"What word are you thinking I am including in the conversation?" Kaylee asked; she showed her ignorance and her lack of participation.

"I guess it is not that I hear your voice. It is that I hear your words in their voices," Saia admitted.

"It is possible their word use is influenced by my instruction of our language to them," Kaylee admitted too.

"That is true. Their language was taught by you. There were fewer contractions and less vocabulary mistakes. I guess I was used to the mistakes; it makes more real and more human." Saia softened in her speech, and she showed some aggressive thoughts at Kaylee.

"Are you still angry at me?" Kaylee opened the jar of potential of aggressive behaviors.

"No," Saia stated with a smile on her face. With her hand, she indicated an invitation to sit on the porch of her home. Then she resumed the discussion. "I am not. I may have some residuals from the events off the spaceship. I would like to say I am sorry for those episodes." The depth of her apology was not making Kaylee feel better, as she was a robot, but it made her feel better. It lightened her up.

"Thank you." Kaylee felt she had to say this.

Both of them sat there on the porch and looked at the midday sun shining. There were two suns bombarding arrays upon the dirt. Kaylee observed nothing new about the whole situation. Then Saia returned to the conversation.

"I thought of planting wheat and maybe oatmeal."

"Oatmeal requires a cool weather and a lot of water. As we are not sure whether we are in summer or spring, it may be more cautious to plant corn. It demands more water, but it is hardier." Kaylee gave her advice.

"Are you giving me farming advice?" Saia uttered out and laughed at the same time.

"I guess I did." Kaylee did not laugh, but Saia did for the both of them.

"Thank you. Thank you for having a normal conversation with me. Thank you for accepting me as the asshole who tried to rule over the planet." Saia tried to punch the shoulder of the robot, but it was not a good idea.

"Do you see yourself living here, starting a family?" Kaylee wondered out loud.

"I do, but does anyone want to have me as their wife?" Saia wondered.

"I am sure Bilo likes you. His heart rate was elevated every time he was near you," Kaylee stated.

"You see, this is what I mean. You make no mistake about anyone or anything," Saia came out.

"I am just stating facts." If Kaylee could smile, it would have been a sarcastic comment.

"I feel sometimes you are not a robot," Saia said with a smile on her face.

"Once upon a time, part of me was human," Kaylee informed Saia.

HENRI NGUYEN

"I know. They gave us that information," Saia admitted.

"Did you stir the rebellion?" Kaylee asked.

"Yeah, I did. You want to know why?" Saia asked but did not expect an answer; she took a deep breath and continued, "This reason was the selection of people for the colonization. It seemed we were the last one. The planets appeared to be more difficult, and I wondered if we could get to a place, it would be it. The rest of the colonists agreed with me."

"I see," Kaylee uttered out.

"I am sorry for having done this to you, but I felt imprisoned and trapped," Saia said.

"Do you feel the same now?" Kaylee asked.

"No, I do not. I have what my mom wanted and what I wanted all my childhood," the seventeen-year-old said calmly. Then a thought crossed her mind. "The Wshlng are good people. They accepted me and worked with me to free me from the idea of persecution. This can be haunting at times. Also, they are dying." The words came out with sadness in her voice.

"What do you mean?" Kaylee wanted more information.

"I saw it in their minds. They are dying, not soon but dying." The emotions of sadness and grief appeared on her face. Tears drew and dripped down her face. It was the first time she showed humanity.

"Thank you," Kaylee said and got up.

"Will you come again?" Saia asked.

"I think you are all doing well and on your way to better times," Kaylee reflected.

"So this would be the last good-bye?" Saia asked.

"I guess it would be." Kaylee seemed to have an end.

Kaylee turned to say those words, and Saia opened her arms. A hug happened. Hugging a piece of metal was never that emotional and never that warm, but this one was.

Kaylee walked back to her shuttle and took a last look at Saia. She marveled at the strong little woman who had to deal with a lot of issues within herself. This was a reality for every one of them, Kaylee thought. Then Kaylee got in the shuttle. The door shut under her feet. A few seconds later, its engine roared and it lifted up.

Kaylee felt she should have a last conversation with Jwar. The shuttle trip lasted less than a minute. It took her longer to land the craft than the flying took. She came down and walked toward the purple Wshlng. Inside her brain, Kaylee squealed, and this meant, "Jwar, can we talk?"

Jwar met Kaylee. It was joyful. It seemed they found solace for their lives. This was too huge to be it. How can anyone feel solace for their lives? Kaylee was unable to process the information as an answer.

"Hello," Kaylee squealed out.

"Hello to you, Kaylee," Jwar responded.

"I came back from Saia's place. You have done a good job with Saia," Kaylee expressed.

"Thank you. She is a fragile woman. She needed some help with her traumas. This was not hard when you realize every living being has trauma to deal with," Jwar squealed back.

"Indeed, we all have issues. Can I ask you a question?" Kaylee asked.

"Of course, you can," Jwar answered.

"Saia told me that, through her therapies, she saw your death," Kaylee put it shortly.

"Yes, we are dying. We all are. That is the problem being living beings," Jwar answered without skipping a squeal.

"She said it was not coming soon. Is that true?" Kaylee needed to know.

"Saia is a strong woman. She understood the situation well. We, the Wshlng, were a species not that different from what we show here. However, after many, many, centuries, we faced the end of our time. We found a way to stay 'alive' for a millennium longer. This is what you see now," Jwar admitted.

"The oil and the ternary code mean you are robots too." Kaylee put it altogether.

"In a shape and a form greater than yourself, yes, we are," Jwar answered her question.

"When is your time over?" The question was brutal, but she was Kaylee.

"We believe we have another seventeen years or so," Jwar responded.

"Is this why you accepted the colonization of the planet?" Kaylee added on.

"Indeed, we knew we were soon to be done here. Therefore, it would be easier to ease the integration of another specie," Jwar answered wishfully.

"How was your world before you became robots?" Kaylee wondered.

"This was a long time ago. There were towns and roads. There were ways to travel faster, and we ended up living a life no one wanted to live. There were stories about one bad person, and this became a tradition. We wondered if the whole world was bad. There was no trust left. This led us to war, and war was unlimited. The cruelty of living beings can only be measured by the good they do. Our scientists came to the conclusion that we damaged our world and only a few of us would survive it. This was the age of the robot. We have been alone ever since. When you came, it was like the sky opened. We saw the devil inside Saia, but we also saw her pains. This was the ultimate dilemma for us as we saw each other in her pains and her evil ideals. This was the world to us," Jwar squealed out. This was heavy stuff.

"Thank you." Kaylee absorbed the telling of their history.

The suns passed over their heads, and the afternoon progressed as usual. There was nothing to stop the suns from crossing their skies, but tomorrow was another day in which the suns would do as they pleased.

The children of this world were about to disappear, and what about the children of her world? Would they burn the planet and break apart? This was up to them. She could only take them here. She had no mission related to their survival. This was up to them and their memories.

The locals were gentle, but even this would not be enough. What if they were evil? What if they lured them here to take them for food? This was ludicrous. There was nothing she could do at this point but leave.

CHAPTER 48

THE NEXT MORNING came, and Kaylee was on the spaceship. The colonies were all on the planet. She would have to leave them alone. She would continue to be in space. This did not bother her as much as it did Saia.

There were a few things left to complete, but Kaylee's biggest problem was, *Where would you go?* A debate began in her head. This was between her human side and her robot counterpart.

"Where do you want to go?" Kaylee asked her robot side.

"Do we need to go anywhere?" Robot responded.

"Ah, yes, you are being logical again." Kaylee snorted at the robot.

"We have completed the mission," the robot responded.

"You are way too logical about this. So let us address your issue. You are correct, we have completed the mission. Second, we are free to go anywhere we desire. Three, why not go anywhere?" Kaylee made the argument a little more ridiculous than it needed.

"So what is your point?" The robot was not sure what she tried to say.

"Evidently, we have nothing left to do. Let us go out there. We have some nuclear bombs left. Let's use them," Kaylee said with a tone that indicated she wanted to see the universe.

"What if one of the colonies needed our help?" the robot hypothesized.

"They can't even communicate their problems. They will have to survive, and that is it," Kaylee put in short words.

"You speak the truth. There are many troubles they can run through. Should we not be their failsafe measure?" This question was a pause in Kaylee's fight with the robot's mind.

"Maybe, but our mission was to establish three colonies. We did this. Now we have the freedom of going our own way," Kaylee responded to her robotic half.

Silence fell between them. There was little she or it could say that would tip the balance of power for one another. Then an idea came to Kaylee.

"What if we went back to earth and rescued more people to settle them on a different planet?" Kaylee suggested.

"Good idea. I agree," her robot side stated.

"All right. All we have to do is trace our steps back," Kaylee stated.

"Or we could shoot to our solar system," the robot indicated.

"Would this be too much to ask for our engine?" Kaylee asked the robot side.

"It may be, but if successful, we will save a lot of time and bombs for the next travel," the robot mind responded.

"All right. What can we lose in all this?" Kaylee expressed.

"Actually, we would be able to confirm the theory of parallel universe," the robot enunciated.

"How?" Kaylee wondered, as if she knew what the theory was.

"It was theorized in the early twenty-first century that the universe was a series of two-dimensional universes and we perceived them as one. If this theory is true, we could make the distance in a few days." This was the theory. Kaylee had no choice but trust the robotic side, as all this was spaghetti to her.

"All right, let's do it," Kaylee agreed.

The calculations took about a day, and then another day was taken to move away from the planet and wait for the fourth planet to move along to shoot for the bottom of the sun. At the speed they were about to travel, a turn was not the easiest thing to complete.

Two days later, Kaylee and the robot was the only person on board, and then the ship dropped the nuclear weapon. It exploded. The thrust was enormous. They were beyond the speed of light.

C was the symbol for the speed of light. This would be 299,792 kilometers per second. This was fast; at this moment, they traveled faster than the speed of light. This was not the time to stick a head or a limb out the window.

The trip was nearly forgettable as it was so fast. There was not much to recall. The light, photons, was seen almost going backwards. This was an odd experience. Kaylee admired this moment and when she crossed the depression of the sun in the fabric of space. This was not a moment you would remember, but it was a mark in time. One second, the suns bombard your vision, and the next, you were in the dark.

Traveling in the dark was not terrific, but it had its poetic moments. If only one of them could write a poem. Kaylee was never taught by her father, and she never went to school, where this art was no longer taught. The robotic side was not even in the ball park to have this debate.

An hour passed, another hour passed, and another. It seemed lost was a possibility. This was part of the calculation; mistakes were possible. As the hours elapsed, the possibility grew. The robotic side did not panic. For that matter, it could not feel a thing. It could only calculate. All was a probability, for all it cared was the proof of a place or a theory of humankind. This was the only way it could be.

If not for those ideals of science, it would have no thought. Kaylee was its soul because she was human. Her expression of ideas and concepts of emotional feelings were difficult with the robotic side. On the other hand, it maintained her mind in focus. This was a strange marriage.

Finally, a source of light came into focus. They moved toward this source of light. This came dramatically harsher. The shield held, but the light around it was blinding. They came closer and closer to this source of light. Then it went from darkness to light. This overwhelmed all but Kaylee the robot.

They emerged and flew away from the sun. The location was not clear. A few minutes were required to address this issue. The robot was hard at work. Then it became true. They were in their original star system. They began slowing down. Then Venus came into view. Earth was next.

In orbit, they tried to follow any communication. And there was plenty of it.

The thought of going to Earth again was appealing to the human side of the robot. Kaylee wanted to see her old world; this was a reality that she never thought she would ever do again. As she floated in the air, her robotic side was dominated. There were feelings. She thought she lost those feelings.

There was a moment of eagerness, but this moment fleeted away. It was not reality; it was like a feeling, difficult to assert what it was, but it was not real. The robot was in charge of the shuttle and its entry in the atmosphere.

The shuttle landed in Australia. It was a desert; how can one continent become this pile of sand? This was human making. The sand blew against Kaylee's body. Every grain of sand made a small sound on the metallic body. This was an instant of reflection, but this would not happen. Kaylee headed to the train.

The train was older, and this required some readjustments to make it functional. Finally, it went; she reached the tunnel of life. There was some of it. The people were hidden and darkened by this last attack. It was not nirvana; Kaylee and the robot never saw nirvana, but they were sure this was not heaven.

The lights were off. The darkness reigned. The people tried to stay away from the light, as it would bring the North American Army. This was a reality to manage. Management was not the word they used; instead of the word "reality," they used a different word—"nrk." This nrk was a Thai term for "hell." This was not far from the truth.

The remaining people were left alone. Their AI ran out; there was no more electricity. There was no light; barely any food to talk about. This was arduous; beyond arduous, it was nrk.

Kaylee entered the tunnel. No one came out; they hid, and there was not one person who dared change this situation. Kaylee turned on her lights. Upon the lights hitting the broken stalls, cracked woods from a table, half a chair, and clothing were revealed to Kaylee's eyes. This would bring anyone to sadness; Kaylee was a robot, and this was not making her sad.

Kaylee lifted pieces to make her way through the shambles. Despite all this disorder, she looked for survivors. This was her new mission. There was hope as long as she had energy in her.

Nrk was no place for anyone to live. Nevertheless, there were people left here; this was the thought running across her mind. Her mind was complicated; no one really knew how it would end up when you crossed a human into a robot.

Another stall was lifted. A child was there; he looked very weak and terrified. Kaylee knew it was not going to be that easy for her to calm the child down. Over her left shoulder, Kaylee could see the mother with a broom about to swipe at her. Immediately, she pulled up and looked at the woman. There was no facial expression that she could ever give to reduce their terror.

As the broom landed on her left side of her body, there was no pain. There was no effective way to indicate her compassion and kindness. There was about to be a second broom hit when a man came out and said in Laotian, "She is the one." This must be some sort of code, because more of them came out. As they moved toward her in the dark, there were voices chanting, "Hara, Hara, Hara."

Kaylee was emotional in her mind, and the robot showed nothing. There was no way for her to show anything.

Kaylee counted the crowd. There were 169 people left. Among them, ninety-four of them were children. This was potentially another colony. Computing all these people for two months, she came up with the results—she did not have enough food, as there was no food on the spaceship. This would be a problem.

Taking 169 people to anywhere was difficult. Moving these 169 people was not just difficult; it was excruciating. The pain of walking; the open sores that could not be repaired, as the body did not have enough calories to even make the person not lose weight. This was terrible for Kaylee; it was a good thing that she was a robot at this time.

Taking the train to Australia was long, and no one complained. This was the resilience of people who were trash. There was a sense of being dumped on every day and why this would ever change, until Kaylee

HENRI NGUYEN

or Hara came to save them. They were willing to put up with hunger if this situation would improve the chances of their children to make something for the future. This was a strong feeling in the parents on this train. For Kaylee, none of those thoughts existed. There was an idea for getting food for the next trip. This was her only thought.

Kaylee felt different from her previous human life. Her robotic side focused her ideas, and there were little or no fleeting ideas. Her sexual desire was extinguished. Was she happy about it? She was a robot; how could she ever be happy about anything?

At the shuttle, Kaylee helped everyone to get onto it. The walking up was accompanied by tears and words equivalent to good-bye and kissing the sandy ground. They knew there was another world out there. This one was over.

The shuttle took off and climbed in the sky. Finally, the craft arrived at the ship. Docking was easy, and the unloading was easier for the people. Space came without gravity, and this lifted them. It was not always funny; it was surprising and disorienting for some, while others could see a future in the lack of gravity.

Settling everyone in rooms was easy. Telling them she had to recharge to go down and get them food was not as easy. The words came easily, as her databank of languages was wide enough for communication. The hard part was their anxiety.

There was a feeling of being lost without Kaylee. She was the most important person for all of them. Kaylee had to reassure them of her return with food. This was a difficult motion to complete. Finally, she went to her recharge platform. If Kaylee could, she would have been relieved.

Three hours later, some of the children stared at her as Kaylee began moving. She wished she could smile. This was among the cards for her.

She could only be the robot they knew as Hara. Their parents were resting; at least she hoped for a temporary rest. Kaylee swung herself in the direction of the shuttle bay. The children followed her.

Most of the food were in North America. They produced in Pittsburg or in Cheyenne. These were two bases she needed to break into to get them food. There would be armed men and a lot of weapons. She had none. This was not a fair battle plan.

Within the next twenty minutes, Kaylee hacked into their AI. She changed the guard schedule for the Cheyenne manufactory. Food was a commodity, and this meant workers and security could change. There were no questions from the workers and the guards. When was the last robbery the guards ever witnessed? This was no big issue.

The next evening, Kaylee flew the shuttle to Cheyenne and thought of a way into the food deposit. There was no need for weapons, Kaylee thought. However, speed was the main issue. Kaylee decided to land the craft not near the factory but directly at the back door of it.

Most of the food manufacturing was completed in the building, but it was moved in large casings at the back of the building. She was alone, and this would take a little more time. The guard, because she could not change it to zero guard, would be suspicious and call out the army, and this would take them about twenty minutes to reach the factory. This would be enough time to get two casings into the ship.

The plane was twenty thousand meters above the factory. It waited, and this was no difficult moment. The radars could locate the shuttle, but because Kaylee had a connection with the AI in charge of the Interweb, she was able to disable the radar pickup and missile response. Indeed, there was a bling with the radar; immediately, Kaylee shut it off. There was nothing to see here.

HENRI NGUYEN

The third shift of guards came in. There was only one guard. Kaylee descended from the stationary place to the back of the building. The landing was close enough to the door. Kaylee lowered herself to the ground and moved as fast as she could to break in the doors. This was no hard thing. The door was open, and Kaylee saw two casings of food ready for shipment. She pushed the first one, and it came near the craft. Kaylee kept pushing when a voice came into her auditory instruments. It was the guard. Another casing should be sufficient.

Kaylee returned for a second casing and pushed it. The minutes passed, and this was anxiety ridden for the guard. He shot two magazines of energy. He was not able to hit Kaylee, who was not a small robot, and, of course, there was a series of swearing and bad words accompanying the shooting.

The second load was on board. Kaylee's auditory receptors could hear the cars of soldiers headed to Cheyenne. There was not enough time to calculate how much food she just stole. There was enough time for her to run to the cockpit. She got to the cockpit. Then something was wrong.

The cockpit was locked.

Kaylee was not surprised, but she recalculated. This was not expected. The calculations were useless. Someone closed her hack of the AI and rode back on the link. Kaylee was in control of her body, but the control of the plane was lost for now. This was not a good moment.

Soldiers got closer, and this was getting worse for Kaylee. However, per her robot shape and being a robot, there were no emotions and no facial expressions.

CHAPTER 49

THE COLD NIGHT in Cheyenne transformed into a heated night. The army surrounded Kaylee and her craft. The shuttle was not accessible to Kaylee. The link with the Interweb to the AI was lost. No calculation would be enough to regain control of the shuttle in the next five minutes.

Four minutes elapsed. Kaylee knew she would have to do something out of the box. Hence, thinking outside of the box would be necessary.

Kaylee calculated, if she was to be taken, she would end up in Chicago, and General Sihi would use her as a trophy for the robbery. This was going to be difficult to absorb, as the shuttle would be dismantled and the food recuperated.

Her mind scanned all access to the shuttle system. Then Kaylee reached an unused lavatory evacuation subroutine. Could this be the one door no one ever considered? Kaylee entered through the subroutine and got to the lavatory routine and entered the access code. The next second, she was in the system.

The soldiers were now surrounding her. They screamed and yelled for her to remain still or she ran the risk of being shot. She had yet to move for the last minute.

Now she was in the system; she ran across the software. She had the choice of sending the shuttle back to the spaceship or make it fly until she could figure out how to get out of jail. She elected to send the craft back to spaceship. Her thought was *If I returned it, there will be a chance for the people to live.*

The next second, the shuttle lifted, and this made a noise that the soldiers were deafened by. This gave Kaylee the chance of running away. The running was not difficult, but was it fast enough to lose the soldiers behind her?

Kaylee ran and ran; she never checked behind her. There was no sound of anyone chasing her. Then a car sound came into her listening devices. They were coming, and she would have to hide. There was no way to reach the kind of speed the cars engendered. Kaylee was closing on a forest. This could be her hiding place.

Ducking into the woods, her eyes perceived darkness. This was a decent forest for hiding. There were logs on the ground. This would be an adequate visual hiding spot, but her metal would reveal her so quickly. She would have to find a location with a lot of metal.

The thought crossed her mind; a metal dump would be a better hiding spot. At that moment, Kaylee reviewed the map, and there was a metal dump about sixteen kilometers away. There was a thought of sprinting for it, but she knew they would catch up to her in a split. If she maintained an unpredictable path, she had a chance.

At that moment, Kaylee began a running pattern that made no sense. Kaylee used her human side. She became artistic. The car sounds were at a distance of four kilometers, and she attempted to maintain them at that distance.

The patterns made straight lines and changed only if they were closing in at less than four kilometers. The problem of having no planes but only drones. You could lose yourself with a fat running a frequent direction changes. The following cars would struggle to maintain their speed. And this happened. She was close to the metal dump.

There was a secondary issue. If the metal was plenty in this dump, her energy would give her away. She would have to shut down. The robot had a wake-up call, but this was not fully tested and only worked if she was in the charging station. She was not going to be in the charging station. Kaylee had little choice; she would have to shut herself down. This was a danger.

At the edge of the metal dump, Kaylee knew her victory could be partial. The shutting down of a robot was not difficult; it was the waking up. When the robot was in the charging station, it was easy to have the wake-up function linked to her energy level. At 100 percent, the software would kick in. In this case, there would be nothing kicking in. As Kaylee ran into the metal dump, she wrote a piece of software. This was a dangerous moment. What if she wrote a wrong instruction or one that did not work with the wake-up software? She did not have the luxury of time to test her software. It was in.

In a flash, Kaylee jumped into a pile of metal, and at the same time, she shut off her systems.

The search went on, and there was no one to find.

The second day, they went in visually. And nothing was found. There was too much metal.

The third day, they maintained soldiers present at the metal dump.

The fourth day, the metal looked alike to everyone.

The fifth day, General Sihi ran another squadron of drones to pick up any signs of energy. There were no signs to find her.

The week followed another one. After three weeks, the soldiers were gone. The drones were still present. After the fourth week, even the drones were reassigned.

The robot did not move because there was no energy running through her circuits. The fifth week ran through. Then a radar function came on. There was nothing to pick up. This was Kaylee's point. She knew it would take them up to five weeks to leave this place. She did not write the software to wake her up in five weeks. Kaylee wrote the software to scan for any activity in the area, and if there was no activity for a week, then she can be awakened.

Kaylee climbed out of the metal where she hid for five weeks. Checking her battery level, it was at three days. This was not too bad, if she knew how to get out of this place. Kaylee got up and moved toward the woods to elude any drones leftover.

In the woods, Kaylee took a position of moderate rest to conserve her energy. Then she proceeded with calculating what options were available.

If Kaylee stayed on Earth, she would run out of energy within the next three days. This was not a good option.

If Kaylee maintained her function at a low level, she could make it to five days. The question was, why? Why would she reduce her function to make her life longer? This made no sense to her; her mission at this point, although it was written by herself, was to make a fourth colony. Hence, Kaylee needed to return to the spaceship.

This was the problem. If she communicated with her ship, then the army would locate her. Kaylee had to figure out a way to communicate with them but not be detected. This was not evident for anyone, although, except for a robot, no one else was here.

Kaylee ran across all her communication devices, and they were all bad options, except one. The naval code was sent for years through lighting system. It was like Morse code on flap lights.

At that moment, Kaylee calculated the rotation of the spaceship with her position. There should be six passages of the ship above her. Of course, there was the chance that no one would care to look down or even no one would pick up the light signal. And what if the lights would be picked up? Would it be understood? These were hard questions to answer.

In her mind, there was a sense of achievement. Kaylee was a robot, and it made it simpler to live her life. She would complete her goal and fight for her goal to the end of her life. This fact did not escape for the robot; no matter if you were blind or not, there would no way for a human to see any of those emotions on her face and behaviors. She focused her energy to use the best of her abilities to complete her mission, even the one Kaylee and the robot wrote for themselves.

CHAPTER 50

T HE DAY CLOSED on the afternoon, and the evening was about to open its hours. Kaylee climbed on top of the tallest tree and looked up. She waited for the right moment. Then she flashed the message, "Send a shuttle. I am free and alive."

The message was sent three times. Of course, no one responded to her. She waited another four hours and repeated the message again.

The first day was over. She had another two days of function. Kaylee was not sure if anyone would see her message. Every four hours, Kaylee would send her message, and after the few minutes it took for the three messages to be sent, she would wait another four hours. This was a desperate move; if she could pray, she would have done so.

The second day went the same way. Despair was not part of her function. Kaylee knew what it meant. The meaning of the word did not give you the definition of the mind shattering and confusion that accompanied it. It was hard for humans stuck on a spaceship or ship that was out in the elements where control was lost.

This was a moment of remembering emotional souvenirs of the past, realizing the running of the ship was lost at a precise instant, running all the system to save your life was useless, and, the most important, the praying to the maker of their choice. Acceptance was the last moment, the time when life was about to be lost. Despair was not a pretty picture, but it was a real image of human death.

Kaylee was no longer human; robot, as she was, was stoic to the end. Stoicism was the human word attributed to robots to make them more human; but to them, it was a normal life. There was no confusion until the energy was no longer running. Their circuits kept them from panicking at the nearing end.

The third day was nearly over. It was her last day. Kaylee was still in the tree. Her message was sent again. There was no one to show her compassion, although there would be no feeling for this demonstration of feelings. If Kaylee would shut down, it would be the end for herself. No one would ever know what she had done for humankind.

On top of her tree, Kaylee sent her last message. After this last one, there would be no need to climb up again. She would be out of energy before the four hours would elapse. The truth was she was proud of herself. She fought to the end and was true to herself. Although Kaylee did not know all these adventures would land on her lap.

Her batteries ran to 2 percent. Kaylee sat down and looked forward. She sensed the end approached. Then she listened to the birds and forest and the sound of a shuttle.

Was this possible?

The next seconds, Kaylee calculated. She understood landing a shuttle was not going to be easy when you were being shot at. At that instant, missiles exploded in the sky. Her thought was, *Can I reach wherever they land?* Calculations ran across her mind. She had less than two and a half hours left of battery. This was not going to be easy.

The shuttle moved in erratic motions. This was due to being shot at and their desperate attempts to avoid being hit. Mathematics helped everyone in this world and time, but it did not help Kaylee. There were six potential landing areas. These would have to be reached soon, as Kaylee estimated the time on the ground would be about ten minutes before the army showed up and locked them all.

The areas for landing were scattered. There were two of them that were less than a kilometer apart. This would have to be the best shot for them and her. Kaylee began moving, and almost immediately she was running. The closest location was about seven kilometers away.

Each step got her not only closer to an escape but also closer to doom. This was a dilemma Kaylee would have to accept. It was easier when she was human. Human 6; robot 3.

It was about a kilometer away. There was no one waiting for her. She would have to signal them. This was not evident when your battery was running low. Kaylee kept on running; the advantage of being a robot was there was no fatigue until the battery died. Breathing was not shallow or deep; there was no breathing, no inhalation or expiration. There was just a back-of-the-neck exhaust and intake of air for Kaylee's brain.

It was dangerous, but Kaylee came up with an idea to attract the attention of the pilots to the landing spot. Kaylee was sure this was the craziest idea ever. There was no way it could ever work.

Kaylee hit the brakes and changed direction. She ran to the enemy. A missile launcher was rolling around and tried to aim for the spaceship in the sky. Kaylee could see it. It was about four kilometers away. This would be a stretch of her batteries, but not being seen by the craft would kill her anyway. Kaylee resumed running, but this time, she went harder at it.

A kilometer away, Kaylee thought she could just topple the truck. Then after calculations, it would be difficult to topple a six-ton truck. Even if you enter her speed with maximum acceleration and her weight, it would not be sufficient. However, would it be enough for the crew of the flying craft to see her?

At five hundred meters away, there was really no other choice but to hit the truck. It would put a dent into it.

With four hundred meters to go, Kaylee could see the truck's cloud of dust behind it. This would have to do. Kaylee held her acceleration for the last 250 meters. It should be enough to put a significant ding into the truck. There was no anxiety toward it, even in the human brain.

Three hundred meters before the huge hit. If sweat would ever be included for robots, Kaylee would be the first one. Running decreased her battery; the meter showed 1.7 percent. This would be enough for her to be on the ship. After this, Kaylee thought she would pass out and it would be up to the rescued people to figure out how to place her in the recharger.

At 252 meters to the truck, Kaylee began to accelerate her speed. She was increasing her pace, and this kept on increasing her near out-of-battery moment. The truck was visible, and for one reason or another, they had not spotted her yet.

One hundred meters away, Kaylee was near her maximum speed of 50 kilometers per hour. She was not tired but could see her battery disappearing very quickly.

Then ten meters away, they saw her. Kaylee could see their faces and their moment of panic. A few meters less, the people in the truck were still panicking, and this was about two seconds away from a bang that they would remember if they survived this accident.

Kaylee's left shoulder hit the truck's front grill of the engine. A loud bang exploded. Smoke lifted in the sky. The rockets began to be shot randomly. The following explosions were not on target. The robot hit the engine, and the noise continued to be heard. The noise of metal on metal was a screech of terrifying and annoying levels. Finally, the truck began to decelerate.

Clouds of dust came up into the sky. Kaylee was not sure if they saw her, but they saw the truck accident. She counted on some reasoning to figure out why the incident happened. She pulled out of the engine. There was a return of the loud and high screech of metal on metal. This was not easy to get out of, as metal shards were stuck in her sides. Then when she pulled out of the truck's engine, Kaylee realized that the shaft of the engine came into her robot torso.

This did not hurt her. Human 6; robot 4. Her energy was lowered by this accident, and the injuries were shutting down some of her systems. Her left upper extremity was not moving, and trunk rotation was offline. Her vision was also damaged. It was blurry, and occasionally there was outage in the feed. This was not a good thing. Kaylee stepped with care and slowed her pace.

A second into the careful stepping, Kaylee realized the feed of the visual instruments were off. She did not know how to manage this situation.

The running needed to be resumed, but without vision, there was no way for her to do so. It took her about three seconds to come to the realization that there were no easy answers.

The problem was easy to put down. Kaylee needed to get to the shuttle; however, she could not localize the craft, as she had no visual input coming in. What did she have available?

Kaylee saw in her guidance system that there was a map of the area and her hearing skills were still active in her right mechanical ear. Her radar was off, and as Kaylee knew very well by now, her vision was off. She had to deal with what was in front of her; there was no point in asking for better function when no one gave a care about it.

Memory of the area did not mean a complete mapping of holes and grass potholes. The walking was slow, but with her hearing, she could feel the sound of the shuttle door opening. In the background of all this sound were the soldiers of the North American Army shouting. Discerning the sounds of one area versus the overall noise was not easy.

Kaylee walked fast. Her energy meter was near below 1 percent. This was a problem. Kaylee needed to trust her auditory skills that she could locate hypothetically the shuttle. This was no real setting; it was her trusting her own self.

It was 330 degrees northwest from her position; or at least that was her thought. Kaylee began running. If she was a blind human, there would be anxiety of falling and tripping. For her, there was no anxiety, just calculations.

Kaylee ran with an exaggerated knee elevation. This would help her avoid falling, she thought. She was about three kilometers away. It got nearer every second. The only small problem was her energy level; it was getting lower and lower; this was in direct relationship to her energy-consuming run.

Despite having a close encounter with near complete shutdown, Kaylee did not know what would happen to her brain if the robot got to zero and everything would shut down. What would happen to the human brain after the zero mark would be reached? No one knew. Kaleah was the only other one who transferred her brain into the AI. No one would know; she would be the first to know.

The running continued, and the decreasing energy reserve continued too. Kaylee was not worried about all this; she wanted to get to the shuttle. Then out of nowhere, there was a banging sound. Was this noise a guidance? Or was it a diversion? How was she to know which was which? The human side had to take a decision.

Human 7; robot 4.

Kaylee turned slightly to 270-degree direction. The noise was rhythmic. It went on, and if the surrounding noise was not as loud as it was, she could hear a voice saying, "We are here. Come to us." It had to be them, whoever them was.

HENRI NGUYEN

The running was nearing its end. The battery was so low; the meter said 0 percent. Systems shut down one after another; they were coming offline to allow Kaylee all the energy left for her escape. Her arms were no longer working. Her trunk was off. Her neck was locked in. There were never sensations in her body, but now she could not see or hear. She was running ultimately without any guidance. Now her map was gone. Kaylee ran to the shuttle without any idea of where it was.

CHAPTER 51

A ROBOT COULD ONLY work if there was energy. Kaylee was out of energy. Her human brain needed the energy to provide her some oxygen. It was needed to keep her alive. However, at this point, she was out of it. Was she dead?

The human brain was not alive; it was positronic, but her substance was human. If the positronic brain was out of energy, would it come back as soon as energy was provided? Again, Kaylee would be the first one to answer this majestic question.

Her mind was in a body at 0 percent energy. Kaylee did not know what would happen after the zero mark was reached. Did she ever make it to the shuttle? Did the army catch up to her? Did they place her in a research facility? Where was this facility? How would the rescued people on the spaceship survive or even go anywhere? All these questions would go through her processing centers, and answers would be obtained. However, Kaylee was not among the living anymore. Again, was she dead?

There were many ways to look at what would happen to her soul. There were the Buddhist beliefs, Zoroastrianism, Jewish religion, Christian religion, Muslim religion, and atheism. There were many more belief systems out in the world, but which was the true one? Was there a place for a soul that was transferred to a robot?

How could it be anticipated in any religion? The religious texts were written centuries ago. Did they have the vision of a robot? Did they ever see the world in a shamble as it was? Were food produced out of bacteria? There was no way for any of it to ever be imagined. There was only the way of the present that could explain any of these events.

Kaylee was a hero. In a heartbeat, she accepted to be transferred into a robot. It was for all the right reasons, but there was so much for her to live. Why did she agree to this shift that ended her dreams? It was because Kaylee was a hero.

Heroes were strong and powerful. They were leaders and drove the good into the darkness of evil. These were the images all humanity grew up with. Kaylee was none of those aspects. She was a real human who sought the truth.

The truth led her to become a robot. The robot threw her into a series of adventures. Kaylee was the only being in the universe who knew where the three colonies were. She saw them herself. There were characters who made the world better, but Kaylee created worlds. This was the work of a god. Was she a god?

There would be some who believed this and others who would argue the opposite. This would be the beginning of an eternal argument. This would be the seed of disputes and, eventually, war. Would this ever be needed? For humankind, it seemed an addition that was not needed but part of the recipe nonetheless.

Humankind was a contradiction in itself. It was amazing to see it propagate and create. There had been symphonies and amazing works of art. There were paintings in all sorts of medium, and there was the exploration of space. Yet there were wars throughout its history and, now, pure poverty. One of the most essential parts for humans was to eat; this became a very difficult action to continue life. Humans can be cruel, and today was the best example. There was enough food production in the North America to feed the world but not enough kindness to one another to feed the world. This was a contradiction in all phases of the word itself.

The robot was inactive. No one knew if the positronic brain would maintain Kaylee alive now that there was no energy left. Was this the end of Kaylee? Her body had rotten by now and remained in the Pacific under tons of water. That body was left behind after the transfer and it died. Was this going to happen to the robot called Kaylee or Hara?

CHAPTER 52

T HE TREES WERE away, and the person who banged the pipes to orient Kaylee yelled to her to hurry up. This was not needed. Kaylee could not hear this sound of his voice. Her systems had shut off the auditory sensors. Kaylee ran with all her might. Then the batteries cut out her legs. She fell as if she was a brick hitting the ground.

The men who encouraged Kaylee to run faster were in shock, and their mouths showed this. After a second, they ran out to Kaylee.

Their legs showed the level of hunger in them. They were muscular, but the muscles were weak and needed more energy to bulk up. This was a reality they had to face. They were deprived of food and energy, and yet they were out here to pull Kaylee to the shuttle. This was going to be a difficult task.

The first man grabbed her arm. He struggled to lift her arm. The second one grabbed the other arm, and he strained under the heavy weight of the other arm. This was not going to go well; the North American Army shot at them and the lying Kaylee.

The struggle kept on going; the effort was generous when compared to their progress. There was no movement in Kaylee's position.

An instant after the men arrived to Kaylee, a woman arrived.

The woman was even more disabled from the hunger she had suffered through. Her ribs were visible, despite a gown over her body. Also, her face showed the ravages of lack of food. This was a sad picture—three humans who barely could stand, attempting to save Kaylee, a robot. This was the meaning of heroism.

Heroes were not the superhumans we had always imagined.

Superman was a hero because of his kindness. Batman was a dark hero because of the incident in his childhood. They all wanted to do good for humanity; they were given powers or gave themselves powers. The heroes of today were not chosen or did not give themselves the opportunity to shine. Shining was the last of their thoughts.

Heroism was the act of trying to save someone else without regards for your well-being. It was a mind trick you gave your brain to fool it. You did not care if soldiers were shooting at you; you did not care if you could barely stand; it did not matter. They wanted and would save Kaylee. This was an idea in their mind, and it fooled them.

The woman did not bring her muscles to the game. Struggling to bring the battery to Kaylee, the woman slid and looked at the military fireworks. This terrified her. Nonetheless, she proceeded to open the panel to have access to her battery. Then, calmly, she plugged the wires to Kaylee's battery.

The next second took forever for the three of them. It was not a calm second either. The soldiers were about one hundred meters away from them. The soldiers ran pretty fast.

Within the next twenty seconds, the soldiers surrounded the three Asians. How about that for fooling you? Their Asian brains did a joke on them. It was not funny, per their faces. The woman was still kneeling on the ground. She began praying for Kaylee. This did not move her a millimeter.

The ants of the North American Army called in cars to come pick up three prisoners and a robot. This was a good loot. Furthermore, two soldiers crept into the shuttle. This was the end of a dream, or was it a nightmare?

HENRI NGUYEN

Waiting there kneeling with your hands on your head was not pleasant. The wind grew and blew. The woman felt the wind. Slowly, she began to smile and said, "Ṭhex keid h̄ ı̇m." This meant "She is reborn." The men looked at her, and their eyes went to Kaylee. There was no movement, no evidence of her rebirth; there was not an iota of proof of the statement.

The opposite of hope was this moment. It was a mixture of lies and depression. Their look at the robot was the evidence of this mix. Their eyes went to Kaylee with hope, and they returned to the ground. The vision of the ground was almost the end of this life to them. They wanted to kiss the ground that held them and die in peace.

The cars arrived. The soldiers loaded their prisoners. Kaylee was not loaded in a car. This was because the soldiers struggled too. They had muscles and were not showing signs of malnutrition, but she was a heavy load. They argued with each other, but this was not the beginning of a fight. They were too happy to have completed their mission.

Soldiers laughing at their arduous gains turned their backs to Kaylee's body. No one cared about a dead robot. Then, as if it was a dramatic moment, Kaylee's vision came back online. Then her auditory software was on. She was still on the ground. There were no signs of life from Kaylee. She oriented herself to the events.

It was clear that the North American Army had the crew of the shuttle. Kaylee thought of her options. She could just get up and run to the shuttle and leave the three souls. This was not an option she considered. Kaylee continued to review the options. She was at about 0.5 percent. This would give her about enough energy to knock out five or six soldiers and get on the shuttle.

With her auditory function, Kaylee scanned the group. There were seven soldiers. This was more than expected. Kaylee needed some more energy; she could stay on the ground until the battery charger would run out. This could give her the energy needed to clump a few more soldiers.

Silence was her advantage. The soldiers thought her silence was their victory. For the Asians in the car, silence was their death sentence. The wind was their only sound.

A few minutes passed, and Kaylee was at the battery charger maximum. The charger was dead. She had about 0.75 percent. This would be all she had to make it. Kaylee elected to shut down her mapping, calculation, connection with other computer systems, and facial recognition. These would allow more freedom for what needed to be done.

Kaylee had no idea of where they held her rescuers, but she would have to act on instinct. This was a human character and not a computer or even a robot one. This was not a sentence that the robotic side could understand. Human 8; robot 4.

Waiting for the right moment, Kaylee understood that the longer she waited, the harder all this would be. Hence, she decided to begin the fight immediately.

When Kaylee pulled her arms under her torso, no one saw this. Then it happened. She pushed herself up. The soldiers were stunned. They looked for a second, which allowed Kaylee to come to a stand. The next action came quickly. A shot and then a multitude of shots. Kaylee was a robot; shooting her was nearly useless.

Although there was the stun setting that could knock her of her feet, the soldiers were too terrified and panicked to think about this in time. Two of them were knocked off.

The sounds of weapons gave the Asians hope, and the woman attempted to get out of the car. Being tied did not help her movements; despite all this, she was successful. The men followed, and when they were out of the car, they ran to the shuttle.

Kaylee was busy knocking men to the ground. With a metal arm, it was easy as her arm was heavy. If Kaylee could have the satisfaction of knocking anything, it would have been delicious.

Kaylee knocked off four soldiers and had three more to go. Then she decided to turn around and get to the shuttle. It was about one hundred meters away. Kaylee put the pedal to the metal. She was going like the champions of this old event called the one-hundred-meter dash. Kaylee could feel the zipping of the weapons discharging at her back.

Kaylee was so close to the ramp when a blast caught her in the back. It was a stun shot. It slowed her down. A second shot landed at her back. Kaylee could see her clumsy-looking feet slow down.

The shuttle was on, and the lady screamed, "Mā s̄ạtẇ r̂ āy tạw h̄ ıỳ." Kaylee did not understand, but she had an idea of what it could mean. It was something like "Get your butt on the ship, you cow." Human 8; robot 5.

A third shot hit her back. Her system began to shut down again. Kaylee could feel her legs were about to give out. Then it became dark.

The shuttle took off.

The soldiers shot up in the sky, and nothing happened. Shooting the sky was harder. The distance between you and a moving target was more difficult to judge.

In the shuttle, two men were attempting to move Kaylee. She was shut off and heavy. One of the men told the other one to tie her arms and to put on the pressure suits.

This was quickly done. It was in time before they reached the point of no oxygen left. Then they crossed the stratosphere. Kaylee was much lighter at this point. They pulled her at the edge of the shuttle bay door. It was in time indeed, as they were entering the exosphere.

CHAPTER 53

I T WAS A strange feeling after three hours of recharging. Kaylee felt full and satisfied. However, she was not sure where she was. Was she in the comfort of her own charging station and in the spaceship? Or was she charging in the military installation of Chicago?

If Kaylee ever experienced a hangover, this would be the opposite. Kaylee was full of life, while the hangover person wanted to die. She felt she could conquer the world; the person suffering from a night of debauchery would not even try to conquer his bed. However, one aspect was the same—where was I? This was the question resonating in either head.

Kaylee's visual software and hardware kicked back into action. There was nothing to tell her where she was. The panels could be from anywhere. However, Kaylee did feel, if she could, better as she recognized the panels. Then when her feet came off the platform, Kaylee knew she was in space.

The sensation of being in space was incredible. You could be weighing near a ton, but there you were floating like a cork on a river. Bobbing around like this cork felt amazing. Kaylee's feet, as soon as she hit the command to release, floated up.

Pulling herself across the ship became a usual activity for Kaylee. Gaining speed, she headed to the Ring. At its entry, Kaylee grabbed a sidebar, and this stopped her. Then she pushed to descend into the Ring.

Upon arriving in the Ring, there was a force that pulled her to the ground. This felt good too. It was as if there were two of her favorite moments. When she saw the humans moving, Kaylee thought to herself, *The lack of gravity was better for me.* Human 8; robot 6.

Looking upon the people rescued was a sad sight. They were skinny and sick-looking people. This was after a few days of eating food. How could she ever think of creating another colony with these people?

Most of the people were cold; there were not enough suits and blankets for all of them. But a moment happened that gave her hope again. A woman who barely weighed enough to be considered human walked around rubbing people's back and handed them any piece of cloth she saw. On her own back, she had a raggedy shirt, which was missing most of its buttons except two; one sleeve was missing, and her pants were barely enough to call them pants. This was an odd gathering of people.

At that moment, Kaylee knew what she needed to do. She needed to find them a new home. There would be issues, but they were strong enough to make a new world home. Immediately, she bent her knees, and as soon as she extended them, Kaylee propelled into the sky.

Kaylee floated in space. Her face was stoic or just did not have the muscles to show anger, sadness, empathy, or even joy. This was a hard thing to do—to leave here without any way to show her emotions. Human 9; robot 6.

The human elected to show itself. There was nothing the robot could do.

Within a couple of hours, the people in the Ring were secured. Kaylee turned on the engines. Its gentle roar meant departure. A few hours later, they jumped.

Lightning Source UK Ltd.
Milton Keynes UK
UKHW040625050521
383143UK00010B/158/J